River of Painted Birds

For Lee, a wondrous poet, —Tessa Bridal

by

Tessa Bridal

Praise for *River of Painted Birds*

A good historical novel lets us observe a time and place different from our own, which is occupied by interesting people. A great historical novel, however, does far more. It tricks us into believing that we have been transported to another time where we visit places that are opened to us. Events happen in a special reality as if we were eyewitnesses to them. The author introduces people who are so lifelike that we care for them and worry about what they do and how they feel. They become as familiar as our neighbors. The descriptions of the landscapes of the past are so clear that we feel that we can reach out and touch the birds and plants living there.

Tessa Bridal's *River of Painted Birds* is a great historical novel. She has traveled to Ireland, Paraguay, and her native Uruguay in order to accurately describe the settings of her novel. Her research on the relations between the Jesuits and the Indians is impeccable. Words like "magical, luminous, vivid, and unforgettable" have been used to describe her writing. These are true descriptions. But there is more. Bridal's book inspires, educates, engrosses, and captivates the reader. Her book is one of those remarkable epics of literature that we read avidly. We want to know the ending. We don't want the book to end. Highly recommended!

—Professor Emerita Carol Urness,
University of Minnesota

Spun as delicately as gossamer, *River of Painted Birds* reveals the frailties and strengths of people as strands caught within the mid-18th century web for power, wealth and godliness. Tessa Bridal's intimate narrative brings us into real time as Spain and Portugal, England and France, Catholics and Jesuits maneuver and manipulate for precedence into the reaches of South America. Centered within Montevideo, *River of Painted Birds* presents a necessary and penetrating wisp of history as memoir and legend, mysticism and parable. It enters our cognizance as a last stand for human dignity in a world rushing toward physical conquest, annihilation of spiritual justice.

—Rita Kohn, author, playwright,
and writer and producer of Public Television documentaries

We are made part of this historical novel about Ireland and the Jesuit Missions of South America, the result of a profound investigation into the characteristics of the 18th century, and taking place in the city of Montevideo.

This masterful description of native flora and fauna, and the fusion between human beings and nature awakens in one a feeling of sublime spirituality.

—Lucía Todone, Professor of Biology, Curator of the Department of Zoology at the Natural History Museum "Carlos A. Torres de la Llosa"

The colorful detail, the fluidity with which the story develops from Ireland to the Río de la Plata where Isabel flowers as a woman determined to face her new world, the description and revaluation of indigenous cultures, with their deep respect for mother earth, reaches the soul. Tessa Bridal has managed to narrate, in exquisite detail, the history of the European conquest of our lands from a rarely heard perspective.

Recommended for: Teachers interested in sharing with their students different cultural perspectives not traditionally represented in history books. Teachers interested in exploring South American literature with their students. Teachers in Spanish immersion programs.

—María Alicia Arabbo, Assistant Director, Office of Multilingual Learning, Saint Paul Public Schools

River of Painted Birds is at once an adventure story and a love story, as the spirited Isabel disguises herself as a boy and flees Ireland to find herself landed (by mistake!) in what is now Uruguay. As Isabel's eyes open to her new surroundings, our eyes open to an intriguing history of competing eighteenth-century empires and clashing cultures. This is great reading for history and fiction lovers alike.

—Suzanne Lebsock, PhD, Board of Governors Professor of History Emerita, Rutgers University

ISBN: 978-0-9962849-0-5

Cover art:
Ceibo flowers by Sylvia Crannell
Mate gourd by Heidi Arneson

Author photo by Kent Flemmer. Used with permission.

Interior file design by Patti Frazee.

Project Management and Publicity: BookSmart Publishing Management, www.booksmartpub.com.

www.tessabridal.com

Minneapolis, MN

To my Irish ancestor Kate Hughes,
who began the journey.

And to my sister, Carole,
who completed it,
almost 200 years later.

Other Books by Tessa Bridal

Fiction
The Tree of Red Stars

Non-fiction
Exploring Museum Theatre
Effective Exhibit Interpretation and Design

Contents

City of Montevideo During the Hispanic Period

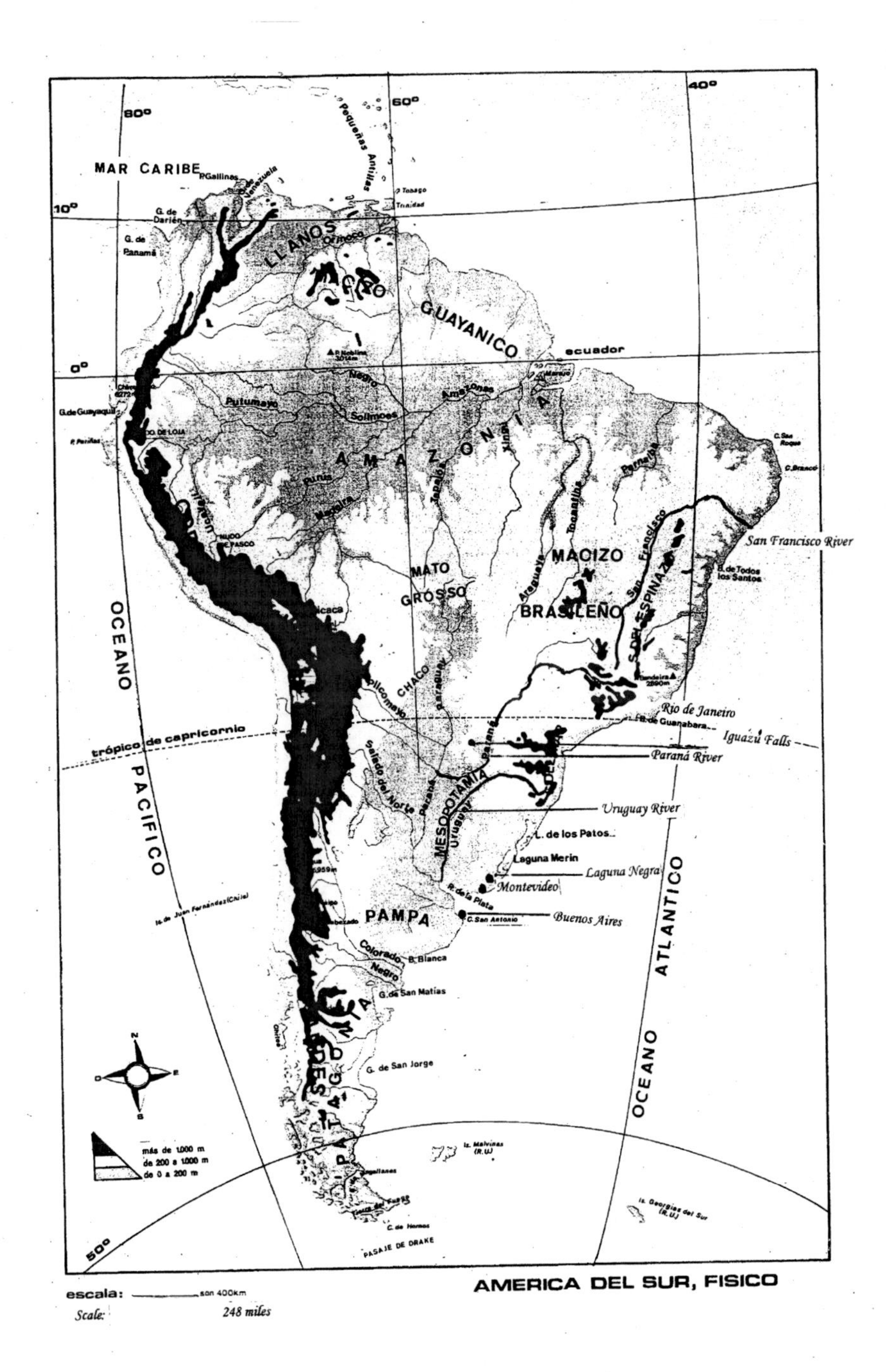

Physical Map of South America

River of Painted Birds

Sweet mate…
You were in our sorrows and our joys;
You flavored every event;
Funerals and weddings,
-From hand to hand and mouth to mouth-
With the bombilla like a weapon at your shoulder
You stood guard
Like a faithful sentinel…

El mate dulce, Fernán Silva Valdés
Translation by Tessa Bridal

Everyone knows that the real literature of a people lies in their origins, in the exact reproduction of types, habits and customs now almost completely extinguished.

Sin pasión y sin divisa, prólogo,
Eduardo Acevedo Diaz

Chapter I

"Boston, did you say? This ship is bound for the other America, lad!"

I had never thought to ask which America the ship was sailing for, and three days into the journey, when the Captain informed me that we were headed for Buenos Aires, a place I had never heard of, I knew that this latest catastrophe was God's punishment for my crime. Perhaps I should simply throw myself into the ocean and put an end to my miserable existence.

My only excuse for the haste with which I had boarded the *Bonaventure* was my husband's murder. Much as I had wished for his death it had not been my intention to kill him, but kill him I had, and buried his body in the cellar. As cold bloodedly as if murder were an everyday occurrence in my life, I'd cut off my hair, put on my brother's clothes, and boarded the first ship I could find bound for America. I had cousins in Boston and enough money secreted in my clothes and trunk to get me there and keep me for a while. But what would I do in a Spanish colony? I spoke not one word of the language and had no more idea of what faced me there than if I had been banished to the Antipodes.

So profoundly had the Captain's words shaken me that I barely felt the touch of the ship owner's sleeve on mine as he came to lean on the rail by my side. Like me, he had boarded the ship in Cork, sporting a brilliant jade suit decorated in gold thread, the minutely embroidered undercoat covered in pink flowers. White lace had cascaded at his throat and appeared in soft folds at his cuffs. My attention had been drawn by the stark contrast between his white periwig and the darkness of his skin, and by the fact that he had carried his own sea chest, swinging it on board as easily as a common sailor.

I glanced up at him. He had removed the periwig and a pair of strangely golden eyes met mine.

"What is your name?" he asked. He spoke English confidently, with an accent reminiscent of the Spanish and Portuguese sailors who roamed the streets of Cork.

"Michael Keating," I lied.

"Will you allow me to advise you, Michael?"

His inflection, so different from the Captain's mocking, jeering tone, was kind and I looked away, afraid that I might cry.

"Whenever I see anyone looking at the sea with such longing and despair I know they are wishing it would claim them."

"Death does seem to be the only answer to my troubles."

"Ah, yes, but do consider me! Cargo if lost can be replaced, but awkward questions are asked about young men who fall overboard, and from the tearful farewell you were given in Cork I assume that there are some who care for you."

"The people you saw were old friends."

"They did not assist you to confirm your destination?"

"I left in haste. I made all the arrangements myself. I have relatives awaiting me in Boston."

He lit his pipe and I noticed the strong and slender fingers, the nails clipped and clean. "Our first stop will likely be Antigua Island. We will wait there until a ship bound for Boston can be found."

"Would it not be easier to return to Cork?" The words had left my mouth before I realized that the last thing in the world I wanted was to go back to Ireland.

"A ship is married to the winds and the tides. The *Bonaventure* is following the trade winds south to the Azores — the route Christopher Columbus took. Turning back could delay us for weeks."

I retired below decks, huddling in my bunk while the hull creaked and what I assumed from the sounds were hundreds of mice and rats frolicked in the holds. My cabin was no more than a windowless closet, a walled-in berth, six by three feet, with a bull's eye of thick glass onto the deck above providing the only light. I could barely stretch out on the narrow bunk and could only pull my trunk out from under it by opening the door and dragging the trunk halfway into the passage, where the crew's hats and sea boots were wedged into every available space, and the low beams strung with nets of potatoes and cheeses swinging suspended amongst the ropes of onions.

I found my journal and put the trunk back, shutting myself in by the dim light of a small lantern. I made myself as comfortable as possible in the tiny space and held my journal to my chest. Force of habit decreed that my bed was neatly made, with the warm blankets that had been my farewell gift from my neighbors the O'Neills tucked firmly round the thin mattress, and Mrs. O'Neill's embroidered pillow resting at the head. The events of the last few days had so drastically altered my circumstances, and my former life seemed so illusory that for a moment I harbored the quite irrational fear that the journal would be blank and even memory would refuse to come to my aid to assure me that I was not a murderess, an imposter, or a liar by choice.

I made myself open the worn cover, and my relief at seeing my own familiar handwriting was so great I laughed out loud.

My last entry was dated April 29, 1745, the day my life had taken a most precipitous turn. I had been summoned to a cottage on the outskirts of the city. As if it were yesterday, I remembered standing in the doorway with a dead baby in my arms, the cold a tangible weight pressing me into the ground. Mist blanketed the countryside, hovering like smoke over the scrub. No breeze rattled the naked branches of the solitary tree nearby and no birds called. I felt as if I'd entered a sad and desolate painting that mirrored my own inner landscape.

I walked to the freshly dug grave behind the cottage and knelt to lay the small body, wrapped in rags, in the cold earth. The bottom of the grave was almost beyond my reach and as I lowered the bundle the rags gave way, revealing a tiny hand. I recoiled and stood up hastily, picking up the spade I had rested against the wattle and daub wall. I said a quick prayer before filling the hole, crossed myself, and returned to the interior of the cottage through the tattered curtain that served as a door. A cold gust pursued me, blowing my skirt into the room ahead of me and stirring up the smell of excrement, rot, and vomit that pervaded the hovel Bridget and her family called home.

This was the third of her newborns I had buried. Four of the others had lived, at least for a while. Bridget had barely had the strength to push this last one into the world, and might soon follow him below ground. I did not even know what I would list as the cause of death. Starvation? Despair? Exhaustion?

I sat on the single low stool in the hut and took my midwife's journal from my basket. Even though I had stuffed my father's old boots with rags to insulate them and make them fit better I could feel the cold earth through the thin soles as I wrote. *Bridget O'Connor, age twenty-four, gave birth to a stillborn child. Child carried to term but very small. Mother undernourished.* I turned back the page, reading my previous entry. *Summoned today to the dockside cottages. Spent the night there. Two births. One stillborn. The other might as well have been.*

The words shamed me. The child had deserved to be celebrated, not discounted as another casualty of the poverty and famine that plagued us.

I had put my journal away and begun the work of disposing of the afterbirth and the bloody rags still lying on the bed when two of Bridget's children crept in out of the cold and began searching on a low shelf for food. There was none, and with a sound like the rustle of dead leaves, Bridget sighed and turned her face to the wall. The children curled up by the fire, their bare feet and hands tucked under one another for warmth, their limbs as brittle as the winter twigs stacked up for kindling by the hearth.

I took the scissors with which I had severed the dead child from her mother, and cut a few of the stitches in my hemline, withdrawing a copper penny. I closed the opening carefully, using the needle and catgut with which I sewed wounds, and approached the children by the fire. I woke the eldest, a boy of seven, and put the coin into his hand, telling him to take my horse and ride to town for bread and cheese, admonishing him to mind that he didn't eat it all on the way home. He ran out and I heard the sound of hooves clopping away in the night. It would take him at least an hour to complete his errand and by then I would be finished.

I found a piece of blanket to replace the rags on the bed and was standing outside feeding the afterbirth to two skeletal dogs when a horse-drawn cart careened out of the night and came to a halt amongst the half dozen hovels. The dogs were torn between the urge to bark and the unexpected banquet provided by the afterbirth. Hunger won, and they took ravenous mouthfuls of placenta, ignoring the man who descended from the cart. He was greeted by the thin wail of a child emerging from an opening that served as a window in a nearby hut. He was not much taller than I and dressed in fine leather boots, gloves, and a well-cut riding jacket designed to protect him from the cold and the snow that had started to fall as he arrived.

I watched one of Bridget's neighbors emerge and approach the wagon, bowing to the young man as he came. A local lord, I thought with disgust, come to exact some payment or other from his miserable tenants. I returned inside to heat water and rouse Bridget, relieved to find that her forehead and hands were cool and the bleeding no heavier than normal after giving birth.

"I've made you some tea, Bridget, see if you can drink it."

"I heard horses."

"Some young lord has come."

Bridget's face lit up. "Is it Charlie FitzGibbon?"

"Are you mad, Bridget? What would he be doing here?"

Charlie FitzGibbon's latest exploit had been to smuggle a priest into Cork for a clandestine mass and a large number of people had crowded into a garret to receive his blessing. The floor gave way under their weight and buried them all in the ruins. Charlie organized the carts that conveyed the dead and dying from the scene and then accosted the Mayor, demanding redress for the victims' families and leading a raid on the city's warehouses to help feed them. He escaped being labeled a traitor for his actions only because no one could be found to testify that it was indeed he who had led the assault on the warehouses, depleting them of the supplies reserved for the English troops fighting the French. A rash of proclamations further restricting gatherings of Catholics had followed, but they only served to add to Charlie's popularity.

Laughter reached us from outside and the sound of voices raised in greeting.

"Do go and see if it's him, Isabel!" Bridget pleaded.

The cart had been uncovered, revealing a quantity of roasted fowl and loaves of bread. Bridget's neighbors were gathered, crowding around the young man, their faces free for the moment of care and worry, patting him on the back and repeating his name over and over like a magic charm. "Charlie! Charlie! Charlie!"

He laughed as he distributed the food. "Make haste!" he said. "I may have been pursued!"

The sound of horse's hooves startled us and several men (Bridget's husband among them) armed themselves with stones, glancing anxiously in the direction of the sound. It was only Bridget's son, returning from his errand on my horse, and a sigh of relief went through the group as the boy dismounted.

"Two loaves and half a pound of cheese, Mistress!" he said proudly before his eyes fell on the cart. "Holy Mary, Mother of God!"

I put my arm around him and hurried him out of the snow and into the cottage, asking the child if he had seen anyone on his errand. He assured me that the surrounding area had been as quiet as a graveyard with no other riders abroad that night. He himself had ridden hard to be home before the worst of the snow overtook us. Before I could stop her, Bridget had left her bed and was making her way to the door, determined to catch a glimpse of Charlie. He waved and smiled as he went by and I stood watching the cart until it was out of sight, as captivated as Bridget by the bright strength, the confidence and energy radiating from him. The spell broken, everyone retreated to enjoy the bounty Charlie had distributed. Bridget and her children ate pheasant for their supper and were sleeping peacefully when I lit my lantern and went to find my horse, which the careless boy had left untethered. I had to wade in ankle-deep snow to find him where he stood eating a hedge unmindful of the sprinkling of white that covered him like a mantle.

Going home was out of the question on such a night, but staying where I was depressed me beyond measure. I kept remembering the baby's tiny hand and imagined it moving in its grave, a fanciful notion that convinced me that I could not remain in the vicinity of the place where the child lay buried. I had friends at the castle nearby. More than once I had attended those who worked there and I knew they would take me in on a night like this and give me and my horse a place to sleep.

I swung the two bundles that served me as saddlebags into place, hung the lantern from the pommel while I mounted, and gathering my skirts about me heaved myself into the saddle. The snow felt cold on my exposed ankles and I pulled at my skirt and petticoat, cursing women's clothes and longing for a serviceable pair of britches and knee-high boots.

"Let's go, Puck," I said. "Food and a warm place to sleep await us both."

Puck shook the snow from his face and moved eagerly into the lane that led to the castle. Wolves had not been seen around Cork for over thirty years, but as a frigid wind swept the sky clear of clouds, exposing stars like icicles overhead, I recalled the stories my mother had often told of wolves stealing into houses to snatch babes from their beds, or lurking in lanes such as this one on the prowl for travelers.

I was glad when Busteed Castle emerged in the moonlight out of the acres of woodland surrounding it, its towers and turrets a pale gray against the dark sky. Deer ran startled from the path as I approached, and horses whinnied softly to Puck from the pasture by the stables. I heard music and saw that a whole wing of the castle was lighted. I dismounted before reaching the courtyard, where several carriages waited. The breath of grooms and horses clouded the air, and coachmen stamped their feet and warmed their cold hands under the horse blankets. The lighted wing could only be reached by climbing up a rocky path among the huge, ancient evergreens, and in spite of the cold that pervaded my whole body, I couldn't resist the draw of the light from the silver candelabras, and what I imagined to be the flash of jewels and buckled shoes beyond the ceiling-high double windows. I looped Puck's reins around a low branch and climbed the path. I was just tall enough for my chin to reach the lowest pane of glass.

Hundreds of hothouse flowers were draped in ornamental swirls across the arched stone doorway that separated the Great Hall from the banqueting hall. There a low fence, designed as a centerpiece for the vast table set in the middle of the ancient room, contained a little brown heifer in a field of grass, with a tiny maid to tend her. Huge platters heaped high with venison, fish, fowl, and beef, surrounded the heifer, and she lowed as if in protest of being made to stand amid the sacrificed remains of her kind. In the Great Hall, a small boy rowed in a pool of champagne. Men and women ate and laughed under the hundreds of dripping candles from the chandeliers over their heads. Yards of fabric passed before my eyes, silks, satins, and brocades, embroidered in dazzling colors. Bare bosoms heavy with diamonds, pearls, sapphires, and rubies, wrists sparkling with emeralds, fingers weighted in gold and silver filigree. Not an item in the hall but could have fed Bridget and her family for weeks to come, I thought, wishing I could be in that room for just one moment, feeling lovely, rich, and self-assured, with a carriage waiting to take me home and a maid to warm my bed and bring me breakfast in the morning. As if to remind me of the gulf that separated me from those within, a clump of snow fell from an overhanging branch onto my bare neck.

I retrieved my patient Puck and made my way to the rear of the castle and the servants' quarters where I knocked on the heavy wooden door and asked Margaret the cook for leave to put Puck in the stable. By the time I had fed and brushed him, I was so tired I wanted to curl up in the hay beside him and not stir till dawn, but I was just as hungry as I was tired.

In the castle kitchen, I sat on a stool in a corner with a cup of hot broth, bread dripping with melted butter, and a juicy cut of roast beef as the work continued unabated all around me. Men in livery ran in and out replenishing the banquet tables with crystal water jugs, butter coolers, and wine decanters. A line of girls standing next to water buckets washed the curved fish servers, ladles, straining spoons, and butter knives while another line dried the red and gold china with rags hung by the fire, replacing the plates in piles, which the men arranged on the silver trays they carried back to the dining hall.

My stomach full, I dozed until well after midnight when the Earl's servants slowed their frantic pace. They were eager to celebrate the part their household had played in that night's exploit. Charlie FitzGibbon's cart had been loaded with the Earl's own pheasants and Charlie himself had stood in that very kitchen, as fine an Irish gentleman as they had ever seen. He had treated the maids as if they were high-born ladies, and the men as his equals. As soon as Charlie gave the call, they said, they would all join his revolutionary army.

"Charlie FitzGibbon surely has more sense," I said, "than to ask half-starved peasants to throw themselves unarmed against the might of England."

"Ah, but we won't be unarmed, Isabel! Charlie will have muskets for us all!"

"Oh, aye," Margaret said, "which he'll no doubt buy by selling that old ruin of a castle he lives in!"

"*A man whose passion for power runs high, bids fair for being no patriot*, the good Bishop of Cloyne has said." The Earl's steward prided himself on being a learned man, able not only to read, but to quote what he read.

It was only right, the men argued, for Charlie to wish for power. It was a disgrace that an Irish lord, even if his mother was a Spaniard, could not hold office, vote, or own a horse valued at over five pounds, all because he was a Catholic unwilling to conform and join the ranks of the Protestants, damned like the Earl to burn in hell forever for their heresy. They fell to toasting Charlie, and I took up my basket and wrap and followed the maids to their quarters, where we slipped between icy sheets, glad for the heat from each other's bodies.

Something about the day's events had loosened the tight grip I kept on my emotions, and tired as I was, I could not sleep. I imagined myself dancing under the chandeliers with Charlie FitzGibbon, our passionate love for one another equaled only by our fervor to rouse Ireland to rebel against England. Ballads would be written about us in years to come, celebrating Charlie for his exploits and immortalizing me as the bravest and best of companions for such a hero.

My own husband, Tobias Shandon, had only one thing in common with Charlie FitzGibbon — his looks. He too had a handsome head of dark hair, a pair of eyes the color of a summer sky, and a ready tongue. We had been married six years before, when we were both fifteen. He had come to Cork from no one knew where, with money in his pocket and a box of cobbling tools on his back, both of which, I discovered soon after our hasty wedding, had been stolen. He married me because he needed shelter, food, and an income, all of which I could provide. I married him in loneliness and lust. I had been left an orphan at fourteen, my only brother dead from the same fever that had carried off my Ma and Pa.

I didn't allow thoughts of my family or of my childhood to surface often. I mistrusted the past. Like a mad relative with unpredictable habits, it was unsafe to bring out for airings. Recalling the days before I lost Pa, Ma, and Michael had become a dangerous pastime for me after I married Tobias. Sometimes I felt thankful for the years we had had together, other times I emerged desolate, knowing I was entirely alone, and afraid that I would always be so. How I regretted my anger at Ma when she began her efforts to turn me into a marriageable young woman! I had taken advantage of every opportunity to escape her, dressed in a pair of old britches Michael had discarded as indecent. They were full of holes, and I cut up one of the aprons Ma had made me and used it to make patches, which I sewed on with messy, uneven stitches in unmatched thread, just to spite her. I braided my hair, pinned it under a cap and in this fashion went roaming the shores of the River Lee.

As often as not, I played on the Earl of Busteed's property, the same Earl in whose house I then lay. He owned practically all the land surrounding Cork, and I would have had to go far indeed to avoid trespassing on his grounds. The Earl was fond of hunting and whenever his horses and his dogs were abroad, we fled. It was rumored that he did not limit his hunting to deer and foxes, and my friend Mary and her brothers were often disciplined with tales of the fate that awaited them at the Earl's hands if they did not mend their ways and mind their betters. I considered myself too knowing to believe the stories told of the Earl's pursuit of children, but I was not above teasing Michael about his fears, sending him running to hide in Ma's lap.

I enjoyed watching the Earl's beautiful hunters galloping across the fields, jumping hedges as if they had wings, their haunches taut, their manes and tails flying in the wind. I often climbed a tree to watch from a high branch until the hunt vanished from sight.

One day, the dogs, followed by the Earl and several of his hunting party, raced into the small copse where I was hiding. It had started to rain, and the thunder and lightning excited the animals. I was a little frightened and overexcited myself, and tried to climb higher. I missed my footing on the slippery branches and fell just as the Earl's horse cantered beneath the tree. The stallion saw me and tried to veer aside, but it was too late, his huge hoof struck my right knee, and I cried out as everything went black and all I could feel was the searing pain in my leg. The Earl cursed me, accused me of trying to spook his horse, and without another glance, left me lying where I had fallen. It took me several hours to crawl home, each yard more difficult than the one before. I arrived on my doorstep wet and chilled, and promptly fainted.

Several long, cold weeks spent in bed followed, a time Pa and I called the Long Winter. In an attempt to distract me and take my mind off the pain, Pa brought books, paper, and pens, and sat with me for many an evening by the light of the fire, teaching me my letters. I learned to read first from the family Bible, later by studying the pamphlets and sermons published by George Berkeley, Protestant Bishop of Cloyne. My mother said Pa and I would be damned for reading heresy, but Pa maintained that the Bishop was the best friend Catholics ever had. It was he who had reported that nowhere on earth could be found a people more beggarly wretched and destitute than the common Irish. By common, Pa said, the Bishop meant Catholic, and he was right. Common as rats we were and with less sense, for rats were not governed by priests. Whenever Pa began to rant against priests, Ma padlocked the door and closed the shutters. It was bad enough that he subjected us to these tirades, intolerable that the neighbors or any passersby might hear. She could not even resort to the excuse that he was in his cups, for Pa never drank, another trait that made him suspect to his fellows. He was as good a Catholic as the Pope, he argued, only he would be ashamed to sit eating beef and drinking wine in a silly hat day and night while his flock starved and just one of the rooms in the Vatican would finance an army able to throw the English out of Ireland and overturn the Penal Laws.

Most of these laws, proposed or actual, concerned registration of the clergy and the annulment of marriages between Protestants and Catholics, matters of not much concern to Pa, but they were followed by a proposal to create Protestant charter schools. I remembered sitting up in my bed, listening to Pa explain the proposal to Michael. The aim of the bill was to remove Catholic children from their homes and bring them up in isolation from their families, fostering in them hatred for their motherland, and abhorrence for their religious beliefs. At first, these schools had been supported only by voluntary contributions from nobles and clergymen, but large parliamentary grants had followed, and families had decided that the time had come to hide their boys.

We dug a cellar, working under cover of darkness, removing the earth in buckets and taking it to the woods behind our house. Ma had long been wanting a flagstone floor and here was her opportunity. Under one of the new flagstones there would be a wooden trap door, with a ladder leading into the hole. We would keep the cellar stocked with ale and hardtack, and as soon as the roundup began, hide Michael there and claim that he had run away to sea. Michael said that he would prefer to run away to sea forthwith and not be shut up alone with rats in a dark cellar, but Pa told him there were more rats aboard ship than under the ground, and he should know, for he made his living stocking ships with barrels of salted pork and biscuit, and armies of rats, bigger than any Michael could imagine, lived below decks.

The cellar was dug but never used, for no Protestants came to take Michael away, which at the time I thought was a pity, believing I could not possibly miss his loud voice and muddy feet. As part of my training in the womanly graces, every evening I was obliged to help Ma prepare the meal and the table. Michael's chest would grow to twice its usual size every time Ma said "Time to serve our men, Isabel!" and he would sit next to Pa with a wide grin on his face knowing full well that all I wanted was to pour the stew on his head. He and Pa would discuss how Protestant freemen had recently been disqualified from carrying arms when in the service of Catholics, and how the wealthier families, who had until then resorted to arming their loyal Protestant servants as their sole means of defense, were now smuggling arms into cellars in wine casks against the day when their sons, their lands, or their lives were threatened.

That day was not long in coming. In 1733 a bill was introduced to annul all marriages performed by Catholic clergy, threatening to make Michael and me illegitimate. Michael was only seven at the time and could not understand how such a measure would affect him, but I knew that illegitimate children could not inherit, and thus all Catholic land would be made available to Protestants. It was difficult enough for Catholics to inherit, for the Penal Laws dictated that wealth was to be divided equally amongst all the sons, ensuring in most cases a continued devaluation of land, as each generation parceled it out in smaller and smaller lots. The annulment bill failed, but its threat remained.

It was then that Ma's brother, our only close relation in Cork, sailed for America and joined the one hundred thousand of our countrymen who had already fled Ireland. Every year since then he had encouraged us to join him in Boston, and finally, when I was fourteen, Pa decided to sell his small provisioning business and make the move. No sooner had he done so than he fell victim to a fever that within three months took him, Ma, and Michael.

After that I worked nursing others, sleeping and eating only when I had to, until the pain of my loss was a dull and distant ache. By the famine of 1740, when I was sixteen and one year married, I had become a skilled nurse and midwife.

Three months of drought had triggered the famine and the poor watched their few crops wither in the ground. Their provisions gone, people ate the cats, and later, the few surviving dogs. As I made my rounds, I saw children hunting rats and mice in the quays and roadways, feeding on nettles and grass as they sat, hoping for the strength and quickness to catch a rat if one appeared.

The English placed an embargo on provisions to Ireland. They feared that the French, with whom they were at war again, might capture the vessels and supply their fleet with food.

Pestilence ran rampant and everywhere I went I met the carts, loaded with dead bodies the color of the weeds on which they had fed, creaking their way to the fields, where kites and vultures grew fat on the thousands of unburied dead.

Determined to escape into sleep and away from such morbid memories, I turned on my side, and felt the bruising on my ribs. Tobias' charm had long ago worn off and whenever I denied him what he called his rights he took them, often including punishment for my reluctance to welcome his rough embraces. Three miscarriages, and his squandering of most of the money Pa had left me, had done nothing to draw us closer together.

As the years dragged by my determination to be free of Tobias had grown into an obsession and I spent most of my waking hours planning my escape. My Boston relatives, unaware of Tobias' existence, had been urging me to join them. Work there was hard but plentiful, famine nonexistent, and Irishmen eager for wives from home. Along with the coins sewn into the hem of my skirt, I had been hoarding many more, some of Spanish, some of Dutch and Portuguese origin. I was not always paid for my work, but when I was, I was miserly with my earnings, and lied unabashedly to Tobias about how much I made. Buried under our hearth and in several hiding places around the house and garden were stashes of the money that would one day buy my freedom from Ireland and Tobias. Many were the nights I spent unable to sleep, worrying that Tobias would find the money and rob me not only of the fruits of my labor, but of the liberty I longed for. I wanted a house I could call my own. A safe haven I did not have to share with anyone, least of all a demanding husband whose every habit filled me with loathing, from his vile eating habits to the contents of his chamber pot. I dreamed of coming home to a well-laid fire waiting to be lit, and to a fresh-smelling bed in which I could sleep alone.

I had shared my plan of escape with no one except my dear friend and neighbor Mary, who had been my companion ever since I could remember.

My work took me to the homes of sailors' wives, and from them I had been learning of the arrival and departure of ships to and from America. As I did every night before I fell asleep, I had conjured up an image of myself safely aboard one of those ships, my money well hidden, my trunk under my berth, and myself in a new pair of boots standing under the billowing sails that would carry me away from Tobias.

~

It was dark when I awoke. I was fully dressed, and as I swung my feet over the side of the bunk they touched my journal. I had fallen asleep before adding a word to it.

I made my way onto the deck. The *Bonaventure* was gliding on the smooth surface of the Atlantic like a giant bird. A warm glow lit the horizon and as the watch changed and the ship came to life, I found a place by the animal pens from which to watch the sun rise. The animals too were stirring and seemed content enough in their pens, unaware that they were aboard to reduce our dependence on dried beef and hardtack. Pa had made his living providing hardtack to ships, and I cut my first teeth on it. The hardtack Pa sold was not baked years before the journey, as was common among other providers, but even his products were not free of maggots.

I did not realize how well hidden I was between the cow pen and the chicken cages until I saw the Captain and the ship's owner approaching, deep in conversation. They stopped a few inches from where I sat. They were speaking English and I was the subject of their discourse.

"How was I to know that anyone would be fool enough to board a ship not knowing there are two Americas?" the Captain was saying. "Am I supposed to be a mind reader as well as a wet nurse?"

"You are well aware of my reluctance to carry passengers. How much did you charge him?"

"Two English pounds."

Liar! He had wanted to charge me six pounds for a private cabin. I had offered two and we had settled for four!

"It will be taken from your share of the profits."

The owner was looking out to the horizon as he said this and missed the look of loathing the Captain gave him. By the time they were facing each other again, the Captain had composed himself. "Perhaps," he said, "he will do well in the Spanish colonies. There are opportunities galore there for young men with ambition and a willingness to work hard."

"It is far likelier that such an effeminate young man will end up feeding the fishes at the bottom of the harbor, and as soon as we reach port I will find him a ship sailing for Boston. Perhaps his relatives there will know what to do with him."

I did not see the owner again that day. He dined in his private cabin, and I in the Captain's, an ordeal I had so far dealt with in silence, unable to converse in the various languages spoken by him and his first mate. Now that my foolish mistake was public knowledge, they spoke English and made me the butt of their jokes for the entire meal.

"You should consider yourself fortunate for boarding the *Bonaventure*," Martínez, the first mate, said, "and not ending up in Boston with the English. What Irishman could relish that?" He himself was Spanish and no friend of the English. "In the Spanish colonies," he laughed, "you can go to Mass every day of the week!"

"And you can exchange that little two-penny iron knife," the

Captain said, gesturing to the pocket knife I was using to skewer my ration of meat, "for two horses! In the colonies silver is cheaper than iron!"

Just as I had done every night, I retreated to my bunk as soon as I had eaten. I had never felt more alone. I reached for my lamp and realized that I had allowed it to burn out the night before. I didn't want to face the Captain to ask for more oil, so I closed my eyes and willed myself back to an old retreat, a magical grove of yew and ilex, ancient trees that grew among artfully arranged rocks, their roots clutching the boulders like gigantic, many fingered hands. It was rumored that Druids worshipped their Sun God there. The last time I had seen it, snow lay in patches in the shade and on the branches above me. A gust of wind had blown it off the canopies and it had fallen in glistening crystals onto my favorite black rock, shaped like a stooped figure. I didn't know what its significance was to the Druids, but to me it represented womankind, bowed, yet powerful, and still standing in spite of the weight of ages. Whenever I felt myself sinking, whenever life seemed unendurable, I came to her. After my night at the castle and before returning to the house where I had been born and lived my entire life, I had visited the old rock. The time was approaching when I would make my escape, and I would need to be as firm as she was. I had brought a handful of the hothouse flowers discarded by the dancers the night before and I scattered them in the snow at her feet before leaving.

As I drew near my cottage I saw smoke rising from the chimney, indicating that Tobias was home. It was here, I thought as I unlatched the gate by the entrance to Puck's small paddock, that Tobias had first pushed me, grasping my arm and twisting it. I heard the sharp crack before I felt the pain, and when I came to, my friends and neighbors the O'Neill's were there with the physician.

I rubbed the slightly twisted place at my elbow where the bone had set crookedly, and opened the front door. Tobias was sitting by the fire. The hearth stone under which I kept my largest stash of money had been removed and he was playing with the pile of coins at his feet. The trap door to the cellar stood open between us, and the drawers of the kitchen dresser had been pulled out. He had clearly searched the house from top to bottom.

I had faced Tobias ugly before, but never as ugly as this. He stood up, putting the coins carefully aside, and came toward me. My ears rang and my sight went black as I felt the pain of his blow and tasted blood in my mouth. I fell against the table. The carving knife was within my reach and as Tobias grasped my hair and pulled me upright, I turned and slashed at his belly. Tobias leapt back, missed his footing, and fell into the cellar. I pulled up the ladder, and slammed the trapdoor shut. Then I sat on it, panting and trembling, fully expecting to hear sounds and feel movement beneath me. Tobias was tall enough to push the trap door open, so I reached for my mother's old trunk and pulled on it until its weight was fully over the door. My head and face were throbbing and my tongue, where I had bitten it, was on fire. I was shaking with fear, rage, and relief. Perhaps, I thought gleefully, I'd killed him.

I went to the water bucket and washed my face. My tongue was still bleeding and I swallowed blood as I filled a basin and rinsed out my mouth. Should I ask the O'Neill's for help? I would have to let Tobias out eventually, and now that he knew that I had been keeping money from him there was nothing he would not do to get his hands on it. If he was dead, I would be accused of murder, and hang for it.

There was a knock at the front door. What if Tobias heard the knocking and tried to push open the trapdoor?

It came again. "Isabel? It's Mary. I saw you come home! I know you're there!"

I threw a cloth over the basin of bloody water and opened the door a crack.

"Let me in," Mary said.

"I am alright, Mary."

She pushed the door open, looking first around the empty room and then at my swollen face. "Where is he?"

"He's gone." The words seemed to come from someone far away.

From the cellar there was no sound.

Mary glanced at the coins, still scattered by the hearth where Tobias had left them. "He found your money?"

"I gave him most of it. He left me those."

"How unlike him."

I shrugged. "I care only that he's left. For good, I trust."

Again Mary looked away. At the trunk this time, conspicuously out of place.

"He searched everywhere."

Our eyes met for a brief moment and she nodded. "I think that you should sleep with us tonight."

"I'll come later. I need the afternoon to tidy up the house. Tobias went on a rampage upstairs."

For a moment I thought that Mary would not leave me. If she stayed, I would be tempted to release the torrent of grief that had been building up in me for seven years, and I could not risk that. Not now, when I had Tobias at my mercy. In those few seconds while Mary hesitated I knew that the moment had come for me to act. Tobias could survive in the cellar for a few days. By the time he was found, I would be gone.

"I'll tell Ma you'll be with us for supper then," Mary said.

I bolted the door behind her and ran upstairs. The beds were torn apart, drawers had been emptied, and wardrobes stood open, their contents spilled across the floor. Tobias, however, had found none of my hiding places. Not the hollowed-out catechism book nor the bag buried in the fern pot by the window.

I returned downstairs, poured myself a cup of cider and sat, looking at the trunk. There was still no sound from the cellar. It was unlike Tobias to remain quiet for so long. What if the fall had indeed killed him? Would I be hunted down as a murderess no matter where I went? The knife still lay on the table where I had put it when I answered the door. I stuck it in my belt and placed my father's walking stick on the floor within easy reach of my hand. I lit a lamp and put it by the stick.

My hands were shaking as I began pulling the trunk across the flagstones. I stopped to listen. Nothing. Was he crafty enough to wait until the trapdoor opened and then leap out at me? The temptation to flee was overwhelming. Only the knowledge that my whole future depended on what I did at that moment made me reach for the trapdoor and pull it open. A wave of cool air came from the hole. Gripping the walking stick, I brought the lamp closer.

There he was, a twisted heap where he had fallen and broken his neck.

For the second time in as many days, I dug a grave. Only this time it took me the better part of the afternoon. I placed Tobias' body in it, covered him up, and said a prayer for both our souls.

In the tenuous light that filtered through the bull's eye as the sun set on the *Bonaventure*, I opened my journal and drew a line across the page. Beneath the line I wrote Tobias' name. Above it I drew the trapdoor with my mother's trunk holding it firmly closed. Perhaps its weight would suffice to keep Tobias below ground, freeing me from him at last.

Chapter II

The *Bonaventure*'s pennant of yellow stars on an azure field flew in the morning breeze from the main-topgallant masthead, and I heard the first mate call, "Fore, main, and mizzen topsails! Off gaskets! Sheet home!"

There were few sights more full of promise than billowing sails. As the wind filled them and the deck rose beneath my feet, I heard the ship owner's voice and watched as he approached me. I found it impossible to overlook the complete transformation of his attire. He was wearing a short jacket with a double row of elaborate silver buttons, a pair of long, loose trousers, trimmed with lace at the hem, and a pair of boots without the high heels common to gentlemen's shoes.

He addressed me in Spanish.

"I speak only English, sir."

"I shall give you Spanish lessons then. It'll help to while away the hours," he said.

"Your English is excellent for a Spaniard."

"I am no Spaniard, and my accent is execrable, but you shall help with that. Meanwhile, may I prevail upon you to assist me with the harnesses?"

"If I can. I know nothing of harnesses or cows."

"You have a lot to learn, young man. Have you ever been aboard a ship before?"

"Not as a passenger, sir."

He went on to explain that animals at sea fall and break their legs, forcing him to have to shoot them and depriving him of their meat further into the journey, when it is most needed. "Now, Master Michael, I wish to test this harness. I have designed it to hold the cow aloft during foul weather when the deck becomes slippery."

I pointed out that the harness that would raise the cow was attached to a brace that would move with the ship.

"Aye, aye, but the cow will be off the deck, and that being the case, she cannot slip and break her legs!"

"Your contraption might cause the very condition it's designed to prevent."

He threw his head back and laughed. His hat fell off, revealing long dark hair held back by a colorful woven headband across his forehead. The wind blew his hat along the deck and we chased and caught it, laughing together. When we returned to the pens he handed me a rope and proceeded to place a wide piece of sailcloth under the cow. "Pull!" he ordered.

With the aid of the pulley we hoisted the cow a foot above the deck. It protested, but the harness had been constructed in such a way that it prevented the cow from backing out of it, and the owner looked as proud and pleased as a boy earning his first penny.

"May I ask your name, sir?" I asked as he lowered the animal back to the deck.

"Garzón Moreau."

"You are French?"

"My father was French."

Satisfied with his experiment, he excused himself rather abruptly, vanishing below decks. I was pondering what I might have said to cause the sudden change in his manner when the sound of shouting reached me and I climbed a pile of barrels to see what was happening on the foredeck. The Captain was hauling one of the sailors toward the ropes used to climb the masts and ordering two of his companions to spread-eagle him across them and tie his hands and feet. A cat-o'-nine-tails appeared in the first mate's hands as the sailor's shirt was stripped from his back. I watched in horror as the whip fell and the man's skin burst open, showering the bystanders in blood. In my haste to back away from the scene, I tripped on a coil of rope and sprawled on the deck. I felt myself lifted and put aside as easily as if I had been a child.

Garzón vaulted over a pile of bales and ordered the Captain to stop the whipping. For a moment the two men faced one another and I feared that a fight would break out, but the Captain reined in his rage, stepped back, and ordered the sailor untied. His companions threw a bucket of ocean water over him and it turned pink as it washed over his back onto the deck. Garzón told them to take the man below, and as soon as he was alone with the Captain, he took the blood-soaked whip and threw it overboard. The Captain's face convulsed and a stream of spittle left his mouth and hit the deck at Garzón's feet. Contemptuous as the gesture was, it could not match the look of disdain with which Garzón met it. "I am relieving you of your command. You will retire to your quarters and remain there until we reach port. Señor Martínez," he said, addressing the first mate, "you will see to it."

"Yes, *monsieur!*"

~

It was noon before I dared venture out once more, and by then I was so hungry my knees were trembling. I took my ration of hardtack and stew and went to sit on a barrel, holding the wooden bowl in my lap. Garzón asked if he could join me and we ate together in silence for several moments. He ate elegantly in spite of the mild rocking of the ship and the wind that blew the steam off the stew. I straightened my back and increased the distance between my mouth and the bowl, wondering if I could manage to eat as he did without soiling my front. I was concentrating very hard on this when he spoke and a dollop of gravy left my spoon and landed on my chest.

"I regret that you had to witness such a scene."

"I'm no stranger to the punishment," I said, rubbing at the mess with my sleeve. "My father was in shipping," I added by way of explanation.

"I should have realized that my order forbidding whipping would not be taken seriously," he said, handing me his handkerchief. "Captains don't know how to control the men without the threat of the whip. As if life at sea were not hard enough already, with sleep hard to come by, the food inadequate, and one man or another suffering from prickly heat or gangrene! Not to mention the sailors' vapors, which affect mind and body alike, making men unpredictable and violent!" He stopped abruptly and laughed when he saw that my efforts had only made the stain on my shirt spread. "Come, we'll wash that."

His cabin was spacious, with a table taking up most of the central area. It was covered in charts, magnifying glasses, a quadrant, and a microscope.

"Take it off," he said, gesturing to my shirt.

I closed my coat, holding tightly to the lapels.

He looked amused as he brought out a clean shirt of his own. "Put this on," he said. "You can go behind the screen if you desire privacy."

I could hear him clearing a space on the table while I changed. When I emerged from behind the screen he announced that this was as good a time as any to begin my Spanish lessons and placed before me two hefty tomes titled *Paradise in the New World*. "They identify the banana as the forbidden fruit, place the Garden of Eden in the center of South America, and include a map with the location from which Noah's ark departed after the flood."

I must have looked as amazed as I felt because he smiled. "They were written by some rogue of a lawyer who was evidently paid by the word, since one has to read ten pages before meeting a single paragraph of matter."

"And I am to learn Spanish from them?"

"Unless you have other books we can use."

"I do! Books have been my dear companions ever since my Pa taught me to read, and I brought with me four volumes of the collected works of Mr. Swift and two novels — *Moll Flanders* and *Robinson Crusoe*. I also own Shakespeare's tragedies, given to me by my Ma, and a collection of Moliere's plays — translated into English!"

"A veritable library! Where shall we start?"

"With Mr. Swift?"

"A sensible choice."

"You have read Mr. Swift?"

"He is passionate on the subject of Ireland. I travel there frequently and have endeavored to learn its customs and its history."

The search for my books uncovered items that could reveal my identity, and I spent several minutes making sure everything was well hidden once again. In the process I came across a necklace my brother Michael had given me, and wound it around my fingers, unable to hold back the tears. Grief, I knew, was skilled at ambush and often surprised me with its stealth.

The necklace was made from the pea-sized pearls harvested by fishermen from the River Lee near the ruins of Carrigrohan Castle. The pearls came from freshwater mussels and sold in Cork for a trifling sum. Michael, however, had been eight years old when he bought the necklace and had worked hard to earn the money. It was the pearls that had given me the idea of pretending to be Michael. I had been sifting through the items I wanted to take with me when I came across them, wrapped in his clothes.

I had discarded my skirt and petticoats and tried on his shirt and breeches, feeling so light that I ran up and down the stairs for the sheer joy of it, something I had not done since childhood. Then I removed my round-eared cap and let my hair hang loose while I found the scissors.

Standing in front of the small mirror in the room that had once been Ma and Pa's I had looked carefully at myself for the first time since their death seven years ago. I was surprised to see a serious old woman look back at me. No white hair, no wrinkles, but a look as old and tired as Bridget's. I was as drab as the hills I had been standing on when I first saw Charlie FitzGibbon. Small wonder he had not looked twice at me.

I took up the scissors and by the time I was finished it was dark and the floor covered in hair. I put on Pa's hat and slipped out the back door, thankful for the thick hedge that grew so close to the cottage that I could leave without being seen by the O'Neill's.

I walked for an hour, surprised at how fast and hard my heart beat. I expected to be recognized, but no one paid me any mind until I reached one of the quays and a woman called from a dark alley inviting me to join her for a cup of ale. I was so pleased with my performance that I smiled and lengthened my stride, swaggering past a group of children begging for pennies. I threw them one and called out a greeting in my usual voice. They turned to look at me and I realized that I would have to be more careful, lower my voice, and speak only when spoken to.

When the O'Neill's saw me in Michael's clothes they could not believe their eyes. I was lifelike, they said, as true a boy as a woman could ever be. Mrs. O'Neill said that if she were twenty years younger she would be falling in love. Mary wanted to try on the clothes but her figure was so feminine that the britches would not do up and there was no concealing the proud swell of her breasts. Just as well, Mary said, or the O'Neill's would have lost us both. Mr. and Mrs. O'Neill tried to talk me out of my madness. With Tobias gone, they said, there was no reason for me to want to run away. Only Mary seemed to understand that I could not remain in my house, or even in Cork.

Tobias had not had many friends, and none of them showed undue concern over his disappearance. It was his enemies I had worried about. Tobias owed money all over Cork, and the day after I'd buried him, two of his less savory creditors had come calling. I had sent them away with Tobias' boots, which fit one of them. They would be back, they assured me, and expected to see either Tobias or their money when they did, preferably the latter.

Mary and I lost no time sewing undergarments with hidden seams and pockets, and her father built a false bottom for my trunk. He also melted down my gold coins and cast them into a small statue of the Virgin Mary. He concealed it in a plaster one and Mrs. O'Neill painted it, making it look like something a devout young woman might have done to while away the hours. I looked at the little statue, with its flowing white robes, blue mantle, and pale outstretched hands. The face was delicate, the smile gentle. My skepticism about the Virgin had grown with time, but Ma had instilled enough religion in me to make me kiss her bare feet and ask for her protection before I hid her once more in the depths of the trunk, picked up my books, and returned to the owner's cabin.

He was a good teacher, patient and encouraging, and I left his cabin in search of Mr. Swift's works, believing myself to be an outstanding linguist, able to master Spanish in record time.

~

By the time we crossed the Tropic of Cancer my stock of Spanish words and phrases had grown considerably, and I was able to understand Martínez when he came to tell me that the sailors had caught a shark and pulled it onto the ship. They were pleased, for a fish that size would feed all of us, and shark meat, he assured me, was nothing if not appetizing.

I arrived on deck just as the beast was cut open. Martínez reached into the carcass with a cry of triumph and held up a partly digested human arm, asking Garzón if he wanted it for study. I vomited, confirming the sailors in their opinion that I was surely the tenderest young man they had ever encountered.

Without the Captain to goad them on, the men's teasing had become good-natured and they made every effort to include me in their leisure activities. They found a fishing cane for me, to which they tied a string with a hook and a white feather — necessary, they explained, to trick the flying fish into thinking the feather was a whiting, which they loved to eat. I hadn't the heart to catch the flying fish, and pretended much clumsiness, finding that Garzón would then stand by me and help me string the feather onto the hook over and over again. I liked watching his sure, graceful movements, and more than once I found myself thinking how much he and Pa would have enjoyed comparing notes about the sea. They were very alike, Garzón and Pa. Not in appearance, for Garzón was dark where Pa was fair, and unusually tall, measuring close to six feet, a trait he had inherited from his French father. He had high cheekbones, and a nose I had heard described as Roman. I had never met a Roman, and from the only book about them I had seen, assumed they were a long-ago people and probably all dead.

Like Pa, Garzón believed that most of the maladies suffered by sailors could be avoided if they were fed and clothed adequately. Whenever Pa attempted to persuade ship's owners to stock up on less perishable fruits and vegetables, like oranges and carrots, he was laughed at and called a crafty devil, trying to make money off expensive items instead of the usual salted beef and biscuit.

While scurvy was an affliction more common to the Pacific than the Atlantic, Garzón monitored our diet closely. We were served the usual salted fare, along with sour krout and malt, and five chests of oranges and five of lemons were delivered at every port along the way. The welfare of the men who served him was of paramount importance to him and between ports we all had to drink wort juice (I held my nose) and air our clothes and bedding. This posed a particular challenge for me, since I had had my monthly bleeding since leaving Cork and had to devise a means of washing and drying my under garments in my tiny alcove, an inconvenience I hadn't properly anticipated.

Buckets of sea water were hauled aboard regularly for bathing, and the ship was cleansed by means of smoking pots set down in all the lower quarters. All forty of the men had Magellan Jackets — named, I think, after the Portuguese navigator Magallanes of two hundred years ago — and none had to go barefoot unless they wished to, which several of them did, having been bred at sea and finding surer footing with the aid of their toes.

Early in June, the sea turned red and Garzón had a bucket lowered over the side. When it was brought on board we saw that it was full of tiny swimming creatures. Garzón examined them under his microscope and invited me to look. Squirming on the glass were beings that resembled minute shrimp. They must have been very tasty because when I returned to the deck the sea around us was filled with feeding porpoises and whales. I could scarcely believe my eyes. There was the ship, floating in a red sea, surrounded by gigantic beings whose backs crested like black waves over which the silver porpoises dived, sometimes alone, sometimes in groups like streaks of light. And there were we, small and helpless, entirely at their mercy and entirely ignored by them.

I had taken to following Garzón from one to another of his scientific experiments, free for the first time since my childhood to indulge my curiosity and to marvel at the wonders of the world, like the creatures being studied by him in an array of buckets of salt water. Garzón explained that collectors killed their specimens and dissected them as a means of classifying and understanding them, but he was far more interested in their living habits. He held them captive for a day or two and then released them. Growing up as I had, among seafaring men, many were the hours I had spent listening to their tales of great tentacled monsters that inhabited the deep, of poisonous jellyfish the size of dinner plates, and of eels that gave off light. Garzón's collection was not representative of any of these. Here were fish and jellyfish of a remarkable variety of colors and shapes, unusual plants resembling insects, and creatures that fed on and often looked like them. He named them, and I drew them, sketchily at first, but in greater and greater detail as he encouraged me and my confidence grew.

Soon after we passed the snow-topped peaks of Teneriffe, off the West coast of Africa, Martínez announced that we would soon be beyond the tropics and in *el mar de las damas*, the ladies' sea, so called because it was free of tempests. I told him that it certainly was not named after any of the ladies I knew, and Garzón agreed. He had made no mention of a sweetheart, and there was nothing I had seen among his belongings that indicated that he might be married, but suddenly I felt peevish and jealous. What ladies did he know? And how well did he know them?

A gust of wind blew me off balance, and gathering clouds obscured the setting sun. I was ordered below as top-men scaled the masts and climbed out on the yards to hand and reef canvas.

I was reaching for my lantern when the ship lurched and I lost my balance, falling into my bunk. The lantern, my boots, mug, and every other article not in my trunk or secured to the walls, flew across the tiny cabin. I held tightly to the bed rail as a roar filled the air outside. The ship began to creak and moan as if the trees used in the making of the vessel had returned to life to mourn their fate. Unable to see out and with barely any light within, I clung to my bunk, whispering Hail Mary's and hearing only the terrifying howls of the wind, the lashing of the water, and the screams emanating from the ship as it fought to keep afloat in one piece.

I couldn't bear the thought of dying trapped below and alone, so I groped my way out of the cabin. I heard the Captain banging on his locked door and calling to be let out. Above deck the wind was so strong I could barely open the hold, and when I did, received a sudden cold soaking of heavy rain that made me gasp and choke. A flash of lightning lit the sky and engraved forever on my memory the horrified faces of the men on deck. They made no sound, or if they did, it could not be heard above the roar of wind and water. All were looking up, their mouths agape and their eyes wide.

Bearing down upon us was a wave so tall its top was lost in the darkness. A solid wall of water, lifted from the ocean by the force of the wind above, it hit the ship and turned it on its side, sweeping me back down the steps. Water poured in through every opening, and planks gave way, their caulking weakened.

The ship righted herself, sending me rolling to the other side of the narrow passage gasping for air, and it took all the strength I could muster to re-climb the ladder leading to the deck. Water rushed in upon me every time a wave hit, and I was half-drowned by the time I reached the top and looked out into the storm.

The lantern on the poop deck had been extinguished by the lashings of rain descending on the ship, and I could only see the men on deck in the occasional flashes of lightning. Martínez was tied to the ship's wheel and several sailors had secured themselves to the masts and appeared to be praying to the statue of the Virgin Mary and the infant Jesus nailed to the small platform where I had stood only a few hours before. His voice impossible to hear in the shriek of the wind and the pounding of the waves, Garzón was giving orders by pointing and clawing his way an inch at a time along the rail. For a moment he disappeared into a wave that washed over the ship and I knew that I was screaming because my throat felt on fire, but not a sound could be heard over the roar of the storm.

He emerged from the foam and found the staysail, while another man took hold of the driver. Together they brought them back to the mizzen. Only then could the ship be made to find her keel and head into the wind, our only hope for survival in such a storm. But the sea was not done with us yet. Another gigantic wave hit us and once more the masts dipped toward the black water, sailors clinging to anything left standing on the canted deck.

The ladder to which I clung flew out and I saw the ocean racing up to meet me as I plunged headlong toward it. With a shudder, the ship righted itself, and the ladder, with me still welded to it, slid in the opposite direction. I felt the unyielding surface of a mast at my feet as several of the ladder's rungs broke with the impact, saving me from serious injury.

With a final gust the wind abated, leaving us in a downpour of rain. Once more, our only source of illumination came from the lightning, and for what seemed an eternity those of us who had survived the storm sat, lay, or stood where we were, not daring to disturb the balance of the ship. As we began to move, moans and cries for help rose like distant, eerie ghost sounds amid the hiss of the rain falling on the ship. Surfaces were slippery and men shuffled their feet, trying not to fall as they dropped below decks to man the pumps.

I pulled myself up and felt a stab of pain in my knee. I limped toward the hatchway, dragging the broken ladder with me. The water below was up to my calves and as I joined the others I saw that the Captain had been released to help with the bailing. The effort seemed fruitless, but we worked without rest until the ship had settled once more into its usual rhythmic floating. The silence was stark after the roaring of the storm, and the water sloshed gently at my feet as I climbed back up to look out at the dawn sky.

The deck had been swept clean of every item, including all the livestock and the holy statue. Remnants of the sails the men had not had time to wrap and secure to the masts hung tattered in the early light. Two men had been lost overboard. One was pinned under a broken mast that had jammed sideways across the rails of the poop deck. Two had broken arms. Others had suffered cuts and bruises in their fight to keep the ship afloat.

Those who were uninjured went to work rescuing the sailor trapped under the mast, and setting the ship to rights. The pumps were started; and Garzón went to the galley. One barrel of fresh water remained, and he set some to boiling after finding a large bin of rice. He brought out cups and served brandy to the crew, who were shivering from cold and fright.

I had said nothing until that moment about my healing skills but could not conceal them when the need was so great. Garzón, though surprised by my offer to assist with the wounded, was too busy to question me, and simply ordered two of the able-bodied sailors to clear a table below decks and bring me the most seriously injured first. I untied my trunk from beneath my bunk and hoisted it out, reaching for my basket and withdrawing the items I would need. For the first time, I noticed that my fingers were throbbing and saw that I had torn several nails during my wild ride on the ladder.

The first man brought to me had a deep gash in his leg. I gave him a stick to hold as I sewed his wound, and his knuckles turned white as the needle moved in and out of his flesh.

"Where'd you learn all this then, master?" he asked.

"From an old Irish woman called Mother Phips. She once paid me the compliment of saying that I can stitch as neatly as a nun."

Mrs. Phips would not have recognized my handiwork that day.

The pain in my hands and the swelling from my torn fingernails made me clumsy and inept. My jacket was soaked and heavy and I removed it as the next man was brought in, carried by Garzón. I turned to assist him and saw Garzón's eyes open wide, staring at my chest. I looked down. My breasts lay revealed under my wet shirt as undeniably as if I had stood there naked. I felt the blood rush to my face and turned my back, fumbling for my coat. He helped me to put it on and said that he would find something dry for me to wear.

I tried to still the trembling in my hands as I ran them over the unconscious sailor. His eyes fluttered open and I asked him to open his mouth. I was relieved to see no blood there, a sign that in all likelihood he was not bleeding internally. His chest wounds were not deep, and by the time I had cleansed them Garzón had returned with a dry coat. Both of us had regained our composure and were able to bind the man's broken ribs tightly in a layer of sailcloth.

The men with broken arms followed, and by then every muscle in my body ached and both my elbows throbbed from my fall down the ladder. The roaring in my ears seemed locked in my head, and I began to shiver as I ate the warm cup of rice Garzón had brought me. He peeled the wet mattress off my bunk, found a partially dry blanket and left me to curl up on the hard wooden planks of the bed.

~

I woke up chilled. My mouth was dry and my clothes damp. I slid off the bunk with an effort and found myself standing in a puddle of water. Thirst and hunger drove me out of my cabin and onto the bare deck of the *Bonaventure*, where tattered sails blew in the afternoon breeze and men were hard at work pounding nails into loose planks and hauling wet canvas from below deck.

I tried to button my coat, but my fingers were so sore I could not do it and had to be content with holding it around myself and avoiding Garzón's eyes when he served me my ration of rice and ale. I felt better after eating and drinking, and went below again to see to the wounded men I had tended earlier. They were in pain, but no danger, and after feeding them and changing their dressings, I assisted with bailing and cleaning the ship.

That night, when the ship was quiet, I went on deck and stood by the railing, hoping that Garzón would come, as he had done every night before now, to give me my Spanish lesson. I was about to give up my waiting when he appeared, looking tired and serious. I asked him if he would stop teaching me now that he knew my identity and he didn't answer.

"Until today, I was merely an ignorant boy to you. Only my sex has changed! I am still ignorant and much in need of instruction!"

"Our lessons will take a different form. But we will start with an explanation, if you please." He coughed, rather nervously I thought, and looked down at the water going by beneath us. "Tell me who you really are and what you are doing aboard my ship."

I was surprised at the ease with which I unburdened myself of my early history, telling him about Pa and Ma and Michael, omitting Tobias entirely, and recounting how I had become a nurse and midwife. I told him how I had been orphaned at fourteen and how out of the misfortune of the fever that had taken my family and so many of my neighbors, had come the work that would sustain me. I had begun by nursing the ill and the dying. Later, I had apprenticed myself to a midwife.

Midwifery had seemed a joyful occupation, as indeed it was on the occasions when I attended the birth of children who were wanted and welcomed. How rare this was became obvious all too soon, as I was asked by one desperate woman after another for the means to prevent pregnancies or end them once begun. In almost every home I visited, women just like me hid small hordes of money in places their men were unlikely to touch — cradles, flour bins, the rags they used to staunch their monthly flow. Husbands were rarely in the house when births occurred, they returned once the labor pains were over, the smells aired away, and the blood washed out the door. Some kissed their wives, some tried to kiss me, a few looked at the latest bundle in the bed. When priests were present it was to baptize the newborn or give last rites to the mother, disappearing again after entrusting the family to the care of God. "When I first started hoarding the coins that would make it possible for me to leave Ireland it was with the intention of ensuring my independence. A woman's only hope for it lies in remaining single and in control of her finances. Once married, a woman becomes chattel. I saw it every day in my work among poor and rich alike."

He focused his eyes on me and listened to my words as if nothing else in the world existed but the two of us leaning on the ship's rail. When I finished, he smiled, and something other than the motion of the ship lifted me closer to the stars.

I had revealed more about myself than I had intended and was quick to change the subject, asking him about his own history.

His father had been sent to sea at an early age to serve under a captain who was stingy with the food and generous with the lash. He survived only because he was befriended by a veteran, a one-eyed sailor named Jacques, who jumped ship one day, taking Garzón's father with him. The two of them ended up on a vessel headed for Buenos Aires, where Jacques became a merchant, and Garzón's father eventually owned ships of his own. He grew rich smuggling the first grape vines and olive trees into the Province. Not being a Spaniard, he had not felt it part of his patriotic duty to pay twenty times the usual price for wine and oil he could make himself. The Spanish trapped him one day when he was becalmed and killed him.

He then embarked on a rather dry explanation of how settlers in the colonies are not allowed to compete with the home country by making or growing anything that can be made or grown in Spain. Goods not only had to be imported, they were heavily tithed, and had to be sent to the colonies from a Spanish port on a Spanish ship. Most ship owners ran a licensed ship that obeyed the regulations and paid the levies and several more which operated outside the confines of the law. These ships came and went in complete harmony with the authorities, who also benefited by using the ships to smuggle and sell their own goods, or by accepting bribes with money or merchandise. All prospered and felt no compunction about circumventing laws imposed upon them from afar by greedy Spanish merchants anxious to corner new markets.

He stopped. "I am boring you to tears."

"Oh no! I assure you, I—"

"I have been careless in both my manner and my speech."

"You have been generous and kind! It would be ungrateful of me to take offence at your behavior when I was engaged in deceiving you." I put my hand on his arm. "You will not stop teaching me, will you?"

"Above deck," he said hurriedly, stepping back from my touch. "We will study the stars."

"No more Spanish lessons?"

"We will study the stars in Spanish."

In his eagerness to escape, he tripped over a bucket. As I moved away from the security of the rail, I was none too steady myself.

~

For a day after the storm we lay at anchor while Garzón and Martínez assessed the damage to the *Bonaventure*. We had suffered one broken mast, and several planks had sprung loose in the stern. All the ropes and lanterns on deck were washed away, our drinking water was almost gone and our food stores greatly diminished. We were placed on a ration of two quarts of water and a cup of rice per day until we could re-supply. The sail room was flooded, so all the sodden sail cloth was brought on deck to dry, preparatory to cutting and stitching new sails. Our cargo of iron, a commodity worth almost its weight in gold in the Spanish colonies, had caused the ship to sit low in the water, which may have been to our advantage in the storm, but almost all of the cinnamon, pepper, cloves, and mace stored in the holds with the iron had been ruined.

We reached Antigua Island three days after the storm. The Captain was paid off and disembarked, as glad to be rid of us as we were of him. Repairs would now be made, the ship's holds would be restocked, and new hands hired, all of which would take some time. There was no hurry, Garzón said, for me to leave the ship.

Now that the time had come, I found that I could not bear to think of it.

News greeted us that England and Spain were fighting again. This time, Garzón said, we had a one-eared English captain to thank for this latest war between the two old rivals. Until recently, the Spanish had had access to a large number of slaves thanks to English pirates who smuggled them into the Spanish colonies from Africa. The Spanish governors tolerated the practice until their own slave merchants complained and captured several English slavers, the

Rebecca and her Captain Jenkins among them. As a warning to the English, the Spanish cut off Jenkins' ear. He took offense and displayed the thing — which he took everywhere with him in a bottle — at the Bar of Commons. Shocked at this affront to an Englishman, Parliament demanded compensation from the King of Spain, who thought this attitude impertinent. After all, the English owed him a vast amount in import duties for the thousands of slaves they had smuggled into his colonies. The War of Jenkins' Ear was the result of this haggling over human flesh and suffering.

"This bodes badly for Ireland," I said.

Every time the English went to war they assumed we would join the enemy of the day and put ourselves at his service. They remained perversely ignorant of the obvious. A nation broken by poverty and a people degraded by servitude viewed these power struggles with the utmost indifference. Nevertheless, a flurry of proclamations and proposals to the Privy Council to massacre all Catholics forthwith would doubtless follow this latest war folly.

"It is the fourth time this century that they have declared war on one another," Garzón said. "It makes life perilous for us all. It is out of the question for you to embark for Boston."

"Will I have to remain here until the war is over?"

We were seated on a small hillside overlooking the harbor, and Garzón reached between his feet to pluck a blade of grass. "Or head south. Spanish America is full of opportunities."

Before I could consider the rush of excitement that flooded through me, or how to respond to the suggestion, a voice came from behind us. "Begging your pardon, but did I hear you mention Spanish America?"

A young Scotsman in cap and kilt, leading a horse wearing a tartan saddle cloth, approached us. "Hamish MacBean," he said, making us a small bow. "Charmed to make your acquaintance."

Was it true, he wondered, that the Province of Buenos Aires was bigger than Germany, Italy, France, and the Netherlands put together, and that vast herds of cattle wandered over it, obligingly covered in valuable hides, and full of fat that could be rendered into tallow?

"A conservative estimate is twenty-five million head," Garzón said.

McBean whistled softly.

"The herds of horses often number ten thousand or more."

"And the land?"

"Is there for the taking, at a dollar per head of cattle grazed on it."

"Extraordinary!"

He was eager to leave Antigua, he said. He had escaped there following the defeat of the Young Pretender, Charles Stuart, when the English had taken stern measures against the Scots. "They no longer allow us to wear our tartans when at home!"

I had not spoken a word so far, but this comment annoyed me. "Irish clans have long been suppressed, Catholics are forbidden from going overseas to educate themselves, and we are barred from purchasing land! I would not whine about a skirt if that was all the English had done to me!"

"A kilt, if you please! If you were a gentleman I'd call you out, you insolent pup!"

"If you weren't a dunderhead I'd meet your challenge!"

I was so incensed that I failed to notice Garzón's amusement. He took my arm and led me away, stopping a few feet down the hillside and turning back to MacBean. "Are you a Catholic?"

"Certainly not!"

"Consider being baptized or consign Spanish America to your dreams. The Spanish don't take kindly to Protestants."

He began to laugh as we continued down the hill and by the time we reached the harbor I was laughing too and my anger had entirely disappeared.

It was madness for me to think of the Province. What would I do there? Garzón had mentioned opportunities, but what could those be for a lone woman?

I had not been to his cabin since he had discovered my identity, and I approached it nervously. His door was open and he was bent over a large map spread on the table. He saw me and waved for me to join him, pointing at the map. "This is the Province of Buenos Aires. See this bay here? There is a small city there, called Montevideo. And here," he pointed northeast, beyond the coastal plains, "is a lagoon, fed by ocean tides, rich with fish and prawns." His eyes glowed as he told me how at sunrise dew drops shone there like strewn diamonds on the grass and wild horses rolled in them and shook themselves, sending the dew flying. Bird song filled the air from dawn to dusk, and at night, under the stars, one could grasp the meaning of infinity and feel oneself small and sheltered within it. In the surrounding *montes*, the woods encircling the lagoon, jaguars glittered like gold in an emerald sea, and the *pampas* rippled to the horizon in an ocean of grass.

"Is that where your home is?"

"It will be, if I can persuade my friend Father Manuel to help me."

Father Manuel was a Jesuit, he went on to explain, and as such had many enemies, whose principal complaint against the priests was rarely voiced.

"The Spanish nobility has kept itself well shielded from its actions in America. They brush aside the bloody history of their enslavement of the Indians as exaggeration, as the necessary price of bringing civilization to the heathen, as an inevitable outcome of war. Colonists consider the Indians so far beneath them that they abuse them with impunity. I have yet to hold a conversation with a Spanish or a Portuguese official in which I can detect even a hint that the natives are in any sense their equals. It's as preposterous to them as suggesting that horses or cattle should be declared free or given rights."

Millions of Indians, Garzón said, had been taken, branded on the cheek with their owners mark, their belongings stolen, their lands ravaged. Most of them were put to work in silver mines and on sugar plantations, major sources of revenue for the Spanish and Portuguese crowns. Most of the output from the mines and huge plantations went to European markets, and the cost in human suffering was equally great for both commodities. When the supply of native slaves easily available to them in their own colonies was exhausted, the Portuguese had invaded the lands under Spain's control, capturing and enslaving hundreds of thousands more. It was then that the Jesuits had obtained permission from the King of Spain to arm their converts and train them in the use of firearms and cannon, successfully driving the Portuguese raiders away and allowing the Jesuit Missions to enter this, their most prosperous, peaceful, and productive era. Those who benefited from slavery, however, were spreading tales about the Order's wealth, claiming that the priests defrauded the King of the rightful, Christian gains from the products of the Missions, and that his coffers would soon be overflowing if land owners were allowed to put Mission Indians to work for them, paying not the workers, as Garzón was proposing, but the King himself for the privilege of using his subjects.

He explained that *changadores*, a rough sort of cattlemen, obtained licenses from Buenos Aires allowing them to harvest thousands of animals from the vast herds, but no one had organized this slaughter into anything like a well-regulated industry. The man who went about it the right way, Garzón said, would be richer than Croesus in under a year. Several had tried, with a contingent of soldiers provided by the Governor of Buenos Aires to protect them from the unconverted Indians. They failed, due he believed, to not bothering to seek out the Indians' only allies — the Jesuits.

"I will not make the same mistake. I have been talking to Father Manuel, suggesting that he allow his Indian converts to work for me for wages, and that he establish a mission on my land to convert others."

"Are there any Irish in the province?"

"Some."

"Do the Spanish not consider us their enemies then?"

"Not the Catholic Irish. They are made welcome in the colonies."

"It is the first I've heard of Irish Catholics being made welcome anywhere."

I stood staring at the map, steeling myself to say the words. "I have money. Could I use it to buy shares in your enterprise?"

"Miss Keating— "

Not Micheal, as he had called me until now, not Isabel, as he knew my name to be, but a formal "Miss Keating." This did not bode well, but I was not going to give up, not yet. I looked him full in the face. "Your wife would object?"

"I have no wife. It's simply that the idea of selling shares had not occurred to me. You took me unawares."

"You told me that Spanish America is full of opportunities. I am a hard worker, I can help keep your books and manage the sale of merchandise. It's what I did for Pa."

"You should know that you might be my only investor."

"That is more appealing to me than otherwise."

"Would you remain disguised?"

"For the time being. Does that concern you?"

"On the contrary. It will make things easier for us both. Fewer questions will be asked of two men." He held out his hand.

I knew then that if I took it I would leave the commonplace forever behind me.

I hesitated only for a moment, just long enough to savor the realization that I was making my first decision as a woman unfettered by her past.

Instinctively, I had answered that I would remain disguised. One reason was obvious and indisputable. Men's clothes offered comfort and freedom of movement. The other went back, I suspected, to those days when I had discovered myself to be much more adept than my brother at assisting our father with his business, only to find that no matter how talented and hard working I might be, eventually Michael would be the one to inherit and manage what I had had so strong a hand in building. If pretending to be a man allowed me to exercise those talents on my own behalf, then so be it.

Chapter III

Three and a half months after leaving Cork we reached the South Atlantic, where currents are hazardous and there is always the danger of falling upon the protruding Eastern coast of Brazil. Sentinels were posted in the crow's nest until the danger was past.

I shall never forget that dawn when the jungle loomed out of the early light, a mass of every shade of green imaginable, majestic, wild, and unlike anything I had ever beheld in sheer natural grandeur. Beyond the wide ribbon of sand by the shore, the impenetrable forests stretched as far as the eye could see, the massive trees reaching for the sun through the web of vines and creepers that rioted at their feet.

As we approached the harbor at Río de Janeiro barges surrounded the ship, their thatched coverings offering shade to the poor and scantily clad families living aboard. They were selling fruit, and I was preparing to buy some when Garzón discouraged me, pointing to the harbor waters, where fruits, vegetables, fish bones, and disintegrating loaves of bread lapped against the boats and pylons. I learned that all the refuse from the city of Río de Janeiro was thrown into the harbor waters, including leftover produce from the markets. The barge dwellers harvested what they could from the water to feed themselves and to sell to incoming ships carrying ignorant passengers like me.

The port itself was teeming with people, offering monkeys, parrots, shoe leather, and fish for sale.

I could sense the sailors' excitement as they buckled on their sandals, brushed their jackets, and tied their hair back with colorful ribbons, joking with one another about the number of taverns they would visit and the women they would lie with.

I saw Garzón glancing my way, worried that I might find such talk offensive, but I barely heard the banter, my attention drawn by a large schooner casting anchor far from the other ships.

"Is there illness on board? Is that why they are moored so far from port?"

Garzón told me what the ship carried. "The odor is too rank even for the dockside."

Only Martínez appeared energized. He hurried to Garzón's side, rubbing his hands. He had learned from one of the harbor pilots that the slaver was fresh from Whydah on the coast of Guinea. He urged Garzón to buy all the women who had survived the journey and sell them to the gold miners, a venture that would ensure that neither of them need ever work again, for the miners considered it essential to have at least one Whydah woman to cure them of venereal disease. If they showed up with several the men would give a month's harvest of gold for them.

I would never have dared to ask what I did had the first mate been aware that I was a woman, but since he thought me a callous boy I inquired whether the women knew of a cure for such diseases. If they did, I was bound and determined to learn of it.

"They are the cure, Master Michael. Lie with a Whydah woman and your health will be restored at once!"

"That is wicked and arrant nonsense, Martínez!" Garzón admonished him. "All that will happen is that the woman will become diseased as well."

"The miners we would sell them to don't know that, and a fool's gold weighs as much as any man's!"

Garzón forbade him from buying any women and bringing them on board, and Martínez retreated, muttering that perhaps the time had come for him to go into business for himself.

I did not see Garzón again until that night, when I waited by the main mast as usual for him to join me. I was disturbed by the muffled cries floating from the dark and distant slave vessel, and it was only when I gave up waiting for him and left my place that I noticed Garzón standing in the prow, still and silent, looking from the slave ship to the Southern Cross.

"The Spanish call it the *Cruz de mayo*," he said as I approached him. "My mother's people see the foot of a *ñandú*, walking across the sky. A *ñandú*," he added, "is a very large flightless bird.

"And who are your mother's people?"

"She was from a tribe called the Charrúa."

The night had turned cool and I shivered. Garzón took off his jacket and put it round me. It was warm from his warmth and I buried my face in the broad collar, inhaling a mixture of wool and tobacco. As I slipped my hands into the pockets I felt a smooth, hard shape and withdrew a highly polished, rich brown agate shaped like a crescent moon. "How it shines!"

"Agates are common in the province."

"Did you shape it?"

"It was a gift."

He did not say who from, and sensing that I had trespassed somehow, I returned the jacket and bade him good night. He called after me that he would be going ashore in the morning, and asked if I would care to accompany him. I said I would, and we agreed to meet early on the foredeck.

The combined smell of raw fish, human sweat, and boiling bones assailed my nostrils as I stepped ashore, and I was glad to have a scented handkerchief to press to my nose as we made our way through chanting, half-naked groups of slaves unloading the *Bonaventure*'s merchandise. We walked along narrow streets with houses no more than four stories high and boasting not a single pane of glass. Behind the wooden shutters I occasionally spotted a female figure. The streets, I noticed, were devoid of all but slave women, often walking next to curtained chairs in which their mistresses were transported by pairs of male slaves. If this was the lot of women in the Americas, I told Garzón, I would never don female clothing again.

We were soon walking among stalls displaying Chinese porcelain, Arabian perfumes, and swords crafted in Toledo. I was struggling to take it all in, when we turned into the tailors' lane. Here velvets and satins, embroidered Dutch cloths and silks from Granada, Neapolitan hose, ribbons, laces, and hats made in London and Paris, overflowed into the narrow street and I was almost run down by what seemed to be an army of servants carrying food for the shoppers on platters the size of small boats. Garzón took my arm and led me toward a modest store front, guarded like a small fortress by two men armed with knives, firearms, and swords. Once inside, I felt as if I had entered an enchanted cave. The room overflowed with solid gold ingots, diamonds from Ceylon, silver buckles and buttons, and Panamanian pearls of every hue from white to rose to gray.

As we stepped out once more into the blinding sunlight we were separated by runners clearing a path for a party of wealthy shoppers. The first glimpse I caught of the lords of Brazil was of their horses with their tall-plumed headdresses and hooves gleaming with inlaid emeralds. More plumes decorated the men's hats, and the embroidery and ribbon work on their clothes was so elaborate the garments stood out stiffly, the coat tails covering the horse's flanks, while the reins looked as if they were attached to the lace ruffles that hid the riders' hands. On their feet they wore fine leather boots, the points tucked into stirrups of gold filigree.

As they passed, I saw Garzón waving to me from across the street where he had been studying a display of glassware. I joined him and he asked me if I had built up an appetite yet. We sat down to eat under a green-and-red-striped awning and Garzón ordered fried bananas. While we waited, he placed a tiny glass seagull on the table between us.

"It is Venetian."

I picked it up and put it on my palm. It was so lifelike it needed only a tiny ocean to soar over.

"It is for you," he said, so awkwardly that my eyes filled with tears and for a moment the little seagull shimmered and blurred.

"It is the loveliest thing I've ever owned," I said, wrapping it carefully in my handkerchief.

The bananas arrived and I was about to pick up a slice with my fingers when I saw Garzón reaching for his cutlery. "My father was strict where table manners were concerned," he said. "The first time he saw me reach for food with my hands he had the table cleared until I learned how to use a knife and fork."

"My table manners leave much to be desired. I am anxious to

improve myself." I picked up my own knife and fork and prepared to eat.

"Never touch the knife blade," he said, caressing the back of my hand. The cuff of my coat reminded him that I was in disguise and he leaned back in his chair, laughing.

Full of fried bananas and sweet coffee we had begun our walk back to the ship when I heard a sweet, high voice singing.

So farewell to my friends and relations,
Perchance I shall see you no more,
And when I'm in far distant nations
Sure I'll sigh for my dear native shore.

It was "The Maid With the Bonny Brown Hair," a tune I had last heard on the shores of the River Lee. We followed the voice to an inn and I looked up in astonishment at a child in a wicker cage hanging outside the door. He was no more than four or five, and he sang as sweetly as any canary as he swayed there in the chilly August wind above our heads.

The innkeeper approached us, speaking in Portuguese and offering us lodgings as he wiped his hands on the dirty apron that covered the large expanse of his belly.

"Why is that child in a cage?" I asked him, using the Spanish Garzón had been teaching me.

The man understood me and explained that the child was being punished for eating earth.

"Perhaps he was hungry," I said, pointing to his stick-like limbs.

"Hungry, *senhor*? Observe the stomach on him! He looks like my wife a few months after I have done my duty by her! And yet he eats dirt! He is worse than an animal, *senhor*, do not trouble yourself about him. He is happy there, hear him singing?"

"Distended abdomens in children are not a sign of good nutrition, you blockhead! Bring that child down at once!"

Rather to my surprise, since in my anger I had reverted to speaking English, the man obeyed me, and untied the rope that held the cage aloft while explaining to me that the child was highly trained. "If he so much as hears a song, in any language, he can repeat it. I cannot part with him for less than one bar of gold."

Garzón told him not to take us for fools.

The innkeeper ordered the boy to climb out, but his legs, cramped from confinement, would not allow him to stand. God only knows how long he had been caged and his legs were atrophied from lack of use. I took him in my arms, resting my cheek on the boy's head. "He weighs no more than a feather."

Garzón took me aside. "If you buy him, the innkeeper will only acquire another."

"May we at least ensure that he is freed from the cage?"

The innkeeper pocketed Garzón's gold coin and smiled, telling me I had a heart as tender as a woman's. I knew then that the moment our backs were turned the child would be back in his cage. His arms tightened around my neck as the innkeeper came to take him, and I released his hold and ran, overwhelmed with rage and helplessness.

~

In an effort to distract me and make up for the sad ending to our first outing together on dry land, Garzón obtained an invitation for us to dine with a Mr. Foley, a Dublin merchant he learned of while being measured by his Portuguese tailor. He was a pleasant, hearty fellow and when Garzón told him about Michael Keating, he received an invitation to bring his *protegé* for a visit to the Foley sugar plantation on the outskirts of the city.

We followed Mr. Foley down a narrow road of bright red earth. He explained to me that soil turns this color in Brazil after the trees are cut down. It is then virtually useless as crop land and erodes during the heavy rains, creating areas of red desert in striking contrast to the surrounding jungle. He guided us into the forest, where the trees were so tall their tops seemed lost in the clouds. Some were connected by vines that sent shoots out from hundreds of feet above to take root below. They were the circumference of my waist, and twisted themselves around the trees tying one to another, so that the jungle resembled a vast crisscrossing of Bush-rope. This extensive family of closely bound giants reminded me of my lonely situation, bound to no one and none bound to me. A sense of loss overcame me, so deep a dagger of darkness that I forgot my moment of certainty in Garzón's cabin, and my hand reached for the little seagull I now carried like a talisman close to my heart.

By the time we arrived at the plantation, sitting at the foot of a hill dwarfed by the jungle of vegetation behind it, the effort to sit straight in the saddle took all the energy I had.

"Are you unwell, Master Michael?" Garzón asked me.

I answered that I was simply a little warm, and focused my attention on the long, whitewashed adobe house. It had ornate bars at the windows and a thatched roof, and it looked striking against the red earth and green trees surrounding it. It was a roomy place, kept cool by the wooden blinds and lace curtains at the windows, with a smoothly swept earth floor reminiscent of Irish cottages, and an air of comfort in the smaller rooms leading off the central courtyard, where a tall, spreading tree with huge round leaves shaded the entire area.

Mr. Foley ushered us in just as several children raced into the patio, dressed in bright red and yellow trousers and skirts. They descended on him like a shower of flower petals, searching his pockets, pulling out ribbons, small cloth dolls, and an assortment of animals carved out of bone. One older girl clung to him long after the children had turned their attention to us, and Mr. Foley explained that while the children spoke not one word of English, his wife did. He was evidently most proud of this as he introduced Mrs. Foley, or Ismelda, as she insisted we call her. On closer inspection, she was perhaps not quite as young as I had at first supposed her, but she had greeted her husband so playfully I had thought her one of her own children. She kissed us both on the cheek and commented on the smoothness of mine, asking if I shaved yet. Garzón distracted her with a compliment on her family. She clapped her hands and sent the children scampering off for refreshments while we made ourselves at ease on the wicker chairs.

The youngest child, Tomás, disregarded his mother's instructions and remained behind, studying me from the doorway. He had a burn on his thigh, and I was about to encourage him to approach me when Mr. Foley asked if I intended to settle in Brazil. "I am traveling to Montevideo to establish a partnership with Monsieur Moureau."

Garzón told Mr. Foley of his plan to hire Indians from the Missions.

"What the Jesuits have accomplished is quite remarkable," Mr. Foley said. "The Mission Indians can read and write — which is more than the majority of Spaniards and Portuguese in the area can do! Many are also expert craftsmen, and one of the priests, a man named Sepp, has discovered how to extract iron from *ytacurú* stones and opened an iron works in San Juan!"

Clearly, Ismelda feared her husband would bore us with his stories, for as soon as he had told us about the mechanical marvel in Father Sepp's church tower — a clock, just like the one Mr. Foley had seen in Munich, with the twelve apostles marching across the clock face each day at noon — she tried to change the subject. "Perhaps, the Captain's people were among those who did not fare well during this long struggle," she said.

"I beg your pardon if I have been insensitive, Captain," Mr. Foley said.

"My mother's people are still free, Mr. Foley."

The conversation threatened to founder, and Ismelda came to our rescue. Her parents, she said, had both been enslaved by the Portuguese. The effect of such a remark in an Irish parlor would have been to silence us entirely by plunging us into the most profound embarrassment, but conversation in this portion of the Portuguese colony was conducted in an altogether different manner. The children burst into sound and motion like a flock of startled birds, embracing their mother and offering her fruit from a painted platter. She accepted their offerings, allowing them to cut and peel the fruit for her, reserving the privilege of putting it in her mouth for the youngest only. Mr. Foley invited her to tell us her story, and the children chimed in to encourage her. "Tell the story, *mamá*," the children cried. "Tell how the Portuguese attacked your village and how you fought back!"

So Ismelda told of the sudden attack, of men and dogs so fast and fierce that the warriors had had no time to arm and defend themselves. Children unable to march were killed. Old men and women died screaming to the others to run and hide, but there was nowhere to go through the ring of whips and swords and snarling dogs. As her parents were chained neck to neck and ankle to ankle with the other survivors, Ismelda saw her village go up in flames. "The dogs tracked down those who had escaped, and brought pieces of them back to their masters. The rest of us were driven through the jungle by day and left to lie at night, too exhausted to do more than rest our bleeding feet and comfort one another with pieces of wormy bread."

Water was scarce and every day empty links of chain clanked along between those who could still walk. The dead were left to feed the ants in the humid heat of the jungle. By the time they reached the small port town of Seguro, only two of the nine children taken were still alive. Ismelda was one of them. She arrived in Río de Janeiro chained on one side to a decomposing body and on the other to a woman made mad with grief during her battle to defend her baby from the rats that swarmed over them below decks.

I sat by Ismelda, prevented by my disguise from doing more than mumble my profound regret at what I had heard, and ashamed of the envy I had felt when I first saw her comfortable house, her prosperous husband and thriving children. My melancholy had caused me to compare my lot to hers, and I had thought myself so poor in the joys of family that I had until that moment acted with the barest civility toward her.

Garzón told her quite openly how greatly he admired her for wanting her children to know that she had once been a slave.

"William would have it so," she said, exchanging a fond look with her husband.

Since his mother was no longer interested in his fruit platter, Tomás brought it to me, and I asked him to help me identify the mangoes, papayas, and coconuts he offered. I tried them all, my favorite being the mangoes. Tomás was amazed that such fruits do not grow in Ireland. When I pointed to his burn and asked how he had hurt himself he hid his face in his mother's skirt while his father explained that Tomás had been running by a fire after being told not to, and had fallen as a result of his disobedience.

I asked for vinegar and cedar ashes, explaining that one of the sailors aboard the *Bonaventure* had taught me his remedy for burns, and I wished to try what I had learned on little Tomás. I mashed a banana until it was creamy, adding a few drops of vinegar, a large dab of soft butter, and a small handful of the ashes to prevent scarring. Garzón distracted him by talking to him in Portuguese and showing him his *boleadoras*. I was surprised by how similar Portuguese and Spanish are, and by how much I understood when Garzón told Tomás how his ancestors, the Charrúa, had developed the *bolas*, using them with deadly effect in their battles against Spanish soldiers. Sometimes, he told him, the stones were shaped into points and given the name *rompe cabezas*, or head breakers. Hoping to catch a monkey, Garzón had wrapped them around the pommel of his saddle when we left the ship. I was as curious about them as Tomás, since I often watched Garzón practicing his aim with them on board. The first time I saw the three lengths of rawhide, with their rounded stones tied on the ends, they were whipping over my head toward one of the masts where they wrapped themselves around it with a force which undoubtedly would have taken my head with them had I been any taller. The children, of course, had to see them demonstrated, and they all ran out clapping their hands when Garzón offered to show them how they are used.

Before we left, I told Ismelda to bathe Tomás' wound in warm water every few hours and renew the poultice. Having done something useful, I was in a much better mood on our ride back to the city, and managed to remain cheerful even when a storm overtook us, with thunder so loud and lightning so violent that the horses took fright and were detained only by a thick hedge in which for several moments the terrified animals tried to bury themselves.

We dismounted in a solid sheet of rain, peeled off our sodden jackets, and covered the horses' heads with them, succeeding finally in quieting the trembling animals and soothing them sufficiently to walk them back through the city streets where pipes running along the roof tops were discharging the rainfall in huge arcs across the unpaved streets, turning the dirt roads into streams of red mud.

~

That night I lay in my bunk listening to the creaking of the ship and the lapping of the water. The harbor, cleansed by rain, was quiet, and only the occasional muted and distant cries from the slave ship drifted over the water.

The unexpected sound of footsteps on deck made me jump. It was too soon for a change of the watch, and when I heard the murmur of voices above my head, I opened my door.

No light was visible in the passage, and I had to feel my way to the ladder leading to the deck. No sooner had I put my foot on the bottom rung than the sudden, rhythmic beat of a drum reached my ears. Another joined it, then another, pounding out a deep, compelling call that made the wood under me vibrate.

I climbed the steps and held the hatch open a few inches above my head. Only the moon illuminated the scene outside, where three drummers stood on the same platform that had housed the holy statue before the storm swept it overboard. They were barefoot and clad in white, their hands like swallows skimming and diving over the tall drums.

As the drumming intensified, the sailors joined in, using barrels, buckets, wooden spoons, bowls, and the deck itself, turning the entire ship into one giant drum beating.

Garzón appeared from the shadows of the fore deck, and the men, never breaking their rhythm, cleared a space for him by the drummers. The heels of his boots began a sharp and forceful counterpoint to the drum beat. At first, his hands, holding the *boleadoras*, were clasped behind his back and he moved only his feet. As the dance quickened, his whole body joined the stamping, pounding rhythm, and he discarded his shirt, holding his arms out and twirling the *boleadoras* until they blurred in the air, forming fiery arcs and circles as they flew around him, their shape transformed by motion. Sometimes, he allowed the stones to skim the deck as he whirled with them, his black hair flying and his shoulders glistening with sweat.

My fear forgotten, I felt myself drawn into the pulse that linked the men on deck, the blood in my veins racing and creating a euphoria that made me a part of the sound itself. Just as I thought that I could not remain below and would have to join in the frenzy, the dancing and the drumming stopped. The stones flew silently to rest around Garzón's wrists and everyone on deck froze, breathing heavily, listening.

A distant echo of the thunder from the *Bonaventure* reached us, an answering call from the slave ship, and the most courageous sound I would ever hear, chained hands and feet beating out a faint response. One free drum from the *Bonaventure* answered, softly, in farewell, and then all was still again.

The drummers returned ashore, their white robes whispering on the deck and brushing my fingers as they passed the place where I stood watching, my eyes level with the boards. Soft farewells were exchanged and Garzón gathered his shirt, wiped his face with it, and gently picked up a bundle the drummers had left behind. Two dark little arms reached up and wound themselves around his neck. The wrappings fell away and I saw that the child he was holding was the one I had held earlier that day.

Chapter IV

Just as the innkeeper had boasted, the tiny boy picked up languages with no apparent effort and with perfect pronunciation, although he gave no evidence of understanding the words he was learning. He was unable to tell us his name, so we selected a few and settled on the one he seemed to like the best — Orlando.

For the first few days after he came aboard, Orlando slept under the table in Garzón's cabin, smiling in a most pitiful and fearful manner if I approached him. He came to me if I held my arms out to him, and a few days after coming aboard allowed me to pick him up and present him to the crew. As he grew stronger, he began to pull himself up to a standing position, and although I feared that his legs would remain permanently disfigured I began to hope that he would soon walk.

We had left Río de Janeiro in September, but a *pampero* wind blew the ship off course and we were forced out to sea again for four days before resuming our approach to Montevideo. Orlando became very excited when birds flew over the ship, and Garzón, who always spoke to him as if he could perfectly understand what was said to him, explained that we were close to shore but by no means there yet, for birds can fly up to thirty leagues from land. He posted sentinels in the crow's nest, and on the third day we passed the Isla de Lobos, an island where hundreds of "sea wolves" as the Spanish call the sea lions, lay basking in the sun. Orlando soon demonstrated that his ear was not only for languages. He imitated the sea lions' barks so perfectly the creatures looked our way, positively bemused.

As we neared the harbor, Garzón prepared to sound. Ten fathoms of water are needed for a ship to enter the channel safely, and finding the right channel is a matter of importance, since the river is a mass of sand banks. We continued sounding until the shoreline was in view, and as soon as we passed the small Isla de Flores, angled right. As we began our approach to Montevideo and the great Río de la Plata, frigate birds and cormorants flew overhead and black dolphins came to greet the ship, making me want to tear off my clothes and join Garzón and the sailors when they jumped off the deck to play with the *toninas* in the water. The dolphins seemed to understand that this was a game and jumped and twisted in the air, vanishing under the waves, taunting the swimmers by appearing in front of them like clusters of dark fruit, their heads nodding and their eyes mischievous and fully aware that the men could not keep up with them and would soon tire.

Once we entered the river itself we had to ensure that we avoided the treacherous *Banco Inglés*, where ships frequently ran aground.

"Aptly named, is it not, Garzón?" I said as we stood on deck in a fine drizzle. "A treacherous bank named after a treacherous lot like the English!"

Garzón was busy and did not hear me. His dark hands were steady on the railings, his whole bearing supremely confident as he ordered the unwinding of a rope, several fathoms long. A piece of lead was secured to one end, dipped in wax, and thrown overboard.

"Twenty fathom clay!" announced the leadsman crying the depth as the rope was hauled back in.

"How does he know?"

"By the color of the earth sticking to the wax."

The sun came out to greet us as a square, rough hewn tower became visible in the distance. Garzón took off his hat and shook the rain from it revealing the bright red ribbon holding back his hair and providing the only touch of color against the dark blue of his coat. He pointed to the rainbow that spanned the sky, joining the tiny city I could just see on the horizon, to the ship bobbing on the waves. He picked up Orlando and tucked him under his jacket. "My mother's people believe that rainbows were born when the bat was still a beautiful creature, sporting a feather from each of the birds on earth. As he flew, his colors painted the sky."

I caught a glimmer of something like curiosity on Orlando's face, and I asked Garzón how the bat had lost his feathers.

"He became conceited, and God punished him by giving the feathers back to the birds."

A small boat was lowered and several sailors prepared to row to the port to make arrangements for the ship's arrival. While we waited for permission to pull into the harbor I drew Garzón's story for Orlando, who studied my sketches intently until the sound of Garzón's voice distracted him again.

"Are the silks ready?" Garzón asked Martínez.

"Yes, *monsieur*. And the dueling pistols."

"What?" I said. "Are you to be involved in a duel?"

Garzón explained that the pistols were for the Colonel at the fortress. "I bring him a gift each time we dock so that his men do not ask to see my license."

I was suddenly quite certain that like his father before him, he did not have one. "Are all those skins you regularly take to Ireland contraband?"

"Spanish merchants in Seville have placed a fifty per cent levy on all goods leaving the colonies, and those goods can only be sold in Spain. The levy only serves to make them rich. The colonies derive no benefit from it."

"What if you are caught?"

"I will be hanged. No goods are allowed to enter the Port of Montevideo. All cotton and iron ware have to cross the Atlantic Ocean from Spain to Panama and be shipped from there to Peru, where merchandise is sent by mule along the Andes to La Paz and from there to Buenos Aires. Nothing may legally bypass what you will recognize is a ludicrous route once you learn your geography."

"You might have shared this information with me sooner! Or perhaps you take smuggling so much for granted that you assumed I would as well!"

His reply was drowned out by the cannon blast announcing that we had been cleared to enter the harbor.

~

The small settlement of Montevideo was only twenty-three years old, a year older than I was when I landed there in October of 1746. It was built on a narrow peninsula protected on three sides by the river and by a high wall on the fourth. Cattle, horses, and sheep grazed on the surrounding plains, the city gates opened and closed at dawn and dusk, and peddlers hawked their wares in the Plaza Mayor.

The vegetation approaching the sand dunes along the coast was a mixture of stately trees and silken grasses, and the little city was as quiet as a lullaby compared to Río de Janeiro. The population consisted of the soldiers manning the fortress, their families, the priests at the Jesuit residence, some African and native slaves, and several families brought there from the Canary Islands to people this outpost of the Spanish empire.

Most of the houses were made of adobe, with straw and hide roofs, with an occasional grander residence of stone and brick. The cries of peddlers echoed along the fourteen narrow streets, picked up by the soaring seagulls overhead. Wagon wheels creaked, and oxen lowed as they pulled their burdens in and out of the city. Time had little meaning, except for the man charged with opening and closing the city gates at dawn and dusk, or for those who rang the church bells calling the faithful to worship. Spanish soldiers stood in groups at street corners, flashing their swords and their smiles at the *señoritas* walking by with their chaperones. Something in the perfumed air of the city, where flowers bloomed in every nook and cranny, appeared to infuse even the duennas with tolerance, and in spite of their severe looks and somber gowns, they strolled by the battlements with unconcern, allowing their charges to flutter their fans and raise their eyes to meet those of the amorous soldiers.

Like Cork, Montevideo enjoyed the advantages of an admirable natural harbor, and trade was based on many of the same items. Beef, hides tanned and raw, and tallow, were the main Spanish exports. With the addition of butter and wool, the same was true of Ireland, which also exported shank bones, mainly to the turners, bead makers, cutlers and toy-men in Holland. The number of hides traded, however, was vastly different. The whole of County Cork exported thirty-seven thousand hides a year, the same amount Garzón alone took to France in the single transaction that had made his fortune.

It was hardly surprising that smuggling was prevalent in both places. Merchants in the Spanish colonies labored under severe restrictions and were prohibited from dealing with anyone except the crown and its appointed representatives, who paid so little for the merchandise that if it had not been for the vast number of hides there were to sell it would hardly have been worth the effort. In Ireland, they were tithed and also forbidden from exporting goods to any country with which Great Britain was at war, which effectively eliminated most of Europe at one time or another.

I made up a list of comparisons such as those that used to delight Pa when I concocted them to weigh the advantages and disadvantages of his business proposals.

Cork	**Montevideo**
Population 60,000	*Population 300*
The River Lee runs through the center of the city and every few years gray dolphins swim upriver, bringing fine weather.	*The Río de la Plata embraces the city on three sides and black dolphins leap toward the sky at all times, whether it be fine or no.*
The streets rise steeply in all directions from the riverbanks and quays, and markets abound.	*The streets are flat, straight and narrow crisscrossing the peninsula as neatly as a checkerboard. There is one marketplace.*

Balconies in the Spanish style grace the houses in both cities.

Pa had used the walls of Cork to point out the various stages of its history, telling Michael and me that those ancient stones were like books stacked high for us to read. Montevideo's walls were new and its history as yet unwritten, putting me in mind of a woman I met in the Plaza Mayor, holding a baby in her arms. Her history was visible in every line of her face, the babe's skin smooth and unmarked.

Just as I had hoped, Orlando was now strong enough to walk, and every day we went further, stopping at the church to rest. We sat in the sunshine while birds flew in and out of the open doors and windows and a local *señorita*, who had taken to appearing at church whenever I did, walked by with her duenna, casting warm glances at me from a pair of slanted dark eyes.

Garzón recommended that I remain aboard ship before I found myself betrothed.

Every evening, before the Benediction, a priest took his place in the beautifully carved confessional at the back of the church. Determined to find the courage to kneel before the curtained little window and unburden myself of the sin of Tobias' murder, one afternoon I joined the faithful waiting for absolution. Long before the last person had received her penance, I was overcome by cowardice. I ran shaking from the church and to the battlements overlooking the harbor. In the distance, I could see the waters of the Atlantic Ocean meeting those of the Río de la Plata. Today, the place where the two giants came together was delineated in two distinct shades of blue, as if the water had been painted on a map. Yesterday, they had merged without a trace, like an old married couple taking on one another's characteristics.

I was still shaking as I took a deep breath and looked to the east, where sandy beaches stretched to the horizon. Behind me and to the west were the *pampas* I was anxious to explore. I had promised myself that I would start my new life by shedding the old with a full confession, but it wasn't shame that had caused me to flee the church but the realization that I was not sorry that Tobias was dead. I had not meant to kill him, and given the chance to save him, I would probably have done so. But that was before I met Garzón. Could I utter words of sincere repentance now, when Tobias alive would have tied me to him forever? It had been at that moment, while rehearsing my confession, that I had come to the realization that I was in love.

Unaccustomed to being idle, I took to carrying my sketch book with me wherever I went. Sketching had been a private pastime for me back home. I had not enjoyed the benefit of lessons, since drawing was an activity reserved for the well-born. But here, my efforts to capture the quiet majesty of the river, the quaintness of the city, and the colorful characters inhabiting it only attracted curiosity and amazement that anyone would think them subjects fit for art. The death of King Phillip earlier that year had prescribed a mourning period for all, and even children wore little black armbands, but nothing could repress outbursts of color from manifesting in the occasional turn of a shawl, the glimpse of a petticoat, and the natural flora of the place, spilling over balconies and climbing the walls.

The piece in which I took the most pride was a pencil drawing of the *Bonaventure*. In spite of shortcomings a tutored artist would no doubt have scorned, whenever I looked at the drawing I felt that I had captured the ship's grace under full sail. When it was finished, I dipped my pen in ink and wrote in tiny letters, *The Bonaventure. 298 tons burthen. 90 feet long at the level of the lower deck. 27 and a half feet at its greatest breadth. 11 and a half feet deep in the hold.*

"I'm amazed that you remembered all those numbers!" Garzón said when I presented it to him.

"I've always had a head for figures. I was a better scholar and bookkeeper than my brother, and Pa knew it. It was he and I who really ran the business, although he would have liked Michael to learn it. Speaking of business," I said, "I would very much like to see what lies beyond Montevideo."

"Nothing lies beyond Montevideo," Garzón answered, walking around the cabin, looking for a place to hang the picture. "The city is an isolated, highly defended island in a sea of hostile Indians." He took down a chart and hung the picture in its place. "Perfect!" He stood back to admire the picture and turned to me with a smile. "I have never loved the *Bonaventure* so much as now that you have seen fit to immortalize her."

I blushed with pleasure. "About our excursion…"

"Leaving the safety of the city walls is not to be taken lightly."

"You went partridge hunting yesterday."

"And intend to go again tomorrow."

"I shall come with you."

"Very well, but if you are carried off by Indians I won't answer for the consequences!"

Next morning he appeared at the ship leading two fine bays attired in saddles and reins glittering with silver. He was carrying two long canes, on the end of which were nooses made of horse hair. He described the maneuver employed to catch partridges as "so simple it could be executed without the horse ever breaking its stride." It consisted of circling a partridge until it came to rest next to a patch of scrub, slipping the noose over its head, giving it a tap with the other end of the cane and watching it strangle itself as it took off.

Partridges were obliging enough to dart all about us, deftly avoiding the horses and appearing more confident of their escape than I was of my ability to catch them.

Garzón was soon circling a partridge and as he had predicted, it froze next to some scrub. He lowered his cane, the bird saw the noose, darted nimbly between the horse's feet, and disappeared. This exercise was repeated several times until I was laughing so heartily that when I quite accidentally succeeded in putting a noose around a partridge's neck (something I had yet to see Garzón do) I forgot to tap it and the bird backed dexterously away, vanishing in the distance with its companions, the game over for the day. There would be no partridges for dinner that night, but that posed no challenge for the ship's cook, who had plentiful meat and game to choose from. Orlando and I were awed by the abundance of food that surrounded us, and had succumbed to greed. He still had not spoken, but he sang occasionally, and in his songs I began to hear the words he was learning. Since arriving in Montevideo, his songs had all been about the good things he liked to eat.

The fish brought to the city every morning by the two fishermen who supplied the residents was of a taste and variety unknown to us. Orlando and I tried them fried in a covering of bread crumbs; marinated in lemon juice; cooked over an open fire; and mixed with shrimp, mussels, oysters, and rice. In the Plaza de la Verdura we chose our favorite vegetables from the piles of produce spread on canvases on the ground, and I thought each time of how Ma would have loved the sight of such plenty. Scattered among the familiar turnips, lettuces, onions, potatoes, and garlic, were unfamiliar strains of corn, pumpkins and gourds of various sizes and colors, beans of every hue, tomatoes, *mandioca*, and peppers. The air was redolent with the aroma of strawberries, peaches, pears, figs, grapes, apples, and melons. On our first trip to the market, we saw gull, partridge, and rhea eggs for sale, and bought three different pastries from the sellers walking by with trays hanging from their necks, offering little tubs of sugar to those, like Orlando and me, who craved an extra sprinkling of sweetness on the paper thin layers of pastry embellished with jams and jellies made from all the fruits of the region.

Michael's britches no longer hung loosely on me, and when Garzón took Orlando to the tailor's to have him fitted for a suit of clothes, we discovered that he had gained considerably in both weight and height.

As the day approached for our meeting with Father Manuel, on whom our future depended in large measure, I questioned Garzón closely about why only Indians and Jesuits could come and go freely from the Missions.

"The Fathers are strict about guests and what they are allowed to see. Even the Bishop cannot enter a Mission without special dispensation."

The King, Garzón explained, expected to receive a piece of eight for each Indian under his jurisdiction — it was called a Capitation Tax — and it was the duty of the Governor of Buenos Aires to visit the Missions every five years to verify the priests' figures. Father Manuel and his colleagues deliberately found ways of preventing him from doing so and had fixed the tax at one third what it should be.

"So suspicious of outsiders have they become that they mistrust even their own Church officials. Hence the restriction on visits, even from the Bishop."

"How did you win their trust?"

"I doubt that I have yet, but my idea about hiring the Indians of Santa Marta to work for me appeals to Father Manuel. He was easier to convince than the leader of the *cabildo*, who has done all he can to hinder me."

"What is the *cabildo*?"

"The Indian council, headed by a man called Cararé. A strict Catholic, unwavering in his devotion to the Church and to the King, even though both Church and King consider him so unworthy that he can neither join the priesthood nor hold public office."

Like Irish women, I thought, also the backbone of the church in spite of being barred from exercising any power within it. "So," I said, "not only did you not inform me that a partnership with you would entail smuggling, but that we have yet to persuade the people upon whom our success depends."

He had the good grace to hang his head, but when he looked at me his eyes were merry. "I am counting on you to charm *Don* Cararé!"

Santa Marta was a morning's ride from the city, and as we approached it I understood how easily the Missions could become targets of envy. Cattle, sheep, and horses too numerous for me to count grazed on the plains, and cane fences extended to the horizon, surrounding the *tupambaé* — the richly cultivated fields used to support the Mission's inhabitants and pay the annual tribute to the Spanish Crown.

High stone walls surrounded the mission itself, with watch towers at each of the four corners. Garzón, Orlando, and I were spotted long before we reached the twenty-foot high double doors barring the entrance, and from the watch towers guards called down a greeting and requested that we wait while they obtained permission to admit us. Soon, the sound of a bolt being drawn came from behind the doors and they swung slowly open, revealing the wide expanse of a grassy plaza with a large cross and a well in its center. Directly across the plaza was the church, an imposing building with several bells hanging from its tower. As our horses were taken from us and led away, I saw workshops to my left, and caught a glimpse of intricate wood carvings, painted in vivid colors. To my right were more buildings, connected by a portico of arched stone running the length of the plaza.

I felt Orlando move closer to my side, and saw that his eyes were fixed on an imposing-looking man bearing down upon us. He was dressed in simple, long cotton trousers and shirt, covered with a woven poncho, and like Garzón's, his hair hung straight to his shoulders and was also held back with a headband across his forehead. He carried a tall, carved stick with a silver apple on top, which he rested on the ground before him as he swept us with his large, widely spaced dark eyes. Then he bowed and addressed himself to Garzón, "Welcome back to Santa Marta, Captain."

"Thank you, *Don*槽Cararé," Garzón replied, bowing even lower. "May I introduce my friends to you?"

Cararé gave a small nod.

"Master Michael Keating and young Orlando."

For a moment, I was afraid that I had not passed muster. As I straightened up from bowing to *Don* Cararé I caught a disconcerting glimpse of such warmth and humor in his eyes that I almost missed his invitation to follow him to the guest house. Orlando stopped on the way and looked up at *Don* Cararé, pointing to a mule with a pole attached to its saddle, circling a press and grinding sugar cane. *Don* Cararé, seeing curiosity in Orlando's eyes but no sign that a question would be uttered, spoke slowly, watching Orlando's expression. He explained how, when the buckets under the press were filled with the resulting juice, they would be carried to several large pots hanging over the fires burning nearby.

There, under a colorful canopy, three women were filling wooden moulds with the syrup from the pots and putting them aside to set. From the pile neatly stacked in wicker baskets at their feet, one of them took a sugar brick and offered it to Garzón, saying a few words to him in a language altogether foreign to me. Her gesture was met with gales of laughter from her companions, and a stern look from Cararé that would have withered me in shame, but had no effect on her except to make her greet Garzón with traditional Spanish words. He had told me what the words meant and explained that it was the way ladies were always addressed in the colonies. Nevertheless, I did not like to hear him say, "I am at your feet, lady," and liked her answer "I kiss my hand to you, sir," even less.

Cararé also seemed displeased, and told the saucy minx, whose name was Itanambí, that he expected her to explain to the *Pa'i Mini* where she had learned such things. (I found out later that the *Pa'i Mini* was Father Antonio, who works with Father Manuel.)

The girl bowed her head, but there was no humility in it, the gesture was designed to conceal her smile. As we continued across the plaza, I asked Garzón what language Itanambí had spoken and what she had said to him when she gave him the sugar brick.

"She spoke Guaraní, and offered me sugar to sweeten my kisses."

My opinion of her did not improve with this knowledge, and I felt almost as stern as Cararé when he left us to inform Father Manuel of our arrival.

The guest house was small, clean, and plainly furnished. Two beds stood against one wall, with neatly folded blankets at the foot and pillows at the head. The supports were made of wood, joined with crisscrossed strips of hide, in a pattern of black, brown, and white, matching the backs and seats of the two chairs. A washstand and table were near the door, and from the ceiling a candle fixture hung from a chain. It was a piece of fine metalwork, perfectly balanced to contain three large candles and their snuffers, and could be lowered and raised by another, slender chain connected to the wall. The only ornament in the room was a wooden crucifix hanging between the beds.

Before he left us Cararé had lit the fire and set the kettle to boiling on the hearth. The crackling sound of wood burning, and the warm glow of the flames made the otherwise rather barren room feel more welcoming.

A few moments later, a tall, slender man appeared in the doorway, dressed in plain dark trousers and a loose shirt. His head showed no evidence of the shaven coronet I had seen on priests in Montevideo and his long brown hair was gathered at the nape of his neck and tied with a black ribbon. He greeted Garzón warmly, embracing him and pounding him heartily on the back.

"I've returned, Father, and brought my friend Michael Keating with me."

I knelt before him and asked for his blessing, my eyes fixed on his rope sandals. He put a hand under my chin and as I raised my eyes to his I was startled to discover that one was green and the other brown. "Welcome to Santa Marta." His English was clear, his accent heavier even than Garzón's. He helped me to my feet and turned his attention to Orlando. "And who is this?"

"My name is Orlando."

Garzón and I looked at one another in astonishment. I knelt by Orlando's side and told him how delighted I was to hear him speak, but he hung his head and said no more.

"I think there is something in this room that Orlando will enjoy." Father Manuel walked over to a shelf and took down a box, placing it on the black and white hide laid out by the hearth. He and Orlando sat cross-legged on the floor together and opened the lid. One compartment held marbles of colored glass; another, clay beads that could be strung onto a cord, and a third, a company of little soldiers meticulously carved, and uniformed in such detail that even their buttons, no larger than a pin head, could be unfastened to reveal the tiny shirts beneath. Orlando was immediately engrossed, and Father Manuel got to his feet and gestured for us to join him at the table.

At that moment Itanambí entered the room. Everything about her invited attention, from her intelligent, piercing eyes, to the rainbow of ribbons sewn around the hemline of her skirt. She was carrying a brown gourd with a silver spoon protruding from it. The gourd fit comfortably in her hand as she packed it full of finely ground green tea; and the spoon was not a spoon at all, but a hollow implement with tiny holes at its bulbous base. She hovered over Garzón until Father Manuel took the *mate* gourd from her hands and led her to the door. With a sudden pang of intuition, I knew that she and Garzón had been, perhaps were still, lovers.

"Have you introduced Master Keating to *mate*, Garzón?"

"Not yet."

Father Manuel took a sip from the gourd, offered it to Orlando, who declined, and passed it to Garzón, who drank and in turn passed it to me.

"It makes those who share it brothers," Garzón said.

"And sisters," Father Manuel added.

The brew was bitter, and I made a face in spite of myself.

Father Manuel laughed. "Some prefer it sweet, like Garzón's kisses."

We looked at him as if he possessed some gift of divination.

"In a small community like ours, nothing remains a secret, and I heard the whole exchange with Itanambí from Cararé and from three separate women who stopped me on my way here."

"Before we go any further, Father, I think it best that you be made aware that Master Keating is a woman."

"I would have been surprised to see you direct such glances at a young man, Garzón." Father Manuel dissolved a piece of sugar in the kettle and added the sweetened water to the tea. "Try it now, Master Keating. I shall call you that until you change your clothing, otherwise I shall forget, and embarrass you."

I tried the brew, and found the flavor, like my mood, much improved.

"One of my favorite heavenly bodies was also fond of disguises. Long, long ago," he said, as I handed the gourd back to him, "the moon wished to visit the earth, which she had never touched, but could see from her place in the sky. Her friends, the clouds, agreed one night to cover the sky, so she would not be missed, and the moon disguised herself as a maiden and descended to earth for a visit. She walked through the jungles, smelling the flowers and marveling at the animals, until she came to a lagoon. The water was clear and still, and seemed to beckon to her. She swam in it, and as she stepped ashore, a jaguar attacked her. An old man, out to fill his drinking gourd, defended her, and drove the jaguar away. The moon was very hungry by this time and accepted the old man's invitation to go with him to his home to eat with his family. After her return to her place in the sky, she looked in the window at her new friends, and was pained to find them sitting round their fire with nothing to eat. Their last serving of flour had been used to make her food the night before. Once more, the moon appealed to her friends the clouds, and they showered the jungle all around the old man's hut with a most special rain. As dawn broke in the sky, new trees covered in white flowers appeared all around the hut. They were *yerba* trees, and from them came the leaf of the *mate* tea. The old man's daughter lived forever. She owns the *yerba* trees, and wanders the earth, offering *mate* to all she meets."

Orlando listened enthralled to this story, and Father Manuel asked him if he had understood his English. Orlando went back to playing with the little soldiers.

"He has an uncommon gift for languages," I said, "but he exercises it mostly in song. And you, where did you learn English, Father?"

"Here at Santa Marta. Sixteen years ago, in 1730, a young

Englishman named Thomas Falkner arrived in Montevideo, charged by the Royal Society in London with studying the medicinal properties of plants in the area. He fell ill shortly after his arrival and lay close to death for several weeks. He was brought to us here at the mission for nursing, and while he regained his health he taught Cararé and me to speak English, and discovered in the process that Cararé's wife Wimencaí was a healer. Dr. Falkner wanted to study her medicinal plants, so he taught her some English as well. His gratitude toward us was so strong that he converted to Catholicism and decided to join the Jesuit Order. He went to Cordoba for his training and ordination and has remained there ever since."

"I too am interested in healing, Father! I have made my living as a midwife, and I would like to meet..." I had difficulty pronouncing her name and Father Manuel came to my assistance.

"Wee-men-ka-ee," he said. "In the language of her people, the Chaná, *wimen* means wise. Every season she journeys to different areas, harvesting the plants and seeds she uses in her healing. You will meet her when she returns."

Garzón was impatient to discuss his proposal to hire Mission workers, and soon the two of them were speaking Spanish. The effort to follow the conversation became too much for me, and I withdrew to the hearth, taking my journal from my bag. In it I wrote the Indian names I'd learned that day — Ca-rah-re, Ee-tah-nam-bee, and Wee-men-ka-ee, and beside them I drew the *mate* gourd, Cararé's staff with its silver apple, and a small stack of sugar bricks. By the time I was finished, the gourd had made its way back to me, and Garzón was looking very pleased.

"Father Manuel has agreed to visit the lagoon—"

"— if Cararé comes too. One thing he will never agree to do is disregard the authorities and harvest hides without a license."

"I am willing to concede that point," Garzón said. "If one of the conditions of a partnership with you is the cost and bother of a license, I will obtain one gladly!"

It was late winter, and a light frost powdered the ground when shortly after sunrise, Garzón, Orlando, and I emerged from the city gates. As

I looked back at the walled-in town the guards waved to me from the battlements, and I waved back, feeling strangely exposed as we left the safety of Montevideo and headed for Santa Marta, where we would be leaving Orlando in the care of Father Manuel's companion, Father Antonio.

Garzón and I had had our first quarrel. I had wanted to take Orlando with us; Garzón had argued that the journey was arduous and that Orlando would be far better off at Santa Marta.

"He's getting stronger every day," I said. "He can easily keep up with us on horseback!"

"We have no way of knowing if he could endure hours of riding. He has only recently regained some use of his legs. What if he falls from the horse and injures himself? He'll be safe at the Mission. He can even start attending school, and perhaps being around other children will prompt him to speak again."

"It may also set him back. He is not used to the company of others."

"It is time, Isabel, for the boy to learn that you will not always be there for him."

"Why ever not?"

Garzón shook his head. "Having Orlando with us will delay us. No harm can come to him at the Mission."

I missed him from the moment we lost sight of the mission walls, and that night, as we sat around the fire my thoughts kept reverting to him. We had left him in the guest house with Father Antonio, who distracted him with the box of toys while we slipped out the door. What must he have thought when he discovered we were gone? I had explained the reason for our journey to him in English and in Spanish, but had little idea if he had understood the phrase I repeated again and again. "I will be back soon! ¡*Volveré pronto*!" Even if he had understood, why would he believe me?

I was unfolding the blanket that would be my bed that night when I heard *Don* Cararé telling Garzón that if he and others at Santa Marta decided to entrust themselves to him and leave the safety of their mission they would need more muskets and cannon. "Ours are made of *tacuara* bamboo. Iron would be better."

I did not like the sound of this at all. Garzon had made

smuggling sound commonplace, until Father Manuel told him that Cararé would never agree to it. For the first time since that day on board the *Bonaventure* when Garzon and I had shaken hands, fear and doubt gripped me. I had entrusted a man I barely knew with my life and future. I had done this once before, and paid dearly for it. I had killed to escape the impulsive gullibility that had tied me to Tobias, and now here I was, alone, friendless, and once more at the mercy of a stranger.

"Why do we need cannons?"

I couldn't see his eyes clearly in the firelight, but I saw *Don* Cararé turn toward me and gesture for me to sit by him. "The King has seen to it that we have been armed since the days of the *mamelucos*, " he said.

"Yes, after losing Guayrá to the Portuguese," Garzón said bitterly. "Along with tens of thousands of your people, *Don* Cararé, murdered or driven into slavery by the *mamelucos*."

"Who are the *mamelucos*?" I asked.

"Slavers."

"Named after the Mamelukes," Father Manuel said, "the slave-warriors of Egypt."

"These *mamelucos* were slaves themselves?"

"Some were, some were freemen."

"It might have taken the King time to respond to the Fathers' request for weapons, Captain, but when he did," Cararé said proudly, "he equipped us with better arms than the *mamelucos* had ever dreamed of! He gave us iron cannons, muskets, sabers, lances, fine uniforms. We left the ground littered with their bodies and chased what was left of them all the way back to Brazil!"

"All very convenient for His Majesty. He now had a standing army in the Missions at his beck and call whenever anyone threatened to compete with him in plundering the colonies."

Cararé shook his head. "Such bitterness must be a heavy burden, Captain."

"Father Manuel shares it! Ask him why he and his colleagues teach you Latin and German and whatever language they speak, while pretending you're incapable of learning Spanish!"

"That is to protect us from dishonest traders, not from the King!"

"They are one and the same!"

Father Manuel held up his hand. “Captain, *Don*槍araré and his family have been zealous servants of God and of the King for three generations. You may not believe the King worthy of such devotion, but *Don* Cararé is rightly proud of his loyalty. Your mother’s people do not agree with him, but they respect him for his integrity. You would do well to ponder that.”

Garzón threw what was left of his meal into the grass and left the fireside to make his bed under a distant tree. His sudden movements startled a lizard feasting on the moths attracted to our fire, and it disappeared like a fleeting glint of starlight in the grass.

Cararé took his prayer book from his pocket, wound his rosary around his fingers, and also withdrew, seemingly lost in thought.

Perceiving my distress, Father Manuel explained that slave traders had been at work in the colonies for nearly two centuries, thwarted only by the Jesuits who had established the mission system that now encompassed twenty settlements in the heart of South America.

“The Missions are home to nearly one hundred thousand Indians, a fact that has not gone unnoticed by landowners in need of slaves. For years, I have been praying for a miracle, and when Garzón approached me a few months ago with his revolutionary idea, I knew that my prayer had been answered.”

“*Don* Cararé does not share your opinion?”

“Cararé refuses to think ill of the royal family he considers his protectors.”

“Whereas, in reality it is the Jesuits who have protected the Indians, not the King?”

“Kings do what is expedient to please the men who keep them in power. I believe as Garzón does that those men will soon find a way of persuading the King that in order for gold and silver to continue to pour into Spain from the colonies it will be necessary to close the Missions and allow the owners of mines and plantations access to the thousands living there.”

“So it is unlikely that Garzón’s plan will meet with any support from such men?”

“They might not bother with one small group, but if we succeed in turning this into a plan for a transition from the Missions into employment for the Indians, we will be opposed at every level.”

I looked toward the tree under which Garzón had made his bed. Night fell quickly in this part of the world, and I could no longer see him clearly.

"Do you still wish to stay?" Father Manuel asked. He saw me hesitate and went right to the heart of the matter. "You are aware of the Church's ban on mixed race marriages?"

I hoped that the darkness covered the sudden rush of blood to my face. "No."

"Garzón is. How much has he revealed about himself?"

"I know that his father was French and his mother Indian."

"A Charrúa. They are among the few tribes that have not joined the Missions."

"Yet he has turned to you."

Father Manuel laughed. "Not for the purposes of conversion!"

He unrolled his sleeping hammock and I assisted him to fasten it between two trees, surprised by its brown and green tints, and the star design that lay at its center. "It is a lovely piece of work, isn't it? It was a gift, from a young Minuán friend — a local tribesman — and my dreams are vivid when I sleep on it."

Since living among the Guaraní Indians many years before, Father Manuel had become interested in the significance of dreams, he said.

"The old testament contains numerous instances of the power and veracity of the world we visit in our sleep," he said.

"Tell me about your friend."

"You are not tired?"

"Yes, but there is so much for me to learn! If you want to sleep I'll wait, and like Sheherazade, you can spin out your stories over the nights to come."

He pointed at the stars. "I rarely sleep on such a night as this. I am as drawn to the night sky as a bee to pollen. I am quite certain that the answer to all my questions about our place in the universe lie there. I haven't found my answer yet, but under such a spectacle as this, it doesn't seem to matter. When I first saw the southern sky at night I thought I was dreaming. Until that moment, I had had no idea that there were this many stars in the heavens. It is a sight that stirs me every time, and on cloudy nights, when all I see is darkness, I give thanks. It means that I can devote myself to the tasks I should do every night and do not do when the stars beckon. But you are anxious to learn, and I enjoy sharing my little store of knowledge!" He took by arm and led me back to the fire.

His friend's name was Yací, and Father Manuel had attempted to make contact with Yací's tribe from the moment of his arrival in the province eighteen years ago. Yací was still a boy when they began a routine that they followed for over five years. Father Manuel would make camp near Yací's village and leave small gifts for him — *yerba mate*, a handsaw, loaves of sugar, a knife. In their place Yací left feathers, shells, the dark tourmalines his tribe used for trading, and some rather crude carvings. "He will become a masterful carver one day, but he is still honing that skill." They didn't speak, and Father Manuel never saw Yací during these exchanges. He was certain, however, that Yací was watching him. They developed the strange sensitivity of being able to perceive when they were in the same vicinity, and eventually prepared for a meeting by making special gifts for one another.

"I arrived as usual at the Laguna de los Palmares..."

My eyes flew from the fire to his face.

"Yes, Garzón's lagoon. Also Yací's. I have a strong motive for wanting to move there quite apart from my concerns about the future."

"The lagoon belongs to the Minuanes?"

"They do not share our concept of ownership. It is as impossible for them to own the land as it would be to lay claim to the ocean, or to the air we breathe."

"How then is it Yací's lagoon?"

"He frequents it, fishes in it."

"Will he still come if we settle there?"

"It is my dearest hope."

"Please go on. Tell me about your first meeting."

"I followed my accustomed routine. I bathed my horse, knowing that when I raised my eyes from the beach to the banks surrounding the lagoon, he would be standing there."

And so he had been, a young man with long dark hair, resting lightly on his lance. He had picked up what looked like a bed roll, and approached Father Manuel. Using the knife Father Manuel had left for him when he was a boy he had cut the grass bindings around the bundle and unrolled the hammock at Father Manuel's feet. Father Manuel took time to admire the craftsmanship and the effort that had gone into making the hammock so strong and light, so easily portable. Then he had rolled it up carefully, and laid out his own gifts.

"We talked almost all night."

"What about?"

"Everything! Nothing! I can barely remember. We finished one another's sentences, we laughed, we cried. We became friends. When he left, I was so elated that I performed a dance around my campfire."

"Had Yací been converted?'

"Converting him was the furthest thing from my mind. I was, and am, far more concerned with protecting him."

"From what?"

"From you, from all of us who have come here."

"I wish him no harm!"

"But he will come to harm nevertheless, just because we are here. Just as your own ancestors' lives were transformed by invaders, so will the Minuanes' lives be changed. If history is anything to go by, the change will not be for the better."

"My people lost everything, even the right to till their fields without paying a tithe for the privilege. Now they starve and multiply and live in dwellings hardly worthy of the name, clad in rags alive with lice and fleas, mutilated by disease and blamed for all the evils that beset them. Are the Minuanes like that?"

The Minuanes, he said, could still freely harvest the largesse that surrounded them, they lived in shelters designed to fit their needs, and took pride in the health and strength of their bodies. "And while there is breath in my body, I will fight for their right to continue to do so." He took a rosary from the pocket of his trousers, kissed the wooden cross, and held it up for me to see the seeds strung along its length. "My nurse María made me this. I wonder," he said, "what would have become of me if she had been a woman of mature years, devout and stern, with hair in her nose and whalebone for armor?"

Instead, his mother had chosen a playful, heathenish young orphan brought up in a most careless manner by an older brother who treated her more like a puppy than a child, allowing her to run wild, and neglecting her religious upbringing. It would be a long time before

Father Manuel understood that the choice of María for his nurse had been no accident. His mother had not wanted him to be a priest, and feared from his youngest days that he would be. He was her only child and she wanted grandchildren and a daughter to sit with by the fire on cold nights.

"It was in María that I first saw reverence, not for the Creator, but for his creations. We built altars in the hollow trunks of trees, our deities were stones with unusual colorations, and fallen flowers, for María could not bear to pick a flower and watch it die, forgotten. We collected empty bird and wasp nests, and the husks of beetles that had shed their old skin, leaving behind a perfect replica of themselves for María to wonder at."

Some of his earliest memories, he told me, were of walking in the vineyards sampling the grapes his father grew, while María listened to the birds. She maintained that she could tell from their sounds which grapes were the sweetest and which would make the best wines. If his father would only listen to the birds, she said, he could dispense with all the wine tasting, for the birds were never wrong. Manuel thought the wine tasters enjoyed their work as much as the birds did, and María agreed. Grapes were generous in the pleasure they gave, on and off the vine. But even María could not change the course Manuel had embarked upon before she ever entered his life. Every morning, no matter the weather, he rose early and attended Mass in the small church near his home. Manuel loved the vaulted ceiling, the altar with its gleaming candlesticks, and the sight of the monks at prayer, as still as the statues that surrounded them. When they chanted, the sound of their voices rang through the aisles, around the walls, and up to the painted arches above his head. He was most particularly drawn to the side altar where St. Francis stood, with a dog at his feet and a sparrow on his shoulder.

It was here that he had first seen Brother Andrés watching him from one of the pews. Many years later the monk told Manuel that he had been trying to decide whether his first impression of a striking resemblance between the statue and the boy was accurate or whether Manuel had simply taken on St. Francis' expression. Spirits were moving all about him, Brother Andrés said, colorful little beings wearing unusual wisps of clothing. At first, he had believed them to be demons and crossed himself, but then he had realized that the billowing robes on the playful spirits he saw were simply different, exotic somehow, in hues he had never seen at the monastery.

"I was the only one he would ever tell about the spirits that visited him."

Brother Andrés' was a humble background and it stood him in good stead where his visions were concerned. He was reticent and private, never putting himself forward, and rarely speaking unless spoken to. Manuel understood why Brother Andrés kept his mouth shut. Manuel's father had taken him once to see a man burned at the stake for heresy and Manuel would never forget it.

They began a respectful exchange of daily greetings that soon grew to friendship. Like Manuel's mother, Brother Andrés feared that Manuel was too serious for his age, and made him a rag ball. They kicked it round the dusty courtyard of the monastery, Brother Andrés' habit drawn up to his plump knees, and Manuel's coat folded on a stone bench nearby, where Brother Andrés told him the colorful spirits that accompanied him often frolicked.

"I would dearly have liked to see them, but they never manifested themselves to me."

Manuel's curiosity about the Church only grew with time, and sometimes Brother Andrés was unable to answer his questions. When this happened he would, rather reluctantly, consult his Jesuit colleagues, whose education was superior to his own. There was a long-standing rivalry between the Franciscans and the Company of Jesus, and when Brother Andrés began to suspect that Manuel would one day enter the priesthood, he delighted in hearing Manuel say that he would become a monk too, even though he knew that Manuel was not suited to monastic life. He began taking him to the Jesuit library where Manuel could look up for himself the answers to his questions. Just as Brother Andrés had both feared and hoped, Manuel attracted the attention of the priests who worked there, and was soon walking down the book-lined corridors hand in hand with men who could answer all his questions without even having to consult the volumes at their disposal.

"I am ashamed to recall that for a while I forgot my friend. It pains me yet to think that perhaps he waited for me with his rag ball on the stone bench where I always left my coat, knowing as the minutes and then the hours went by that I would not come that day, or the next."

Manuel was caught up in a new friendship, more exciting than any he had known before, and in his childish enthusiasm he wanted Brother Andrés to be as thrilled as he was. Manuel invited his new friend to accompany him to the monastery, where he introduced him to Brother Andrés. Father Javier was young and exuberant and threw his arms around Brother Andrés, congratulating him on what a fine boy Manuel was. The hesitation Manuel had seen on his face when Father Javier had first appeared faded away as Father Javier swept Manuel up onto his broad shoulders and galloped into the courtyard, saying that he had come to play the famous rag-ball game. "I laughed so hard at the sight of them, one short and stocky, the other tall and slender, running to and fro, that I could not participate in the game!"

Father Javier had recently come from the Missions where he had spent seven years and to which he was returning as soon as he had prepared the young missionaries who would be accompanying him. From the moment he first started talking of his work in the jungles of Spanish America, Manuel knew what his life's work would be. The sea voyage itself held excitement enough for any boy, with the threat of attack by pirates and the lure of exotic foreign ports dotting the route south. Father Javier told him of journeys he had taken inland, through unmapped territory full of people as strange and colorful as the wild animals and birds that surrounded them.

Most of Father Javier's work had been with the Chiquitos Indians, to whom he had had to learn to preach in two languages, one for the men, another for the women. Their vocabularies were so different that even the word for mother was not the same when used by members of different sexes. He told Manuel that the Chiquitos Indians also played with balls, which they made from the gum of a tall tree resembling a sycamore. "The gum oozes out of the bark, white and as rich as cream. It hardens and turns black very quickly, so the Chiquitos smooth it on their arms, gradually rubbing it off and applying more until they work it into a smooth, round shape."

Unlike Manuel, the Chiquitos did not kick their ball, they used their heads to play.

The three of them tried this with Father Javier's rubber ball, but he was the only one with the skill to keep it in the air for long. The exercise made Brother Andrés' neck ache, so he soon gave it up and watched as Manuel learned the tricks Father Javier taught him.

By the time Father Javier left Seville, Manuel's future was decided. He would become a Jesuit missionary and travel, like Father Javier, to Spanish America.

It took him fourteen years of study to prepare for his ordination, and most of that time Manuel was away from home. He visited Brother Andrés every time he returned, telling him all about his life at the seminary, the trials and tribulations of his friends, the eccentricities of his teachers. "I never asked about his life, nor did I notice that his hair was grayer and his back more bowed each year. Brother Andrés waited until I was ordained, and when he knew that I would be leaving soon, he retired to his cell and prepared himself to die."

When Manuel heard how ill his friend was, he ran to the abbey and begged to be allowed to administer the last rites. Brother Andrés appeared to recover after Manuel arrived, and sat up on his narrow bed, surrounded for the first time with whatever comfort pillows, a wrapped and heated brick for his feet, and abundant food could bring. With nothing left to fear, he spent his last days sharing his love of the spirit world with Manuel, and telling him of his discovery, early in childhood, of what he believed to be a fallacy in the church he loved, the failure to recognize the spiritual dimension of other living beings who accompanied men and women on their journey through this world. It was what had drawn him to St. Francis, who Brother Andrés believed had felt the same.

He asked Manuel to dedicate his life as a missionary to deepening the well of goodness in each being, remembering that it is those who work for good and not against evil who bring redemption to the world.

"For three days we talked, and when he could no longer move his lips, I held his hand and did all I could to ease his passing. His heart was strong and beat long after all other signs of life were gone."

Manuel asked for leave to remain in the cell, and it was granted. He fasted, prayed, and meditated on the sparse contents of the cell that had been Brother Andrés' home for most of his life. The old rag ball was there, as was a packet containing all the letters Manuel had written over the years. He found a pair of rope sandals, some seeds in a small cloth bag, and a book by Bartolomé de las Casas, the first priest ordained in the New World. "He was a fierce defender of the Indians, and excoriated those whose greed, as he phrased it, turned Jesus Christ into the cruelest of gods and the king into a wolf hungry for human flesh." Inside the book was a piece of paper, its worn folds revealing its age and usage. "It was addressed to me, and was a copy of the document the Spanish court required be read to the Indians of the New World, exhorting them to adopt a new faith.

"*If you do not do so, or maliciously delay in doing so, let it be known that with God's help I will enter powerfully against you and wage war everywhere and in every manner I can, submitting you to the yoke and obedience of the Church and of His Majesty and taking your women and children as slaves. As such I shall sell them, and dispose of them as His Majesty decrees. And I will take your goods and do unto you all manner of evil I can.*

"I burned candle after candle as I read and meditated upon the words in the book, those on the paper, and those I had heard Brother Andrés speak. The more I studied the court's exhortation, the more contradictory it appeared, every phrase containing words I could not imagine the son of God, in whose name it was used, ever speaking."

Father Manuel asked for permission to take the items he had found and it was readily granted. He burned the packet containing his letters, and put the rope sandals on his feet. "They were too small but I did not mind."

A few days later, he packed the seeds and the old rag ball in his trunk and sailed for the New World.

"And that is how I ended up here, by the river of painted birds."

Chapter V

The following day was a repetition of the first. We rode, rested, and fed and watered the horses, who did nothing to help relieve the tension between Painted Pony and Garzón. Painted Pony was riding a horse who clearly believed that he should be heading the expedition, while Garzón's mount seemed perfectly content to bring up the rear. Garzón attempted to remedy matters by strapping on a pair of spurs, but Father Manuel refused to ride on until Garzón removed them. Vanity, he said, was no reason to cause pain to creatures free from such a fault themselves. Stung, Garzón tightened his jaw and rode several horse lengths behind, not exchanging a single word with us all morning.

By noon, the sun had warmed the earth, and Father Manuel and I removed the ankle length ponchos designed to protect both us and our horses from the cold.

The wetlands surrounding the outskirts of the city soon gave way to rippling grasses, and after that to the centuries old *butiá* palm forests, where we joined the peccaries and birds gorging themselves on the fallen *coquitos* that littered the grove. The yellow fruit hung in huge clusters high above our heads, and at night the fruit bats came, silent and shadowy, to take their turn at the feast the palms provided.

We spent our second night under the low branches of trees whose squat trunks were split and whose dense branches spread in all directions, low to the ground, heavy with flat black gourds shaped like ears. The gourds were full of seeds and rattled mightily when the wind blew.

The smell of the ocean was sharp and the darkness full of sounds I could not identify. Calls and cries, mingling with the more familiar crickets, the soft snuffling and lowing of the wild cattle, and the occasional whinny of a horse.

Exhaustion had finally brought sleep the night before, but that day several snakes had crossed our path. Garzón assured me that few of them were venomous, and as I was unrolling my blankets and preparíng to make my bed, he presented me with the skin of a *venado de campo*, once a species of deer abundant on the open plains. His mother had assured him that no snakes would come near a person sleeping on such a skin, and he never traveled without one. I lay with the velvety hide under my cheek, listening to the hooting of the owls, and the deathly silence that preceded the jaguar's call. I awoke to find myself staring into two enormous eyes on either side of a flat beak. I dived under my blanket and heard Garzón laughing.

"You can come out now. It was only a *ñandú*. They are very curious."

"Rheas," Father Manuel said.

"In the spring we will eat their eggs,"槽Craré added. "One will feed all four of us."

The tension of the day before had eased, and we followed the coastline, traveling on the hard packed sand next to the water's edge, sending clouds of gulls wheeling to the skies. I had grown up next to the water, but beaches such as these filled me with wonder. They stretched before and behind me as far as I could see, mile upon mile of fine white sand. Along the shores of the Río de la Plata the water was calm and often murky, but as the river lost itself in the Atlantic, clear waves as tall as church spires come crashing and foaming to the shore. Hundreds of sea lions basked on the rocks, their barking cries resonating for miles around.

As a child, I often walked the forests and river banks of Cork, but wherever I went, human beings were nearby. Here, I could feel the force of nature in all its solitary grandeur, and that evening I left the others and crossed the sand dunes to be alone on the beach. The roar of the surf filled the air, and the wind blew my hat off. I felt nine years old again, with burrs in my hair and my pockets bulging with stones and feathers. The same urge I experienced aboard ship came over me and I wanted to tear off my clothes and leap into the waves, but I could tell that the water roiling in deep eddies just off the shore would overpower me. I took off my shoes and hose and began to walk, feeling the grand desolation and majesty of that endless landscape. Just behind me, I could see my journey written in footprints in the sand, until the lapping, crashing waves removed all evidence of my presence on these shores. The light was beginning to fade and when I glimpsed something moving in the distance behind me I thought my eyes were deceiving me. The shadow appeared again, and as it came nearer, I heard the familiar strains of "The Maid with the Bonnie Brown Hair." I was standing on the shore thinking that my mind was playing odd tricks on me when I made out a small figure clinging to a horse and singing for all he was worth. It was Orlando! As I ran across the sand toward him, he saw me, and fell from the horse like a leaf blown by the wind. When I reached him, he was lying unconscious on the sand. I gathered him up and struggled back over the sand dunes with him, the exhausted horse trailing behind us.

Both were much in need of care. Father Manuel took charge of the horse while Orlando regained consciousness and ate an entire loaf of bread before curling up in Garzón's lap and falling asleep.

Garzón stroked his back. "You were right. We should not have left him."

"Perhaps he didn't understand that we would return."

"He understood, he just didn't believe it. I should have known better. I of all people should have known better." He handed Orlando to me and walked away, as had become his custom, to make his bed some distance from our small camp, leaving me to ponder the meaning of his remark.

Next morning, knowing that neither Orlando nor the horse could move on so soon, the men went hunting for fresh meat. Father Manuel and Bararé separated a few wild cattle from a herd and drove them toward a stand of trees where Garzón stood twirling two of the three lengths of his *boleadoras* very fast over his head with one hand. In his other hand he held the third length, anchored between the toes of one foot. As the *bolas* gained momentum he released his foothold, and the spinning weapon blurred as it flew toward the running cattle, whipping around the legs of a cow and sending it sprawling in the dust. They were upon the fallen animal instantly, killing it with thrusts from Climb's lance. As they set to work skinning the beast and quartering it, Orlando and I lit a fire and prepared to cook the meat that would bring a healthy color back to his face. Soon the meat was sizzling and the hide was staked out to dry. If the wild dogs and the vultures left it alone we would collect it on our return journey.

Normally, Garzón said, we would eat the entire animal — tongue, liver, brain — but with only four of us traveling most of the carcass would be left for the scavengers. There was only one delicacy he would not give up — *caracú*, bones rich with marrow. He scraped them clean, put them on the fire, and left them to cook until the marrow was soft. Then he showed Orlando and me how to use a stick to scoop the marrow out. He was disappointed when neither of us evinced much pleasure at the taste.

As we headed inland and away from the coast, palm trees waved in the breeze, flocks of parrots flew screeching overhead, and along the streams the banks erupted in ferns and creepers. The surrounding *montes* were thick with mosses and hanging lianas, their shadowy stillness inviting. Where the sun broke through the thick canopy of green, tiny insects engaged in a frenzied, airy dance.

The land began to resemble a green sea, gently rising and falling, with clustered islands of massive boulders dotting the landscape. Some were too smooth and slippery to climb, but others allowed me to explore their caves and crevices, under Cararé's watchful eye. I would not normally have enjoyed being supervised in this way, but something about his quiet, gentle presence made it impossible for me to feel anything but gratitude. Since our first night out when doubts had assailed me, he appeared to have appointed himself my protector, and I loved him for it.

For a day or two, caring for Orlando occupied all of our attention, but we soon reverted to planning how the settlement by the lagoon would be run, and quarrels between Garzón and Cararé sprang up again. Father Manuel supported the idea of paying wages, but money was unknown in the Missions, which were modeled after the tribal communities from which converts originated. Cararé wanted more time to consider how to introduce it, but Garzón had little patience with this cautious approach. What was there to consider? he growled at槽Cararé. If paying wages caused problems, we would solve them! He would not have slaves working for him! And what was an unpaid worker if not a slave? Cararé attempted to explain the difference between a person who has been bought and sold against his will, and a worker free to come and go, who labors for the good of his community. The calmer Cararé was, the more furious Garzón became, and I noticed that Orlando found ways of drawing him away. He asked for help he no longer really needed, and Garzón, still smarting with guilt over having left him behind at Santa Marta, never failed to provide it. Orlando even began requesting lessons in throwing the *boleadoras* and started plaiting the strips of hide he would use in the making of his own set. Whenever the two of them were engaged in some activity together, peace reigned.

A week into our travels we crossed the Arroyo Maldonado, cutting our way through thick vegetation, startling wood turkeys and plovers as we went. At the stream's edge we were surprised by a riot of kingfishers and heron, and saw turtles lying like stones in the dancing crystals scattered by the horses' hooves as we crossed. As we made our way up the banks of the stream on the other side, parrots chattered around us, climbing in and out of their large communal nests.

I delighted in all the birds we saw, but would not hear of Garzón catching any for me. He picked wild flowers for me instead, and one day we discovered a whole field of macachines in bloom, like a pink and purple carpet covering the ground as far as the eye could see. His pleasure in my surprise was as great as if he had planted and cultivated the tiny wild flowers himself.

We doubled back toward the coast and into the land of floating plants and floating nests, with birds of every size and color flying amongst the bull rushes and grasses. Water hyacinths grew in profusion there, and the shades of green were unrivalled even by those in Ireland. Above the flowering swamp grasses rose the Minuanes' burial grounds, surrounded by low trees ornamented with mosses and orchids, providing places of refuge during the rainy season when the waters were high.

We soon left the wading birds, the storks, and the majestic

guazú-pucú swamp deer behind and headed for the chain of three lagoons a few short miles from the coast, where water pooled from the surrounding wetlands.槽Cararé explained that just three days ride further north lay the Fortress of San Miguel, taken from the Spanish by the Portuguese nine years before, and housing a number of soldiers who would come to our defense if needed. They would not be needed, Garzón said. Our land would lie, a haven of safety in the heart of the wilderness, and from it we would prove that we could be trusted to share in the bounty.

Finally, we reached the place Garzón had chosen for this bold experiment that would bring the Indians of the Missions into the eighteenth century. As we stood by the lagoon's dark waters, clouds of pink flamingoes and white herons passed overhead, and from the shore a family of capybaras raised their heads as ducks flapped noisily by. Behind us in the stillness of the *ombú* forest, lizards and armadillos darted in and out of the trees' welcoming hollows. The ancient *ombúes*, their hollow trunks wider than Orlando and I could span even when we joined hands, had branches reaching one hundred feet or more above our heads, and seemed rooted in time, as immovable and solid as cathedrals.

When Father Antonio saw us returning with Orlando, he wept with relief. He had not realized that Orlando was gone until several hours after they noticed that a horse was missing. To make matters worse, Orlando had laid a false trail, so the party sent out to look for him had returned empty handed.

I could not tell whether Orlando understood the worry he had caused, but from the way he welcomed the embraces bestowed on him by Father Antonio and others at the mission I suspected that the idea that he was no longer alone in the world was beginning to take root in him.

We lodged in Santa Marta's guest house while Garzón traveled to Buenos Aires to lay claim to the land surrounding the lagoon and to obtain the license Cararé required in order to begin harvesting hides. Orlando attended the mission school, where I also went to perfect my Spanish and to assist the two priests with their younger pupils.

Father Antonio, I discovered, did not share Father Manuel's feelings of danger regarding the future of the Missions, and agreed with Cararé that the Crown they had served so faithfully would never turn against them. The Jesuits, he claimed, had been through far worse times than these in years past and still managed to maintain their system intact. More significantly, he saw Father Manuel's decision to move as a violation of his vow of obedience, not only to God but to the Order, and suggested that Father Manuel consider whether he was not abandoning both. While Father Manuel had asked himself this same question more times than he cared to recall, he was hurt and angry to hear it voiced, as he told me one day when I went to fetch wood for the oven and found him working furiously at the chopping block. He looked hot and tired and I insisted that he come to the guesthouse with me, where I sat him at the small table, put the *mate* gourd between us, added sugar to the water, and brewed us a gourd the way we both liked it. Then I cut a piece of fruit cake and put it before him. He took a mouthful, raised his eyes to heaven, and said he could not speak until he had relished the full flavor of the honey and dried fruits I had used in the mix. He was on his second piece when he admitted to having quarreled about his dire predictions for the future with every one of his previous partners. He did not wish to leave Father Antonio, whose patient, gentle nature he cherished, on any but the friendliest terms, so he had consented to write and inform the Provincial, Father Nusdorffer, of our plans, and ask for his blessing on the new venture. Father Nusdorffer was a wise and experienced shepherd, well aware of the machinations of his enemies at court.

"Could he prevent the move?" I asked.

"I doubt that he would choose to do so," Father Manuel answered.

"And if he did?"

"Such an outcome is unimaginable to me."

"Would you disobey?"

"I would do everything in my power to persuade Father Nusdorffer to change his mind."

"But would you come?" I insisted, finding myself close to tears. "Would you let Cararé come?"

Cararé knocked at the open door just at that moment and I rubbed my eyes with my apron and beckoned him in, serving him *mate* and warning him that it was sweet. He declined to try it, but accepted the cake, the aroma of which had brought him to the guesthouse door.

"*Don* Cararé," I said, "Garzón once mentioned the number of cattle we will be entitled to claim once he has received the license. He often makes jests and I think he was jesting then. Tell me the truth. I know that I can trust you not to tease me."

"What number did he give?"

"Twelve thousand head."

"It was no jest."

"And since there is no one counting, the figure is merely—" Father Manuel said.

"I will be counting," Cararé said firmly, and as his eyes met mine, I knew that he had decided to join us in our venture.

~

The weeks passed slowly while Garzón was in Buenos Aires obtaining our license and we awaited a reply from the provincial to Father Manuel's letter. Father Manuel taught me Guaraní and helped me improve my Spanish, and I undertook the next phase of the English language education his old friend Thomas Falkner had begun.

"You are an apt pupil, Father."

"Your words are a balm. Thomas claims that my letters are full of unintelligible and atrociously spelt English."

He showed me the Mission school, the storehouses full of flour and grains, and the workshops where the weavers, joiners, smiths and carpenters worked. We toured the infirmary, the gardens, and the arsenal, all built by the Indians out of sun dried bricks and stone, with roofs of thatch. I made myself useful by helping with the sick, and by tending the animals in the menagerie. Amazed at the number and variety of them, I asked why they were there, and Father Manuel explained that they were part of several celebrations that took place during the year.

"They are not sacrificed, are they?"

Father Manuel burst out laughing. "What have they been telling you in Ireland about Spanish priests?"

I felt myself blushing as I replied that I had not thought that *he* would make blood sacrifices.

"You thought the Indians might do so? Allow me to reassure you. The gods of the *pampas* do not require sacrifice, and since Jesus does not either, we have enjoyed compatibility on that score for many centuries."

The animals in the menagerie were valued pets, most were hand raised and were quite tame, even the jaguars.

Father Manuel invited Orlando and me to accompany him to the aviary and as we walked into the big, thatched enclosure and sat together on a small bench, birds descended from the branches around us, landing in our laps, on our shoulders and heads. Father Manuel filled my hands with seed and fruit, and soon I was surrounded by fluttering birds, their claws and beaks tickling my skin as they searched for their favorite morsels.

"I see why Garzón delights in showing you things," Father Manuel smiled. "When you're happy you glow as if you were lit from within."

My pleasure was as nothing compared to Orlando's. At first, as the birds started to descend from their nests and perches, he was alarmed and hid his face in my lap, but as he saw them feeding his eyes grew wider, and Father Manuel put a slice of orange in his palm. Soon two canaries were perched on Orlando's fingers sipping the juice. He laughed aloud with sheer delight and startled the birds away momentarily. They were soon back, and hoping that Orlando might choose to speak to Father Manuel again as he had on the day they met, I left them together and went to sit in the cemetery by my favorite statue.

I looked up at Joan of Arc, with her rich golden brown skin, black hair, wide cheekbones, and large, dark eyes, one foot firmly planted on the chest of a dying soldier, and one muscular, strong arm holding a sword over her head. Cararé had told Orlando and me the story of how she had disguised herself as a man and led troops into battle, and of how she was sold by her captors and condemned for heresy and sorcery. She was a great favorite with the women at the mission, but since she had not been canonized and could not be openly worshipped, Cararé had carved a statue of her and used it to ornament a corner of the burial ground. He was inordinately pleased by my fondness for it.

I walked through the cemetery and into the candlelit church where the carved and painted columns marched like sentinels to the altar. I loved the vaulted ceiling where every foot of space was occupied by neat squares outlined in shades of brown, ranging from a deep mahogany to a pale cedar. Each square contained a carved flower rendered in intricate geometric designs and vividly painted. The red and gold confessional was decorated with replicas of the twelve columns that supported the church, covered in swirls and shapes that matched the beams arcing over my head. The base and body of the pulpit glittered in gold and blue floral carvings against a sea of forest green, and the side altars were small copies of the main one, sheltering statues of the Virgin Mary, the infant Jesus, and various saints whose names槍raré had been teaching me, since he found that my religious education was sadly lacking.

On feast days, which I had learned averaged six or seven every month, there were concerts, and while Cararé informed me that our choir could not rival the one established in Paraguay by Father Basco, I stood amazed while they sang airs from the Italian masters Scarlatti and Caldara. Their singing was not all that would amaze me.

On the feast of the warrior St. Martin, when Orlando and I entered the plaza to make our way to the church, we saw over the church entrance an arch of evergreens laced with flowering vines, orchids, carnations, and roses. Once inside, sweet aromas greeted us. The walls and benches were covered in fruits and flowers, and we heard birds singing above us, where the canaries, cardinals, doves and mockingbirds we had fed just a few days before flew overhead amongst the colorful, minutely rendered flowers that had lured me in the first time I entered the church. The jaguars were tethered to the side altars, tapirs chewed alfalfa by the confessional, and rheas raised their tall necks and studied us as we made our way to a bench.

I skirted the area containing the *chajás*. Father Manuel had assured Orlando that these large birds with claws on their wing tips would do him no harm, but every time they darted their eyes at him Orlando reacted as if they were about to attack, so I carried him on my back until we were safely seated. No sooner had we taken our places, than the musicians entered, some on foot, some borne along with their instruments on small, wheeled platforms. They played drums, harps, and flutes, and were followed by masked and playful dancers clad in brilliant, life-like costumes, portraying jaguars, parrots, and monkeys.

The Mass was a riotous celebration of God and nature united in a spectacle of color and unrestrained joy. The altar was adorned with embroidered cloths as meticulously executed as paintings, glittering with candle holders shaped like birds with open wings, each feather carved and painted in details so precise the wood appeared to take flight under the candle flames.

槽Cararé, who came to sit by us, took Orlando on his lap and told us that the music played during the Mass had been written by a Doménico Zípoli, the deceased choirmaster of the Church of the Society of Jesus in Córdoba. He had composed it to celebrate the Missions with their wealth of contraltos, tenors, and sopranos. Three soloists were featured in the Gloria and the high, perfectly pitched voices rang amongst the flowers, rivaling the birds.

Ever since I could remember, the Catholic Mass had been outlawed in Ireland, and we attended our few churches for abbreviated services, or met in small outdoor gatherings when even my careful mother felt that the salvation of our souls was worth the risk of arrest for conspiracy. Sometimes, we congregated in forests, posted guards, and smuggled in disguised priests. Michael and I were sworn to secrecy, not only from those who might turn us in, but from our father, who would have died of apoplexy if he had known where we were.

Deprived not only of the right to worship, for I don't know how devout I might have been had I been free to practice Catholicism, but of the rituals of the Church, I was exhilarated by a Mass that celebrated life so exuberantly. I could not imagine what Irish church fathers would have made of Father Manuel, who winked at Orlando when he emerged to celebrate the Mass from among the cataract of flowers around the altar. How would they have viewed the animals in the church, and the dancers and lively tunes that preceded the service in such an unrestrained celebration of the senses? I felt as if a door had been opened into a world so new I could not grasp it all at once.

I decided then and there that this would be the last time I would stay behind with Orlando and the other children too young to take Communion when every other person in the church walked to the altar.

I was trembling when at the end of the Mass I approached Father Manuel and asked him to hear my confession. He inquired if I would like to sit outside while the banquet was being prepared. I must have looked taken aback because he assured me that there was nothing magical about the confessional itself. It ensured privacy for those who wanted it, but since he and I were friends we could converse wherever we pleased.

My mouth was dry when he joined me in Joan of Arc's small grove. He had brought a flask of water flavored with lemons and sweetened with sugar and he poured us each a cup. "Tell me what this burden is that you've been carrying, Isabel."

"I killed a man."

Father Manuel looked grave. "What were the circumstances?"

"He was my husband. He hit me and I attacked him with a knife. He stepped back to avoid being stabbed and broke his neck as he fell into the cellar. I buried him there and told no one of it until now."

"Was it your intention to kill him?"

"No. But I was not sorry he died."

"Has that changed?"

"Now that I've left Ireland, now that I've freed myself from him, I wish that Tobias had not died in the process. But do I wish him living? No, because then…"

Father Manuel finished my thought for me. "You wouldn't be free to marry again."

"Is it possible to be absolved for such a sin?"

"There is no sin too large for Christ to carry. But the truth about confession, Isabel, is very simple and very complex. For some, confession is a formula, an easy way to wash away the wrongs we do. But it was not meant to be that easy. Confession is about self-knowledge, and absolution only happens when we have understood and absolved ourselves. I can say the words and the formalities will have been observed, but only you can know if you repent of the wrongs that have prevented you from feeling at peace with yourself."

"I need to know if you think that I murdered him."

"The Church has never considered self defense in the same light as cold blooded murder. What you have related to me was an accidental death."

"But you, Father, do you think I murdered him?"

"I think you wished him dead, and with reason. I also think that you are capable of having seen that without any help from me and that there is something you haven't told me."

I twisted the end of my shirt into a knot. "I used to put laudanum in his ale. Not to kill him, just to prevent him...just to make him sleep. One night he fell asleep and began to choke. I didn't help him. He turned onto his side and saved himself."

We sat in silence until I could stand it no more. "That would have been murder, wouldn't it?"

"I think you were fortunate. You thought of murder and wished for his death, but ultimately, Isabel, it was the fall and not you that killed him. I have no qualms about absolving you for what you've told me."

I threw my arms around him, sending the flask crashing onto the stone base of the statue, and Father Manuel held me while I sobbed into his cotton shirt.

~

I felt as light as gossamer as we walked together toward the banquet.

It was November, and signs of summer were all around us. Flowers garlanded the porticos and a raucous rainbow of parrots streaked across a sky so blue it felt eternal.

The plaza seemed bathed in gold, people glowed, and I shook my head in disbelief at the array, the abundance, and the gleam of the food put before us. Meat, fish, and fowl; vegetables fresh and cooked; fruits heaped in woven baskets; breads and cakes.

Next day I took Communion for the first time in many years and emerged from the church to find In Carrare awaiting me with a Mission soldier's uniform and an invitation to take part in a sham battle in honor of St. Martin. While I changed into the dark blue coat with its silver and gold piping, I could see the men performing ancient war dances and martial exercises, and hear them setting off fireworks, of which they were inordinately fond, and for which they manufactured their own gun powder. As I emerged from the guesthouse, a body of cavalry and one of infantry drilled by me in orderly fashion, shooting at wooden targets. The infantry performed with bows and arrows, swords, slings, and muskets; the cavalry with carbines, lances, and sabers. They competed with one another, and Father Antonio and Cararé awarded prizes to the winners, who marched by in glittering splendor under Spain's Royal Standard, a purple flag with a golden crown and shield. The sham battle followed and I, in my role as Master Keating, was not surprisingly taken captive very early in the melee. I caught sight of Itanambí eyeing me rather suspiciously as I took my place on the sidelines to observe the rest of the proceedings.

Orlando was cheering and jumping up and down. I had observed that whenever he was exposed to new experiences he absorbed them with extraordinary rapidity, quivering with excitement. Then he slept profoundly for a few hours, sometimes talking in his sleep, repeating word for word what he had heard.

That night, tired and replete with good food, Father Manuel, Cararé and I sat on the steps of the guesthouse and reminisced like old soldiers. I described the Irish castles I had known, built as fortresses, and designed, as was Santa Marta, to support the hundreds of people who depended on them. I found myself speaking with relish and as if I myself had been there, of battles during which tar, stones and boiling water had been poured onto the heads of attackers, and of the Cromwellian army siege of 1646, when even the eighteen foot thick walls could not resist the devastating effect of that new weapon — cannons. That set Cararé off and he recalled the old days, when his ancestors had fought the Charrúa and learned to ride horses stolen from the Spanish. Cannon and firearms of all kinds had contributed to his people's defeat also, but what truly decimated them, he told me, was disease, the plagues and illnesses brought over on Spanish and Portuguese ships, and those they fell victim to when put to work in the bowels of the earth.

Cararé's great grandfather had returned bald and toothless from two years of working in the mines, with a weakness in his limbs and an overall tremor that eventually killed him. He had been among the fortunate ones, Cararé said. More than half of the Indians forced to work in the silver mines in the frozen wastes of Huancavélica never returned, dying after three or four years of hard labor and leaving widows and orphans to starve or sell themselves into similar bondage. In the depths of the hills the miners roasted, carving silver from the rocks and carrying it on their backs by candlelight to the surface, where their companions froze as they ground and washed the rocks in the icy winds smiting the hills. In a landscape rendered barren for six leagues around by the thousands of bonfires that raged over the hillsides, the precious metal was melted down and prepared for shipment to Spain.

After watching his father die as a result of unrelenting labor, Cararé's grandfather had moved his family to the mission and told them to fall on their knees and thank God when the mission gates closed behind them. Only the King had access to those the Jesuits protected, and for three generations Cararé and his family had devoted their lives to being faithful soldiers of Christ and the King.

I felt stricken by these tales. My mother's family were silversmiths. From the time I could walk, I was taken to my uncle's shop and taught to turn over the candelabras, the trays and goblets, looking for a ship between two castles and the maker's initial on the left hand side. It was these traits that denoted very old silver, worked before 1714. My mother had been most particular about this, and it is how I learned left from right. Before my father taught me my letters, which wasn't until I was ten years old, I could recognize the words "sterling" and "dollar." If I could find the word "sterling" on a piece of silverwork it meant it was of the required standard; and whenever I found the word "dollar," I knew that I was holding a rare piece made from imported and recast Spanish dollars of the highest standard of purity. Until this moment when I learned at what cost in human suffering all that silver had been mined, I had been proud of being the descendant of a long line of silver and gold smiths, living in Cork for hundreds of years before Christ.

It was unseasonably warm for spring, and I fanned myself with a woven grass fan as Father Manuel and Cararé went on to talk of their efforts to find a printing press and a telescope. Their books were all imported from the northern missions, and no telescope was available to them at all.

"I am envious of Father Suárez's astronomical observatory at San Cosme, God rest his soul," Father Manuel said. "Perhaps one of your tribesmen who helped make his telescopes could be persuaded to join us for a time, Cararé."

Cararé seemed to think that I would know what he was talking about when he told me that with Father Suárez's help, his people had left one hundred and forty observations of the satellites of Jupiter, and astronomical tables through the year 1840. I was about to confess that

I had no idea what an astronomical table was, when we saw Father Antonio hurrying toward us in the dying light, breathlessly calling out that Garzón had returned. I jumped up and was about to run to greet him when Father Antonio added that history was repeating itself. "He has brought a dying man with him! Not at all like that gentlemanly Dr. Falkner you nursed so many years ago, Manuel. A wild looking fellow!"

We ran to the infirmary, and saw a bearded man with a mass of long and tangled hair being laid out on a bed. His chest was an open mass of wounds.

"Was he shot?" Father Manuel asked.

"Attacked by a jaguar," Garzón responded, bringing the lantern closer to the man's face. The rush of recognition that followed made me forget that I had been longing to see Garzón for weeks. I plunged into the oncoming darkness and concealed myself in the cemetery behind Joan of Arc, my back against the base of the statue and my knees drawn to my chin.

What in the name of heaven, I wondered, remembering the bleak day when I had first encountered him, was Charlie FitzGibbon doing in the Province? Since that day when I had seen him outside Bridget's cottage and dreamed of dancing with him, events had driven thoughts of Charlie from my mind. There was no reason for the cold fear that overcame me now. He knew nothing of me or of Tobias and could therefore reveal nothing.

"Are you unwell, Master Michael?"

It was Cararé, come to find me. I shook my head, not trusting my voice, and he sat down next to me. "That man is familiar to you?"

"His name is Charlie FitzGibbon."

"You knew him in Ireland?"

"I knew of him. He hates the English and was probably banished by them."

"What has brought him here I wonder?"

I shook my head.

"Father Antonio wants to know if you will tend to him. And Garzón has asked after you."

"I will be there in a moment, *Don* Cararé."

As he got to his feet, laughter reached us from the infirmary and his face was transformed with happiness. Putting aside his usual quiet decorum he ran toward the infirmary, calling out to me as he went, "My wife has returned!"

I followed him, and as I entered the room I saw that he had his arms around a woman and knew at once that it had been Wimencaí who had modeled for the statue of Joan of Arc. There were the same strong features, the straight black hair and generously rounded body. As soon as Criaré released her, Garzón put his hands around her waist and twirled her in the air in a swirl of colorful petticoats. He kissed her warmly and Wimencaí laughed and pushed him away. He looked at me, and I wished that he would kiss me as well, knowing full well that if nothing else, my disguise would prevent it.

Wimencaí's playful manner vanished as she approached the bed where Charlie lay. She rolled up her sleeves, and asked for warm water.

"I'll fetch it," I said. I wanted an excuse to leave again, to hide my jealousy and confusion, to compose myself. I tried to think of nothing except the simple task of filling a basin with water from the kettle at my hearth, and I kept my eyes fixed on the steam that rose before me as I walked back to the infirmary.

Charlie had been transferred to a wooden table, and I helped Wimencaí wash his wounds and apply clear *cupay* oil to staunch the bleeding. She explained her treatment to me as she worked, and whispered that in his letters Criaré had told her all about me. While Charlie's chest was sewn back together, she asked me to pound some *zuynandy* bark and showed me how to apply it. "It is effective mostly for wounds made by jaguars. It prevents inflammation and poisoning of the wound and also alleviates the pain, which if he ever wakes, poor man, will be considerable."

Satisfied with her handiwork, Wimencaí pronounced herself almost finished.

She wiped her forehead on her sleeve ,and asked me to hand her a pot containing a thick, reddish substance, cooling after being thoroughly softened by the heat from the fire.

"What is this?" I asked her.

"*Sangre del grad*o, the sap of a tree that grows along the banks of streams and rivers. I harvest it only in the winter months of July and August when the moon is waning." She took a brush from her basket and proceeded to paint Charlie's chest and shoulders with the sap. "It acts like a liquid bandage. It will dry and seal his chest until he heals, preventing the wounds from festering."

I helped her return Charlie to his bed and was instructed to watch his breathing while Wimencaí changed into clean clothes. If he woke, I was to put a cloth moistened with salt, fruit juice and laudanum to his lips and squeeze a few drops into his mouth. He did not wake until the next morning, when he looked at me without recognition. What reason after all would he have to connect the young man he saw by his bed with the woman he had barely noticed standing outside a hovel in Cork during a winter storm?

During my next visit I introduced myself and steered the subject quickly onto what had happened to him.

His Spanish mother had relatives to the West of us in Entre Ríos, Charlie told me, and when the English arrested him and gave him the option to emigrate or be hanged, he had decided to emigrate. "I would have chosen hanging if I could have thwarted them more by it!" he grinned.

After several months spent in Buenos Aires establishing himself as a hide merchant, he had finally been on his way to find his relatives when his guide misjudged the rapids and their canoe tipped. The guide was borne away in the current and lost, while Charlie clung to a *camalote*, a sort of moving island common on the Uruguay River. He was not the only one who had sought safety there. No sooner had he pulled himself onto the floating mass of vegetation than he came face to face with a stranded and hungry jaguar that did not wish to share its refuge. "I had been told that the only way to fend off a jaguar is to piss in its eyes, but I reached for my knife instead!"

I laughed rather too loudly at this, as I imagined my brother would have done, and Charlie changed the subject, asking me to fill in whatever I could about what had happened to him after that. "You killed the jaguar, it seems, and were found by some *camiluchos* — cattle workers — who heard your cries for help. They had intended to take you to Montevideo, but when they came across Garzón and heard that he was bound for Santa Marta, they asked him to bring you here."

Charlie was full of questions about the mission and its inhabitants, and liked having me nearby to talk to, but his presence threw me into confusion. It seemed too fateful a coincidence that we should both have ended up not only in the Spanish colonies, but in the very same location, but the fact that we were both from Cork drew us naturally together. My disguise afforded me protection from the charm Charlie exercised on every woman he came in contact with, while at the same time leaving me vulnerable to his thinking that he could knock at my door at any hour. He even wondered why he wasn't allowed to share the guesthouse with Orlando and me. Father Manuel told Charlie that he was not well enough to leave the infirmary, but as his wounds healed, Charlie suspected that something was amiss and even asked me one day if I found his company objectionable. I made up a not altogether untruthful story about Orlando being afraid of strangers, and Charlie, whose manners were beyond reproach, accepted the explanation, although I sensed that he did not quite believe it.

"An unusual name — Garzón," he said one day as I dressed his wounds. He liked to talk at such times, as a distraction from the pain.

"It's French, but written with a 'z' not a 'ç,'" I said.

"Little Itanambí seems awfully fond of him. He's a Catholic, I imagine?"

"Why do you ask?"

"I've not seen him in the church, and he can't marry her if he's not a Catholic, can he? The ruling council would never stand for it."

So it wasn't only jealousy that had made me suspect that there was something between Garzón and Itanambí. Charlie had also seen it. I knew that Garzón had been baptized into the Catholic faith. His father had been conventional or practical enough to see to it, and it was one of Garzón's more vivid childhood memories: the astonishment of his father's band of renegades as a priest was brought aboard, a tough old man who didn't appear remotely afraid of finding himself surrounded by smugglers and pirates. In fact, before the night was out, he and Garzón's father were sharing a bottle of wine and laughing heartily at one another's jokes.

I finished my work and was preparíng to leave the infirmary when Father Manuel came to tell us that the long awaited answer from the Provincial had arrived.

Chapter VI

October, A.D. 1746

My son,

I opened your letter this morning and its contents troubled me so that I am wasting no time sending a reply.

First of all, let me assure you that you are not alone with your concerns about our future and that of our beloved and faithful converts. I have been positively besieged by anxious pleas for concerted action to protect our Missions on one side, and on the other unequivocal orders from Spain to do nothing to offend the King's representatives in his colonies. Delicate negotiations are afoot between the King's ministers and Father Retz, our General, and I have been instructed to do nothing that might endanger these proceedings.

Rumors abound, and one of the most insidious and contemptible regards the fate of the free (an ungodly reference to their unenlightened state) tribes. I have heard of plans to eliminate them if they continue to resist our efforts to bring them to God. While the massacres would be blamed, as they always have been, on the Indians' aggressions toward settlers, the real culprit would remain greed for the resources available in the territories these tribes control.

The most recent accusation leveled against us is that we are impeding the progress of civilization while failing to look to the future, which in the minds of the merchants belongs only to those who own a material interest in it. We must continue to ask ourselves what kind of future is in store for a continent whose history is being written in the blood of its native peoples.

As for allowing Cararé and those who wish to follow him to work for wages, I am of two minds. I trust your judgment regarding Captain Garzón's and Master Keating's integrity, but you must remember that you will be setting a dangerous precedent. Once taken, this step is irreversible, and less scrupulous landowners will come knocking at our mission doors demanding access to the labor we can provide.

Our enemies in Spain and Portugal are busy circulating rumors of our vast riches. They will not be predisposed to believe that we will indeed allow the Indians to keep the wages they will earn. Just as they accuse us of using the profits from our herds and yerba mate to enrich ourselves, so they will believe that any payment made to Indian workers will find its way into our coffers.

I entrust your decision to God and recommend fasting and meditation before you reach it.

Yours in Christ,

Bernardo Nusdorffer, S.J.

"Is he granting permission or withholding it?" Garzón asked.

"Neither," Father Manuel answered.

"Is the man incapable of an honest answer?"

"Captain!" Cararé said. "You are speaking of the Father Provincial!"

"He could be Pope for all the difference it makes to me! Why can he not give a straightforward reply?"

Father Manuel raised his hand before the quarrel could go any further. "He advises fasting and meditation, and I will follow his advice."

For the next two days, Garzón paced around the plaza, practicing his aim by throwing his *boleadoras* for hours on end, swam back and forth across the rather shallow stream nearby, and began a new experiment with water and steam.

"Now there," Charlie said as he watched Garzón fill one of several metal containers at the well, "is either a man in love or in need of a useful pastime."

I bristled. "Our entire future depends on what Father Manuel decides."

"Perhaps so. But what, pray, is your friend doing now?"

Garzón was leaving the compound. From where Charlie and I stood in one of the watch towers, we saw him approach a large pile of wood and brush, over which were arranged a series of stone steps. It soon became apparent that Garzón was attempting to boil the water he had collected, to what end neither Charlie nor I could imagine.

Two days later, having followed Father Nusdorffer's advice, Father Manuel announced that he had reached a decision. He had prayed and fasted, and seen the future as clearly as if it were written in the tiles at his feet. The days when Indians could roam the *pampas* living off the land were numbered. Settlers were coming, and soon every hectare of land would be owned by individuals anxious to exploit its riches. The Mission Indians had many skills from which a new colony could benefit. They were expert carpenters, masons, and farmers. They could read and write in several languages and many had great musical and artistic abilities.

Garzón started to tap his foot impatiently but Father Manuel appeared not to notice. He had no doubt, he said, that enemies of the Jesuits would prevail and the day would soon come when they would be ordered to open their doors to the eighteenth century with all its ills and promises. He knew that the Indians' only hope for survival lay in being hired by landowners who would pay them for their labor.

"Precisely!" Garzón said, but Father Manuel was not to be hurried.

The days were gone, he said, when to all intents and purposes the outside world did not exist and the priests could continue their work untouched by the times. "We have protected the Indians in the Missions from slavery for over two centuries. The time has come for them to blend into the life of the colonies. If I do not encourage them to do so, everything my predecessors and I have fought for will be lost. I have conferred with Vararé and with the *cabildo*, and we are in agreement. Father Antonio will remain here with those who choose to stay. I will accompany those who accept the offer of work."

The extent of the strain Garzón had been under was revealed in the exuberance with which he jumped up and hugged Father Manuel, pounding him on the back until Father Manuel begged him to stop.

"And you, *Don* Cararé?" I asked. "You will be one of those who come with us, won't you?"

"Wimencaí and I will come," he said.

I threw my arms around him, and he held me for a moment while he whispered, "Itanambí will not be joining us!"

"Thank you!" I whispered back as Father Manuel knelt in front of the wooden crucifix, crossed himself, and invited us to do the same. Charlie, Cararé and I accepted his invitation, but Garzón remained standing as Father Manuel looked up at his nailed God. "The Guaraní call you Ñamandú — the first father. Like all fathers, You operate in mysterious ways, Lord. I have often rebelled against the means You choose to achieve Your ends, and I understand why Father Nusdorffer is hesitant about this new endeavor, but I believe that if we don't move, we will be unable to defend ourselves. I am a good shepherd, and if necessary, I too will lay my life down for my sheep. If I am wrong, You will forgive me. From now on, we will have You, we will have each other, and if I know human beings, we will have Master Keating and Captain Garzón."

"Amen!" Garzón said. "We leave in three days!"

~

It took two weeks to prepare for our journey, and Garzón, mad with impatience, seemed to be everywhere at once. He purchased four large wagons, or *carretas*, and supervised the work of securing to their sides the crates that would transport the chickens, ducks, and geese. The body of each *carreta* was the length of two men. Wooden arches supported the thatch that covered the roof and sides, and hides hung at the front and back for privacy and protection from the wind. Two huge wheels, three heads taller than I, propelled the *carretas*, which would be pulled by teams of oxen.

Precious *yerba* seeds were harvested and packed like so much gold, along with the ploughs and tools essential to our success. Father Manuel's books were wrapped in cloth, and placed in the wagon I would share with Orlando. As my Spanish improved I was looking forward to making my way through Father Manuel's library, feasting on his editions of Calderón de la Barca, Moreto y Cavana, Cervantes, and Tirso de Molina.

The one hundred men, women, and children who had elected to accompany us also began sorting through their possessions, deciding what to leave behind. They would be allowed to take only what each could carry. Between Santa Marta and the lagoon, we would have to deviate from the coast several times due to the large rock formations the wagons couldn't cross. This would entail hitching and unhitching the oxen, struggling back and forth over the dunes, emptying the wagons and carrying the contents ourselves when the wheels sank on that endless ribbon of sand that bordered the ocean.

Charlie announced that he had decided to return to Entre Ríos to continue the search for his relatives, and Garzón seemed much relieved. He had been concerned that I might ask Charlie to join our enterprise.

"Partners do not spring such surprises on one another," I told him, masking my own mixed feelings about Charlie's departure.

From the moment he left the infirmary Charlie had been surrounded by solicitous inquiries and showered with small gifts of food and wine. New clothes had been stitched for him and a poncho woven in red, black and white, the colors of the FitzGibbon coat of arms. On more than one occasion, I had observed mothers leading tearful daughters away from the portico outside Charlie's room. He combined the fatal attributes of being a foreigner of noble birth, gifted with physical beauty and a tragic history. For young women accustomed to having their every move scrutinized and their life laid out with no possible variation from the lives their mothers had led before them, Charlie represented a romantic dream, just as he had for me at a time when my life too had felt circumscribed by conditions beyond my control.

Father Manuel was also preparing to say goodbye, in his case to the mission that had been his home for over a decade. Here he had married dozens of couples and baptized hundreds of children, and before we left, he said mass for the last time at the altar he had helped to build.

That night, when all but his closest friends had retired to their beds, they asked for a final tale from the stock of stories that had delighted them for so many years. Father Manuel chose to tell us of his first contact with a small group of Guaraní Indians. Anxious to count them as his converts, he had introduced them to the teachings of Jesus only to discover that they had been Catholics ever since their ancestors had journeyed with St. Thomas the Apostle across the deserts of the Grand Chaco and over the Andes, bringing the word of Christ to all they met.

"The Guaraní, you see," Father Manuel said, lighting his pipe, "believe that St. Thomas landed with the Jesuits at Bahía de los Santos in Brazil. I even went to the lake near Chiquisaca where they claim that the cross he carried is buried. I, like all Jesuits, they told me, am directly descended from him."

"Impossible," Garzón muttered.

"Faith is composed of impossibilities!" Father Manuel smiled.

Stern glances were directed at Garzón and he subsided with his mate gourd while Father Manuel continued.

It was while he was with the Guaraní that he had first heard of the old religion. It happened quite by accident and only because he was overtaken while traveling by the chills preceding several days of a fever that assailed him on and off for several months after his arrival in the colonies. Father Manuel had left his own mission and was traveling with a guide to Asunción to visit his childhood friend Father Javier, when the illness overcame him.

In a circle outside the thatched house to which he was carried were gathered several men, women and children, dressed in plain Mission clothing. As they changed into native attire, folding their Mission garments and putting them aside, they were surrounded by chanting, dancing men, shaking large rattles. The dancing and singing intensified and Father Manuel heard them exchange their Christian names for Guaraní ones. *Chicha*, which until now he had only associated with intoxication, was handed round, and Father Manuel realized that in this instance at least it had a ritualistic purpose, much like communion wine.

Father Manuel floated in and out of consciousness for several days while the music and the dancing continued. By the time his fever passed, there was no one left but his guide and when Father Manuel questioned him the man avoided his eyes and said he had no recollection of what Father Manuel had seen. It was only when Father Manuel arrived at the mission in Asunción that he knew he had not been delirious, for he recognized one of the men he had seen dancing round the fire. Father Manuel remembered him for the fierce determination of his movements, the intense concentration on his face, and for the fact that when he shed his Christian name and put on the feathered headdress offered to him he did so with the air of a king assuming his crown. Father Manuel knew that what he had witnessed was heresy, a pagan ritual that he had not only failed to put a stop to but been tempted to compare to that most holy sacrament, communion.

Father Javier was gentle with him, absolving him and telling him that he had not even been sure at the time that the incident was real. Father Manuel knew that it was, and more. He knew that he had not stopped the ritual because he had allowed himself to be drawn into it, to be moved by it. His anguish was so acute that he wished he belonged to an order that encouraged self flagellation, and he asked for permission to wear a *cilicio* that would pinch and torment his flesh and help him to feel that he was in some way atoning for his faults. Permission was granted and for days Father Manuel wore the metal belt under his robes, until Father Javier, who had now been in the Missions for most of his adult life, referred him to the writings and reports of his predecessors. Father Manuel found these writings rich with portents, dreams, and visions more vivid than any he had so far experienced. It was not possible, Father Javier explained, to live among the Indians and not fall prey to these doubts. Their lives were guided and shaped by dreams. The Guaraní believed that while awake, they prepared themselves for sleep, and the meaningful dreams that followed. Many fine conversions had come about when entire villages, guided by their dreams, had sought baptism.

What then was the meaning of the ritual he had seen? Were these Indians hypocrites, liars, or simply confused and in need of guidance?

And why, whether this was a dream or not, did he feel unable to judge what they had done, why was he unwilling to expose and punish the offender he had recognized?

Father Javier reminded him of the Sacred Congregation for the Propagation of the Faith. Established by Pope Gregory XV in 1622, the Congregation had been clear in its instructions to missionaries about not bringing "any pressure to bear on the peoples to change their manners, customs, and uses, unless they are evidently contrary to religion and sound morals." There was "no stronger cause for alienation and hate," the Congregation maintained, "than an attack on local customs."

These local customs, along with exposure to a tropical climate, commonly inflamed the senses and changed the perceptions of Europeans, Father Javier said, dabbing the welts around Father Manuel's waist while he told his friend how he had boiled the bark and seeds of the *mboy caá* in wine, setting most of the mixture aside for future use as a remedy against snake bites. It had soothing properties and Father Manuel was to apply more every few hours and give up the *cilicio*. He also recommended that, apart from applications of *mboy caá*, Father Manuel should, before every meal, eat large quantities of the fruits of the *Guembe* bush, followed by a cup of cold water.

Feeling just as hopeless as he had when his mother, as a cure for what she termed his melancholy humors, had had him bled by the local surgeon, Father Manuel undertook the treatment. It had no soothing effect on his senses, and Father Javier gave up his efforts and assigned him instead to work with Father Herrán in the more temperate climate of Buenos Aires, where Father Herrán was seeking to convert, among others, the Minuánes and the Charrúa, who continued attacking settlements in the interior and killing any who encroached upon their hunting grounds.

Father Manuel was elated. Here at last was the missionary work he had dreamed of. Ministering to the converted Guaraní was not unlike being a village priest in Spain. But working with Father Herrán meant contact with those he had come to think of as real Indians.

Father Herrán had succeeded in befriending the Minuánes and the Charrúa but nothing more. They had accepted him as a visitor, respected his knowledge of their language and their customs, and believed him when he told them that if they continued their attacks, the Spanish would raise a force against them calculated to wipe them off the face of the earth. They retreated to the *pampas* from the coastal lands where they had lived from the bounty of the ocean, and learned new ways of survival, made possible by their mastery of the horse. Father Herrán spent his life trying to convert the Charrúa and the Minuánes to Christianity with little success, and instead of insulating Father Manuel and keeping his thoughts focused on missionary work, he challenged him further.

Father Manuel laughed as he remembered the tough old man, who bore a striking resemblance to the wild beings to whom he had devoted his life. "It was Father Herrán who taught me to start a fire with a flint stone, to hunt with a bow and arrow, and to dive for shellfish. Like me, Father Herrán came to the Province believing that he was bringing God's word to the heathen and opening the doors of heaven for them. What the distant, unapproachable tribes were telling him was that he should not have come at all."

"But what if the Jesuits had not been here, would the Indians not be in bondage?" I asked.

"Without a doubt."

"Then surely you have done more good than harm?"

"It is not we Jesuits the Charrúa and the Minuánes object to. It is all foreigners. What are we really doing here? Cararé tells me that it is the devil prompting me when I suspect that I have simply provided a cover for the King's greed. There was a time when I had no doubt as to my mission. God sent His only Son to die for the sins of humankind, and from then on it was clear what each of us must do. Save as many souls as possible and bring them to Christ. I meditated and prayed for guidance for years on the issue of what the Charrúa and Minuánes wanted, and slowly, as my Guaraní and Chaná converts grew to trust me they revealed that not all of them had come to my mission drawn by the power of Christ and His church. Many came to avoid what Christ's servants, the Spanish and the Portuguese, waited to do to them if they persisted in worshipping and living as they had done for thousands of years."

"You must have felt ill-used," Charlie said.

"I cared only that they had come. And with that realization I understood that keeping them safe was all that I could do. Whether or not they accepted Christian doctrine I would leave to God."

Weeping men, women and children surrounded Father Manuel when he left the church next day after celebrating his last Mass at Santa Marta. They carried the gifts they had made for him — an embroidered altar cloth with each of the birds in their aviary represented and all the animals marching around the border; and an illustrated life of the saints, starting with a rendering of Jesus' friend Santa Marta herself.

Accompanied by Charlie and Father Antonio, they walked quietly beside the wagons bearing away family and friends, members of a community that had not been sundered for generations. Finally, they stood and waved until a turn in the road hid us from view.

Charlie was the last to leave us, and as he rejoined the others I saw Itanambí by his side.

During the first hours of our journey, other carts and wagons crossed our path, carrying supplies to the inhabitants of the city, but as the miles went by under the oxen's steady step we left all signs of human habitation behind.

Now that we had acquired all the necessary permits and were on our way to establishing ourselves by the lagoon, I had decided to reveal my true identity. I asked Художник Cararé to accompany me that night as I went from fireside to fireside, and in spite of their efforts to act surprised at my revelation, I began to suspect that in reality I had fooled no one.

"Did everyone know?" I asked him before we reached the next fireside.

"No one knew!"

I burst out laughing. "You are a terrible liar! Did you tell them or did they see through my disguise?"

"It was Garzón."

"Garzón told them?"

"He didn't have to. It is the way he looks at you."

For several days we stopped only at night and once during the day to eat, rest, feed and water the animals. When our supplies began to run low, we made camp and the men went hunting, returning with several cows and a solitary *guazú-birá*, a small deer found along the shores of streams and rivers. While the women built the fires and the men skinned the animals beyond a rise that hid them from the camp site, I acted as lookout for a pack of *cimarrones* pacing nearby, watching for the men to finish their work so they could feast on the remains. Spanish hunting mastiffs had been used to track and kill animal and human prey alike, and when their owners died or abandoned them on the plains they mixed with packs of smaller wild dogs to create this formidable new breed, the *cimarrón*, lithe, strong, and as difficult to catch as quicksilver.

Every time I glanced at the dogs I had the feeling that they had inched closer and would soon be upon me. I was considering firing a warning shot when I realized that in my preoccupation with the *cimarrones* I had failed to notice that the men had left the skinning site. I turned toward the dogs, and they too had disappeared.

All of a sudden I was afraid. So afraid that when I sensed that I was not alone on the prairie only my eyes were capable of movement. Standing a few feet away from me were two Minuanes. They seemed to grow out of the ground, their dark skins scarred like tree bark. The wind that always blew on the *pampas* stirred their hair, long and loose at their backs, and rippled through the *ñandú* feathers that crowned their heads and hung about their bodies.

One of them wore a cross around his neck, and I found my tongue and stammered a few words to him in Guaraní. He did not appear to understand me, and both of them continued studying me in a silence broken only by a long clear whistle. Two horses grazing nearby raised their heads and walked toward them, and the Minuanes mounted rapidly and rode away.

I watched until they disappeared from sight into the *monte*. I don't know how long I would have stood there, hoping they would come back, if the *cimarrones* had not returned to growl and yap over the bones and entrails scattered behind me.

A messenger had arrived from Santa Marta during my absence from camp, and I had to wait until he had distributed his packages and letters before being able to speak to Father Manuel and Garzón. I stumbled over the words as I tried to convey the thrill I had felt at sight of the Minuanes.

"What color were their feathers?" Garzón asked.

"White. Why? Does it matter?"

"They wear colored feathers when they are preparing to fight."

"I will pay them a visit," Father Manuel said.

"Please allow me to accompany you, Father!"

"I will come too," Garzón said.

"Cararé will require your assistance organizing a defense should that become necessary."

"If there is danger, Isabel should not go."

"She is in no danger if she puts on female clothing."

"This is unwise. What if they decide to keep you both there?"

"You will no doubt rescue us," Father Manuel smiled.

I changed my clothes, so excited that I could barely manage the buttons on my blouse. Orlando helped me, his small fingers deft and sure as I explained where I was going. "Garzón needs you here. Do you understand?"

He nodded.

I kissed his forehead. "You are the only one who can keep the peace between Garzón and *Don* Cararé!"

~

I led Father Manuel to the spot where I had seen the two men. Having heard him speak of the skills he had learned from old Father Herrán, I had imagined that he would track down the Minuanes. Instead, he simply began to walk, explaining that since there were strangers in the area, the Minuán village would be closely guarded and someone would appear before long to ask us our business. He was right, and we soon came face to face with a single Minuán.

Calmer now, I noticed details that had escaped me earlier — the small stick, the size and shape of a wooden nail, piercing the lower lip, the war trophies hanging at the man's waist. I only knew what those shapeless clusters were because Cararé had told me of the Minuán custom of skinning dead enemies' faces.

He and Father Manuel exchanged a few words, and soon the three of us were leaving the plains and heading toward the *monte*, parting the thick growth as we went, bending, twisting, trying to see the clearing ahead as the sounds and smells of the Minuán village reached us. Its contours and colors blended with the surrounding vegetation and it was difficult to perceive where the village ended and the *monte* began. It consisted of twenty or so of what I at first took to be rough shelters made of sticks and hides, but as we entered the village, a whisper like wind rustling through reeds ran through the clearing as the rush blinds were lowered, transforming the shelters into neat little houses, and hiding the occupants from view. From hammocks hung between the trees, eyes watched us pass. Women crouched near the cooking fires, tending the meat, and I noticed that many of them had joints missing from their fingers. Several men were seated in a circle, talking, and we were ordered to squat nearby.

This, his first visit to a Minuán village, was a crucial moment for Father Manuel. Absorbed in my own excitement I had not noticed until now how tense he was. There was a worried line between his eyes, and he clasped and unclasped his hands nervously.

He pointed Yací out to me, sitting in the circle by the fire and I recognized him at once as one of the men I had seen earlier. He no longer wore the cross that had given me the courage to address him. In its place was a necklace of what looked like animal teeth.

As Father Manuel translated what he could understand of the conversation transpiring in the men's circle, it became obvious that our situation was precarious. Half of them wanted to force us to turn back, the other half, led by Yací, was for letting us pass. He argued that we were heading northwest, beyond their territory, and should be allowed safe passage.

"What are they doing now?" I asked as Yací and a large, muscular fellow with a long scar across his right shoulder, stood and calmly discarded their weapons, their feathers and loin cloths, until they stood naked before us.

"They are going to wrestle for it," Father Manuel whispered.

"For what?"

"For the outcome. For us! If Yací wins, we pass. If he loses, we turn back."

As simple as that, our whole future dependant on a wrestling match! The two men moved out of the circle and Father Manuel reached for his rosary. He soon put it back. His hands mirrored the struggle, and he would have snapped the cords long before Yací, his body glistening with sweat, pinned his opponent to the ground. The match had been so quick I hardly had time to appreciate that the question had been settled. We had gone from peril to safety in less time than it had taken for me to register what had happened.

The men went back to talking and the light was failing when Yací beckoned for Father Manuel to join the circle. I could only imagine what he must be feeling as he removed his hat and walked toward them. He had been waiting for this moment for over a decade.

One of my feet had fallen asleep, and the air had turned cold. I was breathing on my fingers to warm them when I heard a rustle and turned to find myself looking into a pair of amber eyes accented by three dark blue lines painted from the hairline down the middle of the forehead to the tip of the nose, and on each temple. Her eyes and her lighter skin were the only indications that the woman squatting by me was not entirely of native blood. Her hair was long and dark, and her body bare, except for a leather skirt and a cape that hung around her shoulders. Sea shells dangled from her ear lobes, and her mother of pearl bracelets rattled as she offered me a drinking gourd. Hoping it was something warm I took it and put it to my mouth. A strong smell of fermented seeds emanated from it and I sipped it cautiously. It burned my throat and made me gasp.

"Are you a Spaniard?" she asked, addressing me in Spanish.

"I am Irish."

She didn't know what that meant, and I told her about the long sea voyage that had brought me from my home to Montevideo.

"Every year at this time my mother went to Montevideo."

"To visit her family?"

"We were her family. She went to see her old village. When I was little she took me with her. She had yellow hair like yours."

"Did she dress as you do?" I asked, trying not to look too openly at her bare legs and breasts.

"Sometimes." She pointed toward Yací. "That is my husband."

"He's a fine wrestler," I said.

"Our best. That is his brother, Abayubá."

I was surprised. "The man who wrestled him?"

She dismissed him with a wave of her hand. "Whatever Yací proposes, Abayubá says the opposite. It has been that way since they were children and Yací began learning about the outside world. Abayubá blamed my mother for Yací's curiosity, but she only fed it, she was not its cause. Yací was born curious and restless. What do they call you?" she asked, suddenly changing the subject.

"Isabel. And you?"

"Atzaya. You look cold."

She held her hand out to me and led me to the outskirts of the village, where she drew aside the hide that served as a door to her dwelling. Multiple eyes glowed at me from a variety of clay candleholders, some shaped to resemble owls, lizards and capybaras, others fantastical and unlike any creature I had ever seen or heard of.

I could not stand upright in the small space and Atzaya gestured to a pile of hides lying before a backrest made of the same reeds that formed the walls. She sat cross-legged across from me and put a bowl of berries between us. Then she reached for a small basket and withdrew a piece of doe skin as soft as velvet. She unfolded it carefully and put two faded silk roses in my hand. "They were my mother's."

The dress they had been sewn onto was long gone, but Atzaya remembered it well. It was unlike anything else worn in the village, pale like a winter sky, shiny and soft, with the roses sewn in clusters around the hem. Atzaya had tried to recreate the fabric in leather, choosing the finest pieces of doe skin and pounding them for months on end, rubbing them with fat, and kneading them until her fingers ached. The result was leather softer and finer than anything she had ever handled, but it did not resemble the dress. She touched my cotton skirt and looked disappointed. "It was softer even than this."

"It was probably made of silk."

"Can you make this silk?"

I did not know how, I told her. Disappointed, she nevertheless listened as I explained how the silk that worms spin into cocoons is unwound, washed and dyed, and turned into fabric. "It is very fine, very light and very, very strong."

She nodded. Even after she outgrew it, for she had been a girl when she was taken by the Minuanes, Atzaya's mother had still worn the dress, leaving the village and wandering alone by the ocean. Atzaya always followed her, fearing that her mother might choose not to return. Every autumn, her mother had put on her only gown and taken Atzaya to Montevideo. They never went in, Atzaya said. They stood where they could see the walls and watch the gates opening and closing as people and oxcarts went back and forth. She never explained these visits, but her father told Atzaya that her mother needed to see that the world she had once inhabited still existed.

As the seasons passed, the dress had been transformed into a skirt and later a cape, but the roses remained. Atzaya had loved the dress, which shimmered in the sun and billowed in the wind. When her mother burned what was left of her only gown, she scattered the ashes, but kept the roses for her daughter.

Atzaya removed the top from a covered basket, reached in, and began unwinding seeds, shells, wooden beads, bones, the teeth of animals and fish, all carefully pierced and strung on a fine cord. "Yací believes that the answer to my mother's life lies in her story necklace."

She placed a long strand of it in my hands and there, if only I could read it, was a woman's entire history wound around my fingers. This purple shell, what had it meant to her? Had she been touched by its beauty, or had it marked a significant event? And that twisted root carved with the letters M, V and S, what did it mean?

I found myself wishing that my mother had made a story necklace. There was so much about her I didn't know. She had simply been my mother, the one who made sure our lives were comfortable and orderly, the one who comforted and rarely sought comfort, whose needs and desires were unknown to me because I rarely inquired into them, never imagined she had any desire beyond serving my father, Michael and me. Perhaps her story necklace would have included mysteries and longings as deep as Atzaya's mother's.

"Have you found the answer here, Atzaya?"

She shook her head. "This," she said, indicating a fish bone, "is where I began my own story. It's a *pacoú*. Yací carved it to remember our first meal." She touched a little bundle lower down the strand. "This is for my mother. It's one of her rose petals. I bound it up with horsehair."

"What was her name?"

"Mariana."

"How very extraordinary! My mother's name was Marion!"

We smiled at one another and I realized that I had not enjoyed the company of a friend my own age since leaving Ireland, and certainly had not expected to find such a blessing here, in this wild place. As we sat talking and eating berries I forgot that only a few moments before I had been cold and anxious. In the flickering shadows, speaking a language foreign to both of us, we were communicating as easily as if we had known each other all our lives.

"How did your mother come to live with your father's people?"

"There was a fight between some settlers and our tribe, and she and her two brothers were brought to live with our clan. Her brothers were younger than she, and had dark hair and skin. My mother was light skinned and had hair the color of the *aromo* flowers. I asked her once how members of the same family could look so different from one another, and she told me that her relatives were seafarers who brought back wives of many colors from distant places."

Atzaya had inherited Mariana's amber eyes, and while her hair and skin were dark, they were not as dark as her father Calelián's, and as a child, she had rolled in ashes in an attempt to be more like him. Once, she cut off her hair hoping that when it grew again it would be black, not the brown that made her head stand out at gatherings and caused visiting tribes to look at her and want to examine her more closely. She had not understood that curiosity and disapproval were not the same. To her each look had been an accusation, each finger pointing her way a reminder that the blood of invaders runs through her veins. Anyone wanting to anger her, Atzaya said, had only to mention her heritage for her to fly into a rage. Only Yací could calm her. He knew that it was just her wish to be the same as everyone else in the clan that prevented her from showing her love for her mother. The feeling he and Atzaya shared was sweet beyond any sweetness Atzaya had ever known, and as that feeling grew, she had understood just how desolate her mother's life must have been.

I told Atzaya how I had resented learning all the things Ma had wanted to teach me, of my anger at her for wanting me to cook and sew when what I loved were the columns of figures and lists of supplies in my father's warehouse. One day, we agreed, we would be mothers ourselves and perhaps our own daughters would have cause to wish us different than we were.

Atzaya gestured in the direction of the circle where Father Manuel was still sitting. "Are you his wife?"

"Oh, no! He's a priest. Priests have no wives."

"He has a fine face, almost as brown as ours."

"I think it is from spending so much time out of doors."

"His eyes frightened me the first time I saw them!"

"I was startled by them too! I had never met a man with one brown and one green eye before."

"The shamans say that with the green eye Father Manuel sees the past and with the brown one the future."

"He thinks very highly of your husband. Every night he sleeps in the hammock Yací made him."

She was pleased, and told me how it had taken Yací several weeks to gather all the rushes he had needed for the hammock, and days of dyeing and weaving to make the star pattern that decorated it. "He has never taken that much trouble over anything else. It was worth it, he said. He knew from the way Father Manuel handled it that he liked it, and that he respected the work that had gone into it."

It was warm in the shelter, and mention of sleep had made me stifle a yawn.

"Here," Atzaya said, offering me a mixture of leaves crushed with a white powder.

"What is this?"

"Ground bone and tobacco. We put a wedge of it under our top lip and whenever we feel drowsy, we draw down on it to keep ourselves awake."

Before I could decide whether I wanted to try the remedy, the hide curtain parted and Yací himself stepped into the house, bringing with him the faint aroma of wood smoke and tobacco. He was so close to me I could have reached out and touched his smooth, bare legs. "Manuel wants to know if you are hungry."

I shook my head. The image of him wrestling naked moments before kept intruding on my thoughts and I was relieved to see that, small as it was, he had at least put on his loin cloth. He folded his body in one easy movement, and reached for a handful of berries. "You were speaking Spanish and talking about me."

"I was telling Isabel about the hammock you gave Manuel."

"He gave me a cross." Yací pointed to the cross he had been wearing earlier, hanging on one of the posts that supported the roof. "And something else. A more mysterious gift."

I waited for him to tell me what that had been, but when it became clear that he was waiting for me to ask I obliged him.

"It was a man," he said, speaking softly and leaning close to me, "a little man, carved out of wood and painted, and I knew at once that it was me, standing on a rock, leaning on my lance." He saw me glance round and shook his head. "It's not here."

"He keeps it in a cave full of bats," Atzaya said.

"I was afraid of it at first. When water takes my image it returns it as soon as I move away, but the carving was something anyone could hold. And it has magical powers." He paused.

"What kinds of powers?" I asked.

"It sings! Not in words, but in music like water running over a slow fall onto rocks. And only when I ask it to."

"How do you ask?"

"There is a little piece of gold at the base. Whenever I turn it, the statue sings!"

A music box. Very clever of Father Manuel, I thought.

At first, Yací had wondered if Father Manuel was using some evil power to make the statue sing, but the frogs cried just as loudly and the wind sighed just as sweetly as it had before the statue's speaking. The eyes of the jaguar still shone in the sky and the earth felt firm under his feet. The Earth Mother seemed unconcerned with Father Manuel's power to make sounds come from a piece of carved wood, and who was Yací to question her wisdom? The Mother never failed to signal her displeasure. Sometimes, her signals were subtle and hard to read, only the wise ones could sense and interpret them. "But when she is truly angry," Yací said, "her voice is loud and clear. She sends floods to drive us to the hilltops, or parches the land until it cracks and only the birds can fly to water. But she always warns us. Those who live inside the earth know of her anger first. Months may go by without our seeing any of the creatures that live below the surface, but when the Mother is angry, they crawl and leap their way out of her body. Birds become silent, and the jungle cats wary."

By now I was entirely under his spell, all desire for sleep banished, and I was startled when Father Manuel's voice came unexpectedly from outside. "Is Isabel there?"

Yací pulled back the hide curtain and made room for Father Manuel to enter. It was crowded in the tiny house, and our knees touched as we arranged ourselves on the carpet of animal skins.

Yací continued with his narrative as if there had been no interruption. "The cross I wore, and it caused concern. There are those among us who remember the stories told by the ancestor after whom I am named."

This ancestor had been among the first to see white men when they began appearing along the coast. According to the elders of their tribe many men had put out in canoes and ventured near the visitors' vessel, but only the first Yací had gone aboard. He swam out to the ship in the night, and was invited into its very entrails, returning years later with garments such as white men wore, and full of stories to tell.

"I believe," Atzaya said, "that Yací's curiosity about the world around him comes from this ancestor. He was a daring traveler, and came back to our village with tales of wonder and of horror after many seasons of wandering among the people of the cross."

"He had seen marvels, like suits of armor and long tubes through which he could look closely at the stars; he had witnessed death in many forms, and told of a god that demanded the blood of his own son as sacrifice; and of a king who had caged his shamans when they displeased him, and watched them die of hunger. My ancestor became a storyteller, just as I want to be."

"You have told me that he talked of people not unlike yourselves," Father Manuel said, "who think the cross good, because it represents a sacred confluence of earth and water."

That was so, Yací said, but his brother Abayubá believed that nothing good had ever come to them from those who used the cross as a symbol of their beliefs, and for Yací to wear one was an insult to the many who had died since the cross was first brought to their lands.

"Have you brought your tools with you?" he asked Father Manuel. "You promised to show me how you made the statue sing."

"You can come and see the tools at the new settlement. I shall be there attending Isabel and the others who will be living there."

"You are their shaman?"

"Yes."

"We have given Father Manuel our word that we will not disturb you," I said.

"They are honorable people, Yací," Father Manuel said.

"There is no honor in the buying and selling of the Mother," Atzaya answered.

"Europeans do not see the earth that way."

"Then they should stay amongst their own kind."

She spoke the words simply, without anger, bringing home to me the elemental truth Father Manuel had also shared with me, that while we might wish them no harm, harm would come to them whenever their beliefs and ours came into conflict.

Would their fate be exactly like my own peoples'? As we walked back to our camp site, Father Manuel reminded me that this was precisely what our experiment was designed to prevent. If we could prove that it was possible to live peaceably with the Minuanes, to establish bonds of mutual respect for our differences, then perhaps we could alter the course of history.

The moon was so bright there was no need to light the lantern carried by our guide, and he left us as soon as he had led us safely back to the open prairie.

"Our messenger brought some news today that you should hear," Father Manuel said.

Just as he had said he would, Charlie had left Santa Marta to continue the search for his relatives, but he had not gone alone. Itanambí had accompanied him.

No one doubted that she had gone willingly, but the *cabildo* viewed Charlie's behavior as a profound breach of trust. He had been taken into the community, treated as one of them, and repaid them by dishonoring one of their daughters. Her enraged father had gone after them to ensure that Charlie did what was right by her.

"He will never marry her," I said.

"No," Father Manuel agreed.

"He comes from a noble family. Such a marriage—"

"—is out of the question. I know."

Nothing further was said, and back at our camp site I lay awake for a long time, gazing out the back of the wagon at the stars scattered like diamonds in the velvet blackness of the sky. In the distance, several dogs set up a melancholy howling.

I sat up in my bed of sheep skins and glanced at Orlando, who was breathing peacefully beside me. I put on my boots and left the wagon, slipping past the sentinels and out of the sleeping camp. The yellow *pampas* moon hung huge over the never-ending vista of palms, bathing the groves in a glow of light. Somewhere under that same moon, unless her father had caught up with them, Charlie was lying with Itanambí.

There was a time when I would have given much to be in Itanambí's place, but now I would not be her for all the tea in China, as my Ma used to say.

For the second time that night I felt Ma's presence strongly, just as I had in Atzaya's little house. Strange that I should think of her so often in this outlandish place where she had never set foot. What would Ma have made of me sitting on the ground speaking a foreign tongue with a bare breasted woman and her nearly naked husband?

My rambling thoughts had brought me to the palm trees, where bats flitted like flying ash around the fruit high above my head, and fire flies turned the grove into a firework display of flashing white and gold. I had not expected to find anyone else there, but as I was drawn by the fireflies deeper into the grove, I saw Garzón there, dancing.

The last time I had seen him dance had been aboard the *Bonaventure*. His movements then had been angry and sad; now they were full of joy. He had been wearing boots and twirling a set of *boleadoras* in each hand; now he was barefoot, and his hands, wide open to the stars, looked full of fireflies. He saw me and stopped, his chest heaving in the moonlight.

"I am glad to see you dance again," I said.

"I was celebrating FitzGibbon's departure," he said, walking toward me.

I hesitated. "Do you know—?"

"That he took Itanambí with him?" Garzón laughed. "It made me dance twice as much!"

"But I thought you and she—."

"Even if I had wanted to, I couldn't have competed with

FitzGibbon for her affections. He is precisely the means of escape she's been searching for these five years past."

"So she is using him? Poor Charlie!"

"I doubt that he is feeling too sorry for himself at this moment."

He picked up a blanket from under one of the palm trees and spread it on the ground. "Come, watch the fireflies with me."

It was a request, but spoken with a new certainty, as if we had reached a decisive moment in our lives. I didn't hesitate, and we sat, resting our backs against one another, facing opposite ways, yet headed, I was beginning to feel, in the same direction.

I closed my eyes, wishing I knew how to dance the joy coursing through me. Itanambí was gone, and Garzón was glad of it!

He put his head back onto my shoulder and brushed his cheek against mine, touching his lips to my ear and warming it with his breath. "Remember when I said you could not come to my cabin any more, that we would read the stars instead of books?"

"I remember."

"I couldn't trust myself to be alone with you." He turned, and was on his knees beside me. "Could you love me, Isabel? *Porque yo estoy perdido de amor por tí, chalona*."

I too was lost in love and answered yes with all my heart.

I knew that a woman who gave herself before matrimony was a fool. Many were the times I had attended the broken hearted births that followed, despising the weakness of the women, wondering how any man could be worth such suffering. But I was overcome with desire long denied, by an insatiable hunger, a burning wish to be ushered, body and soul into his keeping.

As the sun came up and I lay admiring the rich brown of his skin against the rose of mine, I understood why the wedding vows include the words *with my body I thee worship*, and knew that if he stirred and looked at me I would be back in the hollow of his arms before my conscience could prevent me.

Chapter VII

I was back in the wagon before Orlando awoke, and the next thing I knew he was tapping me softly on the shoulder. "Isabel! Isabel! Indians!"

Orlando had not spoken since introducing himself to Father Manuel, and for a moment I thought I was dreaming. My eyes were stinging from lack of sleep and my mouth felt dry. The memory of all that had happened the night before came rushing back. I sat up and found myself face to face with Atzaya, Yací, and a brace of dead ducks.

"I had a dream!" Yací said, depositing the ducks in my lap. "I was wearing the cross and riding with you!"

I put the ducks aside, found a bag of oranges and some dates to sweeten my breath, and helped Orlando fetch live coals for the pot of water Atzaya was preparing. Garzón was nowhere to be seen, and I was glad, not knowing how I would face him or what we would say to each other in the clear light of morning.

The water was set to boiling and I peeled oranges for us while Yací elaborated on what he had told me about wearing the cross and riding with me.

In his dream, Yací hadn't known exactly where we were bound, but it was for the same place, and we were on the same quest. Convinced that this was a good omen, but well aware that dreams are serious portents, he had asked Atzaya if she thought this particular one contained a warning.

"Because her mother was Spanish, Atzaya's opinion about Spaniards carries a great deal of weight," he said.

I opened my mouth to tell Yací that I wasn't Spanish but Atzaya was already explaining where I came from.

Yací looked concerned. "You knew she wasn't Spanish when you told me that the dream wasn't a warning?"

Atzaya nodded. "Her people are in bondage to invaders."

"Are the invaders African? Is that why your son is not like you?" Yací asked, looking at Orlando.

"Orlando lives with me, but he is not my son."

"Is this your husband?" he asked, seeing Garzón walking toward us.

I busied myself helping Atzaya place the ducks in the boiling water for scalding. "No!" I said.

Atzaya looked at Garzón closely as he came to sit with us. "I can see our cousins the Charrúa in you."

"My mother was Charrúa."

"As soon as Yací went through his manhood trials," Atzaya said, "he left us to visit your tribe in Entre Ríos. His lip was still swollen when he rode away."

"Why?" Orlando asked, startling Garzón.

"I think he's decided to speak again," I whispered. Any awkwardness I might have felt vanished with the warmth of Garzón's smile.

Yací pointed to the small wooden nail in his lower lip. "It was put there during the trials that turned me into a man."

"Did it hurt?"

Yací nodded. "But I wasn't supposed to show it."

"Tell me," Garzón said, "what form does asking for a wife take among your people?"

I kept my eyes lowered, hoping that the sudden burning in my cheeks would be attributed to my closeness to the fire.

Yací described how, on the day he had decided to ask for Atzaya, he had got up with the sun and cleared underbrush and stones from the place he had chosen for a house. Then he had cut four forked branches to brace and support their home, and from the marshes harvested the mass of rushes Atzaya would later weave with horsehair to make walls and a ceiling. Since this would take time, he had prepared several deer hides and two hammocks. "Then I put on the cross and a headdress Atzaya's mother helped me make before she died. We had collected shells and feathers—"

"What kinds of feathers?" Garzón asked.

"Flamingo, parrot, spoonbill, cardinal feathers. We had cut and shaped them, and attached them with horsehair to a headband. When I was ready, I packed all my belongings onto my horse, and decked the horse with feathers too!"

The horse was not used to such finery and kept shaking his head, dislodging the feathers. Yací had had to explain the importance of the occasion to him. After that he had stood and allowed Yací to decorate him, not shaking his head once until it no longer mattered. "He is a good horse and we care for one another."

"I was lying in my hammock when Yací arrived," Atzaya said.

"She sat up so slowly I thought it was because she was in no hurry to leave with me!"

"I didn't want to be spilled out of the hammock on the day of my marriage like a hasty child!"

"I asked her father for permission to take her, and showed him the horse."

"My father was slower even than I was! He looked at the horse, at its decorations, its burdens, even its teeth, and told me to serve food. Yací swallowed the rhea meat as if he had not eaten for days and drank the water in one swallow. But still my father took his time. He lit his pipe and invited Yací to smoke while I gathered my belongings. I was going to string my ears with some new parrot feathers I had just found and sewn onto cord so fine it was almost invisible, but I didn't want to resemble the horse, so I put on the mother of pearl bracelets Yací likes instead."

She had placed her bone needles and her scallop shell ladles inside the clay pots she would use for cooking and storing food, and wrapped them in the jaguar skin that would hold their first-born child. From a basket she had woven especially, she withdrew the piece of doe skin she had hammered until it was as soft as swan's down, and from the doe skin she took her mother's silk roses, whispering to Mariana that she was marrying Yací, just as Mariana would have wished. She loaded her belongings onto the horse, and followed him as Yací walked through the ring of houses toward the place he had prepared for them.

"Now that I was a man with a wife, I would be allowed to sit with the elders around the fire at night!" Yací said proudly.

Under a spreading *coronilla*, he buried the ends of the branches he had cut earlier that day. Atzaya covered them with hides, and lay the deer and capybara skins on the ground. With a big, pointed stone she dug a hole, lined it with rocks, and prepared to start a fire. She looked at him, expecting that Yací would unload the meat, and he was humbled. "I had forgotten to hunt for our first meal together!"

The sun was setting fast and soon the villagers would start arriving with gifts for them. They would bring food but it was traditional for a couple to eat a small meal together first to initiate the new hearth.

Atzaya led him to the river and asked him to wait while she went a little further, around a bend in the water, where she pulled out a basket with two big fish in it. Yací was surprised when she handed them to him. "*Pacoú* are one of my favorite fish," he said, "but difficult to catch, because they will not take a hook!"

"I had caught them by floating Carapá seeds on the water. When the *pacoú* came to eat them, I shot them with my arrows."

By this point in the story, the ducks had been scalded, plucked and gutted, and Yací and Garzón were putting them on spits for roasting. From the collecting basket that had been strapped to her back, Atzaya took mussels and clams and placed them in the pot of water boiling on the fire.

Their arrival had attracted attention, and while the ducks sizzled and browned several children gathered, first to gaze at the two strangers, and then, as they grew bolder, to ask questions. The girls wanted to know about the blue lines painted on Atzaya's face. They were made, Atzaya said, on the first day of menstruation, to mark a girl's transition from childhood to womanhood. She described how she had been taken away when she matured, for days of storytelling and feasting and dancing.

"Who took you?" the girls asked.

"My mother and the other women."

"Did your friends go too?"

"There were this many of us," Atzaya said, placing six duck feathers on the ground before her. "When we returned to our village, we were covered in feathers and shells and flowers, and felt very tall, very proud. I knew that now the gift of life was mine to bestow, and that my body would grow and become like my mother's."

The boys were interested in the stick in Yací's lip, and Yací asked Orlando if he remembered its significance. Orlando said he most certainly did, and proceeded to tell the amazed boys everything Yací had shared with him.

"It hurt a lot," he concluded, "but Yací didn't cry."

"I cried later," Yací said, "when no one could see me."

Less forward than the children, the adults contented themselves with viewing Yací and Atzaya from a discreet distance, until Cararé and Father Manuel brought gifts for Yací to thank him for his intervention on our behalf. Then they crowded round to watch as Cararé presented Yací with a handsome blanket and a bunch of tobacco leaves, and Atzaya with a dozen wax candles.

While we ate, Yací asked for information about another group of settlers he had seen cutting trees and clearing a place on which to build their houses. The location they had chosen was far enough away from the Minuanes' usual hunting and gathering grounds to make immediate action unnecessary, but the threat of their presence troubled his tribesmen. Father Manuel knew nothing about this particular settlement, but he cautioned Yací that more Spaniards and Portuguese were coming and that their numbers would only increase. Cararé invited him and his clan to join us or at least to settle nearby, where we could offer protection should it become necessary.

"We have always protected ourselves," Yací said. "And your settlement will be too near the ocean to be safe for us."

"When my father was a boy," Atzaya said, "we lived near the water. He used to go out in a big canoe with the other men. Our nets were so wide that twenty men could barely haul them in, full of fish to keep our village alive for weeks to come."

"The spirits of the ocean were our friends then. The shamans don't understand what we did to offend them."

Since the arrival of white men on their shores, the Minuanes had avoided settling near the ocean they had once revered. It was easier for them to hide in the interior, where settlers seldom ventured. They had adapted to a roaming life style, but didn't like it. Women complained of having to pack frequently and reweave the rushes for roofs and walls. They often warned the men that the recently departed did not appreciate having their bones transported from place to place, a necessity while they lived a nomadic existence that often took them far from their burial grounds.

"Last night after you left us we talked of the jaguar and Botoque," Atzaya said.

"Who is Botoque?" Orlando asked.

Yací pretended to be surprised that Orlando had never heard the tale, and the children, who had been solemn during the previous conversation, brightened at the prospect of a story.

"My father told it to me," Atzaya said. "Botoque was a Kayapó—"

"He wasn't even one of us!" Yací said.

"A jaguar found him when Botoque was dying of hunger, and —"

"Those Kayapós can't throw a spear to save their lives!"

"—and carried him on his back to his home, where he served Botoque roasted meat. Botoque did not know what cooking was—"

"They only learned to make fire—"

"If you keep interrupting you can't stay. You have been talking all morning. It is my turn to tell a story!"

Yací covered his mouth with his hands, but I could see from his eyes that he was smiling.

"Botoque liked the cooked meat, and stayed with the jaguar, who taught him not only how to tame fire, but how to hunt with a bow and arrow. Botoque used his skills to kill the jaguar's wife. The he fled back to his own people, returned with them to the jaguar's house, and stole the fire."

"So apart from being ignorant and ungrateful, he was a murderer and a thief as well!" Yací said. "What do you think the lesson is in this story, Orlando?"

"To trust no one?"

"That's what I think too. But Atzaya thinks that the story tells us that new discoveries, like fire, only come to us by wronging others."

"There is always a price to pay for new knowledge, but my mother warned us that we could not fight the Spanish with ignorance."

"She knew so much! She could sew leather gourds so tightly they hardly leaked! And it was she who taught us how to make light from bees wax!"

"*Velas*. Like these Cararé has given me."

Atzaya remembered her mother showing her how to make candles, her fair hair blowing in the wind as she bent over the fire, dipping wicks into a gourd of melted beeswax, the candles forming like solid petals in her hands. They lit the candles later and filled their house with light, but her father Calelián had blown them out, saying they were only another example of the white man's sorcery. That night, when Mariana thought Atzaya was asleep, she knelt by her and murmured long incantations in her own tongue, swaying back and forth as she did so. Atzaya had not made candles again until she married Yací and he encouraged her to make candleholders of the little clay animals he shaped.

A loud and sudden hiss made everyone jump, and Yací leapt to his feet, his spear at the ready. Realizing the source of the sound, we all began speaking at once, explaining that it came from the steam escaping from Garzón's ongoing experiments with boiling water. The children scattered to help calm the horses while the rest of us covered our ears and shouted at Garzón to do something.

Convinced that if he could boil water at a sufficiently high temperature, the resulting steam could be put to a useful purpose, Garzón had brought along a set of pots he himself had designed and which produced a shrill series of whistles. Garzón went to see whether the steam had activated the small set of wheels placed underneath the spout from which the steam was emanating, and from the cry of triumph we heard moments later we assumed that something momentous had happened.

"Now if I can only design a wagon powered by steam we will no longer need oxen or horses!"

Why would we want to do without them? several people asked him.

Garzón pointed at the speed with which the wheels were turning. "Because steam will help us move faster!"

"Faster than a galloping horse?" Yací asked.

"Much faster!"

We said goodbye to Atzaya and Yací next day and left the palm groves, heading inland toward the lagoon. I rode anxiously, straining my eyes for a glimpse of the lagoon through the dense *monte* surrounding it. It was not until we were nearly upon it that I caught a glimmer through the trees. I took a machete and rode alone ahead of the others. I wanted to be the first to cut my way through to the open plains on the lagoon's west side, and I walked ahead of my horse, parting the thick lianas and ferns that obstructed my passage. The dark seclusion of the jungle ended almost as suddenly as it had begun and I found myself on a small rise looking out over miles of grass and wetlands. I tied my horse's reins loosely to a branch and was listening to the rustling of the leaves, the trills and liquid laments of the birds around me, when a cloud of butterflies surrounded me. They settled on my arms and in my hair, miraculous breathing jewels, a cathedral of stained glass on the wing.

I felt myself turning into a creature of gossamer and air, a rapid, fluid thing, as light as breath and so much a part of the world around me that when the sounds of the others approaching reached me I wanted to cry out to them to stop, to allow me to remain a while longer in this reverie in which I knew myself a part of all creation, with needs no different from those of the grass at my feet or of the deer grazing upon it.

The butterflies disappeared, the sounds receded, and I sat down and closed my eyes, unwilling to return from the magical place where the butterflies had taken me. I must have fallen asleep, because when I woke, the sun was high in the sky.

I was about to get up when I heard Механизм Cararé's voice. I should have known that he would follow me, and I nearly called out that I was all right when I realized that he was talking to someone.

"My position on the *cabildo* is what gives me the authority to question your behavior," he was saying, "and I will not stand by and watch Isabel wronged."

"You are a presumptuous fool, *Don* Cararé." The voice was Garzón's, and he sounded furious.

"I know what you think of me, Captain. It will only make me watch over Isabel all the more closely. She has no family to guide or protect her, and no old friends here to take their place as her defenders. But she does have new friends, and we will not stand idly by. You may wish to forget that I have known you and of you for many years."

"What are you insinuating?"

"Isabel would not be the first you have seduced and abandoned."

"Be very careful where you go with this."

"I am not afraid of you, Captain. It may be convenient for you to forget Itanambí and that girl who died miscarrying your unfortunate child, but I remember them, and if Isabel shares their fate I will horsewhip you myself."

There was a sudden sound of crashing vegetation. I thought they were fighting and ran to intervene, but when I reached the spot Cararé was alone.

From then on, he and Wimencaí guarded me as jealously as if I were their own daughter, sleeping outside my wagon and riding by my side. As for Garzón, he seemed to have taken Cararé's warning to heart, for he made no effort to challenge them. There was no mistaking the longing I saw in his eyes if I caught him looking at me unawares, but nothing was said about what had taken place between us in the palm groves. Perhaps Cararé's warning had meant more than I realized. Father Manuel had already cautioned me about the Church's ban on mixed marriages, and Garzón could not afford to antagonize Father Manuel or Cararé, the two people on whom our whole future depended.

More than ever, I wished that Ma were by to advise me. I had grown in the shelter of her strength and kindness like an acorn under an oak, and when she fell I knew only that my task was to remain standing. Being her seed, there was no other course to follow. For a year after her death I had borne the loss and the loneliness, but when Tobias came I clung to him as a drowning sailor cast adrift upon the seas clings to any piece of driftwood that might save him. Garzón had come into my life when I was once more alone and vulnerable. I had shown myself a poor judge of character the first time I had been in that sad situation, but this was surely different. When he met me, Garzón hadn't known that I was a woman, allowing me to gain insights into his character that might not have been afforded me otherwise. He had no need or desire to impress me, thinking me a poor Irish boy emmigrating to the colonies, yet he treated me as an equal from the beginning, allowing me to study marine specimens under his microscope, and explaining his reasons for being so particular about the running of his ship. But the part of him I grew fondest of was his ferocious kindness, which I first witnessed that morning when the Captain whipped the sailor with the cat-o'-nine-tails, and then had amply confirmed when he rescued Orlando from the innkeeper. It was also his kindness that had prompted me, for the first time since their deaths, to speak of Pa and Ma and Michael. I had kept my sorrow secret, afraid that if I let it loose it would destroy me, and I would become one of those women who always frightened me so much. They hovered in the alleys of Cork, grasping at our clothes with bony fingers, arms like twigs, clad in rags that often failed to conceal their sex. Stoned, reviled, and starved, they went mad and were often found frozen when the snow melted. I once asked Ma where they came from and why they didn't go home and she told me that women driven mad from loss had no home and could do no more than die. I dreaded becoming one of them, and when Ma left me I was miserly with my sorrow. Only aboard the *Bonaventure*, my hand held fast with kindness, had I begun to spend it. It was my great joy to return the favor, for Garzón too had losses to grieve. Until I came along he had retold none of his mother's stories, nor shared with anyone her vast knowledge of the stars. Until he spoke of her to me, he had believed that he had learned about the heavens from that master navigator, his father. But when we left Río de Janeiro and he pointed out the constellations to me in his mother's tongue, he remembered that it had also been his tongue, until his father taught him another.

Until I had a better grasp of the complex rules of behavior governing life in the Spanish colonies I would have to trust that Garzón cared for me. Meanwhile, I would do nothing that might threaten the success of our enterprise.

~

Our settlement on the western border of the lagoon was speedily mapped out. Just as it had been at Santa Marta, the central plaza would be constructed around a freshly dug well. The church, workshops and granaries were to be at one end, at the other the infirmary, the school,

Orlando's and my little house, and Father Manuel and Garzón's rooms. Bordering this large rectangle would be the Indians' homes, temporarily made of adobe, thatch, and hides. They would be replaced with brick and stone houses as soon as the workshops were operational. We would then secure the settlement by means of a stout reed fence with a watch tower at each corner. A trench would be dug around the fence, and a stand of cacti planted beyond it, a formidable deterrent to man or beast, needing no upkeep, and designed to grow bigger and stronger with time.

Until the surrounding land was cleared, plowed and seeded, we would live off the meat provided by deer, peccary, and cattle, eat fish from the lagoon, and harvest wild and domestic eggs. The women had packed sufficient grain and flour to assure us frugal amounts of bread until after the first harvest, and under Wimencaí's watchful eye a kitchen garden was planted with seeds and cuttings from the endive, parsnip, spinach, cabbage, beetroot, aniseed and coriander plants that grew year round, plants Wimencaí considered essential to the good health of our community.

With fifty skilled laborers to draw upon, the houses went up rapidly, and Garzón soon left with a dozen men to set about herding the allowable maximum of twelve thousand head of cattle onto our territory. Most hide merchants would have slaughtered the entire herd, but we would establish at least one third of them as our breeding stock.

槍araré tried to dissuade me from witnessing the first hide harvest, but I was determined to understand every phase of the work.

The sun was shining bright and hot, making the prairie grasses shimmer and dance, when we rode to the place where the men had gathered for the slaughter. Cararé helped me to climb into the branches of an *ombú*, and I heard the distant sounds of lowing as a cloud of dust in the distance betrayed the presence of a large herd. The men had fanned out behind them, and once in place, urged their horses into a canter. Soon the thunder of hundreds of hooves sounded as the herd raced to escape its pursuers.

Cows, calves and bulls, a living sea, rippled past beneath me. Toward the rear of the herd rode the ham-stringers, wielding their scythe-like lances, long, stout canes, with half moons of sharp iron bound with rawhide. Behind them came the skinners, who dispatched the hamstrung animals with long, thin daggers designed to cause minimum damage to the hides.

It was impossible to see anything until the end of the herd came in sight, and then the ground appeared as full of fallen animals as it had been with running ones moments before. Bellows filled the air until the last animal was dead, and then the prairie was silent except for the voices of the men as they called to one another for occasional assistance over the barking and howling of the *cimarrones* who had gathered nearby, impatient for their share of the kill.

As the dogs fought over the innards thrown to keep them away from the hides and the meat, the smell of the slaughter reached me. Waves of nausea rose in me every time I breathed, the foul smell becoming a part of me until I feared I would never be rid of it. I covered my nose, determined not to vomit, and through my open mouth tasted the blood that covered the ground beneath me, the tinny flavor lying on my tongue and choking me. A flock of vultures settled in the branches above my head, and I climbed hurriedly down from the tree, looking for a pathway through the carnage around me. Finding no clearing, I walked in the direction of a stream, past the men already staking out the harvested hides, and the children standing guard over them to keep away the scavengers.

Once dry, the hides would be folded and transported to the workshops, to be thoroughly cleaned before being weighted, cured, and prepared for shipment. The meat was being cut from the bones, shaped into portions, and draped over long lines of low fence posts for drying before being piled into brine pans, covered with salt, and placed in the sun until acquiring the consistency of leather.

My horsehide boots were soaked in blood by the time I was clear of the scene, and when I stepped into the water, it turned red around me.

~

Atzaya and Yací were observed fishing by the shores of the lagoon, and Father Manuel, knowing how anxious I was to see them again, invited me to accompany him. We found Yací collecting bird feathers and snail shells along the shore and Atzaya standing knee deep in a small cove.

They waved when they saw us, and Atzaya left the water, graceful as a gazelle. She was carrying a small basket full of dried herbs.

"What do you have there?" I asked.

"Watch," she said, tossing a handful of the herbs over the surface of the pool.

It was soon bubbling with fish, competing for the morsels. The food gone, the fish began to swim rapidly and then floundered, gasping for breath. Before long, they were floating belly up in the water. We scooped them onto the sand with Atzaya's net and she showed me how to gut them to eliminate all traces of the *sacha barbasco*, a poisonous yam with extraordinary properties that she had used to kill them.

While the fish baked on the stones that had been heating in the fire, we joined Yací and Father Manuel.

"You need special tools to make a gun," Father Manuel was saying.

"Like the ones you have for making music boxes?" Yací took tobacco from a pouch around his waist and packed his clay pipe.

"Different tools. Even the Indians at the Mission don't have them."

"Then how do they get guns?" He lit the pipe, put it to his mouth, puffed, and passed it to Father Manuel.

"We trade for them, with other white men."

"Could I?"

"They trade only with Mission tribes."

"Would you trade with me for a gun?"

Seeking to avoid an answer, Father Manuel brought out the tools Yací had wished to see, but he no longer seemed interested in making music boxes. "I want to make guns and see if they will kill for me."

"Guns kill for anyone. There is nothing special about them."

Yací looked doubtful. "Why do you not carry one?"

"I do not carry a spear either. I am a man of peace."

"You mean you do not own a killing stick?"

"I have chosen not to."

"Can you not learn its magic?"

"It is no magic. Shooting a gun requires less skill than it took me to make a music box. You load a gun, point it, and press the trigger. The gunpowder within ignites and the gun jumps."

"How does it kill?"

"Something called a bullet leaves the gun and enters the body."

"Like a stone leaves the sling. I have seen bullets. They are small and hard."

"Yes."

"I want a gun."

"I will give you one if you will live at the settlement."

Yací looked at Father Manuel intently. "For how long?"

"Until you choose to leave."

Yací glanced in the direction of the settlement, from which we could hear the sounds of flutes and drums as the workers returned after their morning toil in the fields.

I noticed a look of concern on Atzaya's face, and followed her as she returned to the cooking fire. "That's the music my mother described to me," she said. "It's different from ours, but Yací believes that if he learns it he will receive the gift of his own song."

He had been particularly convinced of it since Father Manuel gave him the little singing statue, and Atzaya knew that of all the lures Father Manuel could have used, the music and the little statue combined were the surest.

"Does he know that Yací has still not received his own *porahei*?" Atzaya asked me.

"Tell me what that is."

"The song that will become his most treasured possession."

I must have looked mystified because Atzaya stopped turning the steaming fish to explain the significance of the *porahei*. "It is the song that will reveal Yací's essence, and the identity of his guiding spirit."

Only after he had composed this song would Yací have attained maturity and entered fully upon his life's journey.

"Has Garzón received his *porahei*?" she asked.

"I don't know," I said, handing Atzaya the palm frond on which she was preparíng to lay the fish for serving.

She took my hands and turned them over, pointing at the calluses. "You didn't have these when I met you," she said.

"I have been working on my house."

For weeks now I had been smoothing the earth floor, mixing mud for the walls, and gathering grass for the thatched roof. My front door was to be made of leather, and I had been pounding it until it was so pliable that槽Cararé complained it was better suited for clothing. "Like the leather you made when you wanted a dress," I laughed.

"You are angry at Garzón?"

I was surprised at her insight. "I fear that I may be carrying his child."

"That doesn't please you?"

Past experience, I told her, had taught me that I would not remain pregnant for long. During my years with Tobias, I had miscarried three times, always toward the end of my third month. "And if now, by some miracle, I am allowed to keep this child, I will have to face Father Manuel and all these new friends at the settlement whose good opinion is so important to me."

Atzaya looked at me questioningly.

"They will reproach me for becoming pregnant without being married," I explained.

"Then you must ask Garzón to marry you."

"Can women do that among your people? It is not done amongst ours."

"Could I ask him for you?"

I smiled. "I wish you could! But no, he must ask me himself."

What if he didn't ask and I did not miscarry? I turned the question over and over in my mind, just as Garzón turned the agate in his hand when he was worried. I could not bear the thought of compelling him to marry me, and suicide I dismissed almost as soon as it entered my mind. I didn't want to die, and I couldn't abandon Orlando. He and I had both faced loss and adversity before, we would face it and survive again. I still had the little statue Mr. O'Neill had forged from my gold coins. The rest of my money I had given to Garzón as my share of our partnership. He had insisted that I keep the statue, and in the event that I had to leave the settlement I would use it to establish myself elsewhere. I would revert to using Tobias' name and play the grieving widow. No one need know that my husband had been dead long before I conceived a child.

~

I was assisting the women with decorating the altar for the first Mass to be celebrated in the newly finished church, when the men walked in, behaving strangely, fluttering their hands over their hearts and raising their eyes. From the windows boys grinned at me, and a flock of little girls like giggling geese ran round me and out the door again. Perhaps, Wimencaí said, a proposal was afoot. Had anyone seen Garzón? she wondered. What would Garzón have to do with a proposal, the women wanted to know? He was a seafaring man whose heart was out of reach as they well knew since Itanambí had tried for it, and if she did not succeed what hope did anyone else have?

Feeling that these remarks were directed at me, I burned with shame and did not join in the banter, turning my back and busying myself with the altar cloths. I wondered at Wimencaí, who I thought was my friend, consenting to participate in such a public humiliation. Determined not to cry in front of them, I focused on the relief I had felt when my monthly flow returned and I had known that Orlando and I would not have to leave. At least not yet. I couldn't bear the thought of staying if Painted accusations turned out to be well founded and I was just another in a long list of women Garzón had wronged.

When he appeared, hat in hand, followed by the men, I leaned over to adjust the drape of the altar cloths. The women put their disheveled hair in place and straightened their sashes as the men walked down the aisle offering to escort them out. Garzón took my arm, but I refused to look at him. I raised my eyes only when we joined the others outside the church, where the women were clapping their hands and kissing their men. Garzón walked to a mass of flowers lying on the ground nearby and brought me an armful. "We thought it fitting that you make the first offering."

He led me round the corner of the church and there, surrounded by leather buckets full of water, stood my old friend Joan of Arc. Overcome with emotion, I stood speechless as the others crowded round to hear how the men had hidden the statue in one of the wagons, and on more than one occasion cursed Garzón for bringing it. It had taken six of them to load it, and when the wagon got mired, they had had to push and pull it out without emptying it, causing the women to make unflattering comments about their brains and their brawn alike, comments for which they expected apologies now that they were all weeping so happily around their beloved statue. Their tears allowed me to give free flow to mine, and my eyes were red and my nose running when I stepped forward to place my flowers at Joan of Arc's feet.

Garzón accompanied me and asked if I would walk with him. We walked in silence to a nearby grove while I took a firm grip on my emotions. When we reached the trees, I turned to face him squarely as he removed his hat and wiped his forehead with his sleeve. He hung his hat on a branch and clasped his hands behind his back. "Will you marry me, Isabel?"

My response was as unexpected to him as it was to me. "I have decided to leave."

As if I had rendered him a physical blow, he stepped back and sat down on a fallen tree trunk. "Why?"

"Because you have barely spoken to me since—since—!"

"I have thought of nothing but you!"

"You did not say so."

"And so you won't have me?"

"No!"

He stood up and snatched his hat back from the branch where he had hung it.

"I don't mean no! I mean yes! But only," I said, stepping back as he swung round and moved toward me, "after you hear what I have to say."

I had imagined the moment of my truth telling at least a thousand times. Somewhere in the recesses of my mind were several well-rehearsed and embroidered variations of my story, but they were lost to me. "I was married when I was fifteen to a man called Tobias Shandon. I thought I was in love with him. Perhaps I was, for a few weeks. Our marriage lasted six years and during that time I miscarried three times, so I might never give you children. A few days before I boarded your ship I killed him — unintentionally. He had found some of my money and he would have beaten me until he found the rest. I fought him off with a knife and he fell and broke his neck. I buried him in the cellar and told everyone who asked that he had left me."

A flock of parrots burst out of the treetops and flew over our heads. Neither of us spoke until their cries had died away.

"Is that all?" he said.

"It's quite enough I think!"

"There are things about me you should also know."

"If these things concern Itanambí, I'd rather you didn't tell me."

"They concern me. I am half Indian."

"I am aware of that."

"I have petitioned to be allowed to marry you. My petition was refused."

"Father Manuel refused you?"

"Cararé informed me that a dispensation would have to be granted by the Provincial allowing Father Manuel to perform the ceremony. I petitioned, but the Provincial is not inclined to disregard Church ordinances."

"I don't understand. How then — ?"

"Would you honor me by marrying me in the way of my mother's people?"

I was so relieved I would have fallen if he had not caught me.

Later, I couldn't for the life of me recollect any words we may have spoken, I remember only a sensation of a long thirst being quenched, of breathlessness and much kissing. In a daze of happiness, I stood under the trees until he returned leading his horse, a sturdy, hard working stallion I was accustomed to seeing in simple attire. Today every inch of his chestnut coat gleamed, and his black mane and tail moved like silk in the breeze. His saddle and stirrups were made of silver, and a spray of *ñandú* feathers dyed blue and yellow burst from a silver shield on his head. Painted sea shells and little silver bells ornamented the reins, tinkling softly as he walked.

Garzón helped me into the saddle and mounted behind me, turning the horse's head toward the furthest corner of the settlement where a small plot of land had been cleared and the contours of a house were outlined with stones laid out on the ground. In the center lay a crimson and indigo blanket. From a small bag tied to the silver saddle, Garzón took out bread, and wild berries he had gathered that day, and together we sat in what would one day be our kitchen, and ate our first meal together as man and wife.

When we returned to the settlement it was to find Father Manuel rummaging about in an old trunk searching for the chasuble his mother had embroidered for him. He had learned from Wimencaí of the Provincial's refusal to grant Garzón permission to marry me, and roundly upbraided him for not having come directly to him. He cared little for what he called the irrelevancies of the Church, and he would be proud to perform the marriage ceremony. "It will be the first wedding held in our new church!"

Flowers were borrowed from Joan of Arc to decorate the altar, and from the brocades and cloth of gold reserved for the saints' robes, a dress had been quickly fashioned for me by the women, who regretted only that they had not had time to embroider my wedding gown, and that some of the seams were basted and not properly sewn.

As I walked to the church, the moon rose and glowed in a liquid shimmer on the waters of the lagoon. Every candle and lantern in the settlement had been used to light the church and it too shone yellow against the darkening sky.

Cararé was waiting by the steps, dressed in his Mission soldier's uniform and carrying his staff of office. I had asked him if he would honor me by walking down the aisle with me in my father's place, and as I took his arm, the doors were flung open, and the choir burst into the "Gloria!"

The air vibrated with the sounds of harps and drums, and the ribbons on the tambourines danced in the flickering light. I walked down the aisle in my purple and gold dress to meet Garzón waiting by the altar in the jade suit in which I had first seen him.

Chapter VIII

Garzón went to work on our house the very next day, but he had many demands on his time and the work progressed slowly. He received offers of help, but turned them down, wanting to do everything himself with the result that in the months that followed he managed only to lay the foundations. Meanwhile, we lived in my little house, in which Garzón built a partition to separate our sleeping quarters from Orlando's.

Our first harvest promised well. We would be able to feed ourselves, and put grain aside for times of need. The second harvest should yield enough grain and flour to sell.

Along with the millions of cattle that roamed the area, a few thousand sheep had also been introduced, and I was dismayed to find that they too were slaughtered, for their fleeces. As a result, their numbers had not increased greatly, and I was determined to change that, recalling the old adage that a sheep feeds its shepherd many times over.

Meanwhile, cattle corrals were going up all around us, and Garzón was surprised one day when Pararé took him aside and suggested making them of *butiá*.

"The palm trees?"

"We will plant them close together. They have no low foliage to get in the way, and in between them we will pile stones. Every year, there will be fewer rocks and fatter trunks."

Garzón remarked, quite unfairly, that it was the first sensible suggestionCararé had made. I had hoped that our marriage would mark the beginning of a greater tolerance for one another, but if any existed, it was soon tested again.

In tribal systems, decisions were made communally, by means of councils of elders. In the Missions, the priests had set up *cabildos* to replicate the councils. Garzón proposed to our *cabildo* that now that they had begun a new way of life, people could not spend quite so much time in church, but were needed for work in the fields and with the cattle.

"Everyone, including Father Manuel, agrees," Garzón said. "Cararé, however, has announced that the others may do as they please, but he will continue to devote as much time to prayer and worship as he has always done!"

"He works twice as hard as any of you, so you have no cause for complaint."

Garzón threw up his hands. "I should know better than to seek any sympathy from you where Cararé is concerned!"

"Have you consulted him about the *cimarrones*?"

Garzón wanted to catch a pair of *cimarrones* and breed them. He had been observing the men struggling with the cattle, especially the bulls, who charged whenever their patience was tried, causing more than one injury to men and horses. Remembering the dogs he had seen herding sheep in Europe, he saw no reason why the same couldn't be done with cattle.

"I consulted him only to please you. I've been watching a dog pack, and tomorrow I'm catching a pair and showing that old pedant what initiative and determination can do!"

"Cararé is your age!"

"It's his pedantry that makes him seem ancient."

"What you call pedantry is wisdom to many."

"He tries my patience, but as I said, asking sympathy from you is useless."

I couldn't help but laugh.

"And now you laugh at my trials with the man!"

I put my arms around his neck. "I laugh at your description of yourself as someone having any patience to try!" I said, and stopped his protests with a kiss.

Next day, Garzón killed a cow, left it on the plain, and hid with two men down wind of the carcass. By the time a pack of five dogs approached the dead animal, sniffing the air, it was almost noon and the vultures were feasting. Garzón waited until the dogs had chased away the birds and ripped and gnawed the carcass to the bones, before preparing to catch the two he had selected. He twirled the *bolas* over his head while the men stood by ready with the ropes. The instant the dogs saw them, they bared their teeth and backed away, but it was too late, the bolas were already spinning through the air.

A snarling, shaggy brown dog fell to the ground, the leather tight around its hind legs. Although it could not run, it lay writhing in the grass, howling as it tried desperately to stand. At sight of this, the rest of the pack turned to flee; the second set of bolas spun toward the male Garzón had spotted, and he fell in his companions' dust.

The men approached the twitching animals cautiously, avoiding their bared teeth and the powerful front legs clawing at the ground. They threw themselves simultaneously at the male dog and tried to wrap it in the large, tough hides they had brought for the purpose, but its teeth tore through the leather, and sank into Garzón's bare arm. One of the men pulled him away, leaving the dog convulsing itself in fear and fury on the ground. Garzón sucked at the wound, spitting out a mouthful of blood and using his bandana as a bandage, before arming himself with a second hide. This time they were able to subdue both dogs and truss them with a heavy rope.

When槽 Cararé saw the sweaty, disheveled men and their sausage-like bundles, he burst out laughing. "I thought you were a sailor!" he said to Garzón. "I've seen children tie neater knots than these!"

"Next time, you try tying forty kilos of squirming dog into two puny hides."

"There's more rope here than on a main sail!" Father Manuel chimed in.

"I think you've killed them," Cararé said, prodding the dogs with the toe of his boot. "They're not moving."

Garzón wiped his face with his bandana. "Why don't the two of you unwrap them?"

Father Manuel pulled a knife from his belt. "How about it, Cararé?"

Garzón smiled. "Allow me to put them in the enclosure first."

It was solidly fenced with the bones harvested from the slaughtered wild cattle, and it had a wooden floor Garzón himself had made to prevent the dogs from digging their way out. In one corner he had built a shelter, open at the front and filled with straw. He thought it looked comfortable enough to receive a human family, but Cararé had already expressed his opinion that wild dogs would not go near it, since their preference for underground burrows was well known.

The bundled dogs were placed in the center of the enclosure, and Father Manuel and Cararé stood ready with their knives while the men who had accompanied Garzón on the dog hunt positioned themselves safely on the opposite side of the high gate. Crowded all around them were the inhabitants of the settlement, some with their children perched on their shoulders, looking through the openings in the criss-crossed bones.

There was no movement from within as Cararé and Father Manuel started cutting through the ropes.

"Are there really live dogs in here, Garzón?"

"You didn't wrap some dead ones by mistake?"

"I tamed them especially for you!" Garzón replied.

"I think—" Father Manuel started to say, but what it was he thought we would never know.

The dogs burst out of their wrappings like enraged banshees. The male threw itself at the bone fence, making the entire structure shake and rattle, sending those near it screaming to a safe distance in a flurry of whirling skirts and ponchos. Father Manuel fell flat on his back at Cararé's feet, where the female lay growling, her eyes, as he would later tell it, fixed on his throat, and her fangs glinting in the sunlight.

A group gathered at the gate, gesticulating wildly to Father Manuel and Cararé to make their way toward it. The male dog, more frantic to get out than to attack those within, continued to race round the enclosure trying to jump the fence. Whenever he approached the gate, everyone there screamed and slammed it shut, depending on a lookout stationed on the shoulders of two friends beneath him, for advice on when to open it again. Since they found it necessary to dance about in order to keep their balance and sometimes struck out in different directions, leaving the lookout hanging from the fence posts, his instructions were subject to misinterpretation, and at one point the gate was flung open when the male dog was headed straight toward it. Faced with a horde of screaming humans, the dog turned in mid-leap and ran back into the enclosure, while the gate guards collected themselves and slammed the gate shut once more.

Father Manuel and Cararé made a break for the gate, clawing their way out into the open, but not before the female had taken a piece out of Cararé's leg. He marched up to Garzón and knocked him to the ground with one blow, splitting his lip in the process.

Wimencaí and I were so annoyed with both of them that we refused them any *coca* to dull the pain when we treated them. They sat staring at one another, Cararé gripping his staff of office while Wimencaí sewed his leg, and Garzón holding a bloody rag to his mouth while I stitched up the dog bite on his arm.

"How could you do this?" I asked him. "You know how vicious those dogs are and you shut Father Manuel and Cararé up with them! Have you taken complete leave of your senses?"

"Two grown men behaving like irresponsible boys!" Wimencaí chided. "You could have been killed!"

Father Manuel, who had been standing quietly by until now, uttered a strange, explosive sound. We all looked in his direction and discovered him attempting to stifle his laughter, which burst forth in uncontrollable guffaws as he pointed at the four of us.

"For shame!" I said. "I think all three of you have gone mad! What is there to laugh about?"

Father Manuel was beyond speech by then, and before we could say anything more, Garzón and Cararé were also roaring with laughter. Cararé howled in pain as Wimencaí jabbed the needle into his leg, but this only made the three of them laugh the harder.

"I am leaving!" Wimencaí said. "You!" She pointed at Father

Manuel. "I've taught you to sew wounds. Make yourself useful now and see how my husband likes your handiwork!"

"This one needs only a stitch or two more," I added, gesturing to Garzón.

I didn't have the heart to stab him as Wimencaí had done to Cararé. In fact, I was perilously close to joining in their laughter and Wimencaí knew it.

She wagged her finger at me. "Don't you encourage them! They are childish enough already!"

~

Garzón couldn't say why, but that day, he and Cararé became friends. For weeks afterwards, they sat by the enclosure, talking to the dogs and lowering food and water over the fence to them until they stopped growling at sight of them and took food from their hands. Father Manuel called them Charrúa, and Añang — a native name meaning evil spirit.

Añang soon presented us with a litter of eight, and Orlando and Garzón devised tricks, most of them involving food, by means of which they distracted her and handled the pups from the day they opened their eyes. Añang endured their rough games in a truly matronly fashion and eventually even allowed Orlando and Garzón to enter the enclosure. Not so her mate. Like his namesakes, he wanted no part of life at the settlement. Well satisfied, Garzón set Charrúa free and he returned to the plains, where Añang joined him as soon as her pups were weaned.

Garzón began by training the young dogs to herd sheep, and when they showed themselves adept at that, moved on to cattle. Unlike sheep dogs, that nip when necessary at the sheep's legs, these dogs turned bulls by going for their noses.

Orlando had become attached to the smallest of the pups, and Garzón allowed him to keep her for his own. He called her Zule, a name we were not familiar with, and which he said he had made up.

As Zule grew bigger, Garzón made a harness for her, with a brace attached for Orlando to lean on. With the dog's help, Orlando walked further and faster, and children who had ignored him before became interested in him now that he had a large companion who he taught to do all manner of tricks. Zule exulted in bringing back anything Orlando threw or dropped, she could leap over barriers without apparent effort, and best of all she loved to swim, pulling Orlando behind her and depositing him on the shore when she tired.

Garzón considered exporting trained dogs to Ireland, but I pointed out that my countrymen had only recently eliminated wolves there and were unlikely to appreciate packs of *cimarrones*, however well trained, disturbing their placid cattle. Horses were another matter, and Garzón bought two more ships in which to accommodate them. The ships were also needed to ferry our hides to Spain and return loaded with merchandise for the colonists. Spanish merchants had long ago been persuaded by their correspondents in Panama and Peru that trade with the Río de la Plata would hurt the rest of the vice-royalty, thereby ensuring that we would continue to sit with one of the best natural harbors in the world without being allowed to bring goods in through it. As a result, Garzón licensed only one of the new ships. With the other he began transferring hides at nearby El Castillo, avoiding the tithes and saving the weeks of labor required to transport them to Montevideo. Several ships had run aground at Puntas de los Castillos, but there were other, less perilous areas of the coast and Garzón knew them all.

Pa would have been proud of the reforms and improvements we were making on our ships. It earned them a reputation as humane vessels and Garzón had no difficulty finding sailors wanting to serve on them. Since they were too poor to provide their own clothing, and suffered greatly in extremes of temperature, being wet most of the time from working on deck, we provided four sets of trousers, shirts, and short jackets for each man, all made at the settlement. We also outfitted the men's hammocks with more than one blanket, and enlarged the usual allowance of fourteen inches per hammock to eighteen. Knowing the hardness of their lot, we provided a good supply of chewing tobacco for them, since smoking aboard ship was forbidden. Sailors spoke of fire with awe, as one of the great hazards of the sea, and it still seemed incredible to me to hear Garzón say that by the time the water that surrounds a ship can be brought aboard to quench the flames, it is often too late, and the vessel lost in the battle between the two elements.

He continued to forbid flogging, and one of the captains he hired sailed with a small pistol strapped to his knee under his britches, and a half dozen knives secreted on his person. None were needed. He found that locking a sailor in the hold for a day on half rations, or docking his pay, was far more efficacious than flogging. Surgeons were hired to sail with each ship, and while the captains at first complained about having what they considered a useless mouth to feed, they soon found that the surgeon paid for himself in preventing the gangrene that led to loss of arms and legs and therefore of work, and that having men in good health, able to shoulder the burden of life at sea, meant more money in everyone's pocket at the end of their journeys. I was pleased mostly for the sailors' sake. It was rare in Cork for a sailor to return home healthy, and many were the times I had been called upon to saw off a gangrenous limb, knowing that with it went the family's livelihood.

In July of 1747, our licensed ship, the *Trapalanda*, sailed from Montevideo bound for Spain. She was loaded with hides and abided by all the regulations. Our unlicensed ship, the *Isabelita*, left for Cork, also loaded with a cargo of 6,000 hides, and captained by Garzón himself. In Cork, he sold the hides for a guinea a dozen, recovering our investment in the ship in a single journey. He loaded the *Isabelita* once more, and sailed to Buenos Aires, where he was detained while he negotiated a good price for the hemp, wool and iron that filled the holds. Hoping to expedite matters, he called at the Viceroy's mansion with gifts for the Viceroy's lady and her daughters. *I was invited to dinner,* he wrote, *and told that I was welcome to return at any time. Before visiting the Viceroy I had stopped in Río de Janeiro to pay a visit to my tailor. I ordered something for you too, although I confess to liking you best clad only in my kisses!*

~

Thus our first year by the shores of the lagoon went by. We were housed, our crops were planted, and our herds grazed all around us. Our leather workshop was full of hides, being cut under the Captain of Leatherwork's direction into squares to fit chair backs and seats. They were stripped, pounded, oiled and softened to make them malleable, then molded into examples of the local flora and fauna, so that chair backs and arms looked like rivers full of fish, or tree branches covered in birds and vines.

In the second month of 1748, accompanied by a small group of outriders, Wimencaí,Ცararé, Orlando, and I traveled to Montevideo to replenish our supplies of articles not produced at the settlement. We wanted pitch and paper, and were in need of ironware for tools, door and window clasps, a small amount of glass for the church, and a few articles of finery for our own clothes and those of the saints.

The workers wages had begun to accumulate, and Wimencaí and I carried many commissions. In a well secreted corner of our wagon lay a stash of gold coins to be used for purchasing cloth, thread, tools, nails, beads, mirrors, hair brushes, and buttons.

Yací chose this time to visit Father Manuel. The Minuánes had been talking of attacking the new settlement Yací had questioned Father Manuel and Cararé about, the one guarded by soldiers. A scouting party had revealed that it was well fortified, and that the men in it carried weapons of the kind Yací's clan wished they also owned. Yací believed that once he had seen a musket at close quarters, especially if he could take it apart for study, he would be able to reproduce it and the tools necessary for making more. Whenever the old people gathered to tell stories, Yací listened closely for one that included a Minuán visiting a white settlement for the purpose of acquiring knowledge. It is possible that many had done so, but only his ancestor, the first Yací, was remembered.

The old people spoke of spirits, of battles and hunts, but mention of white men was always accompanied with warnings that they could not be trusted, and were to be treated with caution. Even after Yací met Father Manuel, and Atzaya and I became friends, they continued to take the warnings seriously.

While Yací considered whether to visit our settlement, he climbed every day to his cave. Sometimes he took Atzaya with him, and together they parted the honeysuckle that grew over the cave entrance, and uncovered the treasures they both kept there. Yací would wind his little statue, letting its music play, while Atzaya unwrapped the handful of agates that had been in the pocket of her mother's dress when she was taken.

He and Atzaya believed that every object, every dream, every change in the weather and the landscape, every encounter with a bird or an animal, was significant, suggesting not only the physical path each person should take, but guiding their spiritual journey. In Yací's case, everything seemed to indicate that he was meant to follow in his ancestor's footsteps. Not only did he bear the same name, he had already proven himself as a traveler with his youthful journey inland to visit the Charrúa. His meetings with Father Manuel, and more recently with me, were further proof that Yací was destined to benefit his people by learning all he could about the foreigners overrunning the Minuánes' territory.

On the day he set for visiting the settlement, Yací attired himself and his horse with care. Strapped to his waist was the knife Father Manuel had given him, and on his head waved the long, full feathers of his personal totem, the *ñandú*. In his right hand Yací carried his lance, leaving his left free to hold the horse's reins.

Father Manuel was waiting for him outside the gates, knowing, as he always did, that Yací was on his way.

Yací's heart was beating very fast. He rode forward slowly as Father Manuel opened the gates for him to enter the plaza, where men and women stood around the well, talking and laughing. They didn't want to stare at him, but they were as tense as cornered peccaries. Yací dismounted but declined Father Manuel's invitation to go inside any of the buildings. A table with fruits and bread was carried into the plaza, and Yací sat on a chair for the first time. Father Manuel summoned the musicians, and before they played they showed Yací their harps, lutes, and violins, and taught him their names.

When the music began Yací felt just as he did when his tribe played their deer skulls, their rattles and sea shells. All music had the effect of transporting him to a different place, and these new sounds embraced him, filled his body, entered his blood, rang sweetly in his ears. He breathed them in like perfume, and was soon floating, formless and free, one with the music that possessed him. The sounds flooded through him, dissolving his senses, turning him and the world around him into a single entity.

Yací traveled to a place he had heard his shamans describe but never thought he would visit, not being a shaman himself. Yací and his people believe that the Earth Mother's home is deep in the heart of the mountains, as far away almost as the setting sun, a place where water freezes and where the cold is so intense a person can die of it. The elders had taught him that the Earth Mother's home is the birthplace of all the rivers and streams that give life to the land, and the waterways are her veins, her life blood. Yací felt himself floating in the water, the music carrying him along. Atzaya's mother, Mariana, appeared, to guide him, and a most wondrous thing occurred — as Yací left the water and followed Mariana into the jungle, she and I became one, and stood between him and the god Ñamandú's most powerful attendant, the Blue Jaguar.

At first Yací thought that Ñamandú was displeased with him, but when Mariana and I stepped aside, the jaguar opened his mouth and instead of the roar Yací had expected, he heard the first words of his sacred song.

The settlement was the last place in which Yací had expected to receive his *porahei*, and the way it came to him so different from any other experience he knew of, that when the lyrical prayer he was composing in his altered state was finished, he was not ready to return to his body.

The musicians told Father Manuel that he and Yací fell asleep during their playing. Nothing could be further from the truth.

When Yací entered into his trance and drifted away, the men played on as if nothing were happening, while Father Manuel felt himself being lifted after Yací by a pull of water and of air. He didn't know if he floated or flew, but somehow he too left his body behind and could see himself sitting in the plaza with Yací by his side. When he looked up again, Yací had disappeared.

Father Manuel felt desolate and abandoned until a ray of light enveloped him and he was back in the vessel of his body as if he had never left it, except for a feeling of such profound well being that for a moment Father Manuel wondered if what he had experienced was sudden death.

The musicians were gone, and he and Yací were alone in the empty square.

They went into the *monte* together and Yací sang his song as if he were the tallest *ombú* in the forest, with roots so deep he knew his incandescent core, and branches so tall he could smell heaven. Words fell from him like leaves and opened like flowers as Yací prayed that the earth would offer wisdom, promising in return to fortify himself with songs and dances as varied as thunder, dew and wind.

His song ended with the desire that out of the ancient mists of creation he and his people would make their way toward a greatness of heart that would pacify Ñamandú and prevent him from unleashing the Blue Jaguar that waited to devour the earth if people displeased him.

As Yací sang, something came to rest in Father Manuel that had been sad and anxious before. He had heard others speak of mystical experiences, and listened with longing as they told of visions, of guiding voices, of certainties that came to them in their altered states.

Perhaps, for great minds, the idea of God as separate from all our fumbling desire to quantify Him was an obvious one, but until that day it had not been so for Father Manuel, or for me. We believed in the God we had known from catechisms memorized by rote since early childhood. The God Yací helped us to glimpse breathed as simply as a newborn within us, was in fact so all pervasive we could no longer think of him in human terms, but simply as a spirit of creation, no matter what name or form we gave it.

Just as I would later, when Yací recounted all this to me, Father Manuel knew then that he was the recipient of a gift beyond price, and wondered how he would ever repay it. He told Yací about what had happened to him during his vision, and of the dreams that had troubled him when he had first arrived in the land of the Guaraní. Yací explained that it is by interpreting dreams, by composing music and by dancing that each person grows to adulthood and develops the philosophy that determines the path he or she wishes to follow.

It had not occurred to Father Manuel that he had been doing this all along. Not the dancing, for he is not nimble on his toes, nor has he composed much music, although in his elation, and with Yací's help, he tried it that night. But Father Manuel had been troubled by dreams and sought advice about them from his own elders since first arriving in the Missions. Now he realized that when he moved from Santa Marta without his superior's permission, he had begun living the philosophy his dreams had taught him.

Yací carried his music back to the village proudly, repeating it over and over, changing some of its rhythms and words. He felt powerful and grown into full manhood. The settlement was no longer confining to him, since he had had the most liberating experience of his life there. It was still difficult for him to accept that a closed place could free the spirit, but Yací believed that there was a lesson for him in that as well.

Atzaya prepared Yací's favorite foods and invited everyone to eat with them while Yací recounted his experiences. When he revealed the part Mariana and I had played in his dream, his brother Abayubá waited only until Yací had stopped speaking before expressing his disapproval and suspicion of the place and the way that Yací's song had come to him.

The elders agreed that the manner in which Yací received his song was unusual, but so, they said, were the times in which they lived, and his relationship with Mariana was almost that of a son toward his own mother so it wasn't strange that she was the one to guide him to his song. Calelián thought that Mariana's choosing to do it while Yací was at the new settlement was also significant, and Atzaya added that my presence in Yací's vision was an indication that I would protect him if he chose to go back there again to complete his quest for knowledge.

Abayubá reminded the elders that nothing good had ever come to them from contact with foreigners. "It would be prudent for us to remember that before sending him back!" he said. "Bestowing a song upon Yací at the settlement was a warning to him to return to us."

The shamans said that this interpretation was possible, but since it is up to each person alone to decide the significance of their dreams, they advised another test, another journey to the settlement, during which Yací would read the signs offered to him as he traveled and examine his dreams. No one doubted that his first experience there had been a powerful and unusual one. All the more reason, they advised, for him to take his time creating the right atmosphere for the dreams to return.

Yací followed their advice. He fasted, sang, and danced before choosing a day for his next visit to Father Manuel. The night before their departure, as they lay in their shelter, Atzaya took his hand and put it on her round belly so he could feel the movements of the child stirring within.

Months would go by and many things would happen before I learned why it was that the next time we saw him he was attempting to terrify us into leaving the lagoon.

Chapter IX

The residents of Montevideo were out of the mourning prescribed by the death of King Philip two years before, and the city had erupted in color like a garden in springtime. Red and yellow parasols bobbed along the narrow streets, and greens and blues were worn again in aprons and head scarves, in skirts and shawls.

Before he left, Garzón had given me a bag of gold coins and told me to buy myself the finest cloth I could find for a new gown. I asked the innkeeper's wife to recommend a seamstress, and she clasped her hands and with shining eyes referred me to the Calle San Luis where the city's first and only European dressmaker resided. As I approached the street, I saw a small crowd gathered around the dressmaker's window, admiring a mannequin attired in a low cut golden gown that shimmered in the sunlight. The close fitting bodice, styled like a short jacket, revealed a stomacher in sharply contrasting shades of purple, tapering to a V below the waist. The sleeves were elbow length and finished with several layers of lace, and the wide skirt was draped over a metal framework. Seen from the side, the front view rendered the figure totally flat except for the breasts, which were raised as high as possible in the low neckline. The back view, revealed in the dressmaker's window with the aid of an artfully placed mirror, was also flat, with a small ruffle where the jacket ended, just below the waist.

The gown recalled me to the night when I had stood, feet and hands frozen, and rested my chin on the stone lintel of Busteed Castle, watching the dancers drifting by in just such gowns as these, never imagining that one day I would have the means to acquire one.

I approached the small door next to the window and knocked. A few minutes later I had been persuaded by the proprietress of the establishment to buy, not the gown in the window, which was already spoken for, but her latest acquisition, a *robe a la française*, or sack-backed gown, with a full length of blue silk damask from shoulder to hem. Every inch of the vast skirt was embroidered by cloistered nuns, the dressmaker said, and the wide blue silk ribbon used to trim the sleeves and the round neck of the gown was the exact shade of my eyes. She was a cunning and persuasive saleswoman and by the time I left her, I had also acquired a pair of hose embroidered in crimson and yellow clocks, and several lengths of lace, which was just what I had been looking for as my contribution to the wedding gowns of the women at the settlement who were getting married later that summer.

When Wimencaí and Cararé saw the new gown they told me that I should waste no opportunity to wear it since from its dimensions it would be impossible to fit into our wagon and would have to be left in Montevideo. I explained that the enormous structure used to support the gown was collapsible. Wimencaí showed great interest in the unyielding framework of whalebone that encased my upper body, and I told her that in Europe this framework would have been reinforced with steel. Here, the proud little dressmaker had boasted, the supports were made of silver.

Knowing that the dress would cause a sensation, I wore it that evening, barely able to accommodate the voluminous skirt in the inn's small dining room. The innkeeper's friends were called in to see it, and I spent a most enjoyable evening being admired. Several times, I withdrew with the ladies to a private area where they could lift the skirt to examine the layers of petticoats and the collapsible structure that sustained them.

I was preparing to retire after a late dinner, when I caught the eye of a man studying me. He had entered after the last of the gown's admirers had left and sat in a corner by the fireplace. As I dropped my napkin on the table and finished my wine, he saluted me, lace cascading from his wrist as he raised his wine cup in a silent toast. I acknowledged the toast by inclining my head, and he approached me. He had a long, concave face, with crowded features, giving him the appearance of an amused and surprised infant.

"Allow me to introduce myself. I am Ernesto Zubillaga, physician to the City of Montevideo."

"*Beso a usted la mano, caballero.*"

"*A sus pies, Señora.*"

I began to introduce myself but it was clear that *Don* Ernesto knew who I was.

"In a city this size, there are no secrets," he said, and asked if he might sit. I gave my permission and he raised his cup once more and proposed a toast to the late King Philip and to his successor, King Ferdinand.

"What is a man of your obvious accomplishments doing here, sir?" I asked, glancing conspicuously from the gold rings on his fingers to the silver buckles on his shoes.

"A vain lover of luxury, do you mean?" he replied, carefully moving the skirt of my gown out of the way as he crossed his legs.

We smiled at one another and raised our wine cups once more.

"I came to Buenos Aires," *Don* Ernesto said, "with the idea of purging that fair city of hucksters in physic and of the wretched quacks I saw there, attending their murdered patients to early graves! It was a losing battle, and when my brother, who is a priest, was assigned to serve in Montevideo, I decided to accompany him."

The city had had no physician and *Don* Ernesto, who had taken an instant liking to the quaint little place, decided to remain. He had inherited sufficient money to keep himself comfortably for the rest of his life, and a small and undemanding practice allowed him time to write his elegiac poem about the conquest of America. It was over fifty pages in length and he had only just reached the seventeenth century.

"Are you not afraid," he asked, "living alone amongst hostile Indians with only your husband and a priest to defend you?"

I told him that no one had shown any hostility toward me and that I felt perfectly safe at the settlement with Father Manuel and his followers. King Philip's death was worrisome, I admitted, for the King and his confessor Father Ravago, had been strong supporters of the Jesuits.

"King Ferdinand may allow himself to be persuaded by those who believe that the priests run their own independent empire here and thumb their noses at all authority not their own," don Ernesto said.

"From what I have observed, the Missions are Spain's strongest hold in the Americas."

"That is an astute observation, and I share your opinion. My poem in fact, begins shortly after Columbus' arrival in America, when the kings of Spain and Portugal — with papal approval — divided the lands of the Guaraní, of the Charrúa and the Minuanes, equally between them. Later, when it dawned upon them that millions of people inhabited what they had deemed a wasteland, they dealt with the inconvenience by considering them part and parcel of their new acquisitions, and decreeing that they would either become subjects of King and Pope, or slaves. The decree was read everywhere, despite the fact that most of their new subjects spoke neither Spanish, nor Portuguese nor Latin. This in no way gave them pause. They were genuinely surprised when the Indians refused to be parceled out and assigned foreign masters."

I was enjoying the little doctor's history lesson and asked if he would care for another cup of wine. He declined, explaining that his delicate constitution would not allow him to indulge in more than one cup with each meal and he had already exceeded his allowance.

He cleared his throat and lowered his voice. "My I presume on our slight acquaintance to issue a warning?"

"A warning? Of what kind?"

"Father Manuel's association with your husband has been noticed by those who wish your experiment to fail."

"And who are they?"

"Their names are of no consequence. They are powerful men, with friends at court. The death of King Philip revived their hope that they would at last be allowed access to the Indians of the Missions. Unlike your husband, they are after slaves, not workers."

"Is Father Manuel in any danger?"

"He could easily be recalled, banished to a place where he could do no harm. With him out of the way, confiscating your property would be quite simple. Prejudice runs deep, *Doña* Isabel, and seeing a man of your husband's heritage succeed, not only with his investments, but by marrying a beautiful, rich and mysterious Irish lady—"

I laughed. "I am neither rich nor a lady. Has no connection been made then between me and my brother Michael?"

"The young man who arrived here with *Monsieur* Moureau over a year ago?"

"I was that young man, *Don* Ernesto."

"The devil with my constitution! I will have another glass of wine!"

While he drank it, I told him my history, and asked for his advice.

"Draw as little attention to yourself as possible. Recommend to your husband that he do the same. It would do no harm to speak only of your difficulties, to give the impression that the Indians are lazy and troublesome, and that living in the wilderness is exceedingly trying. Stress the fact that you are barely surviving. Steer clear of the cities, and spend little when you are obliged to go there."

"In other words, do exactly the opposite of what we have been doing?"

He nodded and rose to go. "I would be honored if before you leave you would join me for luncheon. Pray tell my friend Wimencaí that I have found some *macaguá caá* and will be honored to hand it to her in person. Tomorrow at one o'clock then?"

It was raining heavily when the cannon signaling the opening of the city gates woke me the next morning. The doctor's warning troubled me, and I had slept poorly, deciding to conclude our business in Montevideo that very day and leave as soon as possible.

When I posed the question of lunching with the doctor to Wimencaí she said she would be glad to accompany me, especially if the doctor could provide a supply of *macaguá caá*. This snake grass, as she called it, was named after the Macaguá bird, which frequently battles with snakes, and when bitten eats a grass which serves as an antidote to the poison. The potion made from the grass is also good for headaches, and since Father Manuel often suffers from those she could not lose an opportunity of acquiring some relief for him. In exchange, she would offer the potent *mboy caá*, another type of snake grass known for dissolving kidney stones and difficult to come by in the Río de la Plata.

槽Cararé declined the doctor's invitation. The two were as incompatible, Wimencaí said, as the Macaguá bird and its snake. He and Orlando would go to the market instead and eat sweet *pasteles* till their stomachs ached.

Wimencaí and I walked through a fine drizzle to *Don* Ernesto's house on Calle Real San Gabriel. Land was abundant in the small city, and the doctor's house sat in a colorful garden with a large fig tree shading the entrance. The front door had a small window built into it, with an iron cross covering the shutter. Ornate iron railings jutted out over the windows, and a balcony, covered in purple bougainvillea, overlooked the street.

I rang the bell and soon the little window in the front door opened and a woman's voice called "*Ave María Purísima*."

I had learned how to respond to this greeting honoring the Virgin Mary and replied, "*Sin pecado concebida*". One of the door's two tall panels opened and the woman let us in and took our wet ponchos. We followed her through two interior patios where grape vines dripped, heavy with the morning rain. In the small sitting room to which we were led were straight backed chairs with carved legs, Moorish rugs, and fine oil paintings in gilt frames, all imported from Spain. Orange juice was brought to us on a gleaming tray in cups heavy with inlays of silver.

The sounds of soft crying reached us, and I realized that the room we were in must lead to the doctor's dispensary. Moments later, the doctor hurried in begging our pardon, and assured us that he would be with us soon. The crying continued, mingling with the doctor's voice and that of an older woman. Every so often, the sounds would stop and I heard the murmur of a young, female voice. A few words would be spoken and then the young woman, overcome with grief, would sob in a manner so stricken it was all I could do not to burst into the adjoining room to discover the cause of such heartbreak. Finally, a door opened and closed and two figures passed the small window by which I sat, concealed behind the heavy lace curtains. Both were heavily mantled, but I managed to catch a glimpse of the young woman's face. No more than fifteen or sixteen, she was pale, and her nose, pink from crying, stood out above a small, delicate mouth. Her eyes were large, the dark, thick lashes wet with tears. One small, white hand emerged from the black folds of her mantle to hold it close under her round chin. Her face remained engraved in my memory as her companion hurried her away, hugging the wall, two dark smudges seeking anonymity in the relentless rain.

The doctor entered, shaking his head, and sat, looking dejected and sad. "Poor child, poor child," he sighed.

Wimencaí took his hand. "Are you at liberty to discuss the case?" she asked him.

"It is one of the sadder ones I have encountered."

A few weeks previously, the young woman, whose name was María Luisa, had chosen to leave the safety of the city walls, taking her brother with her. She had soon found an excuse to send him back for a forgotten shawl. He returned to find his sister gone. He searched the area, finding no trace of her. A few days later a Minuán guide brought her back to the city. Once safely home, she claimed to have been violated, and a few weeks later revealed that she was pregnant. *Don* Ernesto wished to cast no aspersions on the young woman's character, but his examination had determined that she had been with child long before leaving Montevideo.

Wimencaí crossed herself. "She pretended to have been held captive?"

"Being forced into her pregnancy is far easier than confessing to having lost her virtue."

"What will become of her?" I asked.

"She will return to Spain and enter a convent."

From the look on Wimencaí's face I surmised that she thought convent life insufficient punishment for someone willing to risk bringing the wrath of the garrison at Montevideo down upon the Minuanes in order to save her good name.

The conversation moved on to other interesting cases the doctor and Wimencaí had dealt with, and on a sudden impulse I asked him if he could advise us about Orlando. I described his condition, and *Don* Ernesto shook his head. "Let us give thanks that we are not in Europe! There someone with his gift for languages would undoubtedly be considered possessed and be burned at the stake!"

"Can it be that you have no new tonic you would try on the boy?" Wimencaí said. Turning to me she added, "We are always quarreling about his newfangled potions and his desire to try miraculous cures for any ailment from convulsions to gout. There is only one subject on which we agree, and that is breast feeding!"

Don Ernesto inveighed against modern women, who scorned to give suck to their innocent babes and delivered them into the arms of strangers for their nourishment.

"At our first meeting we nearly came to blows!"

A few years previously, *Don* Ernesto informed me, while Wimencaí was on one of her journeys, a woman at the mission had gone into labor and Father Manuel had asked *Don* Ernesto to attend her. "I arrived at the laboring woman's house to find her up and about, talking to her friends and helping herself whenever she wished to from a dish of fruit. I ordered the friends to leave, escorted the woman to her bed, had the fruit removed, and was preparíng to use one of modern medicine's most useful tools when Wimencaí burst into the room and ejected me from it!"

"And not a moment too soon!"

"What was the tool you wanted to use, *Don* Ernesto?"

"Forceps of course."

"An instrument of the devil!" Wimencaí said, crossing herself.

"Invented by an Englishman, if memory serves me," I said.

"Used to pull babies prematurely out of their mother's wombs, often with damage to both." Wimencaí became heated as she complained that it was just such instruments as forceps, invented by a man and used exclusively by surgeons, that had made it unnecessary for them to learn how to ease a child into the world in the child's good time, not the doctor's.

"Absolute nonsense!" the doctor cried. "You are opposed as a matter of ignorant prejudice to anything new!"

"I am opposed to interfering with nature!"

"Is that how you defend the perverse barbarity of making women squat on the floor like beasts?"

"Only a man would believe the counterfeit that forcing women to keep to their beds during the work of labor denotes progress!"

"Perhaps *Don* Ernesto doesn't know why it became common usage in Europe," I intervened. "The real explanation was long ago replaced by a more socially acceptable one."

Wimencaí and *Don* Ernesto were silenced, and looked at me with unconcealed curiosity. The practice of making women lie down during labor, I told them, had begun at the court of the French King, Louis XIV, who derived a certain pleasure from watching his mistresses give birth. He hid in their rooms to observe them, but when they birthed on a birthing stool his pleasure was diminished, so he ordered a court doctor to persuade the ladies to position themselves on a high table, where Louis could enjoy a good view of the dawn, as Wimencaí had taught me to call the birth canal. Although labor is much more difficult for women in that position, doctors in France were quick to copy court fashion and the practice soon spread all over Europe.

Wimencaí marveled at the shallowness of men of science in general and physicians in particular, while *Don* Ernesto ran to find his notes. He wanted to record the details of my story before he forgot them, even if they contradicted his previous argument.

~

Since my arrival in Montevideo, I had been allowing myself to harbor the hope that I might finally be with child. On the morning of our departure, I awoke with an all too familiar wetness between my legs and began to cry, finding I could not stop even when Wimencaí came to my door. I would not let her in, ashamed of my grief in front of a woman who had confessed to praying for a child of her own for over fifteen years. But Wimencaí would not take no for an answer. She persuaded me to open my door, and held me while I cried, telling me that the worst thing a woman longing for a child can do is worry. Children come, she said, when they are ready to, and in her world, it is only once a man has dreamed of his child that he can give it life.

I cried all the harder. "Garzón never has dreams!"

Wimencaí laughed and informed me that it was time for me to wash away the tears while she laid out my clothes. The mistrust I had harbored toward her since seeing her greeting Garzón in the infirmary gave way altogether that morning as I sat watching her smooth my blouse and shake out my skirt. My question surprised both of us, and after I asked it we stared at each other for a moment before Wimencaí burst into laughter. I was relieved to observe that she was more curious than offended.

"Me? Garzón's lover? Whatever gave you such an idea?"

"The way you kissed him when you came back from your travels last spring."

"Listen, *querida*, when you are no longer young and a handsome man seems happy to have you in his arms, I recommend that you kiss him if you can! That is all there was to it, I assure you." She came to sit by me. "I love Cararé. He can be stubborn, and his feelings for the King and the Church are uncompromising — Garzón would say intemperate — but it is a loyalty he brings to everything, including marriage. I would not betray his trust and his devotion for all the handsome men in the province."

She picked up a brush and went to work on my hair, braiding it with ribbons and pinning it like a crown around my head. I must have been no more than six or seven the last time I had allowed my mother to perform these offices for me, and I was surprised by how natural it felt, how reassuring, to be taken care of this way.

When I was satisfied that no trace of crying showed on my face, I went out in search of Orlando, who had asked if he might make his bed in the stable. For several months now, he had been riding his own pony, a sturdy and single minded little Welsh stallion brought from Ireland by Garzón. The pony slept in the stable, and when Orlando learned that Zule was not to be allowed inside the inn, he asked if he could make his bed with her. I had been reluctant to give my permission, and Orlando had not pressed me, but his cheeks had been wet when I bent to kiss him good night. I decided that he could come to no harm in the stable with Zule by his side, so we collected bedding from our wagon and installed him there, Zule's tail thumping with pleasure against the pony's stall as she lay down next to him.

I found him washing at the well, and helped him to dry himself. We had visited the barber, and his hair was cut shorter than usual. A small triangular birthmark at the hairline behind his ear caught my attention, and when I bent to look at it more closely I discovered that it was not a birthmark at all but a tattoo. I asked him if he knew its significance but Orlando appeared not to be aware of its existence. I left him at play with the innkeeper's children while Wimencaí, Cararé and I concluded our business in Montevideo.

Having discharged our commissions, we were preparíng

to return to the inn when the city gates were thrown open and a contingent of soldiers rode into the plaza. Behind them, surrounded by more mounted soldiers, limped a pitiful group of women and children, covered in dust, and bleeding from numerous small wounds and insect bites. For all that I had heard about them, I had not seen the Charrúa before, and I joined the small crowd gathering around the soldiers, as curious as they for a glimpse of the captives. An overwhelming sense of familiarity pervaded me as I saw Garzón's face reflected in every set of those high cheekbones and dark eyes.

Wimencaí and屈Cararé stood rigidly, arm in arm, watching the scene unfold. Comments from the crowd informed us that this latest battle with the Charrúa had been unusually bloody, with lives lost on both sides. Several of the soldiers bore evidence of the struggle and I heard them boast that in spite of their wounds they had not left a single warrior alive from this particular clan.

The sale of the women and children would begin as soon as the citizens were gathered. No sooner had the announcement been made than a young woman with wild, uneasy eyes pushed a startled soldier aside, and ran toward the city walls. Hands reached out to stop her, but she evaded them.

A man broke from the soldiers' ranks and went after her. By the time he had crossed the crowded plaza, she had climbed to the top of the battlements, where she stood for a moment, her long black hair blown about her by the wind. The man's voice called to her, and she turned, tearing the deerskin cape from her shoulders with one swift movement. Holding her bare arms up to the sky, she jumped, as if wanting to join the seagulls overhead. The forgiving wind seemed to hold her strong and graceful for a moment before she disappeared from sight.

The man who had pursued her stood frozen, looking down at the rocks below, while the women and children left behind in the Plaza began to wail and moan. The soldiers moved amongst them, slapping them with the flat of their swords and striking them with their horse whips.

The crowd, shocked into momentary stillness, came back to life, closing round the soldiers to lay claim to the human spoils of war.

"I asked for a baby, Major!" one man said angrily. "My wife wanted to raise one. These are walking already."

"You know how it is, *Señor*, they hide and even kill their babies when they see us coming."

"Barbarians! Why my wife wants one I don't know. She has a notion that if they are raised like good Christians they won't commit such atrocities. I'll take that young girl there, the one with the clean face."

His words acted like a bucket of cold water thrown at my head. Forgetting all about *Don* Ernesto's warning about remaining inconspicuous, I reached for my purse, and elbowed my way forward. "I offer double!"

The man turned, looking displeased. He removed his hat and bowed coldly. "*A sus pies, Señora*."

"*Beso a usted la mano, caballero*," I replied, mustering a smile as I put my arm around the girl's shoulders.

"*Señora*, do not touch her, she is filthy! She will contaminate you!"

The girl, whose eyes until that moment had been fixed upon the battlements, sighed and leaned into me. She was shivering in spite of the warmth of the day, and I covered her with my shawl, anxious to move to the front of the crowd to deal with the man in charge of the captives.

Cries filled the air as children were separated from their mothers, sisters from brothers, and friends from one another. Heedless of the looks and curses they received, Wimencaí and Cararé began to bargain for the captives with what few coins they had left after having purchased our supplies earlier that day.

Together, we outbid every offer made by the citizens of Montevideo until all our gold and silver were gone. Twice I followed men who were leaving the Plaza with children taken from their mothers, and begged and pleaded with them, offering twice, thrice what they had paid, until they gave them up. I think they enjoyed watching me beg. My hair was by then disheveled, my hands trembled, and they laughed as they made the deals that cost me every last coin I had. Still five women and two children were left. I asked for credit based on Garzón's ships and the man in charge of the sale refused. There were plenty of others, already resentful of my high handed, rude behavior, anxious to offer ready cash for the captives.

Wimencaí would not abandon them. She swore she'd get the money somehow and soon. Again, the game appealed to them. They made bets. If we could return with the money in half an hour they were ours. Wimencaí pushed them aside and we ran, telling Cararé to guard with his very life the ones we'd so far pried from their buyers. We were possessed with a drive and a fury that drove us straight to *Don* Ernesto's house where we pounded on the door until Apolonia let us in. The doctor himself was not far behind her, anxious to see what the emergency was. Wimencaí told him, and he did not hesitate. From a locked drawer he withdrew a bag of gold coins and put it in her hands. We were gone while he was still getting his hat.

Only Cararé remained in the Plaza. He gestured with his head toward the fountain. The captives had been hidden on the ground behind it, a final joke to see what the mad Irishwoman and her Indian friend would do. Wimencaí emptied the bag of coins into the fountain and didn't wait to hear what insults were hurled at her. *Don* Ernesto was there by now and he took charge, chastising the men if they so much as uttered another word, and threatening to leave them to rot in their own pus next time they needed someone to tend to their poxes.

As we gathered our charges and turned away, Cararé pointed to a bedraggled figure standing nearby. It was the man who had run after the young woman. He was gaunt, with heavy shadows under his eyes, his arm bandaged and lying in a dirty bandana tied like a sling around his neck. He removed his hat, and there, looking as ill almost as when I had first seen him at Santa Marta, was Charlie, staring at me without recognition. I realized that he had no idea who I was, never having seen me in feminine clothing. I walked up to him and put my hand on his good arm. "It's Micheal Keating."

In any other circumstances the situation would have been comical. Charlie looked at me as if either he or I or both of us had taken leave of our senses, and it was only when Wimencaí came up to us that his eyes lost their glazed look.

"We will explain everything when we're at the doctor's," she said.

I was faint by then, whether from fear or relief I don't know, and gratefully accepted the brandy Apolonia pressed upon me. *Don* Ernesto sent for his apprentice while the cook was ordered to run to the butcher's to buy meat enough to feed us all.

The women and children gathered in a corner and Craré spoke softly to them, assuring them that they would all be allowed to return to their tribe soon. Wimencaí warmed water and began washing cuts and swollen feet.

Charlie's arm was broken and would have to be set. I prepared a strong drink from the *coca* leaves Wimencaí had only just purchased from the Aymara healers, who periodically brought them to the region. It would ease the pain and help Charlie to sleep.

He uttered a cry when the bone was put in place, and only I, who knew his face almost as well as I knew my own, from having watched over him for hours during his earlier recovery, understood that he had welcomed the pain.

In the days that followed I learned that Charlie had found no trace of his relatives in Entre Ríos. They had moved away years before, no one knew where. Until he began telling me about it, I don't believe he had allowed himself to dwell on all that had happened to him over the past year. Being forced to leave Ireland had been painful enough, although at the time he thought only of his rage against the English and what a relief it would be to be quit of them.

"Where is Itanambí, Charlie?"

"She left me after catching the eye of a Portuguese merchant who bought her rubies and a ball gown. The last time I saw her she was on her way to Buenos Aires."

"What will you do now?"

"I haven't thought beyond seeking Father Manuel's advice. Do you think he'll receive me? I have no one else to turn to."

"Ride back with us. We will be happy to have your company." That was an outright lie. I knew no one other than myself who would be pleased by Charlie's return.

I was considering how I would break the news to Garzón, when his ship put into harbor. As I had already discovered, news traveled fast in Montevideo, and by the time I saw him, he had already heard about the incident with the captives. I let him know that Craré had selected two of the men from our settlement who had accompanied us to Montevideo, and that they would be leaving the next morning to escort the women and children back to Entre Ríos.

"Where are they?" he asked.

"At *Don* Ernesto Zubillaga's."

He ordered his trunk sent to the inn and I did not see him again until the following day when I woke to find him standing by my bed. He looked quite unlike himself, his clothes were wrinkled and dirty, and a dark stubble of beard cast a shadow over his face.

"I'm sorry if I worried you," he said.

"*Don* Ernesto told me that you needed to be alone."

He lay back, throwing one arm over his face, and I pulled off his boots. I dressed and went downstairs for a basin of hot water, and when I returned, he was sound asleep. I sat in a chair and watched over him, wondering what he would choose to tell me when he woke. From *Don* Ernesto I had learned that my husband had asked to see the captives, who were gathered in the doctor's courtyard. A woman had approached Garzón and spoken to him in words *Don* Ernesto did not understand. Garzón did, and answered. His response had brought the others crowding round. They touched and questioned him, and Garzón had backed away. Suddenly, and without another word, he had hurried from the house.

It was noon before he woke, and by then the water in the basin had cooled. I returned downstairs for a fresh supply, and ordered food for us. He said little while I shaved him and combed his hair. It was only later, after we had eaten, that he began to talk.

"I have gone nowhere near my mother's people for almost twenty years. When a woman came up to me yesterday and said 'You are one of us,' I could only think of everything my father had said about them — that they were dirty, primitive, ignorant, base in their habits."

He had wanted to run away, but instead found himself saying, "My mother's name was Analona."

The woman's eyes had filled with tears. "Analona," she repeated. Then she had turned to the others. "This is Analona's son, Napeguá's grandson!"

They had gathered round him, touching him, asking if he had come to take them home. No, Garzón said, someone else would be doing that. Why not him? they wanted to know. Did he not wish to visit his grandfather?

"I had never imagined that he might still be alive. It was too much for me."

He fled, taking with him a final memory of a boy staring fixedly at him. He was about the same age Garzón had been when his father took him away, and his eyes were full of loss.

"Had I remained with the tribe, I would probably have died as his father did, defending a son of my own."

It was not his intention to wound me with these words, but I felt them as a wound nonetheless. There was a longing in his voice that he was perhaps unaware of.

"Like that boy, I had not shed a single tear. My father claimed it was because I understood that as the son of a civilized man, I did not belong amongst savages any more than he did. I believed his explanation, although I slept for years with the stone my mother gave me knotted in my shirt. But when I walked into *Don* Ernesto's and saw those women and the boy, dry eyed, hiding his terror, the memory of how I hadn't allowed myself to think of my mother for fear that I would cry, came back to me as if it had happened yesterday."

Garzón remembered how his father had refused to call him by the name his mother had given him, saying that he would give his son a proper French name once he forgot her and her language, once he proved that he could be civilized. "Until then, he called me *garçon*. I disguised it later by changing the spelling, because he never did rename me or use the name given to me in baptism. Perhaps he forgot, or perhaps I never lived up to his expectations."

Nevertheless, fine clothes had been bought for him, and a sword with a hilt that fitted his small hand. He was taught Spanish and French, given books, and allowed to share all that his father knew about ships and the sea. It hurt too much to think of his mother, and so Garzón told himself that he had forgotten her, forgotten his grandfather, and would never seek them out or make any effort to return to her.

"Last night I prayed for the first time since I can remember."

"To whom did you pray?"

"To Tupá, an ancient spirit whose name means simply — 'Who are you?' It seemed fitting for someone who doesn't know who he is to appeal to a god whose identity is also a mystery."

"You could visit your grandfather."

"I'm afraid to, Isabel. I'm afraid of being sucked in and never feeling free to leave, of having to abandon everything I love — you,

Orlando, the settlement, my ships. You are my wife and Orlando is my son. I am what circumstance and place have made me, neither white nor Indian, just a painful mixture of both. Last night I realized that I will only ever belong wherever such things don't matter, and that my own small kingdom by the lagoon must be that place."

~

I dressed the following morning to the sound of jangling harness, the creaking of wagon wheels, and the clatter of horse's hooves on the cobblestones in the inn's courtyard, where Garzón and Orlando were supervising the packing into the wagons of the ironware and glass we had bought. Our supplies of rice, hemp, dyes, and molds for making candlesticks and chalices had also been boxed and were ready for loading.

On the dressing table I found a package, a small leather casket, and a note from Garzón. *I visited Michael and your parents' gravesites while I was in Cork. And Mary sent this package.*

I opened the casket first, and the faint, earthy aroma brought back to me the bleak, rainy day when I had laid Ma and Pa to rest. I ran my fingers through the rich old soil and wondered what had possessed Garzón to bring me such a gift.

I would mix it with new soil and plant something in it, a tree perhaps.

Mary's package contained a Callamanca petticoat with quilted leaves of blue satin.

October 1747

Dearest Isabel,

I begin all my letters the same way, with the woefully inadequate words 'I miss you.' It has been so from the moment we saw your ship put out to sea, with your small figure standing on the crowded deck between a mooing cow and several crates of chickens.

We are moving. Reminiscent of you, this old house makes us sad and dreary. My father is transferring his shop nearer to Pope's Quay, for the good of the business, he says. Ma claims it's so that he can be nearer the theatre and the coffee houses and sit by the River Lee all day reading the Dublin newspapers.

You will be anxious for news of our fair city and county.

Do you recollect the two thousand or so Frenchmen and Spaniards I told you of in my last letter, the ones being held prisoners by the English at Kinsale after their failed attempt to possess themselves of the gaol there? Fifty-four of them perished, poor souls, in a fire. At such times I curse Ireland and the English both! Who benefits from these constant foreign wars? Certainly not those who have to fight them, like the wretched prisoners at Kinsale, and assuredly not the common folk like us.

How does it suit you to live in a territory ruled by Spain after all the wars there have been between us? I say 'us' meaning our English neighbors, who are surely the most bellicose nation on God's good earth.

As further evidence of the troubled times we live in, we were visited by various marvels this past summer. First of all, a yellowish substance, with a vile, sulphorous smell, rained down upon Doneraile. No one was harmed and after lying on the ground for a brief time, it disappeared. We also had violent storms, with hail stones of five inches in diameter and spikes to match. Many windows were broken all over town and Ma's roses destroyed.

Your handsome Captain delivered your gifts to us. How thrilled we were to meet him! Your romance is reminiscent of that play we went to see when we were little more than children. Do you recollect it? It was about a young woman named Violette who fell in love with an Indian and ran off to live with him freely in the Americas, just as you have done. I believe it was written by a Frenchman and entitled "Wild Harlequin."

I have made use of the soap you sent me for everything, from my face to my clothing, for it is delicate and sweetly scented. One bar I keep, to show everyone here what fine soaps the Indians make.

You would not recognize your old friend! I am learning to dance the quadrille and wear my hair in the French style, with a becoming (if I do say so myself) cap of tight curls framing my face and an intricate knot at the nape of my neck. And do you remember how we detested sewing? Well, I myself quilted and lined the Callamanca petticoat I am sending you.

You could have knocked me over with a feather when I read your news that Charlie FitzGibbon had turned up in your part of the world! Everyone here believes he went to the American colonies. His brother Ronan, as you know, conformed and became a member of the Anglican Church of Ireland, so he has inherited everything and their father until his death will be no more than a life tenant on his own property. Good Catholics shun Ronan, but the troublesome puppy cares not, for his friends are all Protestants now, and with Charlie gone he can do as he pleases. The news nearly killed old Sir Charles. The entire family went into mourning and even had a Mass said for Ronan FitzGibbon as if he were dead, which to them he is. It was bad enough to have a son exiled, but to see the younger conform and cheat Charlie out of his inheritance was more than the old man could bear and he was found half frozen, wandering distracted as a ghost in the vast recesses of FitzGibbon Castle.

I have not seen the Earl's cook Margaret recently, but the Earl himself, no stranger to cozenage as you well know, has recently acquired more property. Do you recollect that act passed by the English Parliament after the British army was defeated at Fontenoy by the Irish brigade fighting for France? The one disabling all Irish officers who had served from holding any real or personal property? (Our officers would all have quitted their service for the French quite happily if they had been able to make an honest living in their own homeland!) Well, Johnny Busteed, the rogue, denounced several of our poor boys and was thereby entitled to all of their property!

Speaking of property, my father informs me that you are a rich woman now! When the Captain was here he told us that he brought five thousand fleeces with him, having paid a shilling a dozen for them and that he sold them here for five times that amount on your advice. He tells us that the Indians won't eat mutton so he dries it for use on his ships. He has loaded his ship, named after you, with Irish cambric and fine woolen yarn. He says you are a brilliant advisor with a head finely turned for trade, an inimitable clear way of reasoning, and a sharp legal mind. I agreed!

And dear one, do not worry – the children will come when God sends them. Ma waited almost eight years for me, and did not stop bearing for five years afterwards!

Will you return, my darling Isabel? The voyage is long and perilous I know, but what a joy it would be to wake one morning and find you singing in the kitchen as of old.

I think you would want to know that the old oak behind your house was hit by lightning and destroyed everything in its fall, including your house and our garden wall. Our landlord repaired the wall but is doing nothing to rebuild the house, which has stood empty since your departure. Anything that was in it is well buried now.

I have written the ink well dry!

Your fond friend, Mary O'Neill.

P.S. Your faithful steed Puck is as round as a barrel and in fine fettle. I have vowed to ride him more now that summer is here.

So Mary had known, and this was her way of setting my mind at ease about what had lain buried in the cellar.

The sobs that racked me as I sat with the letter clenched in my hands were not for Tobias, but for the ancient, sheltering giant, and for the house I had once shared with Ma, Pa, and Michael.

A crowd of well wishers and curious bystanders assembled to see us off, and last minute gifts of flowers and fruit were handed up to Wimencaí by grateful patients she had attended during her weeks in Montevideo.

The three *camiluchos* Cararé had hired to replace himself and the two men he would take to Entre Ríos, arrived. One of them explained to Garzón that his friend had been taken ill and could not make the journey, so he had brought along another friend willing to work for him. The new man offered to take his shirt off to prove his honesty and

Garzón told him that that was quite unnecessary. When we returned to our room to collect our belongings, I asked him why the man had made such a strange offer.

"He wanted me to know that he hasn't been branded."

"With an iron do you mean?"

"On the shoulder for first offenders."

"For what crime?"

"Cattle thieving."

"Who meets out such barbarous punishment?"

"The owners of the cattle."

"What would you have done if you had found a mark?"

"Congratulated him. The punishment is reserved for Indians, slaves, and half breeds, like me. Cattle and horse thieving is a sport amongst Spaniards." He pointed to the panniers, draped over my trunk like a set of gigantic, collapsed ribs. "And those?"

"They are for my new dress, which I will show you once we're at home."

He groaned as he heaved my trunk onto his back. "What is it decorated with? Cannon balls?"

"It was you who suggested I should buy myself a dress!" I reminded him as I carried the panniers to one of the wagons, already full with the dozens of cushions put there for Charlie by the young ladies of Montevideo. When they heard that our wounded Irish nobleman couldn't ride because of his broken arm, they had raided their trousseaus, competing with one another to see who could produce the most elaborate cushion cover. They stuffed half a wagon full of cushions of varying sizes — a veritable sea of improbable flowers, butterflies and birds. Charlie burst out laughing when he saw them, removed his muddy boots, and stretched himself out on the cushions with every appearance of contentment.

Orlando was saddling his pony with the light, compact saddle Cararé had crafted to accommodate the weakness of his legs, when *Don* Ernesto appeared with a hamper of cold fowl and cheese packed by Apolonia, and a very special gift for Orlando. It was an addition to the saddle, intended for Zule — a combination between a small padded platform and a basket with high sides, designed to be strapped to the saddle and sit on a blanket over the pony's rump.

Orlando threw his arms around *Don* Ernesto's waist and hugged him in a display of emotion unusual for him.

Knowing the pony's uncertain temperament, I held tightly to the reins as Orlando called encouragingly to Zule. A grin of pure enjoyment broke out on Orlando's face as she leapt into her aery.

Don Ernesto wiped his eyes and blew his nose. Garzón gave the signal to depart. The wagoners called to the oxen, the men clicked their tongues to the horses, and amid shouts of farewell and the creaking of the wooden wheels, we wound our way slowly out of the city. The summer air was fragrant with the smell of salt from the ocean and the sun shone brightly in a cloudless turquoise sky.

For the next three weeks, we traveled by the water, falling asleep every night to the dull roar of the waves on the sand. At the end of the third week we stopped to collect the shallow containers of water we had left among the rocks. The water had long ago evaporated, and the containers were covered in a fine film of the salt we would use until we reached the settlement.

We crossed the dunes and entered the palm groves to rest the animals before beginning the journey to the lagoon. While we rested, the *camiluchos* prepared a banquet. They preferred their meat rare, and chewed large mouthfuls of dripping red meat off whole racks of ribs. But that day, they gutted a steer, removed the intestines and the fat, and packed them into the stomach. Once the innards were loaded, they ignited the fat and sewed the stomach back together, leaving an opening for the smoke to emerge. At the end of the day, they would each cut their favorite part out of the cooked stomach.

Charlie told us that on his father's estate a similar method of cooking meat was employed. A pit was dug and lined with heated stones. The meat was wrapped in straw, put in a pot in the pit, and covered with water. The heated stones kept the water boiling and cooked the meat.

It was while we were resting in the groves, that Garzón brought out the gift he had had made for me in Río de Janeiro. It was the most beautiful riding habit I had ever seen, a fawn colored wool jacket with velvet collar and cuffs, decorated with silver buttons in the shape of crescent moons. The buttonholes were finished in silver thread, and all of it was lined in pink taffeta. The bodice was of pink silk and matched the facing on the pleated skirt, which was to be worn over a hoop petticoat.

"I shall keep it for special occasions."

"I know what that means," Garzón said. "You will put it back in the trunk with mothballs for company."

I already felt extravagant owning a set of panniers, adding a hoop petticoat to them was more than I would be able to manage in our small house, so I carried the hoop petticoat into the nearby *monte* and tied the waist ribbons to a low branch, covering the tent-like thing with branches. Garzón had accompanied me and he burst out laughing when he saw what I was doing.

"It may be useful to some wild animal!" I said.

"I would pay my weight in gold to see a *ñandú* running in that!"

"Not as a garment, you fool! As a shelter!"

As we began the final lap of our journey, Charlie complained of being jolted in the wagon and said he couldn't stand the noise of the wheels one more day. The drivers wouldn't oil them because they claimed the oxen liked the sound and responded to it as if to music. I thought it likelier that the poor beasts moved forward in the hope of escaping the noise.

Charlie's arm no longer pained him but Wimencaí had ordered him to keep it immobile for several more weeks. Garzón nevertheless had a horse saddled for him and after that he rode by my side, asking questions about the settlement. I sketched a picture of the compound for him, and in case he had any illusions about what he was going to find, prepared him for the fact that it was nothing more than a fortified village. Marauders might cross the surrounding ditch on foot, I told him, but there is no horse alive that could be coaxed or forced to jump the prickly pear we had planted just beyond the ditch. The attackers would also be easy targets from the watch towers.

In spite of everything I did to prepare him for what he would find when we arrived at the lagoon, Charlie's eyes widened when he saw the settlement. The neatly plowed and planted fields lay in small brown and green swirls all around us, and there was a comforting familiarity about them, but there the familiar ended. Out of the midst of the friendly fields rose the prickly pear hedges like barbed sentinels, their thorns thick and menacing, surrounding the tall, thatched fence enclosing the settlement and converging round a twelve-foot-high gate made entirely of bone. At intervals along the fence, the whitened skulls of steers were set, a decoration Charlie found gruesome. It spoke of death and was reminiscent of the heads of criminals he had seen impaled on stakes.

Greetings met us from the watch towers, and soon the wagons were drawn up in the square for unloading. Father Manuel hurried with the others to greet us, a look of grave concern crossing his face when he saw Charlie. His was not the only greeting lacking in warmth. The elders had already heard that Itanambí had disgraced herself further by leaving Charlie for another man, but this only made him appear worse in their eyes. He had corrupted her and she had only continued along the path on which he set her.

While a fire was lit in the guesthouse, and children brought supplies of fresh bread, fruit and vegetables to fill the baskets hanging in the pantry, I attempted to make Charlie feel welcome. "We are making more chairs, but meanwhile, large skulls serve us well for sitting," I said, pointing to the skull of a bull lying in a corner. He smiled, but his eyes remained thoughtful, and I touched his shoulder, feeling the muscles like taut cords under his shirt. "There is a Mass of Thanksgiving planned for our safe return, and later you'll have an opportunity to speak freely to Father Manuel."

Many wistful and longing glances were cast in Charlie's direction as he took his place with the men on their side of the aisle, but he was on his best behavior and kept his eyes on his prayer book. When the mass was over we accompanied him and Father Manuel to the guest house. As the sun set, I lit a lantern and placed it on the table between us.

Charlie wasted no time. Nothing else could be addressed, he said, until we accepted his apology for having betrayed our community's trust. If we would allow it he intended to devote himself to being of benefit to us. In the year he had spent in the Province he had restored, and would soon surpass, the fortune his family had lost in Ireland. With it, he planned to assist us in establishing a model provincial town, right here, on the shores of our lagoon.

"Isabel and I have often talked about the similarities between these colonies and Ireland, between what is happening to the Indians and what happened to our people after the English invaded us. I share her belief in our capacity to learn from the mistakes of the past and not repeat them."

"I see no evidence that people in the New World have learned from their mistakes in the old," Garzón said. "Pillage, greed, and overbreeding are destroying Europe and will eventually destroy the colonies as well."

"That is a view I cannot share!" Charlie said. "And surely you don't believe it either, or else what would be the point of all this?" he asked, gesturing to the settlement outside the window.

"A man must work, regardless of his beliefs."

"In my opinion, there are two kinds of men in the world: those who wish to exploit what they see, and those, like you, who know how to do so without destroying what benefits them."

"Regrettably, the world is ruled by a third, far more dangerous kind — those who don't understand the difference."

That night I woke to find myself alone in the bed. Garzón was standing by the window, passing his agate from hand to hand.

"Charlie's proposal worries you," I said.

"FitzGibbon himself worries me, Isabel."

"His idealism has cost him much."

"It isn't his idealism that concerns me. I haven't told you, but he chose to confide in me about the young woman who killed herself."

Before the raid that killed her father, her brothers, and her uncles, Charlie had known her, lain with her, smelled and tasted her like the forbidden and exotic fruit she seemed to him. He had defended her from the soldiers who tried to violate her and his arm had been broken in her defense, but he wasn't innocent.

"He talked to me as if I were a priest able to assign him punishment for his sins. I recommended confession, but it wasn't absolution he was seeking. He craves a penance that will draw blood, a hundred Stations of the Cross on bare knees, nights spent in prayer, a tortuous fast."

"Perhaps giving his all to our community will satisfy that craving."

"Why do you want him here, Isabel?"

"I have no romantic feelings for Charlie, if that is what you fear."

"I have feared it."

"I was foolish enough once to think myself in love with Charlie, but that was long ago. My motive for wanting him to stay is a self-interested one."

I had been turning *Don* Ernesto's warning over and over in my mind. I had seen enough in Ireland of laws legalizing the confiscation of property to understand how easily it could be done. Having Charlie with us gave us invaluable protection. He was a nobleman with all the assurance of his aristocratic background and the confidence to challenge anyone who might defy his right to establish himself wherever he pleased.

"Would he consent to being used in this way?"

"I shall ask him if you want me to."

"I think it only fair."

~

Charlie was thoughtful when I told him of my conversation with *Don* Ernesto, and not in the least certain that his presence would help prevent what I feared.

"I don't possess that kind of power, Isabel."

"You have always possessed it, that's why you're unaware of it."

"I meant what I said last night. My wish is to serve you. My life and all I own are at your disposal."

Charlie's formal apology to the *cabildo* was made at their next meeting and accepted. He repeated his pledge to serve us, and when the workshop captains arrived to review their activities, he was invited to stay and hear their reports regarding our crops, livestock, and the disposal of the products of our workshops.

The Captain of Leatherwork spoke first, reporting on the design and manufacture of household furnishings, saddles, reins and harnesses. He was followed by the Captains of Carpentry, Blacksmithing, and Silversmithing, who described the building and making of furniture, the design of tools and locks, and their progress with the decoration of the church. The Chapel Teacher, who led the choir and taught the reading and writing of music, displayed the new music books his artisans had made, and the Captain of Topographers laid out maps of the territory, describing its features in minute detail.

From Carаré the *cabildo* heard that the warehouses were piled high with hides, some weighing as much as thirty-five kilos, plus barrels containing thousands of kilos of tallow for the European markets.

Charlie learned we were already selling jerked beef to the Indies and Havana, a profitable venture since the average yield from a single bull was ninety kilos, that from a cow, sixty.

At the end of the meeting it was decided that Charlie should apply for a license, just as Garzón had done, and add another twelve thousand head of cattle to our stock. In exchange, we would provide the labor, and the shipping of his exports.

Charlie left the next day for Buenos Aires and returned with such speed that Garzón recommended that the *cabildo* examine the license he bore. It was duly presented to them, and Garzón concluded that I had been right. Charlie wielded more influence than money alone could buy. The license, requiring weeks of waiting even when the petitioner was generous with his gifts, had been issued in three days.

That evening, as Orlando and I walked by the guest house, we heard lively singing coming from the open window and Charlie gestured to us to come in to look at the drawings he had been working on. At first, I thought they were sketches of his old home in Ireland, but they turned out to be pictures of the castle Charlie planned to build on the shores of the lagoon. It was strangely suited to its surroundings, a combination of Irish impregnability, and the open design of Spanish courtyards. Tall towers fronted the prairies, and behind them, overlooking the lagoon, rose the main body of the castle, revolving around a large central courtyard paved in brick, where trees, shrubs, and flowers were to be planted. The castle walls, Charlie said, would be eighty centimeters thick, and it would have a grand hall, banqueting rooms, a library, drawing room, and dining room. Brick would be extensively used, and a high stone wall would surround it.

All the windows were to be deeply recessed, with window seats and carved wooden cornices, inspired by the carvings being done in our workshops to ornament the church. These works of art, so lifelike they looked as if they could come leaping and flying out of the carvers' hands, were painted in reds, greens, blues and yellows, depicting fish and birds, fruits and flowers.

Charlie went every morning to watch the Indians cut stone, mold and bake bricks, and care for our precious *yerba* plants. The *mate* made from the *yerba* tree is used as a cure for all ills — sleeplessness, indigestion, and melancholia. We still bought ours from the traders for a high price, since it would be another three years before our own seedlings, taking root in a sheltered area, were ready for transplanting, and five or more after that before the leaves could be harvested. Charlie asked Father Manuel if it was worth the effort, and was assured that if we succeeded in establishing a *yerba* plantation not only would our workers get rich off it, since it is the most valuable commodity produced in the colonies, but we could cut back on the far more arduous work of harvesting hides.

The Indians drink *mate* without embellishment, but like Father Manuel, I add sugar to mine. Sugar is one of Father Manuel's few indulgences. He carries a little bag of sugar squares in his pocket at all times, not only to sweeten his *mate*, but because he knows the horses like it. Recently, he had heard that a German chemist by the name of Marggraf had discovered that sugar could be extracted from beetroot, and Garzón was already growing some in an attempt to reproduce the experiment.

By the end of that season there was no doubt that Charlie, who rose at dawn each day and worked side by side with the men, was gaining everyone's respect and even their affection. The Chapel Teacher had been pleasantly surprised by the sweetness and power of Charlie's voice and soon had Charlie singing solos during the Masses. Before long he was composing music, and I began to hear an Irish strain in the familiar old Italian airs that floated from our little church onto the surrounding pampas.

When the *butiá* flowered and were crowned with heavy clusters of small, yellow fruit, sweet and rich in possibilities, Charlie went to the palm groves every day and brought me a basketful, knowing how I love these *coquitos* fresh off the tree. Wimencaí cooked the fruits with sugar to make a honey-like jelly soothing to the throat, and Charlie himself liked the liquor the Indians made from the fruit.

~

It rained very hard that winter, and I thought our little adobe houses would surely crumble. Perhaps, Father Manuel said, it was the rain that was keeping Yací and Atzaya away, or perhaps they had roamed far afield. He had not seen Yací since his visit to the settlement, and the last time Atzaya and I had spoken was before my marriage to Garzón.

Between sea voyages Garzón occupied himself by making a canoe from the trunk of a *timbó*, and we used the few fine days we had to further explore the lagoon. No one knew why its waters were almost black and retained their dark color even when boiled. It gave my hair a silkiness unlike any I'd ever enjoyed, and Garzón would wind my plaits around his wrists, binding himself to me, he said, with chains of honey. Sometimes I wished the chains were real and I could use them to make him keep his promise that each voyage would be his last. Perhaps then the child we longed for would come.

The shores of the lagoon were sandy, like the ones by the ocean, with rock formations and an abundance of caves, into which I did not venture because they were the favorite haunt of vampire bats, which emerged at close of day in search of food. I would never forget the horror with which I woke one morning as we neared the lagoon for the first time, to see Father Manuel's hammock all stained with blood. I was certain as I ran to him that I would find him with his throat cut or the victim of some horrible animal attack. Instead, he was sleeping peacefully, quite unaware that during the night the bats had fed upon his exposed toes.

Wimencaí calls the bat a gentle surgeon, secreting a substance that not only prevents pain, but often causes its victims to sleep profoundly. There were healers in her tribe once who knew how to extract this essence from the bats' saliva, but it was a long lost art.

The woods surrounding the lagoon were magical, rife with birdsong and decorated with lichens that hung over the water in lacy wreaths, gray as morning mist and fully as ethereal. The woods themselves were strewn with orchids and ferns, and an odd tree that grew in gigantic twists along the ground.

Lizards abounded, glittering like scattered gems amongst the fallen leaves and on the trunks of trees. They ranged in color from the richest browns to gleaming copper and sparkling green. Some were smaller than my little finger, others the length of my arm.

When I first arrived at the lagoon I thought I would be unable to sleep in its vicinity, being almost deafened by the frogs. Until I spent my first night out of doors I had no idea how full of sounds the night could be. Between the high, unrelenting call of the frogs, owls hooted, and the *uru* bird mourned. Creatures I could not name and whose habits were unknown to me, rustled in the undergrowth, clucking, snapping, and murmuring to one another in a range of voices, blending so naturally into the shadows that they became a soothing starlit music that awakened my senses while lulling me into a semi-slumber that proved remarkably refreshing considering its lightness.

I felt compelled to draw everything I saw, as if, Charlie said, I was afraid that it might disappear, and all that would be left would be my imperfect memory of so much beauty. The first time a flock of flamingos flew by, turning the sky pink with their numbers, I knew that I wanted more than anything to preserve their flight toward the setting sun. They were like a curtain being drawn endlessly across the sky until all I could see were flamingos and my neck hurt and still they came and finally I simply lay upon the ground to see them go by, believing that perhaps they never would come to an end and I would grow old watching them.

In the trees near the lagoon I discovered oyster catchers, herons of various colors, and blackbirds. Most of the birds I had never seen before, like the *federales*, with their scarlet heads and necks, and the saffron-trimmed *dragones*. *Viuditas*, white "widows," with flashes of blue, darted by me when I rode, as did the orange and black tanagers, and the blue cardinals with brilliant red crests.

I also drew flowers, and Garzón brought me paints and dyes with which to capture the iridescent shades of the blooming meadows, and the wildness of the imaginative creepers resembling feathers, beaks, butterfly wings, bells, and feather dusters. Craré told me the story of the passion flower, which first came to earth after the crucifixion, and showed me in its configuration the stripes of the whip, the crown of thorns, the spear, and three nails.

When the *ceibos*, the coral trees along the shores of the lagoon, were in bloom the banks turned red, with a rare touch of white from the clustered blossoms hanging in the heavy canopies of the luxurious old trees.

Contentment caused me to blossom also, and Michael's clothes lay unused in my trunk. I still wore britches when I rode, but more often I dressed in bright skirts like the other women and wore earrings made of shells and feather work, and combs in my hair carved from horn. Garzón said we were blindingly beautiful, like the birds and wild flowers I drew. He was leaving again soon, and it truly would be one of his final journeys he assured me.

"You have been saying that ever since we settled here. Meanwhile our house sits unfinished, twenty months after our wedding!"

"I am determined to have enough money put by that you will never know want again."

"We have more money and land than I ever dreamed of possessing. I want you at home enjoying it with me. If you were here more, perhaps—"

"I know how much you long for a child, Isabel." He put his arms around me. "One more journey and then I will never put out to sea again."

"I do not ask that. I ask only that you not make these journeys that take you away for so long. You forget that I grew up amongst sailors and their families. So many of the women I knew never found out if their men had died at sea or simply found a greener shore or a softer love than theirs."

"That you need never fear. There is no love comparable to yours, and no sea that could keep me from you. I would return to haunt you if I had to." He drew me to him and untied my hair ribbon. "And to make sure that you had not taken up with FitzGibbon in my absence."

"Now there's a thought!" I laughed. "At least Charlie is always here, and I do believe that his castle will be built long before you finish our house!"

We had just retired behind the partition when Orlando burst into the house.

"Cararé is back from Entre Ríos! He says that the Minuanes are coming!"

He had barely finished speaking when a deep tremor made its

way through the ground to our feet, and a sound reached us unlike anything I had ever heard, between a roar, a howl, and a chant, between a trumpet of pain and the visceral roar of some ancient monster.

Garzón reached for his gun. "The Minuán war cry!"

We ran out into the plaza and saw Charlie making his way swiftly up one of the ladders to the battlements, filling rapidly with men from the settlement. We followed him, and my heart gave a lurch as I looked out across the prairie. Hundreds of warriors, more Minuanes than I had believed existed, were thundering toward us, they, their spears and their horses decorated in white shells and feathers. As they reached the prickly pear barrier they rode round and round it like dervishes in a growing cloud of dust. It was like being in the eye of a storm. The horses' hooves pounded, spears glinted like bolts of lighting, and the bone fence began to shake, with a sound like hail falling on a brick roof.

The men in the towers and on the battlements seemed turned to stone, while below the horses danced and reared in their stalls, roosters crowed, and dogs howled. The fowl ran to and fro being trampled by the oxen, usually as placid as clods of earth, now being driven mad by the war cry. I hurried back to the plaza to assist the women and children in their efforts to keep the animals from injuring themselves. Suddenly, amid the noise from the Minuanes without and the animals within, a shot rang out. I looked up, but could see nothing clearly through the dust. I was choking with it, and ran to the well to soak my apron. I was washing my eyes, when I heard Father Manuel give a shout and hurl himself off the battlements into the plaza. I thought he must surely have broken his legs, but he leapt up like a cat and was across the plaza before I knew where he was bound. He scaled the ladder on the other side and fell on Charlie, taking his musket and hurling it over the fence before going for his throat. Along with everyone else, I stood frozen with surprise, and then all of us reacted at the same time. Garzón pulled Father Manuel off, and Charlie, pale with shock and gasping for breath, struggled to his feet. Cararé took Father Manuel in his arms and held him while Garzón led Charlie away.

I fully expected to see a hoard of Minuanes come tearing through the gate, but outside there was an eerie silence. I looked through an opening in the fence and saw that the vibrating, swirling circle outside had come to a silent halt. Only the horses' sides heaved, and feather head dresses stirred in the breeze. As if upon some silent command, the Minuanes looked up and met the eyes of the men on the battlements. For what seemed an eternity, they stared at one another. Then a small group made their way on foot through the prickly pear, crossed the ditch, and approached the body of a dead comrade lying by the gate. They returned him to his horse and rode slowly away, disappearing into the *monte* around the lagoon.

The battlements emptied and everyone found something to do restoring us to order, leaving Father Manuel alone with his grief and Химнэ Cararé.

I asked Garzón what had happened. Father Manuel, he said, had been searching for Yací among the riders when he heard Garzón shout Charlie's name. He turned, and there, on the opposite side of the plaza, he saw Charlie, raising his musket. Father Manuel pushed his way through the men crowding the platforms between the towers, calling out warnings to the Minuanes below, but it was impossible for them to hear him over the cries of their companions. Charlie fired, and a Minuán fell. Father Manuel had recognized him as Yací's brother, Abayubá.

"Why didn't they attack?"

"They were not arrayed for battle. Did you not notice their white feathers? I think they only meant to scare us."

"But why?"

"I don't know, Isabel."

Father Manuel had closed himself up with Cararé and refused to see anyone else. The following morning he left in search of Yací.

He began by visiting all their old meeting places. The stream by which they first spoke, the *cerro* where Yací had stood so proudly when he gave Father Manuel the hammock, and the cove where they had sat, fishing and teaching one another so many things, from the words for fish and teacher, to their deepest meanings.

There was no sign of Yací or of his clan.

We tripled the watch, men slept with muskets at hand, and scouts rode out at dawn and dusk to patrol the area, returning with nothing to report. As the days and then the weeks went by, life gradually returned to normal.

Father Manuel returned briefly to collect supplies, and then declared that he would search the entire Province if he had to. Charlie tried to see him, but Father Manuel would not open his door. Charlie banged on it and shouted, "I know that you can hear me! I fired only when I thought they were going to break down the gate! I didn't know about the white feathers! It was not my intention to kill anyone!"

No response came from within, and I took Charlie away, speaking useless words of comfort.

"It is important to me that you believe me, Isabel!"

"I do believe you."

"When I saw the Indians heading for the gate and fired, I fancied I was protecting you. Nothing else seemed to matter. You have been so kind to me. You are being kind now, when I least deserve it."

"Perhaps Father Manuel has not told you of his very personal interest in the Minuanes, of his friendship with one young man in particular."

"Why were they trying to frighten us if they're Father Manuel's friends?"

"I don't understand it either, Charlie. If he can find Yací perhaps he can explain it."

Chapter X

Work at the castle site resumed with increased vigor and before long the sight of trees being felled and the sounds of incessant hammering ringing across the lagoon became unbearable. I asked Garzón to accompany me to the ocean. I was anxious and confused about recent events, and needed to consider them in a place that never failed to bring me clarity and peace.

Orlando would not leave Zule, who was due to have a litter at any moment, and said that he would remain with Wimencaí and To Cararé. Recalling the last time we had left him, we questioned him closely about his decision. We thought it a very good sign when he became rather cross with us.

"I am not a baby any more!" he said. "And Cararé has already told me that he needs me to help him with the harvest."

By the time Garzón and I had crossed the wetlands and reached the palm groves a sense of freedom had come over us. It was the first time we had ever been entirely alone together, and we were unusually silent as we chose a camp site near a stream. I unpacked our sleeping rolls and blankets, and Garzón prepared his line and sat fishing by the stream. As soon as our meal was secured in a basket at the bottom of the stream, we headed for the ocean, leaving the horses in the shade of the palm trees, and walking hand in hand down to the beach, the sand hot on our bare soles. In the shelter of the dunes, we took off our clothes and raced to the water. We swam together as far as we dared, returning breathless to spread our quilt in the soft curves of the dunes.

We made love as if pleasure were something of our own invention, an ecstasy only we had ever known, finally falling exhausted side by side, reaching for our clay bottle, and drinking it dry. There was no racing this time as we made our way to the water, welcoming the waves that washed away sweat and sand, leaving only a feeling of completeness and satiety.

That evening we visited the highest rock formations, watching the gigantic plumes of spray reach for the peaks on which we stood, sending mist into the air around us. As the sun went down, we sat side by side before the spectacle of color unfolding in the sky. The ocean turned dark blue, straying clouds glowed pink and lavender, and the sun streaked the horizon red and orange.

We retired to our camp, ravenous, and Garzón started a fire while I salted the fish and washed fruit in the stream. Oblivious to my presence, dark *caraos* danced with open wings on the opposite shore, their courtship punctuated by graceful cries of *rau, rau!* directed at the flocks of black necked swans flying low over our heads. I filled our clay bottle and hung it from a tree limb where the cool night air could surround it. Resting on clay polished to the consistency of glass, the water would be icy cold by morning.

By nightfall we were wrapped in our light blankets, listening to the sounds of the *monte*. Crickets, frogs, an occasional bird call, the soft neighing of the horses, and now and again the cry of a jaguar.

I woke before Garzón did the following morning, and when I opened my eyes, there was Yací, sitting within reach of my hand, watching me. He looked less vital than before, as if some essential force had drained away from him.

"Atzaya wants you," he said.

"Is she ill?"

He shook his head and linked his fingers, holding out his arms and making a large circle.

"Have her pains begun?"

"No. But she wants you," he repeated.

I woke Garzón, and we wasted no time gathering our belongings and following Yací into the *monte*. Yací's clan were camped in a place so well hidden it was no wonder that Father Manuel had been unable to find them. Pits covered with stones concealed their cooking fires, and very little smoke emerged, lost in the air before it could rise above the trees to give away their whereabouts.

Atzaya and I stood for a long time with our arms around one another. So close was our embrace that I felt the child kick in her womb. She said nothing until Yací and Garzón had left us alone in her small shelter.

"What of the child you feared you were carrying?"

"There was no child. But Garzón and I are married."

"You asked him?"

"He asked me! And I accepted."

She reached into a basket and withdrew a small bag. "This is for you," she said. "Take some every day."

"What is it?"

"*Caá parí.* It encourages children to take their place in our wombs. Now," she said, "I want to tell you why I sent for you."

"Yací has changed."

She nodded. "His souls are lost. What he was sure of is uncertain now, and he misses his friend Manuel."

I told her about Charlie, and how he had not meant to kill Abayubá. I told her too, how Father Manuel had attacked him, and spoke of his grief and of his search.

After the receipt of his song, Atzaya said, Yací had planned to return to our settlement, taking her with him. On the day he had chosen for the visit, he woke early, filled his jaguar skin bag with cassava bread, and put on his pink feather leggings. A careless young man had died of snakebite in their village the week before, having neglected to dye and string the *ñandú* feathers that could have deceived the snake into spilling its venom before touching his leg, and Yací, who had always had a healthy respect for snakes, was making sure that his leggings were in good order. He had found their horses grazing nearby, and by the time he brought them back, Atzaya was ready.

"He asked me if I would ever leave him."

She had been surprised by such an unexpected question.

"Where would I go? I could no more leave him than I could shed my skin and grow a new one. It was I who worried that he would stay at the settlement and I would have to choose between him and my life here."

They had wondered what had brought about these sudden fears. They had loved each other since childhood, knew one another's every thought and impulse, were as closely mated as the pairs of swans flying over them as they rode. Yací had assured her that he would only consider remaining at the settlement if she stayed with him.

On their second day out, he took his *boleadoras* and went in search of food. They had seen deer, partridges and capybaras all around them as they traveled, and Yací was displeased when two hours later they still had nothing to cook over their fire. Yací and his stomach were both grumbling when he took a fish line from his pouch and went to sit by a stream. Nothing bit. Finally, Atzaya picked some wild berries and they made a meager meal out of them.

Dark clouds moved in to cover the sun and they could hear the rumble of distant thunder. They decided to make camp early. Atzaya pulled hides from their packs and Yací was preparing to cut some long branches he would strip and use for building a shelter, when his eyes fell on a strange shape under a tree. He and Atzaya approached it cautiously and moved aside the dead branches that covered it.

Atzaya pointed to a corner of the shelter as she told me this, and there I saw my own discarded hoops lying in a heap.

Yací had cut a few of the canvas strips and disengaged several of the bone sections to make a doorway, covering the resulting little tent with hides and creating a shelter in which he and Atzaya could spend the night.

Atzaya woke when Yací began to thrash in his sleep. The storm had passed and Atzaya could just see him in the moonlight. His movements were wild and threatened to bring the little tent down around them. Atzaya reached for him and Yací threw his arms around her, gasping for breath, and repeating over and over that he had had a dream.

In his dream, Atzaya had been holding their child. They were in an unfamiliar place, isolated from their people, and Father Manuel was talking to a group of outsiders who Yací sensed did not like what they were hearing. A monkey, larger than any Yací had ever seen, was sitting in a pit below Father Manuel, and he knew that it was somehow very important. Monkeys are rare beyond the River Uruguay. Only when heavy rains cause flooding to the north does a monkey sometimes get carried along in the current, usually in the branches of an uprooted tree. A ritual was about to take place connected with the monkey, and Father Manuel wanted to stop it. The others would not. Atzaya urged him to help her hide the child, and as they did so, the realization came to them that no matter where they hid him the gathered strangers would find him. They stood, staring in helpless terror at one another as Father Manuel appeared, carrying the bloody corpse of the monkey and weeping.

Certain that the dream was a warning that Yací should not return to the settlement, they waited for first light, gathered their belongings and started their return journey. Yací had been very quiet.

When they arrived back at their village it was to find a gathering of clans. More settlers, accompanied by Spanish soldiers, had been seen moving inland, and Atzaya's father, Calelián, had come across hundreds of cows stripped of their hides and left to rot in the sun. In itself, this was not an unusual sight. Whole herds were often slaughtered, but this was the third time that season that it had happened within the Minuanes' territory. Kurupí, the protector of animals, would surely be enraged now.

That night, the shamans wore ceremonial attire. Their long deerskin capes touched the ground, and the leg bones of jaguars, along with necklaces made of shells and carved roots, hung around their necks. Their heads were brilliant with crests of parrot, flamingo, and swan feathers. They had fasted, and received a vision. In it, the Earth Mother had walked with her most powerful spirit, the jaguar, and signaled for the shamans to follow. She took them to the edge of the world and showed them another world, like a rotten corpse, alive with maggots.

The Earth Mother told the shamans that the people of this other world reproduced without thought, enlarging their numbers even when their gods could not supply food enough to feed them. These hungry people then overran the world of the Minuanes, the Charrúa, the Chaná, the Guaraní, and all the people of the anaconda and the jaguar, crowding them out and scaring away the animals and the spirits that protect them.

The elders had advised moving to the *cerros*, but Abayubá had said that the warriors must prepare their weapons, and light the bonfires to summon the Charrúa to help them drive the settlers away. "We've already given them the ocean! Are we to give them the plains as well and become hill people?"

The elders talked all night before reaching a compromise. They would neither retreat to the *cerros* nor attack. They would issue a warning, a scare designed to allow settlers to see the Minuánes' numbers and understand that they and their ways were not welcome. Then, if the settlers did not return to Montevideo, the Minuánes would attack. In deference to the place where one of them had received his *porahei*, they had visited our settlement first.

"Abayubá and some other warriors weren't satisfied, but they couldn't go against the whole tribe. To show their unhappiness with the decision, they wore one colored feather among the white, and they made a very powerful offering to leave at the gate, to serve as a further warning."

"What was it, Atzaya?"

"The women were not allowed to know, but Abayubá's wife said it contained several skins."

"Like the ones they take in battle?"

She nodded. "When Abayubá went to the gate and was shot, the elders were not surprised. He had gone against their counsel."

"Is that why they didn't reciprocate and attack us?"

"Yes, they had not prepared themselves for battle," Atzaya explained.

Evil can result from initiating a conflict without the necessary rituals, so they had picked up Abayubá's body, and withdrawn to perform the funeral rites and consider their future.

While Abayubá's wife put her hand on the sacrificial block, offering a joint from one of her fingers to her dead husband, the shaman had prepared the splinters Yací and his father would use during their sacrifice.

"I offered Yací *chicha*, but he refused."

He had wanted no relief as the shaman began inserting the splinters above his wrists, up his arms and across his back. Again, Atzaya had offered *chicha* and again Yací had refused it.

The singing and dancing had lasted well into the night, and then Yací's father and Yací left the camp to stand in the pits they had dug to be closer to the Mother. They spent the night there, mourning Abayubá and sending his souls on their journey to the world of the dead. Atzaya had waited nearby, and when Yací was ready, she had led him back to their shelter, removed the splinters, and washed his wounds.

"He's haunted by the memory of his dream. It was a warning and he interpreted it wrongly, thinking it was about me and the child. He thinks that if he had meditated more on it and sought counsel, instead of believing the first interpretation that came to him, Abayubá might still be alive." She got up. "I want you to tell him what you told me."

A spasm of pain passed over her face and she reached for support. I put my hands on her belly. Her labor had begun, and all thought of a conversation with Yací vanished.

She asked that I remain with her, and for several hours I sat by her while other women came and went, giving advice, relating their own birth stories, offering food.

When her waters broke and the pains began in earnest, Yací returned, and Atzaya squatted by a tall stake in the center of her house. To the stake was tied a thick leather thong shaped like a figure eight, which she wound round her wrists, holding the leather tightly in her hands. Yací sat behind her, his legs under her buttocks, supporting her back. When Atzaya's womb was active, Yací sat very still, but as soon as her breathing quieted, he either rubbed her belly with strong, downward strokes, or picked her up from behind and tossed her gently in the air until labor began again.

I wiped her face, fanned her, and fed her fruit, and as the evening progressed we saw the dark, moist crown of the baby's head appear between Atzaya's legs.

Not long afterwards, her daughter's long, slender little body slipped out of her, twitching with sudden freedom, and Atzaya fell back onto the *aguará* fox pelts covering the ground beneath her. Yací picked up the child, caressing and soothing her. He washed her face, and the baby opened her eyes, startling us with the sudden midnight of her gaze. He lifted her onto Atzaya's breast and waited for the placenta to be delivered. When the cord stopped beating, Yací took his knife and severed it, leaving me to tie it while he cut a small piece of the afterbirth to feed to Atzaya later as an aid to healing. The rest he wrapped in a piece of tapir skin and set it apart for burying.

I took a piece of soft leather and washed her body, and Yací replaced the moist pelts on which she lay with dry, soft jaguar skins. Atzaya was trembling and weak, so Yací lay down by her side and held her, the child lying quietly between them. Together they examined her closely, admiring her long fingers, her nails like tiny sea shells, and her hair the color of black swan's down. Atzaya began to cry. There was nothing about the child to worry her, she said. No light skin, no brown eyes, no fair hair. She was as like Yací as Atzaya could have hoped. She offered the baby her breast and she sucked hungrily, her tiny fingers closing around Atzaya's thumb as Yací sat up and reached for his musical arc. He had made it from the trunk of a palm tree. A piece of *caraguatá* leaf covered the mouth of the hollow base, where the instrument's only string, woven from hairs taken from his horse's tail, was attached. In his left hand Yací held the stem of the arc, the other end he placed in his mouth after moistening a small, straight wand with saliva. As the string began to vibrate, Yací added his own voice to the sounds that emerged.

A murmur reached us from outside. The song had communicated the successful birth of a daughter, and the women had returned with thistle tea to ensure that Atzaya's milk descended quickly to fatten the child. While she received them and drank the tea, Yací took the baby outside for her dedication to Zobá, the spirit of the moon.

~

Cararé met us at the gates to the settlement. "Father Manuel is back. You must prepare yourselves. He is changed."

He had always been lean, but now he was gaunt, his eyes sunk in two dark rings of shadow, the lines on his face etched more deeply than before. The most startling change in him was that his hair had turned almost entirely white.

I told him everything I had learned from Atzaya. "She knows what is best for Yací and she will guide him back to your friendship, I know it."

Garzón left a week later, but not before riding to the Fortress of San Miguel and bringing a dozen soldiers back with him. It pained him to see the settlement he had envisioned as an oasis of peace guarded by Portuguese soldiers, but it was the only way he could conciliate his fears for our safety with his need to return to Ireland to close out his business there. It would be his last trip, and his pack mule would be loaded with gifts for Mary and her parents. Letters, drawings of my new home, three pairs of horse-hide boots, a leather waistcoat for Mr. O'Neill, embroidered ribbons, lace as fine as a spider's web.

As a parting gift to me, Garzón brought me an orphaned wild foal to mother. She was dark brown, with one white stocking and a single splash of white on her rump. Garzón had rescued her from the *cimarrones*, and she kicked and whinnied in protest when I tried to tend her wounds. This, he said, was my opportunity to prove that mares need not be bred only for slaughter. Neither Indians nor *camiluchos* would ride them, so mare hides were tanned, their grease used for lighting lamps, their tongues sold as delicacies. Mare bones and hair were exported, and their knuckle bones became part of a gambling game called *taba*.

I named the colt Chalona, the Charrúa word for girl, and put her in a corral with mothers and their foals. I visited her every day until she ate out of my hand. Her wounds were superficial and healed well untended. Soon, she was following me everywhere, even inside the house, where Charlie found her one day and chased her out, complaining that Orlando and I had turned our house into a menagerie. Zule had chosen to have her pups under Orlando's bed and all five of them romped at our feet, dragging at my skirt and chasing my broom. It was worth every annoyance and discomfort just to hear Orlando laugh. With the puppies swarming all over him, pulling at his clothes and licking his face, Orlando laughed with the pure joy of childhood, a sound I had heard from him all too rarely.

Two months passed without any signs of my monthly flow and I tried not to allow myself to become too hopeful. I drank my daily infusion of *caá parí*, took particular care to engage in no strenuous activities, and as the end of my third month drew near, waited anxiously for signs that I would miscarry. The days, and then the weeks went by, and finally as the fourth month of my pregnancy drew to a close I was unable to contain myself any longer and shared my news with

Orlando. We were singing and dancing when Wimencaí came to our door accompanied by Cararé.

Orlando threw his arms around them. "I am going to have a brother!"

"Bless me, dear friends!"

Wimencaí and Cararé stood frozen for a moment and then Wimencaí buried her face in Cararé's shoulder and burst into tears. Thinking I had been insensitive in sharing my news so suddenly and without any consideration for her I began to apologize, but she shook her head and cried all the harder. Still holding her close to his side, Cararé ushered us back into the house. He helped Wimencaí to a chair and turned to face me.

"You know that *Don* Carlos has messengers traveling back and forth on business for him. They have brought bad news this time."

Two sailors had come ashore off the coast of Brazil, suffering from terrible, disfiguring burns. They carried a tale of fire and shipwreck, how long ago they were uncertain, having lost all track of time floating tied to a mast until it came within sight of the passing vessel that had rescued them. They owed their lives to their Captain, who fought to save those wounded in the explosion that caused the fire. He was last seen lowering the ship's surgeon into the water before the ship sank, leaving debris and bodies scattered wide upon the waters. The sunken ship was the *Isabelita* and the men knew of no other survivors.

~

As June of 1750 came and went, I sat with my big belly and painted until my arms ached and the colors blurred. My art took on an ethereal quality, with birds hidden in the bark of trees, and forms resembling unborn children floating in the waters of the lagoon. Whenever I sat there I could conjure Garzón's presence so vividly I saw him, lying in the palm groves with his arms open to the sky while animals shook themselves, and the palm trees waved their parasol of leaves in the breeze, like so many giantesses greeting one another at the dawn of a new day.

I missed his smile, and the warmth of his voice. I missed his hands, which I desired whether they were wrapping my hair around his wrists, hoisting a sail, or gentling a horse. But most of all I missed his eyes in which I had felt myself to be the most beautiful and accomplished woman in the world.

I don't know what I would have done without Orlando. He was as grieved as I, yet it was he who saw to it that we ate the food delivered every day to our door, he who shook out the rugs and pumped water from the well, he who brushed my hair, and tidied our house every morning and night. It was only when I found him trying to sew the baby clothes that had been lying cut and waiting for my needle, that I was able to release my sorrow. I sobbed and Orlando sobbed with me, until Zule, agitated by our distress, licked away our tears.

Whenever Charlie's messengers arrived from Montevideo or from the Missions, I could not stifle the hope that they came with news of Garzón, that by some miracle he had survived and sent word that he was alive and on his way home. Charlie went himself to Brazil to see what he could learn about the wreck, and wrote often, always hopeful that he was on the trail of information that would help him uncover something that would pinpoint where the ship had gone down.

In spite of the cool weather, Wimencaí insisted that Orlando and I go out every day, taking us for long rides across the open plains. We avoided the slaughtering huts and instead visited the matted, rolling moors where flocks of sheep were scattered, like graying snow on the windy hillsides.

"You have an affinity for my people, Isabel," she said one day, after I chose a local willow, the *sauce criollo* to sit under.

"If by that you mean yourself, Wimencaí, you are quite right."

"I meant the willows. They are people too, you know, turned to trees by Ñeambiú, who was forbidden to love a man from an enemy tribe. She ran away, and her father found her in the *montes* of Iguazú, where she had turned herself into a statue. Her father was sad, for he loved his daughter. He asked the shaman for help, and the shaman whispered to Ñeambiú that the man she loved was dead."

I turned away, wondering why of all the stories she could have told me, Wimencaí had chosen this one.

"Her sorrow brought her back to life, but in her fury at the news she turned them all into willows and herself into a bird. You've heard her I'm sure, calling to her lover in the night."

"The *urutau*?" Orlando asked.

Wimencaí nodded.

"I heard her the first night I ever slept in the *monte*," I said, remembering the haunting cries that had woken me with a start, "but I've never seen her."

"No one has ever seen her. She is a ghost bird. Something you must not become once your grieving is over."

My grieving would never be over. I would smile, even laugh again no doubt, my heart would lift and my spirits soar, desire would visit me, longings and cravings overcome me, but under it all would lie that hollow, empty place Garzón and I had filled together, and like the *uru* I would mourn in the darkness where none could see me.

When it was too cold and windy to go roaming with Wimencaí, Orlando and I stayed home, shelling peas and snapping beans, squatting on the packed earth floor of Wimencaí's house, or tending the physic garden where the scent of mint, sweet marjoram, and rosemary, hung in the air with the sureness of Wimencaí's healing.

Father Manuel and I needed each other most particularly then. Yací had not contacted him, and Father Manuel seemed lost in some painful trance, out of which he emerged only rarely in the evenings when we sat together. He refused to acknowledge Charlie's efforts to make peace with him by sending him a telescope and a printing press, both transported at great trouble and expense.

Tentatively, like two moths flirting with a candle flame, he and I were able to approach our losses and talk to one another about them. We discovered that grief, being skilled at ambush, surprised us at unexpected moments.

Father Manuel would wake and think what a fine day it was to meet Yací by the lagoon, or reach for his tools and remember the deftness of Yací's hands. He would have to remind himself that it was Yací's trust in him, not Yací himself, that was dead. He tried to believe as I did, that Yací would return one day, or allow Father Manuel to find him, and their friendship would be salvaged.

I would see the jasmine flowering by my door, Chalona would look up expectantly when I whistled, Zule would sniff Garzón's poncho, still hanging by the door where he had left it, and the void in the world created by his absence opened and my breath caught painfully, making me believe that unless I could open my eyes and see him again it would not be possible for me to face another day.

I could not bear it when it rained because then he would have run home to dry himself by the fire, using the weather as an excuse to draw the curtains and lure me to bed. Sunshine hurt because on sunny days he loaded the canoe and took me to the beach on the other side of the lagoon, where we could swim and dive until our skin puckered, and joke about being old before our time.

Then Father Manuel would ask me to draw one of the plants he had begun to catalogue, Orlando's coat would need patching, or the child in my womb stirred, and somehow the vacuum into which I had fallen closed, and air returned to fill my lungs with promise.

My old midwife's journal became a close companion, the recipient of confidences and outpourings of grief I didn't want even Orlando to witness. I hid it, with its assortment of entries and drawings, in the false bottom of my old trunk, under the dress I bought in Montevideo, and by the tiny seagull Garzón had given me.

Everyone at the settlement surrounded me with care. They gathered in the evenings to play and sing, and at first, when I wanted to do nothing for myself, they helped Orlando to clean the house, and cooked our meals. They took it for granted that we would do these things for one another, and every so often a woman asked if I remembered when the loss of a parent, or a husband, or worst of all, a child, had rendered her incapable of anything but sorrow and the community had closed about her like the shielding, generous wings of a poncho.

Charlie came home, and offered to take me to nearby Buenos Aires for a visit if I wished, and I considered it. Buenos Aires, being free of memories of Garzón, appeared inviting for a while, until I realized that I had tried that already, by going to places we had not visited together. "He was never here," I would think, and so even his absence became a presence, and I would stand shafted with the pain of it. I could not forget him, and as long as there was memory there would be this empty, stabbing sensation, this darkness I fell into at night and woke to in the morning.

When the setting sun shimmered over the jungle hugging the lagoon, Orlando and I attended evening Benediction in the church and often joined Father Manuel afterwards for dinner, taking our chairs outside after the meal to sit under the stars. Wimencaí would sort through her herbs, while螺araré tuned and played his harp.

"I see that our tree is doing well, Father," I said one day, fingering the cool leaves of the tree growing by his door. When I had told him of my intention of planting a tree in the soil Garzón brought from my family's gravesite, Father Manuel had remembered the little linen bag of seeds he had taken from Brother Andrés' trunk and which had lain in a drawer ever since. With Orlando's help, the two of us had dug a hole together, scattered the soil and the seeds in it, and watered it until we were rewarded with the sight of a small green shoot.

"Planting Brother Andrés' seeds in Irish soil was an act of pure faith! I wondered if they would even sprout after all these years."

"I knew they would," Orlando said, his Spanish now as fluent and precise as it had once been tentative and random. "The little ones told me."

"What little ones?" I asked him.

"The colorful little spirits."

Father Manuel sat down rather suddenly. Then he laughed his old, rich, throaty laugh, sprang up, took Orlando's hands, and performed a little dance with him around the tiny tree.

Wimencaí's eyes filled with tears when she saw her old friend playful again, and Cararé took up his harp and accompanied the dancers until they collapsed breathlessly on the steps.

"A fitting way to commemorate our twenty years of marriage!" Cararé said.

It was not possible, Father Manuel declared! Wimencaí did not look a day older than fifteen, the age she had been when he had brought Cararé with him from Paraguay.

Every year, he explained to Orlando and me, all the young women in the Missions who had turned fifteen were paired with young men of seventeen and married, and Father Herrán had already chosen a bridegroom for Wimencaí.

"But when I saw Cararé I said I would marry no one but him!"

"Poor Father Herrán had no idea how to cope with such subversion," Father Manuel laughed.

"The first thing I saw when I arrived at Santa Marta," Cararé said, "was Wimencaí! I didn't know if what I was seeing before me was a rainbow or an orchid or a bird, or all three combined. I had never seen so many colors on one person. And her hair! It hung at her back like a black sea. I would have died if she had not married me, and I almost died when she did!"

"What was the other bridegroom like, Wimencaí?" I asked.

"Oh, he was handsome, hard working, charming..."

"He had a big nose and an ever bigger opinion of himself!" Cararé said.

"Will I get married when I'm seventeen?" Orlando asked.

"Of course you will!" we assured him.

"And will my bride be as beautiful as Wimencaí?"

Wimencaí kissed him on both cheeks. "She will be as lovely as a flower and as gentle as a prayer!"

Until the day Wimencaí invited me to accompany her to the *quilombo*, a community of escaped slaves Garzón had sheltered in our *montes* before he left, I had not given them a thought, so absorbed had I been with my pregnancy and with my grief. Now I learned that they were a small group, all escaped from the same master.

"Has he not come after them?" I asked.

"He's dead."

From the way Wimencaí busied herself packing her basket with clean cloths and little bags of herbs, I gathered that it would be best not to ask how he had died.

"One of the women has sent for me. Will you assist me?" she asked.

"Yes."

We landed on the sandy shore beyond the caves, carrying Wimencaí's basket and a bag with supplies for the inhabitants. The half dozen small huts, built of leather, mud, and thatch, were in the heart of the surrounding *monte*, a good half hour's walk from the beach. Biting insects were prolific that year and I was glad to arrive at the small clearing where the smoke from the fires kept them at bay.

The woman Wimencaí was there to attend placed her hands protectively on her belly when she saw me, and I noticed that her wrists were deeply scarred. She backed away, and Wimencaí lay a reassuring hand on her arm.

The woman's eyes filled with angry tears. "I don't want her," she said, pointing at me, "to touch the child!"

"Please don't fear me."

"I would be mad not to fear you." She was about to say more when her labor intensified, and the man who had been standing quietly behind her put his arms around her and led her away.

"Shall I leave, Wimencaí?"

Wimencaí shook her head. "No, but don't come in."

I squatted by the adobe wall of the hut, wishing I had stayed at home. It was cold and my back ached. "It is very quiet in there," I said, gesturing over my shoulder into the hut and addressing an old woman sitting nearby.

"If Zulema did not cry out when she was branded, labor will not draw her voice."

"Branded? For cattle thieving?"

"From the time she could walk, Zulema vowed she would escape. So she grew up in leg irons. Her ankles are as twisted as these *coronillas*." She picked up a piece of firewood and ran her gnarled fingers over it. "Every time she ran, they whipped her. The last time, they branded her as well, with an F, for *Fugida*. But she is not afraid for herself. Her fear is for her child. She has lost one already. They took him away from her when he had just begun to walk and sold him."

"No wonder she fears me."

We sat together until from within the house the cry of a new life pierced the stillness of evening, and the old woman smiled a toothless smile. Moments later, the man who had been with Zulema emerged holding a naked baby, his dark skin a gift of ebony against the green of the surrounding jungle. The man held the child high, opened wide his throat, and cried in triumph to the skies.

"*¡Libre! ¡Libre! ¡ Libre!*"

The child, unaware that he could be anything but free, howled in protest at this treatment, and the man, laughing happily, went back inside.

I could not resist the temptation to move aside the hide that covered the entrance and steal a glance in at the door. Wimencaí was washing her hands in a leather bucket, and Zulema lay on a bed of straw on the floor. She opened her blouse and reached up her arms for her newborn child. "Give him to me!" The branded F for fugitive gleamed on her bare breast and it seemed to me that she bore the scar with as much pride as any soldier wore his medals.

At that moment, my own child stirred, and I placed my hands on my belly, thinking that if Zulema could bear so much and still rejoice in giving birth, then surely so could I.

~

Without informing me, Charlie sent a letter to *Don* Ernesto requesting that he leave his duties in Montevideo to his apprentice and pay him the favor of a visit. He mentioned nothing about my condition, and *Don* Ernesto assumed that he was being invited, not in his professional capacity, but as a guest.

Being a man of excellent qualities but unquestionably vain about his appearance, the good doctor decided to outfit himself in a manner he deemed appropriate for a stay at the Province's only castle. Although unfinished, stories already proliferated about its magnificence. Rumor had it that the floors were of solid gold and the furnishings studded with precious stones. Those who traveled made it a point to return to Montevideo with increasingly fantastic stories to add to the fable of the mad Irishman's castle, and Charlie did nothing to dispel them.

Don Ernesto therefore hired a wagon large enough to accommodate his voluminous dressing case, containing an assorted wardrobe he had not had many occasions to display since moving to Montevideo.

Charlie had sent a troop of outriders to accompany the doctor, and he departed in as much splendor as it was possible to muster when riding in a *carreta*. All of this was extremely gratifying to *Don* Ernesto, who felt not only protected but well cared for, since the *camiluchos* did the hunting, prepared the food, and set up camp each night.

He arrived expecting to find himself one of several guests invited to inaugurate the castle. Wimencaí and Father Manuel, who were the first to greet him, disabused him of this impression.

I was extremely fond of *Don* Ernesto and glad I was not present to watch his face fall as he realized that not only were there to be no balls or hunting parties, but he had been invited as a professional man, not as a distinguished guest.

"Whatever possessed Mr. FitzGibbon to send for me?"

"He wants Isabel to have the best care," Wimencaí told him.

Don Ernesto's features were convulsed for a few moments while he wiped his spectacles. "That she had already," he said, looking fondly at Wimencaí.

When he came to see me I was at work on a painting, an angry rendition of a boat assailed by waves in the form of horses with frothing mouths and fiery eyes. I had not intended to show it to anyone, and didn't welcome *Don* Ernesto's interest in it. I threw a cloth over the canvas and was grateful when Wimencaí asked whether I had known that Charlie had sent for *Don* Ernesto to attend me. I assured her I had not, imagining that no one would attend me during my labor but her. Not, I hastened to assure *Don* Ernesto, that I didn't have the utmost confidence in him, it had simply not occurred to me to send for him when Wimencaí was so near at hand.

"I understand perfectly," he said, his child-like face a picture of disappointment. "I shall pay my respects to Mr. FitzGibbon and leave at once."

Orlando, having heard of the doctor's arrival, burst in the door at that moment and threw himself at *Don* Ernesto, nearly knocking him off his feet.

"Who is this?" *Don* Ernesto said, adjusting his spectacles and staring at Orlando. "A new friend of Wimencaí's?"

"I am Orlando!"

"Impossible! The Orlando I knew was a child! You are a tall, handsome young man! Much too grown up for this." From his pocket *Don* Ernesto withdrew a little clay flute shaped like an egret.

Orlando glowed with pleasure and began at once to play his favorite tunes.

Wimencaí and I told *Don* Ernesto that we wouldn't hear of him leaving us. He had been traveling for three weeks, and the least he could do was to give us the pleasure of his company until the end of the year. He admitted to having brought his elegiac poem with him, hoping to find a few moments of leisure to devote to the work. "I would deem it an honor if all of you would read it. It would benefit greatly from illustration, and having seen this painting, *Doña* Isabel," he said, approaching the canvas once more, "I ask you most particularly to consider this as you read."

Wimencaí declined the pleasure of reading the work, saying she had no appreciation for poetry, but Father Manuel and I accepted with enthusiasm.

The poem was written in archaic Spanish, and Father Manuel's help was essential to me in deciphering it. *Don* Ernesto evoked history and legend masterfully in his poem, and before long I had prepared several sketches. From the poem I had learned that before people knew their value, diamonds were used in Brazil as markers in games of cards, and that later it was these Brazilian diamonds that had bought from the Vatican the title of *Rey Fidelissimo* for the King of Portugal.

The first drawing I put before *Don* Ernesto was irreverent, and showed men casting their diamonds on a table under which women and children writhed in chains. Above them hovered the Pope, one jeweled hand covering his right eye, his left cast on the glittering stones. *Don* Ernesto was nonplussed and in his nervousness moved the sketch aside and uncovered my rendition of the Nayarit Mountains, where as his poem revealed, the Lord of the Deer raised the newborn sun on his antlers. The Andean sirens Quesintuú and Umantuú were born of the waters of Lake Titicaca as a result, and devoted themselves to making love to the god of light and fire. In my sketch, the two sirens reveled in naked abandon while tongues of flame sent them into ecstasies.

Beads of perspiration broke out on *Don* Ernesto's brow and he covered the sketches hastily with his handkerchief, assuring Father Manuel that in asking me to illustrate his poem he had had no intention of leading me astray.

Father Manuel and I exchanged a look, and for the first time in many months, laughed whole heartedly. I threw my arms around *Don* Ernesto and thanked him. "See! Your visit has done us good already! And I promise you some chaste drawings for your poem, none of which you need feel any obligation to use!"

I had been most taken, I told him, by the story of Caupolicán, the Chief of the Araucanian Indians who in spite of having been blinded in one eye continued defending the lands beyond the Andes from the Spanish. I thought Caupolicán a most fitting name for our settlement, and that night when *Don* Ernesto and I dined at the half finished castle, I suggested it. Charlie said that he would order an arch made with the name *Caupolicán* on it, to rest on the pillars over our gates. He then moved on to his favorite topic, the rooms he was having prepared for me at the castle.

"I cannot allow Isabel to move into your home, *Don* Carlos. It would be most improper."

"I was not aware that your permission was necessary, *Don* Ernesto," Charlie said, a palpable coldness in his voice.

Don Ernesto was not intimidated. "Isabel is my friend. Friends protect one another from committing improprieties."

"I resent the implication. I have invited Isabel to bring a maid with her, a nurse for the baby, any companion she chooses, and to make the castle her own. It's only fitting. Here we are, fellow countrymen in a strange land, and business partners. We should help one another in times of need, don't you agree?"

"Charlie has been most kind, *Don* Ernesto. He has had a cradle carved, and he himself has made little horses with the most delicate leather saddles and reins, and a tiny wagon for the baby to play with."

Don Ernesto was unmoved. He agreed that Charlie's offer was a kind one and he did not doubt his generosity or his desire to serve me, but if I ever took up residence in the castle he would insist on finding an appropriate chaperone for me himself. Clearly thinking that this had put an end to the matter, he changed the subject by asking if Charlie had heard of a presentation made recently to the Royal Society in London by a Benjamin Robins, regarding the physics of a spinning projectile. It was predicted that before the century was out Englishmen would be flying around the globe.

"If it is left up to English physicists they will devise a means of projecting their cannon balls long before they turn their minds to anything as useful as transporting one another."

Don Ernesto gamely changed the subject again, telling us that King Ferdinand of Spain had acknowledged the growing importance of his southern colonies by creating the position of Governor of Montevideo. The Governor was to represent Ferdinand as head of the armed forces stationed in the city, and —槨Cararé had been proud to inform him — as Protector of the Indians.

"Does Undefined Cararé still maintain that the King will not forget his loyal Catholic soldiers?" Charlie asked.

"Cararé would sooner face death that believe ill of the King," I answered.

"He is in for a rude awakening!"

Don Ernesto could not have agreed with Charlie more, but the question of my move to the castle had created an antagonism between them that led *Don* Ernesto to defend his king. The evening ended with the two men bidding one another a frosty good night.

Later, *Don* Ernesto confided to Father Manuel that he wished Charlie at the furthest Antipodes.

~

Dawn was streaking the sky when my labor began. Soon my arms would be full and my womb empty. My breasts tingled as I thought of the child who would pull at them, and at that moment I knew that he would be a boy. My longing for Garzón had never been greater, but I could not succumb to it. To face the ordeal ahead of me, I had to marshal every ounce of physical and emotional strength I possessed.

Orlando woke as I was opening the chest in which we had placed the baby's clothes, and he and Zule came to stand by me as I reached in to touch the tiny, waiting garments. Orlando placed a shawl around my shoulders, and between my still gentle contractions, we made our way to Wimencaí's house. In the weeks since *Don* Ernesto's arrival we had discussed what we would do, and Wimencaí's eyes were serious as she asked me once more if I was sure of what I wanted. I nodded, and Wimencaí sent a messenger ahead to alert the inhabitants of the *quilombo* that she and I were on our way.

Cararé put the basket containing Wimencaí's store of herbs and implements into a wagon, and we drove slowly out of the settlement. The sky was overcast, and a chill wind blew in our faces as we descended to the lagoon. By the time I boarded the canoe, my contractions were coming faster than I had expected, and I gripped the sides trying not to cry out as Wimencaí and Cararé paddled rapidly across the choppy waters, leaving Orlando and Zule on the shore. Orlando knew that he was to wait with *Don* Ernesto, and he made his way back up the banks of the lagoon, leaning more heavily than usual on Zule's harness. When he reached the top, he stopped, and took out the paper I had folded and put in his pocket.

You are not to worry. I will be back soon with a brother for you! I am counting on you to teach him to read and write and ride. As soon as he is old enough we will swim together and play with Zule. You and I have been all in all to one another, and my love for you will never change.

We were well out on the lagoon when Orlando turned and waved to me, a big, happy wave, as if his heart felt lighter.

Our walk up the steep grade from the beach and through the *monte* was not an easy one and I was thankful for Cararé's strong arm around me. Seeing Zulema watching me from one of the huts when we arrived, I disengaged myself from Cararé and walked with as straight a back as I could manage toward the tiny hut that had been prepared for me. There was a pile of straw in one corner and the skull of a bull in the other. Bare feet had worn the earth floor smooth, and the one small window had a cloth nailed over it through which the wind pursued us.

Cararé brought a fresh supply of wood for the fire, and Wimencaí unrolled her blankets, clean and fresh smelling from the little bags of dried flower petals she stored among them.

Between contractions, she and I walked back and forth in the tiny space, until time held no meaning for me. I was in a world of my own, neither knowing nor caring where my body was or what my surroundings. The fire made the hut too warm and Wimencaí pulled back the hide covering the entrance until the rain blew in and she was forced to close it. Heavy gray clouds moved in and now and again I heard the clap of distant thunder. For a brief moment I slept, and dreamed that the waves of pain were *cimarrones* eating me alive, and that Garzón was there, pulling them away. I woke with a start and called for Wimencaí. It was the last thing I consciously remembered before my waters broke, and until I felt a relief so all consuming I never wanted it to end, and wept with wonder at the familiar eyes of a baby boy, looking up at me as if he knew my every thought already. I held him to my breast and he sucked strongly, causing my contractions to begin again. I barely noticed.

From a pot of boiling water Wimencaí withdrew a leather thong and a knife. "The cord has stopped beating. It is time to sever his bonds with your body and make him a son of the earth."

Wimencaí assisted me in cutting and tying the cord, reminding me that I had yet to pass the afterbirth, but I was too absorbed in the miracle I had created to heed her, and she went to the fire and dropped some *macaguaá caá* leaves into the water laced with vinegar that boiled there. Not long after the smell reached my nostrils the afterbirth followed and Wimencaí cut several strips of placenta, mixed them with wild onions, garlic and rice, and made me a stew to heal my womb and stop the bleeding. The remains of the afterbirth she placed in a small hide bag for burial later. As I watched her I thought of the baby whose afterbirth I had fed to starving dogs. He would have been four years old this last Irish winter.

Holding Sebastian's fist warm in mine, I emerged from the hut several hours later to find the inhabitants of the little settlement gathered to congratulate me. Round my neck they hung a shell necklace, and on my head they placed a garland of feathers. The old woman who had kept me company the last time I had come, had made a tiny leather waistcoat, and once more she grinned her toothless smile as she handed me the gift.

"Tell Mister Charlie that it is made from the only hide we didn't leave whole."

"I doubt that he noticed."

"Oh, Mister Charlie noticed, of that you can be sure. Nothing escapes him. He has already been up here to tell us that in future when we need leather we're to take a whole hide and not leave remnants hanging on his fences."

I glanced round to see if Zulema was among the well wishers. There was no sign of her, and I followed Wimencaí and Cararé toward the waiting canoe, ducking now and again to avoid the overhanging branches, heavy with the recent rain.

Just as we were about to leave the *monte* and descend to the beach, a figure emerged from among the trees. It was Zulema, her baby tied to her back, his little head nestled against one shoulder, an arm flung sleepily over the other. A tiny bracelet circled his wrist. Zulema stepped up to us and thrust a small bundle into my hands. "Our sons were born in the same village. Among my people that makes them brothers." She disappeared before I could speak.

"What did she give you?" Wimencaí asked.

Inside the little leather pouch I found a band of iron, twin to the one Zulema's baby wore. Wimencaí told me what they were made of. Born free, Zulema's son would never wear irons, but Zulema would not let him forget that his mother once had, and that many of his people still did. The bracelets had been made of the irons Zulema herself had worn. I took Sebastian's tiny hand and slipped the iron onto his wrist, thinking as I did so how pleased Garzón would have been with such a gift. Throughout my labor I had felt his presence strongly. Now he vanished, as suddenly and as completely as if the universe had swallowed him. Without the weight of Sebastian in my arms to keep me rooted to the ground, the next gust of wind would have scattered me into a million tiny pieces.

Nearly a year in the making, Charlie's castle was almost finished and towered over our landscape, the bricks glowing warm and red in the sun, and the stones glistening gray and cool when it rained. The wide staircase curved gracefully from the upper floors in its long sweep to the great hall, the only place where wood had been lavishly used. White jasmines and purple and red bougainvillea flowered in the courtyard; pink and yellow roses were planted round the eight columns that surrounded it, and water lilies bloomed in a small pond in the center, where, Charlie said, there would soon be fish.

Whenever he went to Montevideo or to Buenos Aires he was treated with awe. Even the wealthiest of the men who came from Spain and Portugal to seek a new life in our colonies, did not live in, and in their wildest dreams never thought of building, a castle in the wilderness. It was a masterful stroke of genius on Charlie's part, and it established him as the preeminent nobleman in the region.

He now owned two ships, and they continued to ferry hides, amethysts, furs and arms to Ireland, where according to Mary O'Neill he was fast becoming one of the major financers of the Irish cause, keeping the fires of independence hot and burning. She wrote to tell me that the aurora borealis was so immense and stained the sky so deep a scarlet they thought Cork was on fire. Instead, it was under water, four to five feet deep on Dunscombe's Marsh, and three in the center of the city. It put me in mind of the flood we experienced when Mary and I were six or seven years old, a trial for our father's, a thrill for us, since we had to go from house to house by boat, which we thought far more exciting than walking.

The worst of the summer heat was behind us and intoxicatingly sweet perfumes blew across the flowering prairies and from the canopied *montes*. Everywhere I looked I saw festive and riotous colors, and my paintings resembled pictures executed by a child run amok with a paint box. It was difficult to work at summer's end. The intense heat had hung for weeks like a shimmering crown over the horizon, sapping me of energy, and when the welcome breezes began to blow, bringing memories of the ocean to haunt me, I found myself stopping in my tracks to breathe the cool air, imagining the taste of salt and of Garzón's skin upon my tongue. For the first time since his disappearance, I longed to visit the beach again and rediscover that elusive self that emerged whenever I was by the ocean.

The soldiers had long since returned to San Miguel, their pockets jingling with gold, and leading a string of mules loaded with *mate*. Settlers continued to move in around us, and a small fort was being built to protect them at the foot of the range of hills lying a few miles inland from Punta Colorada. When Charlie discovered that one of the new settlers was a young Irishman, he invited him to the castle for a visit. Patrick too had been a part of those working to free Ireland from English rule and lost his lands to a Protestant who claimed to be "willing to abide by the laws his betters had made for that pit of Popish corruption called Ireland." Charlie felt that he had found the very man to assist him with his plans to establish an Irish colony here, and the two of them drank late into the night and woke us all with their loud Irish songs. Then they brought out all of Jonathan Swift's writings and inflamed themselves into a patriotic frenzy by reading his Proposals and Observations. Charlie had just threatened to use his money to arm a fleet and return to Ireland to free it single handed, when he saw me standing in the doorway. He got up on a chair, pamphlet in hand, and proclaimed Swift's words about our homeland, "Whoever travels this Country, and observes the Dwellings of the Natives, will hardly think himself in a Land where either Law, Religion, or common Humanity is professed!" His gestures were too grand for a man whose equilibrium was affected by liquor, and he fell to the floor, curled up, and closed his eyes.

Patrick was already asleep in a chair, so I threw a blanket over Charlie and went back upstairs. Orlando, Sebastian, and I were occupying rooms in the east wing, chaperoned by *Don* Ernesto who, having failed to find a female companion for me, had placed himself between my rooms and Charlie's. He had found a ready ally in Cararé, who watched Charlie and me quite openly through a spyglass when we rode. Charlie referred to them as "the duennas" and resorted to all manner of strategies in order to be alone with me. He employed boys to summon Cararé away, or set the church bells to ringing, feigning some emergency. Once he even started a small fire behind the workshops.

"What do they imagine I will do to you?" he asked me one day, turning to wave and bow to Cararé as we rode out of Caupolicán together.

"They think you wish to seduce me."

"I do."

I blushed and pretended to adjust my stirrup.

"That was an unforgivably crude remark to make to a lady in mourning. Will you forgive me?"

I not only forgave him, my vanity was gratified by his admission. Except in girlish fantasy, I had never allowed myself to consider the possibility that Charlie would think seriously of me. Now, his circumstances and mine were greatly altered. I was no longer a poor girl; he had lost his right to his title and his inheritance. Both of us had recreated ourselves in a place where no one would think twice of an alliance between us that included matrimony.

I had come to care deeply for Charlie, not only because he was a good friend to me, but because he was unusually tender with Orlando and Sebastian. He had ordered the making of a small door, less than three feet high, leading out into a walled-in garden which was to be Sebastian's own. And knowing of Orlando's love of books, he had had low shelves built in the nursery and filled them with volumes of every description. While Sebastian was as happy in Charlie's arms as he was in mine, Orlando was less at ease with him. He appreciated the books, and he and Charlie tried reading them together, but while Orlando could sit quietly for hours, Charlie could barely keep still for five minutes.

Occasionally, he spoke of returning to Ireland, and I reluctantly reminded him that he was forever barred from doing so. Even if the English pardoned him, his ships flew Spanish colors along with the red and white FitzGibbon coat of arms, and he traveled on a Spanish passport, which meant he could not legally remain in Ireland above forty days. While I had left my homeland happily behind, Charlie could not forget Ireland. His melancholy and restlessness became so intense that autumn of 1750 that I persuaded him to leave Caupolicán for a few short days and accompany me to the ocean, where I planned to sleep again with an infinity of stars over my head. They were the same stars, Charlie said, as looked down upon me at Caupolicán, and I could climb the towers and look at them from there, but it was not the same to me, and I wanted Sebastian to know the vaulting ocean and its crystal breakers from his earliest years.

The "duennas" objected to our trip. Only Wimencaí supported me when I said that I would not allow any of them to accompany us on the journey. I would be traveling in my own wagon with the children, and five *camiluchos* would ride with us. To everyone's surprise, Father Manuel took my side. It had taken a long time, but he and Charlie had made their peace. Hurt as he was by Yací's disappearance from our lives, Father Manuel could not fail to see how sorry Charlie was, and how determined to earn forgiveness.

"It is like blaming a bull calf for trampling on a sapling," Father Manuel sighed. "Both are lethal, and have no awareness of it."

When we set out on our journey, I was alone in the wagon. Orlando was on his pony, and Sebastian rode in front of Charlie, his head covered in a leather hat, beaten to cottony softness by patient, loving hands at the settlement. Wimencaí had woven him a poncho to protect him on cool evenings, and槃araré had made him a pair of tiny, horse-hide boots.

Don Ernesto traveled with us part of the way and then his wagon, surrounded by a mounted escort of *camiluchos*, left us for Montevideo. In his possession was the poem he had completed and I had illustrated during his stay with us. Orlando and I cried when he left us, while Charlie tried not to show his relief to be rid of him. To Charlie *Don* Ernesto was a busy body, a fop, a scribbler of incomprehensible poetry. To me, he represented unstinting generosity of spirit, a sheltering friendship as solid and enduring as an *ombú*. In *Don* Ernesto's company, Orlando was happy.

Early in our travels, I found an oven bird's nest. Of all the birds, I have always been fondest of these golden brown birds, who trustingly build their two room mud nests, the size of a large round pot, within easy reach of a person's hand. They are master builders and loving parents, unpretentious and efficient, just as I wished to be. I was showing the nest, empty now of its young and waiting for next year's tenants, to Orlando and Sebastian, when Charlie accidentally broke it in two, causing the *camiluchos* to shake their heads sadly and unpack their saddlebags, airing their ponchos in the sun.

"I hope you haven't brought bad weather on us, Charlie," I said, surprised at the sudden tightness in my throat. On most occasions I could control memories of Garzón, but the nest brought back his story of how unfortunate it is to damage an oven bird's home. The oven bird, he said, was not really a bird, but a young man, who heard a woman's voice singing to him during his manhood trials. The boy's father wished him to marry as soon as he was mature, but the boy wanted to find the woman whose lovely voice had comforted him during his long fast, so he became a bird and went in search of her. Ever since, they had built their mud homes together.

Next day it started to rain, a slow drizzle at first that made Charlie irritable, and delayed our progress. I rode with Sebastian and Orlando in the wagon, watching men and beasts struggle against the wind and rain that was slowing us almost to a halt.

As we approached the ocean the rain came down in torrents, pouring through the canvas tents, soaking clothes, food, and blankets. It was early autumn and we would have been quite warm were it not for the continual damp and discomfort of wet boots and stockings. The wind roared in from the ocean, whipping sand across our path and salt into our eyes.

Hunting became difficult, and we had to make do with our provisions of powdered beef, dried tongue, bread and cheese. Some of the food turned moldy, and all of it tasted damp. The beef we mixed liberally with wild onions and garlic and boiled it with rice to make a filling, if monotonous meal. After several days without the fresh meat usually provided by deer, iguanas and partridges, Charlie decided to go further afield to hunt. So accustomed had he become to living off the land when he traveled, that he could not believe that a herd of cattle was not within easy shooting range. He rode all day looking for one. When he finally did lay eyes on a herd, his horse, exhausted from having battled through the mud all day, refused to give chase.

I awaited his return with *mate*. The wind buffeted the tall wagon, making it sway, and the loose deer hides hanging at front and back did little to prevent an occasional gust from sweeping through. Sebastian and Orlando lay side by side on their bed of sheep skins. Sebastian's skin glowed bronze in the lamplight. His hair was almost black, with a hint of red where the light fell on it, and his eyes were a rather startling pale green, with a shimmer of gold around the edges. Sleeping next to him was Orlando, the faithful Zule by his side. I had worried that after giving birth to the child I had so longed for my feelings toward Orlando might change. They had, but not as I had feared. I did not love Orlando less, but more. Having now given birth myself, I thought often of his mother. If she had died when he was born, she had suffered no further. But what if she had lived? What if he had been taken from her, like Zulema's first child? As the rain dripped unrelentingly on the sodden leather above us, I lay down by my boys and drew them closer, warming my cold hands on the warmth of their bodies. I was drifting off to sleep when Charlie pulled aside the hides and climbed in.

"If I cannot escape this wind and that smelly dog I shall speedily go mad!"

He looked so unhappy, so unlike the young man I had seen four years ago elated by his theft of a wagon full of pheasants, that my heart went out to him. I reached out to brush the wet hair from his eyes, and heard my name called. For a moment I thought I had imagined it. The wind was howling and the trees hissed in the rain. There it was again! Orlando had heard it too and he rubbed his eyes and moved to the rear of the wagon to pull aside the hide. Father Manuel was dismounting a few feet away, asking the men to unsaddle his horse and prepare him a fresh one. We waved to him, and he removed his wet poncho and hung it outside the wagon before climbing in with us.

After the briefest of greetings, he reached into the pocket of his trousers and took out a small leather pouch. "This came for you."

In the soft light cast by the lantern, I untied the drawstring and withdrew a long string of painted clay beads. A little wooden seagull dangled from the end.

I did not dare to move, to speak, to disturb the air around me in any way.

Orlando crept softly to my side and touched the little carving, making the little bird fly.

"There is a note." Father Manuel unfolded the soiled and crumpled piece of paper that accompanied the beads.

"Please read it to me," I whispered.

"Querida, *I am on my way home to you. Fate has restored me to the world of memory and of the living, and nothing can keep me from you now. Garzón*."

Orlando gave a whoop of joy. "He's alive!"

"So it seems," Father Manuel said.

"Aren't you happy, Isabel?"

"When did it arrive?"

"A messenger brought it two days ago. He had received it from someone riding from the Missions."

Suddenly I needed to be in the open with emotions so vast I could no longer contain them. I vaulted out of the wagon and into the rain. Within seconds, as I ran blindly through the downpour, I was soaked to the skin. I reached an *ombú* and threw myself against it, sobbing against its rough bark as I held tightly to the beads.

Garzón was alive! Somewhere in the vast world he was alive and on his way to me!

I felt a touch on my shoulder and turned to see Charlie standing there. He held his arms out to me, and it was only when I felt his breath mingling with mine that I tore myself away and ran back to the wagon.

Later that night, when the children were asleep and we had changed into dry clothes, Father Manuel told us that news of Garzón was not all that he had brought. King Ferdinand had signed a Treaty with the Portuguese. Under its provisions, Spain was to regain possession of Colonia, a small, strategically located coastal city the Portuguese had stolen from their Spanish rivals and used as a center for smuggling and contraband. In exchange for Colonia, Portugal would receive twenty thousand square miles, and seven prosperous Missions.

"The fact that the Missions are home to thousands of his most loyal subjects means nothing to Ferdinand! He is washing his hands of the consequences, bartering away their lives like so many sheaves of wheat, uncaring that he is handing them over to the tender mercies of their oldest enemies. Twenty-five thousand souls!"

"What is to become of them?" Charlie asked.

They could stay, the king was magnanimous enough to grant, if they swore allegiance to Portugal. If not, then they must leave, taking with them all of their belongings and their cattle, but with no compensation for their houses or for their land.

"Painted Carar\u00e9 is convinced that there has been a mistake and that the King's orders are being misinterpreted. I entertain no such illusions. It amounts to an abominable betrayal, and I am riding at once to join Fathers Balda and Henis, who run the Missions most affected."

"What can we do?" I asked.

"We must prepare to receive as many of the disinherited as we can accommodate," Father Manuel said. "Carar\u00e9 has already begun the work of building more homes for them."

With Charlie he exchanged a look of despair and appeal. We both knew that this was what Charlie had been waiting for, the cause that had so far eluded him. He was energized, his face taut, his eyes alight, no trace in his demeanor that he and I had forgotten ourselves so entirely as to kiss without restraint. He gave an almost imperceptible nod, and Father Manuel turned away, knowing full well what Charlie would do.

That night I lay with the message beads wound round my fingers, counting them over and over. They were a calendar of sorts, Father Manuel had explained, commonly used to convey time and often sent from one relative or friend to another to communicate an upcoming visit. Each bead represented a day. On the day the beads were all removed, the visitor's arrival was imminent. There were twenty-five beads on the string, and we had no idea how long had passed since the message had been sent and Father Manuel had received it. Garz\u00f3n had clearly assumed that the beads would travel faster than he could. Messengers rode hard, and were able to change horses frequently. Weather permitting they could travel between Montevideo and the Missions in less than a fortnight.

Perhaps Garzón had been delayed by illness or injury. Or perhaps he was at Caupolicán even as I counted the beads. I was torn between a desire to follow the trail the letter had taken and find him, and the certainty that all I could sensibly do, was wait.

Chapter XI

The clouds unfurled at dawn, revealing a sky luminous in its turquoise glory. From the leaves of the trees all around us hung thousands of rain drops, shimmering in the sun like crystals. Flocks of parrots streaked the air with flashes of red and green, and the *ñandúes* shook the water from their feathers and stretched their long necks. The bird chorus that had so enchanted me the first time I awoke out of doors was in full voice, the chirps and trills of the flycatchers and *monjitas*, the calls of the black and gold King of the Forest, and the long, clear cries of the kiskadees. I looked into the haze of pink and lavender in the sky above the jungle of the hills and my heart stirred at the sight. The secret stillness of the *monte* was as alluring on that day as it had been the first time I stood at its edge and looked beyond the thick vegetation into the flowering glory within.

The oxen lowed softly, blinking their gentle eyes as I glanced hopefully at the sky, noisy with the clouds of geese that had replaced the rain clouds. They flew low, honking under the predatory eye of the hawks soaring on the air above them.

For a moment I wondered if I had dreamed last night's events. Somewhere in the vast world Garzón was alive! Mixed with the strange blend of joy and apprehension was the knowledge that our colony would soon be at war. The news Father Manuel had brought would transform our lives in more ways than we could imagine, and he was counting on me to assist屋Craré in receiving the displaced Indians who chose to come to us.

Charlie did not need to tell me his plans. Now that Father Manuel's worst fears about the Missions had come to pass, Charlie was leaving immediately. He knew that a force would be mustered to resist the Treaty's provisions, and he would be putting himself and all his resources at their disposal. He asked if I would break my return journey by stopping at the new fortress to give the news regarding the Treaty to his friend Patrick. The detour should not take more than half a day, and anxious as I was to be on my way home, I nevertheless agreed.

Our parting was awkward and cool. I was ashamed of the desire that had swept over me when I kissed him, and what Charlie felt I could only guess. I made sure that no occasion to be alone with him presented itself before Orlando and I laid our wet clothes to dry on top of the wagon and struck out.

The heavy rains had made a mire of the terrain, and almost two days passed before the walls of the small fortress appeared in the distance. No movement was apparent around the stockade and no smoke rose to indicate that life proceeded as usual in the makeshift houses obscured by the surrounding trees. The men exchanged silent glances, and two of them rode ahead to investigate.

It was not long before we could see through the trees to what remained of the fortress. It and the five houses it had been built to protect were burned to the ground.

Suddenly, the man riding ahead called a halt. In a deep ditch crossing his path he had found the bodies of the male settlers and five soldiers. One of the men hurried back to tell me that Patrick's body was not among them.

"Orlando, I need to enter the settlement. You and Zule are to stay here with Sebastian until I return."

I handed the men a spade so they could begin digging graves in the slippery mud, and approached what was left of the houses. Clothes and cooking utensils lay sodden by those walls left standing, and a small black dog barked half heartedly at me as he limped away. Odds and ends of the settlers' possessions were scattered all over the ground. A shoe here, a tin mug there, a hoe, a hair ribbon caught on a branch.

My eyes were following a piece of charred cloth blowing by my feet, and I was hoping that Patrick had somehow escaped the massacre, when I heard a soft groan from beyond a crumbled wall. I ran toward it and saw him, lying there soaked in the blood and rain of several days. Two arrows had pierced his chest, the shafts lying broken nearby where they had snapped when he tried to pull them out. I knelt beside him and took his hand.

"Minuanes," he murmured.

I urged him to conserve his strength, but he wanted me to know all that had happened.

The Indians had pushed ignited grass with their lances under the eaves of the houses, and when the smoke and heat became too great to bear, the settlers had run out. The men had been killed, the two women and their three children spared, and allowed to run into the fort, where he himself had been sleeping that night. The survivors had retired to the one room barracks, barricaded the door with a table, and stationed three men at each narrow window, one to shoot, two to reload. From there they could see the Minuanes tearing down the fence, and then, silencing their war cry, momentarily disappear.

The next thing they knew, the silence was shattered as the Minuanes came screaming through the torn fence, torches held high. All the men had been killed. The women and their three children taken.

Patrick had tried to keep track of time, and believed it had been four days ago, just before the rains began.

Before he died he grasped my sleeve. "The women and children," he said, "you must send your men to save them!"

I assured him that I would, but the effort had been too much for him and he was gone.

Saying nothing to the *camiluchos*, I took my horse and slipped away from the site.

The Minuanes had made no effort to cover their departure and I found their tracks easily. As the trail through the open plains and across the moors became more difficult to follow, I grew absorbed in my task and before I knew it I was near a small valley. I saw smoke and tethered my horse, moving forward cautiously to look down at the camp site from which I had observed the spirals of smoke.

When it became apparent that no guards had been posted, I climbed a tree where I could lie concealed and watch what was happening below. About two dozen men were gathered, with many more women and children squatting nearby. I picked out Yací, but saw no sign of Atzaya or of the captive women and children.

Seven warriors had been prepared for burial and loud wails rent the quiet as several women approached a block of wood in the center of the circle of mourners and put their hands on it, offering joints off their fingers to their dead relatives. The warriors' knives and spears lay by the block, and after the wives, sisters and daughters had each made their offering of flesh, they picked up the weapons and stabbed their arms and breasts with them. The male mourners then began their own ritual flesh piercing.

Atzaya had told me about these burial rites, and I remembered that the men would retire now to stand throughout the night in holes they had dug for the purpose. The splinters covering their arms were part of this offering to the dead, and when they were removed, the men would begin their fast.

I made sure I was well hidden as the whole band escorted the mourners from the camp, heading toward the hills and the burial mounds and away from my hiding place. I was wondering what I should do next, when Atzaya appeared in the clearing below.

The noise I made climbing down the hillside startled her.

"What are you doing here?" she asked. "Have you come from the settlement?"

"From the one that was burned, yes."

I asked her to tell me what had happened, and she explained that the shamans had experienced many dreams and visions, some full of dire portents, and scouts had reported that other tribes were gathering in large numbers on the plains. In Montevideo, soldiers appeared on the city ramparts more frequently, and large numbers of ships had been sighted making their way to the town. They had heard that the Mission tribes were finally rebelling and would be joined by large numbers of free tribes, including their cousins the Charrúa.

I told her about the treaty, and Atzaya sighed, a deep, wrenching sigh. "Is that what you came to tell me?"

"I'm looking for the women and children who were taken during the attack."

"I set them free."

"When?"

"During the sacrifices, when no one was looking."

"Where did they go?"

"They ran away from me." She pointed toward the hills near where I had lain hidden.

We went looking for them and found them huddled together under some bushes, the children clinging to their mothers.

"I am taking you to safety," I told the women. "I have a horse and a wagon nearby."

"We don't want to be hunted down like animals! Take the children, *Señora*, we will run in the other direction and they can chase us!"

"No one will chase you. You are free to go. Atzaya will not send anyone after you."

Still they did not move. Their eyes were fixed on Atzaya, and I wondered if I could persuade them to leave their hiding place while she was there.

I took her aside. "Will you be punished for this?"

She shook her head. "I am doing it for my mother. Perhaps now her souls will rest." She smiled and touched my blouse, damp from the milk leaking from my breasts. "The caá parí did its work?"

"Yes! I have you to thank for a healthy son. And your daughter?"

"She is walking, and curious like her father. Her name is Yandibé."

"What can I tell Father Manuel about Yací?"

"His souls are scattered still. Tell him to be patient. They will come home."

The women watched her walk away, and it was only when we could no longer see her that I was able to coax them out. Thorns and branches tore at our clothes and hair as we began the trek through the underbrush to the place where I had left my horse. I placed the children on it, and we were half way to the wagon when the search party sent out by Orlando found us.

That night we posted guards and doused the fire that could reveal our location in the unlikely event that the Minuanes decided to interrupt their mourning and pursue us.

Exhausted as they were, the bereaved women could not sleep. They rocked their children, fed them cold meat and rice, and told me of their home in the Canary Islands, and of their long sea voyage south. They spoke of their delight when their first crop of wheat was harvested and their houses built outside the walls of the little fortress. Until the day the Minuanes attacked, they had not even seen an Indian, they said, and then one dawn they awoke to a sound they would remember to their dying day.

"Like thunder, or the roar of a bull," one of them said.

They described what followed in the manner of people trying to recollect a dream full of conflicting images and emotions. They had run with their husbands and children through the sound, amid the horses, and over the bodies of the soldiers who had left the fort to assist them, expecting at any moment to be speared or trampled, only to find themselves in the stockade at last, untouched, but without their men. All of them lay dead behind them, along with one woman who perished defending her husband.

In the days that followed, they had often wished they had died too. In Atzaya they had seen their future and that of their daughters, and death seemed preferable to mating with a savage and bearing half-breed children.

Orlando walked up to me at that moment, carrying Sebastian in one arm and leaning on Zule with the other.

"My sons," I said.

They were in my debt and at my mercy and they knew it. Only that kept them from voicing the distaste that widened their eyes and pursed their mouths at the sight of Orlando's dark skin. Murmuring excuses about the lateness of the hour, they gathered their children and moved away.

Exhaustion overcame me like a fog, and I turned my back on them, took Sebastian from Orlando, and returned to the wagon.

I slept poorly, starting at every sound, my eyes and ears straining in the darkness, listening for anything that would reveal that we were under attack. It seemed an eternity before the jingle of harness and the smell of roasting meat greeted me. The men had been hunting and two racks of ribs were cooking over the fire when I emerged.

I had decided to part with the wagon. Two *camiluchos* would accompany the women to Montevideo, the other three would escort me back to Caupolicán. I would travel faster without the oxen to delay me and I wanted to make up for lost time.

We continued our journey along the wind swept beaches toward the distant lagoon, with one of the men crossing the dunes and looking out every so often over the palm groves in search of Minuanes. Only cattle and wild horses were in evidence, grazing on the green and purple grasses, their occasional bellows and whinnies cutting through the whistling, singing wind as it stirred the palm fronds and held the soaring *gavilanes* lightly on the clear autumn air. A day later, we saw the towers of Caupolicán Castle in the distance, and Orlando clapped his hands.

"Will Garzón be there, Isabel?"

"I dare not hope so," I said. "But he's on his way!"

We returned to a flurry of activity. Cararé was preparing for the arrival of the homeless Indians by building houses and stocking supplies for use in the months to come. Charlie had come and gone. None of us expected to see him again for the duration of the war, and we were surprised when he returned a few days later.

He and Cararé were in complete disagreement about the Treaty of Madrid, and tensions between them ran high. Cararé maintained that since it seemed to be no more than an accommodation of boundaries between Spain and Portugal, we should do the best we could for the dispossessed Indians, and avoid a war.

"Surely you realize, *Don* Cararé, that if twenty-five thousand displaced inhabitants of the Missions decide not to honor the Treaty, and the free tribes and the thousands of Indians in the Missions all around us join them, they will muster a force even the Spanish and the Portuguese combined cannot match!"

"I do not doubt that you will do all you can to ensure that outcome, *Don* Carlos."

"I will! We shall use the arms the King has provided to beat him and his Portuguese friends at their own game!"

I could not overcome a feeling in the depth of my soul that the Indians would lose such a war. Spain and Portugal had too much at stake to permit any other outcome. And what would Cararé do? Would he fight for the King he had served all his life with unwavering devotion, or with his own Mission forces arrayed against that King?

Several of our young men, fired by Charlie's passion for the cause, decided to join him. Together, they rode out of Caupolicán under the white banner made for Charlie by the women at the settlement as a gift of farewell. It was emblazoned with the black ermine prints and the bright red annulets of the FitzGibbon coat of arms and rippled in the air behind him as he cantered away.

He had left me a small package and a note, and asked me not to open them until after he was gone. I opened the package first and was surprised when a document ornamented with various seals fell into my lap. It certified that *Don* Carlos FitzGibbon and *Doña* Isabel Keating were man and wife. The note was brief.

> *Dear Isabel, I shall not return from this war. I will either be killed or move on elsewhere, far from any memory of what might have been.*
>
> *I want the castle and its lands to be yours, and can think of only one way to make sure of it. I paid dearly for the enclosed marriage document in more ways than one. I would have given every last ounce of gold I own that it were true. Use it if you need to. It would please me to know that I had been of service to you and yours.*
>
> *Think well of me if you can. Charles FitzGibbon*

I folded the letter and pressed it to my mouth, opened it, kissed and folded it again and again into ever smaller pieces, as if each crease would serve to enclose more and more tightly all that was Charlie, and by putting the letter and the certificate into the hidden wall recess of my room at the castle, I could tell myself that I would forget them.

I paid off the servants, sent them back to Montevideo, and returned with Orlando and Sebastian to our little house. The first thing I did was change out of my mourning clothes into the skirt and blouse I had been wearing the day Garzón proposed to me, and then I slipped the message beads over my head and got to work preparing the house for his arrival.

I was brushing cobwebs from the corners and shaking dust from the rugs when Father Manuel returned. The Indians of the Missions had burned the decrees ordering them to leave, he told us, and they had refused to observe the new colonial boundaries.

The Governor of Buenos Aires and several influential Jesuits at the Spanish court pleaded with the King to allow the Indians to remain on their land, but he turned a deaf ear to their entreaties. The Treaty stood, and if the Indians refused to leave peacefully they would be forced into compliance.

Singer Cararé was not alone in refusing to believe it. He and others like him had fought for the Crown so often they thought their loyalty returned, and would battle anyone who told them otherwise. It was not the King, but his ministers, who had given these orders, and as soon as he understood that it was his most loyal subjects who were being turned out, he would remedy the situation.

The greatest irony was that in the war moving inexorably toward us both sides would be fighting for the same monarch. Ferdinand ill deserved such devotion and sacrifice.

Father Manuel decided that he would join the Mission forces, taking with him every able bodied man who wished to accompany him. They knew that if they lost the war, all of us would be branded as enemies of these new allies, Spain and Portugal, and neither the rocky moors nor the deep blue ocean would protect us then.

Preparations for war began. We lay out lances for the foot soldiers, swords for the cavalry, powder and shot, and as many muskets as we could muster. We prepared two bows, four strings, and thirty arrows for each archer. For the *pedreros*, who would wield the slingshots, we packed thirty stones per man.

"Why thirty?" Orlando asked while he helped count out the stones.

It had always been so, the men said. Thirty arrows, thirty stones, thirty *desjarretaderas*, the scythes they used for disabling cattle, now destined for maiming horses and unseating their riders.

The sounds of cannon and barrels of gun powder being rolled into the plaza woke me before first light on the day of their departure. Women and children, wrapped in ponchos, moved to and fro out of warehouses and homes, packing hampers with food and filling water gourds at the well. I bundled a sleeping Sebastian onto my back, and Orlando and I went to see the men off. They had been transformed overnight into the company of well drilled, smartly outfitted soldiers I had fought next to at Santa Marta in what seemed a lifetime ago.

Two hours later, in perfect formation, with the *caciques* riding ahead, the little army marched out of the gates. Those of us left behind crowded into the watch towers and onto the battlements. We would have liked to shower the soldiers with flower petals and cheer them on their way, but the solemnity of the occasion weighed too heavily upon us. We rang the bells instead. They tolled equally at births and funerals, at celebrations and at times of danger, and seemed the most fitting of farewells.

Everyone believed that Cararé had decided to remain at the settlement, but just as the last soldiers rode out of the gates, he appeared, his uniform impeccable, his stirrups and scabbard gleaming. A cheer went up and grew louder as he cantered past the soldiers. The standard he, Wimencaí and I had worked on the night before unfurled over his head, and Joan of Arc billowed into the wind, her sword held high. For our motto, we had chosen the words *¡Alta la llama!* Hold the flame high!

Cararé took his place with the other *caciques* at the head of the departing troops, and turned back to wave at Wimencaí who stood still and silent in the watch towers, the only one amid the cheering women and children who really knew what the decision had cost him.

That night, Orlando and I removed another message bead and put it in a gourd by my bed. Over the gourd, we hung the two little seagulls, the crystal one Garzón gave me in Río de Janeiro, and the wooden one he sent with the beads.

Since the castle's towers were the highest points for miles around, Wimencaí and I regularly climbed the narrow winding steps to the turrets to watch the sky fill with smoke signals by day and the glow of distant bonfires by night. Each was either a call for help, a beacon lit by one group of Mission fighters summoning another to their aid, or a means of informing on the movements of the troops that hunted them.

We were standing there a week after the men had left, sipping *mate* and trying to interpret the smoke signals in the sky, when we heard a rustle on the stone steps leading to the tower. It was Zulema. Her man Lauro had gone to join the Mission tribesmen in their fight against Spain, and she had heard that the best place to watch for smoke signals was at Caupolicán. We welcomed her and her little son, who was now a year old. He kept all three of us busy making sure he didn't fall down the steps as he practiced his walking. Eventually, he exhausted himself and after a satisfying feed at Zulema's breast, fell asleep. Zulema wrapped him tightly in her poncho and placed him at her feet. The three of us were standing together passing the mate gourd from black hand to brown, from brown to white, and back again, when I heard the familiar irregularity of Orlando's step on the stairs.

Sebastian was sleeping soundly, he said, and he had left the window open and asked the neighbors to tend him if he woke. I introduced him to Zulema, and Orlando who was fond of babies, immediately knelt to examine the bundle at her feet. Zulema squatted down next to him and uncovered the baby's face so that Orlando could see him better. As he bent over the child she gave a cry and fell back, her hands clasped over her mouth.

For a moment she remained that way, as if turned to stone, then she shook her head and wailed, suddenly throwing herself toward Orlando. He lost his balance and fell over, clutching my skirt.

"You are my son!" Zulema cried. "You are my son!" She tried to take his face in her hands but Orlando would not let her. He burst into tears. "Don't cry! Don't cry! We have found each other! Look!" Zulema said, turning wildly to Wimencaí and me. "Look behind his ear! I put that mark there myself when he was born!"

Again, she tried to touch Orlando, and again he withdrew, hiding behind me. Wimencaí picked up Zulema's sleeping baby, and led Zulema to the stairs. "We will find a light and examine the mark properly," she said. She glanced over her shoulder at Orlando and me. I don't know which one of us was the more terrified.

Once in our house we found a mirror so that Orlando could see the mark for himself. At first, he didn't want to look and neither did I, so fearful was I of what we would find, but eventually his curiosity got the better of him.

"What does this mark mean? Why did you put it there?" he asked Zulema.

"I put it there because I knew that you would be taken from me. The owner of the plantation where your father and I worked sold our babies as soon as they could walk, and you not only walked before you were a year old, you talked and sang. You could repeat anything that was said to you. You were valuable, and I'm sure he got a good price for you. So I marked you, in case we ever met again. Your father knew how to make tattoos and we did it together."

"Where is my father?"

"He became ill and could no longer work, so he was killed." She began to weep again, and Zule, sensing her distress, came to nuzzle her hand.

"Zule," Orlando said. "Zulema." His eyes were wide as he looked from one to the other. "I remembered your name."

Zulema laughed through her tears. "Would you like to know your birth name? The one your father gave you?"

"I like the name I have."

"I like it too. You don't have to change it."

They sat quietly, studying one another. Every few seconds she would shake her head in disbelief and touch him, caressing his cheek, kissing his hand. At first Orlando was unsure what to make of her attentions, but as the night wore on he returned them in full measure.

Wimencaí put her arm around my waist and pulled me to her, holding me tightly. I was trying not to cry, not to spoil Orlando's joy, but it was all I could do not to grab him and order Zulema to leave, to let us resume our lives, to let me keep him.

Suddenly, he turned to me. "Will I have to leave here?"

"Don't you want to come with me?" Zulema asked him. "And with your brother?"

He pointed to Sebastian, sleeping with Zulema's baby in the crib under the window. "I have two brothers. And I can't go without Zule and her children."

"Her children?" Zulema asked.

"She has five. And I want to be here when Garzón returns."

"I will come for you as soon as he arrives," I said, regretting the words the moment I had spoken them. They sounded so easy, as if his departure meant nothing to me, as if the desire to fight tooth and nail to keep him were not tearing me to pieces. "I will miss you every minute of every day."

Orlando looked at Zulema and back at me, unsure. "Can I still be married here when I am seventeen?"

"Of course you can," Wimencaí said. "I myself will be looking for a bride for you!"

"And you can come and visit us whenever you want to. You and your mother will always be welcome here."

"Perhaps it would be best if you slept here tonight," Wimencaí suggested.

Zulema nodded, her eyes full of understanding.

"Tomorrow, Orlando," I said, "we can show Zulema your books."

"You can read?" Zulema asked him in surprise.

"And write. In Spanish, English, Portuguese and Latin," Orlando said proudly.

"You left me a slave and return to me a scholar. I am very proud of you, *hijito*."

"I will teach you if you want to learn," Orlando said. "And my new brother."

I insisted that Zulema and Orlando take my bed. I fed Sebastian and curled up on Orlando's bed, behind the partition, burying my face in his pillow. Sometime during the night, he crept in beside me.

"Isabel," he whispered, "what if I don't like the *quilombo*?"

"I will come to see you in a few days," I whispered back, "and if you are unhappy we will decide what to do about it."

I lay awake until dawn, holding his hand. How could something so shattering have happened so fast? Yesterday he had been mine, now he was Zulema's. Could he possibly understand what his departure would cost me? Or was the transition to his real mother so natural, so desirable, so like a dream come true, that only joy was possible?

When the babies began to stir, Zulema and I fed them, while Orlando made *mate* and cut slices of the bread we'd baked the day before. Wimencaí joined us for breakfast, and then Orlando buckled Zule into her harness while I folded the old burlap *mate* bag she had appropriated for her bed.

"What about my pony and my saddle?"

"They will stay here, ready for you whenever you visit us."

He held his arms out to Wimencaí. "Remember, my bride must be as beautiful as you," he said.

When she released him he turned to me again. "I wouldn't leave you for anyone else, Isabel. Please don't cry."

But I was still crying when Orlando and Zulema paddled away together across the lagoon, Zule and her offspring barking their goodbyes.

Chapter XII

In the days that followed, I took to joining the women in their field work. Every morning we filed out of the settlement's gates carrying jugs of water and baskets of bread, and made our way to the fields of winter wheat and the rows of vegetables, where we chased the parrots away and sang to the crops as we weeded, or harvested potatoes, carrots and pumpkins. At noon, the children, escorted by their grandparents, ran to find us and bring us home for our noonday meal.

Three beads were added to the gourd by my bed, and then another three, and still there was no sign of Garzón and no further word from him. I had no idea where the note had originated, no information that could guide me in beginning a search for him. Even if the beads had reached me in the shortest possible time, he should not have been so far behind them. Wimencaí reminded me that we were at war, and that even at our two-day distance from the coast we had seen Spanish and Portuguese soldiers on patrol. A lone and unallied rider trying to make his way through the fighting to us would have a difficult time of it. My greatest fear remained the same. He lay somewhere, ill or wounded, and could not come to me.

Soon, only two of the twenty-five beads remained on the cord.

Whenever my anxiety became more than I could bear, I left Sebastian with Wimencaí and walked the *montes* along the lagoon, throwing stones at the water until my arms ached. Sometimes,

I knelt in the church and prayed under the fine linen paintings the settlement's inhabitants had made in place of stained glass windows, while the instruments wove their silken thread around the voices that fell and softy faded, leaving the air vibrating and myself motionless. I had always found this music and the smell of cedar from the carved and painted columns soothing, thinking that if angels sang they must sound like this, their harmony perfect, their tone simple, rich, and as light as air.

I was strewing herbs over the church floor and sprinkling them with scented water, when a shadow fell across the doorway. I looked up to see Father Manuel standing there. He had no news of Garzón. He had come to bring the wounded, friend and foe alike, for us to tend.

Until that moment the war had seemed distant and unreal, an exercise not unlike the one I had participated in when I had dressed up as a soldier and marched with the troops at Santa Marta. When I stepped outside the gates of Caupolicán all such memories fled.

The ground was covered with men, sitting or leaning on their weapons, their wounds ranging from bruises and scratches to severed limbs and gun shot wounds. Exhausted horses hung their heads, and even the oxen bore the marks of battle. At first I couldn't place the sound I heard hovering in the air, a low keening moan that rose and fell, rose and fell again. It was the begging sound of pain, and it hovered in the air mingling with the smell of festering wounds.

Every man, woman and child able to walk was put to work. Blankets were turned into stretchers and tables set up in the plaza to receive the most seriously wounded. Children pumped water and kept Wimencaí and I supplied as we went to work cutting away clothing and cleaning wounds. Women prepared bandages out of every available piece of cloth we had, and carried food and water to the injured waiting their turn outside. Father Manuel and the younger children tended to the animals, and the elders began the task of taking down the name of every man who could still give it.

I lost track of time, days and nights blending into one another in a blur of exhaustion. Father Manuel established a relay team of horses between Caupolicán and Montevideo, and sent for don Ernesto. He was no horseman, and when he arrived a week later I barely recognized him. He was dirty, unshaven, and saddle sore, and I burst into tears of pity and relief at sight of him. That night, Wimencaí and I slept without interruption and when I felt a hand on my shoulder I awoke with a start. "How long have I been asleep? What has happened?"

Two children were bending over me. "Father Manuel's friend is here!" they said. "He told us to come and wake you!"

"What friend?" I said, swinging my feet to the floor.

"His Indian friend!"

"Yací?"

They nodded. "He's hurt."

I had fallen asleep fully clothed and reached my door as Father Manuel and Yací entered the gates. Yací was limping and had a bloody piece of rawhide tied around his thigh. He was leading a horse, and draped across its back was a frighteningly familiar figure. Yací saw me in the doorway and called out. "He's alive!"

I remember little of what followed. I was of no use to Wimencaí and *Don* Ernesto as they cut away Garzón's blood soaked clothes and prepared to wash his body. All I could do was gather up the torn clothes and hold them tightly. He was painfully thin and covered in scars, and the soles of his feet were leathery. Wimencaí said he looked as if he had walked from the other side of the world. His hair was very long and braided with beads, and a joint was missing from the small finger of his left hand.

My own fingers, running over the remnants of his shirt as if it could tell me where he had been these eighteen months past, came upon a hard knot. I worked it open and found the agate I had so often seen in Garzón's hands. He would want it by him when he woke, so I took a nightshirt from the trunk where I had put all his belongings and sewed the agate into the pocket.

Garzón began to stir and moan when *Don* Ernesto removed a musket ball from his shoulder and another from his back, and Wimencaí made me wait outside until their work was finished. I looked in through the window, and for a moment his eyes met mine. I was about to run back in, to offer what comfort I could, but the look in his eyes was distant, as if the pain had taken him to a place where nothing else existed, and he fainted into merciful oblivion.

Just as I had promised, I sent word to Orlando at the *quilombo*, and he came that very night, accompanied by Zule and carrying all of his books.

The first thing Garzón saw when he opened his eyes was Sebastian, pulling himself up to stand tentatively by the bed, his eyes barely reaching the quilt. He lost his balance when Garzón reached out to touch him, and sat down hard. Orlando hurried to comfort him while I knelt by the bed.

"Are you real?" Garzón whispered.

I put his hand to my face and let him feel my tears.

"What date is it?"

"The sixth of June."

"What year?"

"1750."

"I've longed to touch you for five hundred and forty three days."

I kissed first one scar and then another, wanting to know everything that had happened, and preventing him from answering for fear that he would tire himself with conversation.

"Where are my clothes?"

"In pieces on the rubbish heap. But," I said, seeing alarm leap into his eyes, "your agate is here." I touched the pocket of his nightshirt and his hand closed over it.

"There was a bag."

I brought him the little leather pouch that had been tied to his belt. "This one?"

"Yes." He opened it and spilled a collection of little animals and flowers out on the blanket for Orlando and Sebastian to see — a tiny tapir, a jaguar, parrots, toucans, orchids, nightshade and trumpet vines. "I made them on my journey home. They helped to while away the hours." He asked Orlando to pick the ones he would like for himself, and he chose the jaguar and the trumpet vines. Sebastian looked at the rough carvings and reached for the toucan, holding it tenderly and saying something Garzón pretended to understand. Sebastian saw through the pretense, and gave his father a look full of suspicion.

"Did you make that one too?" Orlando asked, pointing to the wooden seagull that hung by the bed along with its glass companion.

Garzón lay back on the pillow. "It was the first one I made. The two resemble Isabel and me, don't you think? The rough brown bird and his crystalline mate."

During the next few days he slept so much and so deeply that I became worried. *Don* Ernesto reassured me. It was the very best thing for him, he said. Whenever he woke, I was to feed him beef broth and fruit, and when the pain was very bad, soak a wad of cotton in coca juice and rub it on his gums.

As soon as he could sit up he asked me to cut his hair and shave him. He suspected that it was his wild appearance that made Sebastian wary of him, and he was right. As soon as Sebastian could see his face he no longer shied away when Garzón tried to touch him, and even consented to sleep with us, so long as I placed myself in the middle and we kissed him instead of each other.

Orlando waited patiently for Garzón to tell us what had happened to him. He sat by the bed, playing with his carvings or reading aloud, but Garzón soon noticed that he would ask where the wood used to make the jaguar and the trumpet vines had been found, and that when he read, it was always from *Gulliver's Travels*.

One afternoon, when my work at the infirmary was done for the day, and I was playing Sebastian's favorite game of hiding his cloth doll for him to find, Orlando could contain himself no longer and asked Garzón if what we had heard about the *Isabelita* was true, and she had indeed gone down in flames.

"I have never seen a ship catch fire so fast."

He had no idea how long he had been in the water after the ship sank and before losing consciousness. He remembered wondering if he was in his mother's womb enjoying a vision of all that was to come. Could it be that this was what the time before birth was like — an opportunity to experience one's life before emerging to live it? Was that why incidents and places sometimes seemed familiar? The sounds he heard were comforting, like his mother's voice, which returned to him in all its force of sweetness. There were other voices too and suddenly a bright and painful light which he knew was the sun. If this was birth he would soon forget the visions and the water that held him safe against all harm.

He had cried out, surprising himself with the depth and anguish of the sound he made. Hands had lifted him from the water and he wanted to demand to be put back, but the effort of that one cry took all the voice he had, and he fought to remember whether he should know who he was or whether he was indeed a newborn. He awoke to a ring of faces painted in brilliant reds and yellows, like the macaw that was also studying him from the shoulder of one of the children. A woman was fanning him with a palm frond, and as he opened his eyes the faces receded to give him room and then closed in again before being pushed aside by an old man with a feather headdress and earrings, speaking a tongue Garzón could not understand. He was given a sweet milky substance to drink and drifted off to sleep.

It was dark when he opened his eyes. A woman sat on the ground near him nursing a baby, and watching her Garzón recalled how soft his own mother's skin had felt against his cheek when he had rested his head on her shoulder to look at the stars. He felt the warmth of his tears and wondered why it was that he could remember his mother's skin and yet had no idea of where he was or what had happened to make his memory play such tricks upon him. He knew now that it was not birth he had experienced, but some strange accident that had deprived him of movement and speech. He tried to lift his hands and was so relieved to feel his fingers he almost cried again. Slowly he touched his bare chest, his face, and his legs, which were wooden. He tried to focus his thoughts. Not wooden, splinted. His legs must be broken. No parts of him seemed to be missing, yet his body was as strange to him as if he lived outside it and was seeing it for the first time. He tried sitting up, and with the dizziness came an even greater stab of memory. Flames and screaming wind. He fell back against the soft skins cushioning him, and the woman put her baby down and hurried to his side, her hand soothing on his forehead.

Seeing a face in the mist, he cried out my name, his head aching so acutely he thought it would burst, and then the old man was there with his milky drink that brought solace and sleep.

"All through the seasons of planting and harvesting," he told us, "I drifted in and out of consciousness, watching the blow-pipe over my head swaying back and forth on its cord of silk-grass."

By the time he could sit up unaided, he had learned enough of his rescuers' language to understand that they were as mystified as he by his survival.

With each passing day, the memories returned. The first thing that came back to him was the memory of his agate. What if he had lost it? He clamored for help and several people came running. Where were his clothes? What had they done with the clothes he had been wearing when they found him? Nothing, they assured him, they had done nothing. They were there, under his head, serving as a pillow. Garzón grabbed them up and found his agate in the tail of his shirt, where he had knotted it as he clung to the ship's mast. He wept with relief and passed it back and forth between his hands, waiting anxiously for flashes of memory, clinging to them when they came, and weaving them together with the same care the women took with the long fronds they braided into baskets. He sat for hours in the mottled shadows of the forest, watching the men preparing their weapons for the hunt, returning to camp with deer, tapirs, monkeys, and birds to roast over their fires. He saw them make, clean and repair arrows, spears, and clubs; heard them sing, and decorate their bodies with dyes and feathers.

One day, when his host reached for the quiver of arrows hanging near the blow-pipe, Garzón asked if he was correct in supposing that it was the jawbone of a *perai* fish that was tied with a little bunch of silk-grass to the quiver's brim. His host sat on the ground next to Garzón and placed the round box quiver between them. It was almost as long as his forearm, made of wood and coated in wax, with a round piece of tapir skin to cover it. Round the middle of the box a loop was tied, long enough to hang over a man's shoulder. His host removed the tapir skin top and turned the quiver upside down, releasing the hundred arrows it contained. Since contact with the needle-sharp points would cause death, the arrows were strung together with cotton, and rolled round a stick, each end embedded in small wheels designed to prevent the hunter's hands from touching the poison, and allowing him, by turning the wheel, to release one arrow at a time. His host then demonstrated how the jawbone of the *perai*, with its vicious teeth, was used to sharpen the arrows.

By then, Garzón had remembered his name, and that he had once lived in a village much like the one he was in now. He knew that he recognized the stars because his mother had taught him their names, and that he had been on a ship that had caught fire. But he could not remember why he had left his village, or what he had been doing on a ship, or why at night he often dreamed of a blue-eyed woman. He began to wonder if his confusion was due to a blow to his head, to the drinks the old man gave him, or both.

At night, when the urge to go south was so compelling he couldn't sleep, faces without names haunted him, and he learned not to wrestle with memory when it teased. Like mist, it was ethereal and impossible to catch. When the time was right the pictures appeared, vivid and almost tangible in their clarity, and with them came the feelings that made them real.

He knew that he had to start using his legs, but when the splints were removed he was so stiff that it took several days of exercise before he could bend his knees. Whenever the children crowded round him, Garzón put them to work kneading his muscles as he told them stories of life at sea, even though he had no inkling of whether what he told them had happened to him or was the product of his imagination. It was when the pain was fiercest that the memories came, so at night, while the village slept, he walked. One night, as he was returning to his shelter weak from his exertions, he saw rush lights glowing in one of the houses. Women were moving back and forth, and as he went by the cry of a newborn cut through the silence.

"I was overcome by a rush of memory so strong it felled me. Images poured in one upon another, names, places, and my connection to them. Suddenly, I remembered you Orlando, and Father Manuel, and Cararé and Wimencaí. I saw Isabel walking toward me in Yací's village, to tell me that Atzaya's baby was a girl. I remembered the letter that had reached me a few days before I sailed, and how it was the news it contained that had kept me hanging on to the plank that brought me to shore."

From that moment on not a day passed when he did not work on reconstructing his life, one memory at a time, until the only blank that remained was of the hours after he had lowered the surgeon into the water, and been found by his rescuers.

As soon as he was strong enough, he climbed into the jungle canopy to study the stars and saw from their position that he was much further south of the Equator, and far closer to home, than he had imagined.

"I saw the swarm of bees, the group of stars my father called the Pleiades. Nearby were Alpha and Beta, the eyes of my mother's people's great jaguar, and part of a creature my father said was a Centaur, half horse and half human. And at that moment, remembering my parents, I also remembered my Charrúa name."

Orlando had sat enthralled as Garzón spoke, and when Garzón said that he could talk no more that day, he made me promise that no matter what he was doing or what time it was, I would call him to Garzón's bedside the moment he decided to take up his story again.

A day passed before Garzón felt able to continue. Sebastian was with Wimencaí, so I sat on the bed next to Garzón with my sketch pad, and Orlando made himself comfortable at his feet.

Garzón had debated whether to return to the nearby coast and attempt to make his way south on the Atlantic Ocean, or whether to canoe down the river that ran by the village. The villagers traveled on the river all the time, and explained that it led to an even greater body of water that from their description Garzón deduced was the Paraná. If this was so, that mighty river would take him within easy reach of the Missions, where he knew he would be provided with everything necessary to make his way home. He decided to use the rivers for speed. They were fraught with rapids and falls and it would often be necessary for him to walk with the canoe on his back, but even so, he believed he would make better progress that way than on the ocean.

He began by taking short journeys, testing his endurance and his skills, and calculating what he would need to take with him in the way of weapons, clothing, and food.

"Knowing that I would soon be leaving, the villagers honored me by allowing me to enter into the full mystery of the blow pipe and *wourari*. The ritual would delay me, so I tried to find a way to refuse."

"Weren't you curious?" Orlando asked.

Garzón smiled. "I was. Perhaps that's why none of the excuses I came up with proved adequate."

The ritual began with the building of a small hut where the poison would be prepared. On the morning after it was completed and without breaking their fast, Garzón and his host entered the jungle to harvest the *wourali* vine.

"We dug up a bitter tasting root and two bulbous plants, which we put in a small basket. Then we captured some large black ants and some small red ones."

"How?" Orlando wanted to know.

"With great care! The bite of the black ones causes a fever and the red ones give you a nasty sting."

They returned to the village to harvest the necessary pepper plants and then retired to the hut, where they ground the fangs of a Labarria and those of a Curucuru snake, shredded the *wourali* vine and the roots, and put them, along with the fangs, into a leaf colander.

"We held the colander over a new clay pot and poured water over the mixture we had made. Then we added the juice from the stalks, the fangs, the ants, and the bruised pepper plants. We boiled it over a slow fire, using leaves to remove the scum that floated to the surface, until the pot was full of dark brown syrup. We took great care not to inhale any of the vapor and once the syrup had cooled, we poured it into a gourd, covered it with leaves and a piece of deer skin, and tied the opening tightly shut with a cord."

From the banks of the river, Garzón's host selected a bright yellow *ourah* reed several heads taller than he, perfectly hollow and without knots or joints. The *ourah* was then encased in a polished, brown *samourah*, a palm reed from which he was taught to extract the pulp after steeping the reed for several days in water. He was instructed in how to tie the end to which his mouth would be applied with silk-grass to prevent it from splitting, and protect the other end with an *acuero* seed, filled with beeswax. About an arm's length from the mouth piece, two agouti teeth, serving as sights, were fastened.

The hollow arrows he made from *Coucourite* palm leaves. They were about a hand in length, and as sharp as needles. The ends he dipped in the *wourali*, but not before filling them first with the wild cotton that would absorb the poison. It took him many hours of practice to do this well, for the cotton had to be large enough to fit the end of the arrow while tapering off to next to nothing before being threaded in place with more silk-grass.

Several more days were required to make his own round box quiver and blowpipe and learn to use them, and during that time he thought much about what his host had told him. Because *wourali* has the power to bring about death, women and young girls able to create life, cannot come into contact with it, lest it do them harm. Men with pregnant wives also abstain from its preparation, and the shelter in which the *wourali* was mixed was burned after they had finished.

"I wonder," I said, "what would change in our world if the making of gunpowder was approached with a similar acknowledgement of its deadly properties? What if men with pregnant wives weren't allowed to touch it? Imagine if we had to fast before preparing our deadly weapons and make all anew each time, because thoughts of killing had corrupted even the tools we touched?"

Conscious that he had been allowed entry not only into a science, but into a philosophy whose sacredness he had only just begun to understand, Garzón knew he was not worthy of carrying *wourali* out of the jungle with him.

"I presented my blowpipe and arrows to the village elders before leaving, and took with me only a simple bow with a new kind of arrow I had also learned from my hosts how to make. It was nicked just below the point, designed to break off when it struck and leave me with a reusable shaft."

On the day of his departure, they dressed him in a loincloth made of tapir skin and shod him in a pair of woven sandals. His canoe, loaded with food, was waiting at the banks of the river. The entire village turned out to see him off, and his final glimpse of them came just before the river took a sharp bend to the west.

The tribes he met on his way south were curious about him — a bearded, solitary stranger, dressed like a native, speaking a smattering of several languages, and clearly of mixed blood.

"They listened to my story of shipwreck and survival, and understood that, like the god Coniraya, who pursued his love until his feet bled and the animals of the forest mocked him, I was seeking the woman I loved and had far to travel before finding her. They were kind and helped me on my way, loaded with provisions of cassava bread and dried fish."

In the months that followed, he felt himself trapped in a rushing, relentless waterfall of memories, some his own, some prescient, pulsating images that came from within people, plants, and animals. When he remembered someone it was not only a face and a voice that came back to him, but the whole being. He saw plants and animals as fiery, pure essences, and wondered if the substance the healer had given him had permanently altered his perceptions. Drinking from a clay vessel he could feel the hands that shaped it, and when he breathed the scented smoke of the *acaiari* tree he felt the rustling shapes it had once sheltered.

"When loneliness or pain kept me awake, I willed myself back here, to the lagoon. I remembered Isabel trailing her hand in the water, and you," he said to Orlando, "swimming with Zule behind the canoe."

He had imagined the music drifting from the church as the choir sang, and the musicians spinning their web of sound, enfolding us in measures as rich as the love beckoning to him so strongly that it was all he could do not to plunge heedlessly into the jungle without stopping until he reached me.

"It is what Coniraya did," he said, taking my hand, "but then he was a god."

His dreams were vivid, and in them he saw his mother standing alone on the shore as his father's ship put out to sea. He felt her death soon after his departure, and in his dreams participated in the rituals that followed, waking up convinced that his skin had been pierced and remembering a vision he received while he still lived with her. The shamans said he was very young to dream so vividly of the future, but several others in the tribe had had similar dreams, and the fact that he shared them could only mean that the ancestors were ensuring that their message was understood in every living generation.

His dreams were of an upcoming time of death and desolation among the people of the jaguar and the anaconda. A long, dark time, longer than winter, drought or flood, and more devastating. In the dreams, he and his tribes-people wandered in a shadowy, forgotten place, like homeless spirits for whom no rites of passage had been enacted. The shamans interpreted these dreams to mean that to the outside world, they would disappear.

"All of you would die?" Orlando whispered.

"That is what I thought, but my mother and the shamans said no. There would be a time of war, a time of bondage, and a time of darkness and confusion, but in the end our voices would be heard again."

He had found little comfort in this interpretation. The shamans could not tell him if the darkness would last a day, a year, or several lifetimes, and he wanted to know that there would be an end to it before he died. Only as he journeyed through the jungle did he understand that his life and death were of consequence only if he ensured that he passed along his reverence and knowledge in the new life of his seed, and in the sharing of his wisdom.

His longing to return to us grew so intense that he drove himself mercilessly. There was not much more to him any more than bone, muscle and sinew, and he was possessed of a strength and determination he believed could only come from Coniraya himself.

As we charted his travels with the help of Father Manuel's maps, we discovered that the river that ran by the village where Garzón had convalesced was the São Francisco. By the time he left it, he had completed one third of his journey and was on his way to the Paraná, the waterway that would carry him within a few days walk of his eventual destination, the Uruguay. The region between the São Francisco and the Paraná was known as the Mato Grosso.

"That's Portuguese," Orlando said.

"Yes. It means 'dense jungle,' and is an apt name. The area can only be traversed on foot, at the rate of a few miles a day."

He regaled us with stories of how he had eaten monkeys, grubs, and raw fish, and been eaten by all manner of crawling, leaping, flying, and swimming beings he couldn't even begin to name.

He had given his canoe to the first villagers he met. In return, they replenished his supplies, and presented him with a sturdy bag of woven *caraguatá* in which to carry them.

The further into the jungle he went, the more tales he heard from the local inhabitants about the falls ahead. They were called Iguazú, and stretched for miles across his path toward the Uruguay. He was taught to differentiate and name the brown water of the Paraná River that fed the falls, the mist that bathed the trees, and the pools and running water that constituted the glorious chain the Guaraní worshipped as the origin of life. For many nights before ever catching a glimpse of the falls, he fell asleep to the sound of their distant roar.

When he knew that he was within a day's walk of the nearest cataracts, he prepared himself by bathing his body, combing and braiding his hair, and selecting an offering from the orchids that hung like rich fruit from the trees, their colors and forms so varied he found himself stopping to study individual petals. Perhaps the flowers were one of the reasons the Guaraní never seemed in a hurry.

"Who would wish to run when he could hold in his palm a work of art so perfect and so intricate?"

There were orchids of all colors, some ostentatious, almost garish, like the young men he often saw on his travels who seemed to want to draw attention to the brilliance of their persons; others modest and retiring, blending in with the muted browns and russets of the trees. He reached up to select what he thought was a bloom, and the entire garland took flight. He was surrounded by butterflies, dancing and fluttering around him, no longer modest in their hues, but displaying their sparkling wings, covered in what looked like tiny jewels of colored light. He stood amongst them until they tired and vanished like a cloud of gold dust among the trees. He would make an offering of a different kind, he decided, and leave the orchids to grace the air.

The roar grew louder as he walked, and soon everything around him glistened with moisture. His skin cooled, and more butterflies floated by, iridescent blue and as large as his hand. A hint of a breeze stirred the leaves as he stepped onto a rocky outcrop and almost lost his balance when the full force of Iguazú hit him.

As far as he could see the green of the jungle was laced with brown and white falling water, some of the falls as wide as the horizon, others delicate ribbons cascading from rocky outcrops into the foaming Paraná. Some fell from so high they misted into clouds where they met the river, others trickled over stairways of rocks, like veils dropped by careless goddesses on their way to swim in the lagoons that pooled amongst the islands of vegetation. Iguazú roared over rocks, sang in the current, and whispered in the tree roots, sending water drops like delicate sequins into the air and massive torrents unleashed into the rivers. Solitary birds soared over the water, floating on the currents of air like kites free of their tether, and watching them, he understood that reverence was the most fitting offering he could make to the spirits of Iguazú.

He spent several days locating a narrow gorge, well seeded with small islands, that would support a crossing. He lost his sandals to the current, but that didn't trouble him. The jungle is generous and would provide material for making more, as well as the wood he needed for a small raft that would carry him further along the Paraná and into the heart of the Missions.

"Is that where Yací found you?"

Garzón shook his head, looking suddenly very tired. He leaned his head back and closed his eyes. "I have yet to thank him for rescuing me."

"I will bring Yací to see you tomorrow," I said.

Orlando smoothed the blanket over Garzón's chest and tucked him in, just as Garzón had done for him so many times before.

I found Yací under a tree, stringing parrot feathers onto his lance, while Father Manuel bathed his leg with a warm infusion of *zuynandy*.

"Your wound is healing well," I said.

He smiled and looked up at me. "Both of them are."

It was undoubtedly true that he and Father Manuel looked healthier and happier than they had since the day of Abayubá's shooting. At least the war had produced the one good outcome of bringing these two old friends together again.

I told Yací that Garzón wanted to see him, and Father Manuel helped him to his feet. We stopped at the infirmary, leaving Yací to proceed alone.

Hours later, when I returned to the house with Orlando and Sebastian, I expected to find Yací gone. Father Manuel, Wimencaí and *Don* Ernesto had joined us, and we all stared at the sight of Yací sitting in a chair by Garzón's bed smiling vacantly into space. Garzón was in the same condition.

"You've been drinking!" I said.

I was looking around for evidence of *chicha* when Yací shook his head and held up some withered plants.

Wimencaí sniffed them. "*Ceibo* shoots," she said. "They do relieve pain—"

"And cause mild intoxication," *Don* Ernesto laughed.

"Bring chairs!" Garzón said. "Make *mate*! I want Yací to tell you all how he rescued me."

"Not until you are yourself again!" I said.

Wimencaí brought meat and cheese from her stores and by the time we had eaten, the effects of the *ceibo* shoots had faded.

"You are quite sure that the *ceibo* hasn't hurt him?" I asked Wimencaí.

"Absolutely certain. Look at him!"

It was true that Garzón had a healthier color and seemed energized.

"Begin, my friend!" he said to Yací.

Yací lit his pipe and waited until the room was quite silent. "I was riding north with warriors from my clan, to join the Mission forces, when some Spanish soldiers saw us. There were many more of them than of us, so we hid in the *monte* and used our slingshots on them."

The soldiers had fired a few random shots into the thick vegetation, and one bullet found its mark in Yací's leg, sending him sprawling to the ground behind a low thicket. Four of the soldiers who saw him fall came crashing through the undergrowth toward him, and Atzaya's father, Calelián, ran to his defense. The soldiers leapt on him, pinned him to the ground, and bound his hands.

Yací dragged himself after them and saw Calelián being tied to the tail of a horse and led away.

"It was getting dark, so they didn't go far. They built a fire, and staked Calelián out with their other prisoner." Yací nodded toward Garzón.

Yací lay concealed in the *monte*, watching the Spaniards bed down for the night. The guard posted by the horses kept himself awake by drinking out of a clay jug, and amused himself by stabbing Calelián and Garzón with sticks he took from the fire.

Clouds covered the moon and little light fell on Yací and his companions when they left the *monte*. Unnoticed by the guard, they reached the sleeping soldiers and before they could raise the alarm, clubbed them to death. A man they left for dead roused himself, and shot Garzón in the back.

"I didn't know that they had shot him once already," Yací said.

"They had captured me the day before," Garzón said. "They didn't believe me when I told them that I had a wife who would pay a fine ransom for me! They were planning to sell me if I survived."

"How did they catch you?" Orlando asked.

"I was stupid enough to walk right into them. They thought I was one of the Indians they'd fought in a skirmish much like the one they had had with Yací."

That was how this war was being waged, Father Manuel said, in a series of small skirmishes, the outcome determined just as much by random circumstance as by skill or courage.

The Spanish sent out scouts and hunters who rarely returned. Father Manuel had stumbled upon more than one of these unfortunate patrols, their throats cut, their eyes glassy and full of flies. Only on the few occasions when actual battles took place, could the Spanish and Portuguese forces fight in their traditional manner, with the cavalry leading the charge, while the infantry waited in trenches dug in the battlefields. The Indians had learned quickly how to turn these tactics against them. They used their knowledge of the countryside, and their horsemanship to full advantage, and dispersed on all sides like water over the field of battle, surrounding the soldiers and trapping them in their trenches, wreaking havoc amongst forces unaccustomed to such methods of attack.

Such had been his own first battle, and the Mission forces had shown no mercy when the Spanish soldiers retreated. They continued the attack until the entire company, a battalion of five hundred, lay dead upon the field and in the graves they had dug for themselves in the trenches. The Charrúa, who had joined the fight, walked amongst the dead collecting the smaller cannon balls to make into *boleadoras.*

"Victories over the royalist forces are rare," Father Manuel sighed. "The war is not going well for us. In his last letter, Cararé told me that in Daymán the Portuguese have killed Chief Paracatú and four hundred of his men."

"Father, did you have to fight too?" Orlando asked him.

"During that battle I mentioned, the one where a whole battalion was lost, a soldier came at me with his bayonet and I shot him. He fell on me, soaking me in his blood and baptizing me in war. He looked surprised, as if in the midst of slaughter he found his own death unexpected." Father Manuel looked down at the seed rosary wound around his fingers. "Until then I had managed to consider myself unnecessary as a warrior, limiting my assistance to caring for wounded men and shooting wounded horses. I was reproached for wasting gunpowder on animals, but I would not leave innocent creatures to pay in suffering for our self-defeating hatreds."

Soon after their victory they had been forced to retreat and had tried swimming to safety across a deep river. All one hundred and fifty of their prisoners had been lost. The wounded drowned, the able bodied escaped. The survivors spent a miserable night soaked to the skin, shivering in their hiding place in a thick stand of trees. Their store of gunpowder was wet and the guns inoperable. When they accidentally stumbled across a company of soldiers, they fought with slingshots and lances.

After that they were often hungry. Wild animals and cattle, once so abundant, seemed to have disappeared. They did not come across deer or peccary once after leaving the area of Caupolicán. As for cattle, the Spanish forces rounded them up and drove them far from the fields of battle. All they saw of them was dust on the horizon.

Their days consisted of rising, walking, riding, hunting, eating, and sleeping, killing or being killed, all with as little purpose as Father Manuel's worst nightmares. Soldiers were sent out onto the plains and into the jungles to kill Indians. Indians waited at every turn ready to kill soldiers.

"I cannot see how such a war will ever end," he said.

"Tell them of your visit to your grandfather," Yací prompted Garzón.

The room was very quiet as Orlando slipped off *Don* Ernesto's lap and went to sit in his usual place at the foot of the bed. For a moment I wondered if Garzón was going to do as Yací asked. He sat staring at the *mate* gourd in his hands as if it could tell him how to begin. Then he handed it to me and began to speak.

"As soon as I reached the mission at Yapeyú I realized that I was near the place where I was born. I sent the beads to Isabel, and simply began to walk in the direction of the village. I told the guards who I was and they took me to where an old man sat on a jaguar skin working on a piece of stone. He looked up when I entered his little house, and his face lit up like a child's. 'How like your mother you are, Tacuabé,' he said. The voice was all that was left of my grandfather that I could recognize, that and his tenderness toward me. He saw at once that I was cold, and he picked up an old piece of blanket and put it round my shoulders.

He made me a meal of fish and *mandioca*, and I asked him to tell me everything he remembered about my mother. She had often dreamed of me, he said, and he had promised her that he would not die until I returned. When my father took her from them, my grandmother had sat by the river and not left her post until a year later, when my mother returned. She had refused to abandon her tribal customs, and when I was born on the floor of my father's cabin, it was too much for him. He took her back to her village and left us both there. My mother never expected to see him again, but nine years later he appeared, saying he wanted his son. My mother refused to give me up, so he simply took me one day when I was fishing alone by a stream. He told me it had all been arranged, and she had sold me to him. My mother didn't live long after I was taken. She wanted to enter the spirit world, where she could take better care of me. I repaid her by forgetting her."

"You kept her parting gift with you always," I said.

"At least I did that. It isn't much, is it?"

"It is only natural for a child to believe what he is told," Father Manuel said.

"I visited her grave every day that I was there."

"And you made her an offering?" I asked, touching the finger with the missing joint.

"Of a different kind. I left her most of the carvings I had made. This," he said, holding up his hand, "this I made to my grandfather. He kept his promise, and lived until I returned. Once he had said everything he had to say, he joined my mother."

~

When a letter came from Charlie, I waited until I was alone to open it. I hadn't told Garzón about the papers hidden at the castle, and I didn't want him to learn about them by some random reference of Charlie's. I need not have worried. The letter concerned only the war, and by the time I reached the end of it I was incredulous and elated.

Just as Painted had always believed he would, the King had taken the side of the Indians, and their lands were to be restored to them. This was an outcome so extraordinary that Charlie was traveling to Buenos Aires to confirm it.

Every day after receiving the letter we asked each other if it could possibly be true, and prayed that it was. I wanted it to be so most of all for Креме, whose joy I could only imagine when he heard of his King's decision. Our prayers were answered. All over the colony the church bells rang, proclaiming Ferdinand's goodness, and an end to the fighting.

Креме came home, and when the long awaited decree arrived from Spain making the King's decision official, it was he, tired, worn, and looking a decade older, who climbed to the top of one of the watchtowers to read it to us. Like his faith in his king, his voice never wavered, and when he had pronounced every word in the document, he carried his standard into the church and placed it on the altar, lying before it on the floor, his arms outstretched, and his forehead on the tiles he himself had made and put there three years earlier.

While Wimencaí prepared his *mate* gourd and his pipe, and fireworks flew from the castle towers, Креме sat outside his house receiving the homage his loyalty so richly deserved from the visitors who streamed in and out until dawn.

As for Father Manuel, his knees were raw. As penance for doubting the goodness of God, he fell on them each time he remembered what Ferdinand had done.

News of the decision gradually reached the fighters in outlying areas, and over the next few weeks we received Africans returning to their *quilombos*, Christian Indians making their way back to their Missions, and unconverted tribes riding to their homes on *pampas* and in *montes*.

Along with their triumph, they carried disturbing news of outbreaks of smallpox in the tribal communities. Epidemics of smallpox had overtaken the Indians ever since Europeans first arrived, but coupled with the decimations of the recent war, this latest outbreak meant that their numbers would be seriously threatened.

The news troubled Yací, and he left us soon after receiving it, to go in search of his clan.

The promise of both springtime and peace brought a surge of activity to Caupolicán. Our food stocks were nearly depleted, but the herds were returning, and the crop of winter wheat had been a fine one. Our wounded were on the road to recovery, grass was sprouting over the graves of the fourteen men from our settlement who had given their lives for the vagaries of King Ferdinand, and Wimencaí had been called to five births in a single fortnight.

Don Ernesto, whose poem was to be published soon, had begun a new work cataloguing the flora and fauna of the area, and he asked if he might stay with us a season or two longer. We welcomed the suggestion, and when Garzón returned Orlando to Zulema, he took *Don* Ernesto with him to harvest plants from the other shore of the lagoon.

I began painting again and one morning I looked up from my canvas and saw Yací, Atzaya and their little daughter Yandibé riding toward the gates of Caupolicán. They stopped some distance away and Yací transferred Yandibé from his horse to Atzaya's. He turned away, and Atzaya and Yandibé proceeded alone.

I ran to meet them, and learned that Yací had returned to his village to find the few living surrounded by the dying, covered in eruptions that sealed shut their eyes and swelled their tongues. At the first signs of the disease, the sick, their belongings, and those who came in contact with them had been isolated, but for many it was too late. Yací and his little family had been spared, but Yandibé was suffering from a bloody flux no one was left alive in her village to advise them how to cure.

Atzaya and Yandibé were beyond contagion, but having been recently exposed to the disease, Yací would be obliged to keep well away until we could be certain that he would not bring it with him to Caupolicán.

Before they parted, Yací and Atzaya had put strings of ten beads into one another's hands, to assist them in keeping track of how many days would pass before Yací could come to fetch her away.

Wimencaí made a drink for Yandibé from tobacco leaves to induce vomiting, and once her system was cleansed she prepared a mixture of milk, lemons, rue, and mint. By the following day, Yandibé was feeling stronger and two days after that she ate her first substantial meal with no ill results.

The last time I had seen Atzaya had been when she released the captive women and children, and I was anxious to hear what her tribe's reaction had been. They were displeased with her, she said, but far too busy to concern themselves with the escaped captives. Word had come that the clans were gathering in unprecedented numbers, and the warriors had immediately gone to work strengthening their spears and preparing their most imposing head gear for battle. The white feathers of peacetime had been put away and colored ones had taken their place. Torn slings were mended, and leather breech cloths decorated with shells and the rattling black gourds of the *timbó*.

While all of this activity was going on, Atzaya had brought out Yací's wooden chisels and the little mall he used as a hammer in his stonework. She had put them before him, wound the singing statue Father Manuel had given him, and while its music played around them, spread her mother's beloved agates on the ground. She told him that now that her mother's spirit was free, she wanted him to make something out of the agates.

Yací had touched the blue stones, arranging them this way and that. "I will make you a star you can hold in your hand, with a heart so pale the light will shine through it, and spokes like the blue of midnight."

It would be shaped like the spiked *bolas* he would soon be using in battle and fit together in five perfect pieces. For days Yací had shaped the agates as they sat by the fire with Yandibé. He had smoothed the rough edges of the stones as shafts of light went back and forth between the flames and his hands, and as the star took shape, the feeling of having lost his way began to recede, and Yací sensed that his souls were coming home from the darkness in which they had been lost since Abayubá's death.

As she was telling me this, Atzaya reached into the pouch tied at her waist and withdrew a parcel of black and white fur, revealing the most bewitching piece of craftsmanship I had ever beheld. I was entranced by the shimmering blue agates, and wondered how anything inanimate could convey both fire and ice so perfectly. I yearned to possess them as I had never yearned for anything before.

Chapter XIII

Sebastian, who had just celebrated his first birthday, spent long hours with Yandibé, playing with carved wooden animals and *carretas*, cloth dolls, and the many stones and feathers they found by the lagoon. We often took them there, where the two of them could wave to Yací at his camp nearby. Yandibé swung from branch to branch to show her father how strong she had become. Atzaya shot arrows across to him with the beads she removed from her calendar necklace, until at last the day came when she shot the last bead. One more night and Yací and his family would be reunited.

Atzaya, Wimencaí and I were in my house with *Don* Ernesto preparing the meal we would all share to celebrate, when there was a knock at the door. It was Criaré.

"This was left at the gate."

It was a stone, wrapped in a page from a book, and with my name on it. In the margins was written a brief message, the writing that of a child or of someone for whom writing was a recently acquired skill. The message read simply, *Orlando has the small pox.*

My knees gave way, and I would have fallen if Criaré had not caught me.

If he had been with me he would not have contracted the smallpox. Why had I ever let him go? Why had I returned him to the *quilombo* instead of keeping him by my side?

"I must go at once!"

"I will go," *Don* Ernesto said. "I have survived exposure to smallpox before. You have Sebastian to consider."

"What if he dies and I never see him again?" I cried.

"What if you die? Or Sebastian?"

I knew that *Don* Ernesto was right, but I longed to be with Orlando, to nurse him, to surround him with my love and protection, to make sure that everything was being done for his ease and comfort, but all I could do was see that the canoe was filled with supplies, with blankets and candles, with dried beef, cheeses, and fruits. I also equipped *Don* Ernesto with paper, quills and ink, demanding that he leave a letter on the shore every day reporting on Orlando's condition.

His first communication made me so angry I could barely contain myself. He reported how Orlando and others at the *quilombo* had contracted the disease from soldiers passing through the area, leaving behind contaminated blankets and clothing. It was an old means of disposing of the unwanted, he said, allowing the smallpox to kill them. Entire villages had been wiped out this way. The disease had claimed Zulema's man Lauro, and Orlando's little brother. Orlando's condition remained the same. The fever raged, but he was so far holding on to life.

Day after day I watched from the opposite shore as Garzón crossed the lagoon to pick up *Don* Ernesto's letters. One morning, as he approached the shore, I saw *Don* Ernesto himself standing there with Zule at his side and Orlando in his arms. He handed Orlando to Garzón, who placed him in the canoe and paddled swiftly back to me.

"He is beyond contagion," he said. "But Zulema is dead."

As I lay him down in the infirmary I realized that I had never entirely forgiven her for taking him from me. Did Orlando know that his mother was dead? Had he witnessed her death, and that of his little brother? I wept with shame as I remembered the resentment I had harbored toward her. She had deserved to know her child, and Orlando had deserved to learn his own history, to hear that he was wanted and loved by his parents. Zulema was the reason I had chosen to give birth in the *quilombo*. The image of her scarred wrists and branded breast, and the old woman's tale of how Zulema's first child had been taken from her, had first put the idea in my head. I had made no connection between that child and Orlando until the day Zulema saw his tattoo, I only knew that I wanted my son born there, in that place where I had seen courage personified.

I was bathing Orlando's scars with rose hip water the next day when he opened his eyes. "Don't cry, Isabel," he whispered. "I'm never leaving again."

Garzón and I carried him home and watched over him day and night. He wanted to become a teacher, he told us, to get married and live with his wife and children at Caupolicán. When he died, he wanted to be buried in the burial ground with a head stone saying Orlando Zumbí, teacher and scholar.

"Zumbí, Is that your African name, Orlando?" Garzón asked him.

"After the last chief of Palmares. He was lame like I am, and his empire was by the river Itapicurú, in Brazil — an entire colony of runaway slaves. Thirty thousand of them! It stood for over a hundred years until—" Orlando looked distressed for a moment. "Until — I can't remember the date."

"1695, son," Garzón said.

"1695, yes!"

It took nine thousand men and many cannon to bring Palmares down, and the glow of Zumbí's city burning was seen all the way to the city of Porto Calvo. The Portuguese thought that if they killed everyone in Palmares they would eradicate the very memory of such a place.

"Instead, my mother said, it lives in the soul of every slave, and at the heart of every *quilombo*. I will write the story of Palmares one day! *Don* Ernesto is going to help me. And perhaps you will draw the pictures, Isabel?"

"I will draw them, Orlando Zumbí."

I had shown Yací my paintings, and he was intrigued by some of the colors I used, so I taught him how to mix the dyes and apply them. He combined colors I had never imagined, and drew on rocks, on pieces of wood, even on his own skin, walking round the settlement like a movable canvas. Knowing how much Orlando enjoyed seeing him painted, he made sure he was wearing his brightest designs whenever he entered the house.

Atzaya always asked Garzón for stories about his journeys, even though she accused him of imagining the ants that build cities and cultivate plants, and the lizards and fish that change colors. Yací, however, believed in marvels, and like Orlando never tired of hearing of fish that flew, of tentacled monsters that inhabited the depths, of whales so large they dwarfed the ships.

One day, he asked where Garzón had first heard the story of the god Coniraya, but Garzón could not remember. In fact, the only part of the story he recalled was that Coniraya had loved a woman enough to follow her for endless days through the jungle. He, Yací said, knew the rest, and would tell it to us.

Like Garzón, the god Coniraya had fallen in love with a woman from a faraway place. He had followed her, walking through forests, tripping on tree roots, stepping on thorns, and cutting himself on rocks. When the skunk saw his wounds he had laughed and called Coniraya a fool, saying no love was worthy of such sacrifice.

"Then Coniraya stopped his journey and told the skunk about the sun that shines within."

Yací opened his left hand and showed us where he had drawn two suns blending on his palm. When beings are very fortunate, Coniraya told the skunk, they meet the sun that is the twin to theirs. If their good fortune holds, the recognition is mutual, and if they are very brave and willing to suffer for their love, they are allowed to live and to die together, renewing the sun itself with their own fire.

"For his failure to understand that even gods must suffer for such a gift, Coniraya turned the skunk into a smelly night prowler, and to this day, he wanders the earth, searching for his own twin sun."

Yací unrolled a soft scroll I had made for him, a picture of him and Atzaya under a *ceibo*, she wearing a crown of its red ceibo flowers, and he painted in all the dyes I had given him. Yandibé stood by them, holding the blue agates in her cupped hands. He had added to my work, and a bright yellow sun now shone above their heads.

"Now we have a gift for you," he said.

Atzaya put the skunk skin pouch in my hands, and I felt the agates resting inside. I cannot take these, I thought. I want them too much. "They were your mother's and should go to Yandibé," I said.

"My mother's souls are all at rest," Atzaya said. "We want the agates to be yours."

I poured the blue stones onto Orlando's bed, and they winked in the sun like newborn stars.

~

All of us wanted to see the marker that established the new boundaries between the Spanish and Portuguese dominions. Survivors of Yací and Atzaya's clan had chosen to settle near there, and when Yací took his family to join them, Father Manuel, Garzón and I rode with them to view the marker.

On the Spanish side it read *Hispaniae rege catholico* and on the Portuguese side *Lusitano rege fidelissimo*. A plain stone slab set in a field few people would ever cross, bearing words for which thousands had died, and which only future historians would bother to read. Pampas grass had already grown up around it and soon wind and weather would obscure the words, and the marker would look no different from any other stone on the prairies.

We all stood and stared at it for a long time, each lost in our own thoughts.

At the Portuguese fort nearby, troops were still camped outside. A white flag of truce had replaced the rose colored flag of war, but Yací suspected that the soldiers had no intention of leaving and were only biding their time before attacking again. Father Manuel explained that orders often took months to arrive, and that the King had recently replaced all of his ministers.

To Atzaya's father Calelián, this simply sounded like an excuse for not honoring one's word. He wanted to muster a contingent of warriors to attack the fort from the rear. Father Manuel asked him to consider that such an attack could endanger the peace agreement and give the Portuguese an excuse not to keep their word. Calelián laughed. The Portuguese, he claimed, had never needed an excuse to break their word before, and the time had come for the tribes to stop dancing like mindless puppets every time the kings of Spain and Portugal changed their villainous minds.

Father Manuel found himself in a painful quandary. He bore no love for the Portuguese, and trusted neither them nor his own countrymen any more than Calelián did. He nevertheless knew that the decree ordering them to retreat was real, and wanted to believe that peace was possible.

He decided to visit the fort in an attempt to discover where matters stood, and learned while he was there that the letter the commander had been waiting for containing instructions to retreat, had finally arrived.

The soldiers left peacefully a few days later, walking behind the wagons carrying their supplies and their wounded, and Father Manuel rode back to the settlement greatly relieved, only to find me waiting to tell him that I had had another letter from Charlie.

Father Manuel received the information I imparted with an incredulity amounting to numbness.

The King had changed his mind.

If the Indians of the seven Missions he had deeded to Portugal returned to their land, royalist forces would be sent to remove them. As Spanish kings before him had traditionally done, King Ferdinand put out the call for warriors from the unaffected Missions to form the backbone of the army that would march against their dispossessed brothers.

Father Manuel lay his seed rosary, his embroidered chasuble, and Brother Andrés' copy of the writings of Bartolomé de las Casas, on the altar. Chararé's banner was where he had put it on his day of triumph, draped across the nearest side altar, a sword resting nearby. Chararé himself stood immobile by it, wearing his plainest work clothes instead of the dark blue Mission soldier's uniform of which he had once been so proud.

Father Manuel genuflected, turned his back on the altar, and came down the steps toward us. Garzón took up the sword and helped Chararé buckle it around his waist, while I slipped a little bag of dried orange peel from our tree into Father Manuel's pocket, to remind him of home.

In the plaza, the men were engaged in the same round of preparations as before, only this time there was no feeling of anticipated victory, no real hope that we would succeed in establishing the peace we all craved.

Garzón would be marching with them, and for our leave taking, he and I walked to the same crest on which we had stood the first time we surveyed the lagoon together. The pastures were covered in long shadows, and cattle grazed in the evening breeze. Sheep drank from the streams, and one lamb stood confidently on its recumbent mother's back. Around the settlement, the fields lay in neatly plowed and cultivated swirls; a thin spiral of smoke rose from the *quilombo*; and in the distance, we saw the Minuanes waiting for the men from Caupolicán to join them.

Overlooking the lagoon stood Charlie's castle, the pale gray stones of its walls glowing in the sunlight, a reminder of the incongruity of the four worlds fate had brought together.

The gold, the silver, all the hides and gems we took from the river of painted birds had after all brought nothing but strife, as all the Mother's gifts did, Garzón's grandfather had warned him, when used without honor. He had believed that when all the sacred gold and silver were gone, men would find the holy plants, and if by then we still had not learned wisdom, a second curse would fall on us as we discovered that the Mother gives us these powerful essences to help us attain perfection, not riches. But so long as the interpretation of wisdom was left not to the wise but to the self advancing, we would inevitably continue to repeat the same mistakes.

I knew that time could not be turned back, nor that moment found when men began to plant beyond their needs and reap beyond their planting. All we could do was find those hearts and minds that questioned and hesitated and do them honor, for only they could save us.

As the church bells tolled their solemn call to arms, Garzón took his place next to the men, and rode out to join the gathered Minuanes on the plains. We gathered on the battlements as before, only this time there were no cheers, only the silence of despair.

The men headed north, to find Alejandro, the commander from the northern Missions. He and his men had just lost a battle with the Portuguese and when the men from Caupolicán caught up with him, they found the Mission soldiers tying up the pontoons on which they had made their escape across the Iguazú River. In their haste, they had left the ammunition for their four remaining cannons on the other side. Only one round had remained for each, so perhaps it represented no great loss after all. The Portuguese fort Alejandro planned to attack had twice that number of cannon, but he knew exactly where the fort's weak points lay, and how to execute distracting maneuvers that succeeded in drawing fire away from the men who breached the rear gate.

In spite of his masterful tactics, his forces were repelled and in the second attempt on the fort Alejandro was killed by a bullet fired from the battlements.

Chief Sepé took over the command, and the assault on the fort did not let up even when half the men lay dead by the walls. Surprisingly, it was the Portuguese who asked for a truce. Sepé retreated to form his escort, and twenty-two men, Father Manuel, Cararé and Yací included, were chosen to accompany him into the fort. Before they went, the Mission soldiers washed in the river and tidied their clothing. Muddy boots were scraped clean, buttons polished, and sashes straightened. Yací and the men from the free tribes restrung their torn shell and seedpod leggings and bathed their horses.

Outside the fortress they hobbled their horses and put down their muskets and sabers, their spears, bows and arrows. The wooden doors swung open to admit them, the only sound the tinkling of the shells and seedpods that ornamented the warriors' ankles. The doors were shut and barred behind them and the men found themselves standing at the center of a ring of muskets, a second ring guarding them from the battlements above.

Before Father Manuel could do more than shout "Traitor!" at the Portuguese captain, his arms were pinned behind him.

The captain laughed and shook his head. "Listen to this, men!" he said. "A Spanish priest fighting with a pack of renegade Indians, shouting treason at a Portuguese officer fighting for his king!"

As Sepé, Yací, Cararé and their companions were tied hand and foot to stakes in the ground, Father Manuel realized that he was to be spared the punishment in store for them, and he tore and bit at the ropes that bound him until his wrists and mouth were red with blood.

Yes, he was a traitor, on all counts, he shouted, fighting his king and breaking his vows. He was the one who should be punished, not Sepé and his followers, and not, he begged, Cararé.

He offered himself in Cararé's place, went so far as to threaten them with excommunication if they punished one of the King's most loyal subjects, but his pleas went unheard.

The air, so still before, filled with cries. Father Manuel was so close to the victims, that like the soldier who told Garzón the story, he too could smell the sweat of the men brandishing the whips, and feel the warmth of the blood that spattered over him.

The sun was setting as the final tired lashes fell on the inert, unrecognizable masses of flesh at his feet. Yací and the others who lay on the ground had long ago lost consciousness, and Father Manuel's voice was a mere rasp in his throat.

He welcomed the bullets that ended his life, and when his body was thrown with the others in a heap outside the walls, the soldiers wondered only at the scent of oranges that lingered in the air. One of them, already terrified by having witnessed the murder of a priest, and thinking the aroma a sign of holiness, wrapped Father Manuel's body in a blanket and took him to where Garzón was waiting with the troops.

When they went to collect the bodies of their companions, they were amazed to find them alive. The miracle of their survival was attributed to Father Manuel and cited in future years as the first of his miracles.

They tended to the men's wounds as best they could, and began the slow and painful journey back to Caupolicán.

Cararé never regained consciousness and Garzón rode by the wagon in which he lay until he died.

Once they reached Caupolicán and lodged Yací and the other wounded in the infirmary, Garzón prepared a mound in the Charrúa tradition for Cararé and Father Manuel, and asked the women and me for permission to put Joan of Arc on top of it. We gave it readily. They had been warriors, just as she had, and she would watch over them and see the two old friends safely on their journey into the spirit world, where Wimencaí believes a very special place is reserved for those who die in despair.

We buried Cararé's harp and his sword with him, and dressed Father Manuel in the chasuble his mother had made when he became a missionary. The choir sang, and Orlando and Garzón danced. Wimencaí prepared a feast of all their favorite foods, and late that night, when everyone else had left, Wimencaí, Garzón and I, sat together under the stars while Sebastian and Orlando slept on the lap of the mound just as they had slept in Carareé's and Father Manuel's laps so many times before.

~

As soon as he could speak, Yací asked for his statue, and Atzaya and I went to find it.

It was deer rutting season, and the air around the cave was redolent with the smell of their markings. A male had visited the area recently and a strong aroma of garlic hovered round the cave opening. Inside, we dug until we retrieved the singing statue from its secret hiding place.

Yací's hands trembled as he unwrapped the soft deer skin and reached for the little golden key, desperate to hear the music he found so haunting and so sweet, but no matter how he tried, the statue sang no more.

~

The final stand taken by the Indians of the Missions took place in Caaibaté, while the tribes of the *pampas* were riding to their aid. Three Africans, five men born in the colonies, and two thousand five hundred Indians fell on the field of battle.

So did a solitary countryman of mine, holding his red and white banner.

Among the imperial forces, casualties were light. Three men gave their lives for the Kings of Spain and Portugal.

As I sat listening to the drums of the victorious Portuguese and Spanish battalions, I wished that they drummed a call for peace and solidarity, a reprise to the meaning of true freedom, and not a blind desire for conquest over my beloved river of painted birds.

I continue to believe that no war will ever succeed in killing the dream Caupolicán represents, and that the song of the harvest and the harp will be more enduring than the battle cry.

Homes are going up all around us for the survivors, and the yield of these rich prairies will generously feed us all so long as we give back as generously.

At night when Garzón and I climb to the highest turret to look out over the lagoon and beyond, fireflies dance round the graves at Joan of Arc's feet.

Don Ernesto was proved right. Men came to claim as theirs the land by the lagoon, and were stopped by the document that proclaimed me Charlie's wife. So Charlie and his castle stand guard over us after all, just as he would have wished.

Glossary

All of these words are used in context and explained in the text. This is to serve the reader as further clarification.

Fr. – French Gu.- Guaraní In.- Indigenous (various)
La. – Latin Port.- Portuguese Sp. – Spanish

acaiari, In. gum of the Hayawa tree, used to produce an aromatic smoke
acuero, In. species of palm
agouti, In. forest-dwelling rodent
aromo, Sp. fragrant bush
arroyo, Sp. stream
a sus pies, señora, Sp. at your feet, lady
Ave María Purísima, Sp. a salute to the Virgin Mary
Banco Inglés, Sp. English bank (as in a river bank)
beso a usted la mano, caballero, Sp. I kiss my hand to you, sir
boleadoras, bolas, Sp. A weapon, consisting of three rounded stones tied to strips of rawhide or rope
butiá, Sp. palm indigenous to Uruguay
caá parí, Gu. Paradise Tree
Caballero, me da una mano? Sp. Sir, would you lend me a hand?
cabildo, Sp. tribal council
cacique, Sp. head man
camalote, Sp. small moving island
camilucho, Sp. cattle man, cowboy
caracú, Sp. bone marrow
caraguatá, Gu. fibrous plant
carao, Gu. limpkin
carreta(s), Sp. wagon

ceibo(s), Sp. coral tree, La. Erythrina crista-galli
cerro (s) Sp. hills
changadores, Sp. hired hands
chajá, Sp. southern screamer
chicha, Sp. fermented grain drink made with wild honey
cilicio, Sp. a metal belt worn under a religious' robes for purposes of self-punishment
cimarrón, Sp. wild, used here for dogs
coquitos, Sp. fruit of the butiá
coronilla, Sp. tree, La. Scutia buxifolia
Cruz de mayo, Sp. cross of May, or Southern Cross
cupay, Gu. oil
don/doña, Sp. equivalent to Mr. and Mrs.
dragones, Sp. (dragon) bird, La. Xanthopsar flavus
escudo, Sp. (shield) a coin
fugida, Sp. fugitive (fem.)
guazú birá, Gu. small deer
guazú pucú, Gu. swamp deer
hijito, Sp. diminutive for son
Hispaniae Rege Catholico, Lat. Catholic Spanish King
Libre, Sp. free
Los Castillos, Sp. The Castles
Lusitano Rege Fidelissimo, Lat. Faithful Portuguese King
macachines, Sp. small wild flower
macaguá caá, Gu. snake grass
mamá, Sp. mother
mamelucos, Sp. slave warriors
Mar de las damas, Sp. The Ladies' Sea
mboy caá snake grass
monsieur, Fr. Mister/sir
monte, Sp. wooded area
ñandú rhea
ombú shady, umbrella shaped, silk cotton tree
ourah, In. a large reed, La. Arundinaria schomburgkii

pacoú, In. river fish, La. Myleus pacu
Pa'I Mini, Gu. minor, or small father
pampa(s), Sp. grasslands
pampero, Sp. strong, seasonal wind
pastel/pasteles, Sp. *sweet pastries*
perai, In. piranha, La. Serrasalmus piraya
porahei, Gu. sacred song
querida, Sp. dear, beloved
Rey Fidelissimo, Lat. faithful king
Robe a la francaise, Fr. dress in the French style
sacha barbasco, In. a plant used to catch fish, La. Serjania piscetorum
samourah, In. a palm, La. Ireartia setigera
sangre del grado, Sp. resin
sauce criollo, Sp. native willow, La. Salix humboldtiana
senhor, Port. sir, mister
señor, Sp. sir, mister
señorita, Sp. miss (form of address)
sin pecado concebida, Sp. conceived without sin
tacuara, Sp. bamboo
timbó, Sp. a tropical tree, La. Paullinia pinnata
toninas, Sp. black river dolphins
uru, Gu. bird
urutau, Gu. ghost bird
venado de campo, Sp. plains deer
wimen, In. wise
wourali, In. also known as curare
wourari, In. the rite for using curare
yerba mate, Sp. a green tea
zuyñandy, Gu. coral tree

Name Pronunciations

Atzaya at-sa-ya
Abayuba ah-bah-ju-ba
Buenos Aires boo-en-os i-res
Calelián cah-leh-lee-an
槽Cararé ca-rah-re
Charrúa cha-rew-ah
Chiquitos chee-kee-tos
Guaraní goo-ah-ra-nee
Herrán err-ann
Itanambí ee-tah-nahm-bee
Javier ha-vee-err
Martínez mar-teen-ez
Minuán mee-nu-an
Montevideo mon-the-vee-deh-o
Wimencaí wee-men-ka-ee
Yací jah-cee

Weights and Measures

It was not until late in the 18th century that anything resembling a uniform system of weights and measures was developed. Even then, countries, and areas within countries, had their own way of conveying weight, distance, and other measures. The human body was often used, as in feet, and (from the Latin for arms) brachia. For that reason, modern weights and measures are used here.

Acknowledgments

Among the many extraordinary encounters over the decades of travel and research for this book, the most unexpected occurred in Minnesota.

I had learned that the James Ford Bell Library in the Wilson Library at the University of Minnesota had in its rare books and documents collection, volumes of Jesuit writings from the time period and locations I was researching. I was sitting at a table, surrounded by documents in Spanish, Latin, and Portuguese, when the Library's at the time, Carol Urness, introduced herself.

Carol explained that the Library was always interested in learning how researchers used its collection. I gladly shared that I was there reading first hand accounts of the Jesuits' travels from Europe to South America, and of the fabled Mission system they established there. Carol told me that the Library had recently acquired a document written by a Jesuit Priest, believed to be the only extant first person account of the Guaraní War of 1754, an important event in this book. The document had as yet not been studied.

Moments later, I watched as Carol opened a box containing the document and handed it to me. I have since revisited it, my amazement undiminished at the confluence of events that brought the writings of an 18th century Spanish Jesuit into the hands of a 21st century Uruguayan writer.

Thanks to a grant from the Central Minnesota Arts Board, through funding provided by the McKnight Foundation, I travelled to what remains of the Jesuit Missions in the jungles of Paraguay.

Nicolás and Tracy Carter put me in touch with Edgar and Noemi Araujo, who became my guides there, intuitively taking me at all hours of the day and night to abandoned ruins still able to convey the intellectual, architectural, and artistic wonder of the relationship between Jesuits and Indians that led to the creation of structures, stone and wood carvings, music, and art work of such depth and beauty.

In Uruguay, with meticulous attention and the intuition of old friends, Raúl and Florencia Rodríguez planned my travels into the areas covered in this book; Lucía Todone shared her vast knowledge of birds, and the flora and fauna of Uruguay; and Rosario Cibils of Uruguay's Biblioteca Nacional, guided and assisted me in locating books and documents pertinent to the 18th century.

In Ireland, Catholic clergy and librarians, especially Kieran Burke in Cork, shared knowledge, objects, and documents. Antoinette O'Leary of Inniscarra researched music and lyrics from the period.

Patti Frazee and Gordon Thomas of BookSmart Publishing Management provided everything necessary to bring this book to fruition; my deep appreciation for their talents, their support and their friendship. And as always, thank you, Carolyn Holbrook, for your decades-long mentorship of this grateful writer.

Sylvia Crannell and Heidi Arneson immersed themselves in the cultures of this book and brought the cover to life with their artistry.

During all the years of research, my brother Dion Bridal, his wife Marcela Dutra, and my nieces Victoria and Antonia, received me in their home and graciously put up with my comings and goings from places distant and various.

Ever generous with her time, Bertha Jackson made herself available to drive me around Montevideo, and made it possible for me to enjoy days of rest at her and her husband Juan's estancia in Río Negro.

Eloise Morley and Anita Ransom have my abiding love and gratitude for reading through various versions of this book and providing the support all writers crave. Estela Manancero Villagrán and Sonia Tuduri gave unstintingly of their time and efforts to assist in the promotion of the book in both languages.

My daughters Anna and Kate were my companions on these travels, making them all the more memorable. My husband Randy was taken by cancer before this book was finished. He had until then kept the home fires burning and our menagerie cared for while our daughters and I went adventuring.

Abiding love and thanks to you all.

About the Author

Born and raised in Uruguay, Tessa Bridal came to the United States for the first time as a foreign exchange student through the Youth for Understanding program. Her Michigan family remains an integral part of her life today. When her mother and sister moved to Washington DC, Bridal moved with them. She began writing as a means of dealing with homesickness and issues of cultural displacement.

After attending drama school in London, she returned to the United States, married and moved to Minnesota, where she had two daughters, and developed a career in theatre in museums, an educational and interpretive technique she was instrumental in developing and for which she became widely recognized in the museum field. While at the Science Museum of Minnesota, she was awarded the American Alliance of Museums' Excellence in Practice Award, which recognizes an individual who demonstrates exemplary service to the public through the practice of education in museums.

Bridal went on to lead interpretive programs at The Children's Museum of Indianapolis and the Monterey Bay Aquarium, and is the author of two books on the use of theatre in museums, *Exploring Museum Theatre* and *Effective Exhibit Interpretation and Design.*

Her first novel *The Tree of Red Stars* won the Milkweed Prize for Fiction, the Friends of American Writers Fiction Prize, and was translated into several languages.